MW01124228

FIRE UNDER HEAVEN
CINDA RICHARDS

AN AUTHORS GUILD BACKINPRINT.COM EDITION

Fire Under Heaven
All Rights Reserved © 1987, 2000 by Cinda Richards
Dillon's Promise
All Rights Reserved © 1986, 2000 by Cinda Richards

AN AUTHORS GUILD BACKINPRINT.COM EDITION

Published by iUniverse.com, Inc.

For information address:
iUniverse.com, Inc.
620 North 48th Street, Suite 201
Lincoln, NE 68504-3467
www.iuniverse.com

Originally published by The Berkley Publishing Group

ISBN: 0-595-09433-3

Printed in the United States of America

CHAPTER

One

I NEVER TAKE cookies to strangers.

Now that would have been an original excuse, Annemarie Worth thought. It might even have occurred to her if she hadn't always felt so sorry for people who had to be far from home. Unfortunately, Annemarie knew what it was like to be bound by one's obligations and to be desperately homesick. She sighed and kept walking, shifting the tin of homemade chocolate chip cookies to her other arm. The thing was heavy. It had an embossed winter snow scene on the lid, and it had once held a five-pound Belgian fruitcake. So far, delivering these wasn't as easy as she'd been led to believe. All she had to do, David Gannon's sister assured her, was to call the American embassy when she arrived in Kharan, and David himself would come and get them. Well, she'd

1

done that—several times. Gunnery Sergeant Gannon was out, and apparently he was going to stay that way.

To make matters worse, Annemarie couldn't locate her brother, Joe, either, and he was the reason she'd come to Kharan in the first place. Joe was an engineer with Aramco Oil, and because of the instability of the Middle East, he'd begged her to come to Kharan and take his two daughters back to the United States. Joe was a widower; he couldn't do it himself now, and he couldn't stand the thought of sending his girls home on a plane alone. So who better to do it than his middle sister, Annemarie—the one who let a total stranger talk her into becoming a cookie messenger, too, while she was at it?

The sun was so bright in this part of the world, and Annemarie shaded her eyes before she crossed the street. She was in a newer part of the city, where most of the Westerners stayed and where the major oil companies had their housing complexes. If she could believe the receptionist at Aramco, she was not far from the American Embassy. The street was wide, and the traffic heavy. There were no traffic signals, and she crossed to the other side the same way everyone else did—when and wherever she could. She had to dodge a safari of orange Land-Rovers and a Toyota truck that was transporting a bored-looking camel. Ah, the modern world, Annemarie thought as the camel passed. Several people in the Land-Rover whistled and waved—tourists, she thought, likely Americans.

She walked on, turning left at a stand of date palms as she'd been instructed and passing a sidewalk café where the strong aroma of coffee and tobacco smoke mingled with the sweet scent of jasmine and orange blossoms. The café patrons were all men, she noted.

She supposed that the women of Kharan took their coffee and conversation at home — or did without.

She could see the embassy now, and was more relieved than she cared to admit. Annemarie simply wasn't the adventurous sort. And if it weren't for Joe and her nieces being God only knew where, and the responsibility she felt for this can of cookies, she wouldn't be out in the hot sun roaming the streets alone in a foreign country.

But, Annemarie reasoned, she had nothing except time on her hands until Joe got back, and she might as well do something with it — such as hike a few blocks to the American Embassy. She could deliver the cookies, and she could help relieve someone's homesickness.

The embassy building was several stories tall, and ocher-colored like every other building in Kharan. It's architectural style was not quite Middle Eastern. The windows were too large and modern-looking for one thing, and yet they were covered with the traditional iron grillwork. The grounds were walled, and several trucks loaded with cement were parked in front of the gate. The gate was open, and Annemarie walked up the sidewalk to the entrance.

It took a moment for her eyes to adjust to the artificial lighting as she stepped inside the embassy doors. The place was crowded enough, she noted as she waited her turn to move up to a glass booth marked Post No. 1. Embassy personnel and several marines in the booth worked busily speaking to the people in line through the circular, louvered metal slot in the glass that reminded Annemarie of the box office at the movies.

"May we help you, ma'am?" a young man asked through the metal disk.

Thinking that he looked entirely too young for the

responsibility that question implied, Annemarie stepped up to the glass.

"Yes, I brought—"

She never got to finish her sentence. As she set the cookie can on the counter, the young man squealed and dropped out of sight. Everyone else in the booth seemed to freeze—except the closest marine, the one who was outside the booth.

"Stand back from the glass!" he ordered, his sidearm out.

Annemarie was still looking for the young man and for the cause of all this alarm.

"Now, please, ma'am!"

"What is—?" Annemarie said, then she realized, *Oh, Lord, he means me!* She could feel the eyes of everyone in the place on her. She knew from the tone of voice that she had better do as she was told.

"Stand back from the glass, ma'am!" he barked again. His voice was too loud for the "ma'am" to be reassuring. She reached to take the cookies with her.

"Don't touch it, ma'am!" he said. "Step away from the can! Identify the contents of the can, please, ma'am!"

"It's only cookies," Annemarie said. "I can show—"

"Don't touch the can, ma'am! Your name, please."

"Annemarie Worth. I have my passport . . ." she said, reaching for her purse.

"Keep your hands where I can see them, please, ma'am!"

"Look," Annemarie said. "This can is full of chocolate chip cookies—a friend of a friend asked me to bring them here—" She realized immediately from the look on the marine's face that that was the wrong thing to say. At best, she'd just made him think that she'd been unwittingly recruited to deliver an explosive device or whatever he thought she had.

"No—no, you don't understand. The cookies are for a Sergeant Gannon. His sister asked a friend of mine if I'd bring them to him. Like an idiot, I said yes—listen, I could just leave them here," she offered hopefully.

He wasn't buying that, either. Annemarie could hear the shuffle of people being herded to safety behind her.

"It's only cookies, for Pete's sake!" she said.

"Your company in Kharan, ma'am," the marine ordered.

"I don't have any company! My brother asked me to come here and get his children, he wants them back in the United States. He wasn't at his apartment when I arrived. He's out in an oil field somewhere. My nieces are off on a school field trip to some Turkish ruins or something. I had this tin of cookies. I was supposed to call—I did call, but Sergeant Gannon wasn't in. I brought the cookies by anyway. I was just going to leave them—"

"Heidi!" the marine suddenly yelled.

"What!" a muffled, faraway voice answered.

"Your brother's name, please, ma'am," the marine said to Annemarie.

"Joe Worth, Jr."

"What oil field is he in?"

"I don't know—he works for Aramco."

"Heidi, verify that a Joe Worth works for Aramco!"

"Junior," Annemarie reminded him. "Joe Worth, Jr."

"Joe Worth, Jr.!" he yelled, but he was looking over Annemarie's shoulder. "Sergeant Gannon, this woman says she knows you," he said in a normal tone of voice, and Annemarie looked around into the most incredible pair of blue eyes she'd ever seen. Black Irish, she thought immediately. She'd never seen a man with such dark hair coupled with such piercingly blue eyes. Stunning was the only word for it. He was muscular and tall. He wasn't dressed like a marine; he was wearing jeans and a T-shirt, but clearly the marine with the gun deferred to his authority. Annemarie gave a short sigh and tried to be reasonable.

"No, I didn't say I knew Sergeant Gannon. We've never met. I said his sister asked a friend of mine if I'd bring him a tin of cookies. And I did—or I'm trying to," she added significantly. She thought she saw the barest of smiles working at the corners of David Gannon's mouth. His blue eyes assessed her worried brown ones intimately—as if he found her an attractive woman instead of a fanatic with a bomb hidden in a cookie can. No one had looked at her like that in a very long time, and she could feel her composure slipping.

Lord, what eyes, she kept thinking.

She couldn't keep from admiring the thick, dark lashes that surrounded the eyes, and for a moment, she forgot the trouble she was in. She could feel her heart beginning to pound, her face grow warm because he was returning her look of admiration—intently. Flustered now, she glanced away, hoping that he wouldn't interpret it as a sign of guilt.

"Ma'am, if you'd wait here just a minute, please," he said. He was deep-voiced, and she tried to identify the accent. She had been exposed to all kinds of accents in her time. His was New York City, she thought. Maybe New Jersey.

She hesitated. "All right," she decided, feeling a little better about the situation. She likely didn't have a choice in the matter, but he made it sound as if she did. He walked off a short distance from her, taking the other marine with him. She watched them both carefully, determined to overhear.

"—you want to tell me why the hell you thought this woman was attacking the embassy?" she made out, half lip-reading. She edged a little closer.

"I didn't, Sergeant," the younger Marine said. "Well, not until Freddie squeaked like a stepped-on rat, I didn't. I thought she must have said something—done something to him the way he hollered and hit the floor. She's lucky I didn't shoot her."

"No, *you're* lucky you didn't shoot her, Hershel. That can she's got is from my sister."

"Oh, God," Hershel observed.

"So now what do you plan to do?"

"Me, Sergeant?"

"Hell, yes, you! You're the one waving a forty-five around, aren't you?"

Hershel thought for a moment.

"Well—if she's not some big-shot senator's daughter, maybe we can get out of it?" he suggested hopefully.

"You wish," David Gannon told him. "How are you going to do that?"

"I don't know, Sergeant."

"That's exactly right, Hershel. You don't know. That's why I'm the detachment commander and you're the lance corporal."

"No excuses, Sergeant," the now somewhat downcast young marine said.

"You give me an excuse and your butt's had it," Sergeant Gannon warned him. "Given the information you had, Hershel, you did the right thing. Your voice was firm enough to get results, but you weren't disrespectful. You did okay—up to a point."

The two of them walked back to where Annemarie waited, and she was beginning to understand what was going on. The younger marine stood awkwardly for a moment, seeming to feel that he ought to say something to her but not knowing what to say or how to say it.

"Welcome to Kharan, ma'am," he finally managed, and Annemarie couldn't keep from smiling in spite of her growing certainty that David Gannon had just used her as some sort of training exercise. She suspected that the sergeant had been listening to her exchange with Hershel a lot longer than she'd realized.

"Thank you," she said dryly. She turned her attention to Sergeant Gannon. "Do you have anybody else you'd like to run out here so we can role-play bombing the embassy?"

"Ma'am?" he queried, leaning closer to her. She got the barest whiff of his masculine scent—very clean, very soap-and-water and manly.

"You heard what I said," she answered, forcing herself to attend to the matter at hand. "I'm not a senator's daughter, but I'm not too crazy about what you just did, either."

"What is it you think I did, ma'am?" There was just enough mischief in those blue eyes to annoy her.

"I think you let this little situation go on a lot longer than you had to, Sergeant Gannon. He could have shot me!"

"No, ma'am. There was no danger of that."

"How do you know?"

"It's my job to know. Hershel's a fine marine. This was a good chance for him to learn. The world situation being what it is—I'm sorry, I don't know your name, ma'am—"

"Worth," Annemarie said, and his eyes were holding hers again. She forced herself not to look away.

"Sometimes, Ms. Worth, a learning situation for an embassy guard is so on-the-job it's fatal. The experience he just got here may save somebody's life someday."

"Oh, you think so?" she asked, still incredulous that David Gannon had presumed to do such a thing.

"Yes, I do. Look, I could have stopped it sooner, but I didn't. I apologize for that—but not for Hershel. He did a damn fine job. Okay?"

"Okay?" he asked again when Annemarie didn't answer him. She was perfectly aware of the world situation—no one could make a trip to the Middle East these days and not consider the dangers. And she understood his reasoning; she just didn't want him to think the knee-weakening looks he was giving her had persuaded her.

"Okay," she said finally, and he grinned what was probably the most disarming grin she'd ever encountered. No wonder people went to all kinds of trouble to see that he got cookies. She didn't grin back. "Wouldn't it be easier just to stop visitors at the front gate?" she asked.

"Yes, it would be easier, but it wouldn't do for us to look like we're worried. We have to be accessible to our citizens, and we have to be prepared—but we don't want to look like it, see?"

"You mean like parking those big trucks with the cement out front," Annemarie suggested with just a trace of irony. David Gannon refused to be baited.

"Yes," he said, fighting down a smile. "Pretty subtle, huh? Ms. Worth, would you step in here just a minute?" he asked politely, indicating an office just down the hall.

"Why?" she asked suspiciously.

"Well—you're looking a little green around the gills . . ."

"My gills are fine."

"Even so, after what we've put you through, I can't just send you off until I know you're all right."

"I'm fine!"

"Humor me, will you? It's part of my job." He walked away to get the tin of cookies. "I want you to have some of these—my sister, Teresa, makes the best chocolate chip cookies in the world."

"No, thank you. It's really not necessary," she insisted, but he had taken her by the elbow, his warm, firm hand guiding her down the hall. She was afraid to put up too much of a fuss—Hershel was still around. All the people who had been in the embassy earlier stared at her curiously.

"It's necessary for me, Ms. Worth. I really appreciate the trouble you've gone to. I know it was a pain hanging around airports and getting on and off planes with this big can—not to mention your welcome here at the embassy. You're not upset—well, you're a little bit upset," he qualified when she was about to protest that assessment of her emotional state. "But you understand how things are and you aren't going to give me a hard time about it—are you?"

She worked to keep from smiling. He was nothing if not transparent. A little empathy, a little personal attention, some cookies—and she was supposed to forget all about this. "I haven't decided yet," she said with as much of a straight face as she could manage. She thought it would do him good to worry a little longer about whether or not she'd write her congressman or ask to see the chargé d'affaires. "I've never been mistaken for a mad bomber before."

"Fair enough, I guess," he said with a sigh. He reached in front of her to open the office door, his head coming very close to hers. He was a big man. He made her feel delicately female, and she was getting those sensations again: slightly weakened knees, addled thoughts, and an intense desire to stand and stare at him for as long as he'd put up with it.

"I think you're giving me the business," he whispered as he pushed the door in, the eyes that affected her so filled with mischief.

He must have women falling all over him, Annemarie thought crazily.

"I think I'm giving as good as I just got, Sergeant," she countered, trying to remember who she was and what she was doing.

He laughed. "Damn, Ms. Worth. They don't get much by you, do they? After you . . ."

She went ahead of him into the office, seeing his reflection in the glass window in the opposite wall as he . . . checked out her legs. So, she thought. He's subtle. He's not the sort of man who leers.

The office was completely devoid of clutter, and David Gannon, showing no trace of the interest she'd just seen reflected in the window, set the tin of cookies down on the desktop and opened it carefully. Then he pulled out a sheet of plain white paper from a desk drawer, folding it in half and stapling the sides together. Into this makeshift bag he carefully placed—*one* cookie.

"Well, what the hell," he said, looking up at her thoughtfully. "Ms. Worth—take *two* cookies, okay? Consider it a token of my thankfulness."

"I'll consider it what it is," Annemarie said. "A bribe. Thank you." She took the cookies out of his hand and headed for the door. She really was out of her depth here. She was a little restaurant owner from the mountains of Virginia, and she'd just come close to being mistaken for a member of some hostile extremist group. She wasn't used to this kind of thing, and here she was —almost—enjoying herself! And she'd only just met the man, for heaven's sake!

She stuck the cookies into the pocket of her skirt. "Good afternoon, Sergeant Gannon. If you and Teresa ever need help recruiting somebody to carry cookies for you, don't give my name as a reference, okay? Oh— and if you don't mind my saying so, Freddie needs to take a vacation."

She was still smiling when she walked outside. The sergeant was pretty cute, all right—cute enough to make her see the good sense in getting out of there before she drooled all over him. Whatever had passed between them came under the heading of a mild flirtation, she supposed. Harmless, and not unpleasant.

"Ms. Worth!" someone called as she walked past the sidewalk café. "Ms. Worth!" She turned around to see David Gannon running toward her with the easy grace of a man in excellent physical condition.

"What?" she asked testily when caught up with her —because he was carrying that notorious can of cookies.

He grinned. His blue eyes were mischievous again, teasing, and she had the idea that they were always that way—whenever he was up to something. "Now, I know how you feel, Ms. Worth, but I was just wondering . . ."

"No, thank you," Annemarie interrupted.

"You don't even know what it is."

"I don't care what it is. I was just saving you time."

"I'm not in a hurry—well, I *am* in a hurry, but however long it takes to talk you into this is okay." He paused, apparently to see if she wanted to say something. "Here's the plan," he said when she didn't comment. "I was thinking—since you went to all the trouble to bring these cookies over here, maybe you'd like to see what I'm going to do with them."

"No, I don't think so," she said, trying not to look at him as if she thought he was out of his mind.

"Wait, Ms. Worth," he said when she tried to walk on. "See, Teresa sends me these for the children at American Hospital. I thought you'd like to go with me to deliver them. I mean, you've carried them this far—you may as well see what you were doing it for."

"Sergeant Gannon," Annemarie began, trying to think of a reason she could give, without being rude, why she couldn't possibly accompany him.

"Come on, Ms. Worth. These kids don't get many visitors. It'll make them happy. What do you say? I'd really like for you to come with me."

Annemarie frowned. "Why?"

"Why? Because you're a nice American lady. They don't get to see many nice American ladies. I don't either," he added in a moment of candor.

"I have to see my brother..."

"You don't know when he'll be back, do you? We can call Aramco and leave a message where you'll be. That way, if he does get back before you do, he can find you or call you. You won't have to worry about missing him or anything."

She was still frowning. "Sergeant Gannon—"

"What?" he asked, giving her a very persuasive grin.

"Don't keep saying 'Sergeant Gannon,' Ms. Worth. Say yes, you'll go with me."

Annemarie looked into his eyes. He gazed back at her. Did she want to go to the hospital with him or not?

She did, she decided, and she wasn't going to let herself think about why beyond the altruistic reason. She wasn't going to think about the fact that she was, for the moment, alone in a foreign country, or that she didn't really know this man. Instead, she was going to dwell on the fact that she rather liked him in a crazy, illogical, spur-of-the-moment way. She liked the fact that his sister thought enough of him to send him cookies, and that he had been gruffly kind to a very insecure Hershel—even though she was certain Hershel would get the dressing down of his life whenever he deserved or needed it. She also liked the fact that for the first time in a very long while, she had met a man to whom she was attracted. And, looking into his eyes now, she could almost swear that he was feeling something, too.

"All right," she said, looking away toward the café.

"You will?" he answered with enough surprise to make her think, incredible as it seemed, that he hadn't been that sure of her, soul-piercing blue eyes or not. For some reason, she found that . . . rather endearing.

"Yes, I will," she answered. She'd probably regret it, but she was going to do it. She let herself look into his eyes again, promising herself she was going to stop doing that.

"Great!" he said, smiling down at her. "We'll cut through the alley—"

"I thought I was going to call Joe from the embassy or somewhere," she protested as he tried to steer her toward a cluttered back alley that ran behind the café.

"I already did that," he answered, still ushering her along.

Annemarie stopped walking. "You're pretty sure of yourself, aren't you?" she said, annoyed that he had the presumptive arrogance of the stunningly handsome after all.

"Well, see, I figured I'd catch you close to this alley —it's a short cut, it runs to the back of the hospital. So, I thought I'd save time if I just had Heidi go ahead and call Aramco and leave the message that you were going to American Hospital with me—you remember Heidi?"

"I remember her voice," Annemarie said significantly, because Heidi had been under a piece of furniture somewhere.

He grinned. "And see, if you'd told me to drop dead instead of saying you'd come along with me—then I could just have had Heidi cancel the message. No problem. See?"

"Oh, I see," Annemarie assured him. "Does your mind always work like this?"

"Like what?"

"Figuring out all these—logistics."

"I guess so, Ms. Worth," he confessed. "Does this mean you'll still go with me? You can't hold it against a guy for planning ahead, now, can you?"

Annemarie didn't answer him. He was smiling down at her, full of himself, aggravating her and loving every minute of it. She felt as if she'd just thrown in with a Dead End Kid or one of the Little Rascals.

"I'm still going," she said grudgingly, wondering all the while if crossing all those time zones was responsible for this total lack of judgment on her part.

"Great," he said, taking her elbow. "Now, remember one thing when we go through the alley here."

"What?" Annemarie asked warily.

"If you recognize it, don't step in it. If you don't recognize it, don't step in it. Got it?"

She stopped walking again, looking up into his teasing eyes and then at the ground while she thought this thing over. "I got it," she said finally.

The hospital was large and modern, and David Gannon seemed to know his way around it. She rather liked the open, airy feel of the place as she followed him down one shiny corridor after another.

"Wait, Ms. Worth," he said when they reached a pair of doors with Arab lettering and the English word *Pediatrics* on it. "These are Bedouin children we're going to see—the ones nobody wants. They've been left here at the hospital. Sometimes they get left at the embassy gate. Some of them have birth defects. Some of them are burned pretty badly—the Bedouins have a lot of open fires. You don't have to go in with me if you'd find it—upsetting."

"I'll go in," she said without hesitation. She met David Gannon's steady gaze, seeing something there she couldn't quite read.

He smiled. "Good for you, Ms. Worth," he said, pushing open the door.

Annemarie followed him inside, smiling a bit at the cheers that went up at the nursing station when he dramatically presented the cookie can.

"Gannon comes through again," one of the younger nurses said, her eyes traveling over him with such longing that Annemarie had to look away.

Sergeant Gannon didn't seem to notice it, and the nurse glanced at Annemarie. "Who's your friend, David?" He didn't seem to notice the importance of her question, either.

"This is Ms. Worth, Karen. She hand-delivered the cookies this afternoon." He put his hand in the middle of Annemarie's back, bringing her forward.

She listened to him rattle off all the names of the people at the nurses' station, nodding politely and returning Karen's not-quite-friendly smile.

"Charlie's in the day room, Gannon," a petite older nurse said. "You got time to take him some cookies and milk?"

"That's what I came for, shorty," he advised her. "I'll get the milk." He opened the can of cookies and took a tissue from the box that sat on the counter, wrapping up a cookie and giving it to Annemarie to hold. "This way," he said, and she followed him to a small kitchen, waiting outside the door while he went in and poured a cup of milk.

The day room was bright and sunny, with an oasis painted on one wall. A tarbooshed Mickey Mouse waded in the water, while Minnie and Pluto rested under the shade of a palm tree.

Annemarie chuckled. "This is nice," she remarked.

"Karen did that," David answered.

"She's very talented," Annemarie said charitably, wondering why she was feeling such a pang of what could only be described as jealousy.

"There's Charlie," David said, walking over to a small child who was sitting quietly in a walker. He had dark hair and olive skin, and great, liquid brown eyes. He wore braces on both legs, and he grinned broadly at David's approach.

"He has spina bifida—open spine," David explained to her. "And what we're trying to do is teach him to feed himself." He took the cookie out of Annemarie's hand and sat down on the floor, looking around for a place to put the cup of milk.

"I'll hold it," Annemarie said. She pulled up one of the child-sized straight chairs and sat down beside him, taking the cup of milk while he broke off a small piece of the cookie.

"See, what we do is let Charlie taste what we got here—don't we, my man?" he said to the child, gently feeding him the piece of cookie. Charlie loved it. "And —maybe I'll give him just one more little piece so he's sure about this deal here—"

"I think he's sure," Annemarie said, smiling at Charlie's pleasure.

"Yeah, you're right, Ms. Worth. See this lady, Charles? She brought you the cookie. What do you think about that?"

Charlie grinned and chewed, losing a bit of cookie, which David wiped off his chin with the tissue.

"Now, what we do with the next bite is, we don't put it all the way to his lips—so if he wants it bad enough, he'll reach for it—way to go, Charlie!" David praised the boy as he reached on cue. "And we keep getting farther away—see, it's kind of like learning a skill backward until he's finally to a point where you can put the cookie down and he'll pick it up and feed himself." He glanced at Annemarie, then back again, as if he'd caught sight of something in her eyes that he wanted to investigate further. Drooling admiration, probably, she thought, still holding his steady gaze. There was more to this man than unusually brilliant eye color and a thick set of eyelashes.

"Ready for the milk?" Annemarie asked abruptly, because she was getting a little rattled. She helped Charlie drink the milk; she had enough nieces and nephews not to worry about how to manage it even if she had to use the same backward technique that David had showed her with the cookie.

"Have you two known each other long?" she asked, giving Charlie another sip.

"Since he was born. Somebody left him by the embassy gate," David said. "He's a little over a year old now. He's had more surgery than any ten people you know." He sighed. "It's better nowadays, I guess. They used to leave babies like him alone in the desert . . ."

They stayed at the hospital for over an hour.

"What's going to happen to Charlie?" Annemarie asked when they walked out of the building and into the bright sunlight. They didn't go back through the alley, taking the longer way around along the palm-lined boulevard. The traffic was still heavy. Compact cars dodged back and forth between buses and trucks, and pedestrians needing to cross the street still took their chances.

"He'll live on the children's ward until they fix everything they can fix. Probably longer. The hospital doubles as a sort of unofficial orphanage."

"I'm glad you brought me. It was nice to see where the cookies were going."

Their eyes met, but Annemarie looked away.

"I thought you'd like it," he answered, slowing his pace so that they were barely walking along.

"And why is that?" she asked carefully.

"Because you didn't put Hershel's or my butt on the chopping block, for one thing," he advised her, and she laughed. "You're a sympathetic woman, Ms. Worth." He made it sound like a very good thing to be.

"Ms. Worth?" he said, stopping in the shade of a date palm. "Would you like to see a little bit of Kharan? If you're not going to be here long, I could take you to the marketplace, if you want to go. You might like to take some things back to your family"—he grinned—"camel saddles, a string of fish, stuff like that. I wouldn't take you to the tourist traps, I'd take you to the real marketplace—what do you say?"

"You don't have to do that, Sergeant."

"I know I don't have to, Ms. Worth. I want to. What do you say?"

CHAPTER

Two

WHAT SHE SAID was yes. Then she sort of got out of the way while David Gannon once again handled the logistics. She called Aramco from the embassy, leaving a subsequent message for her brother, then she met David at an old, bedraggled-looking, spotty gray Chevrolet that was parked a block from the embassy gates. As she walked up, he was fiddling with something under the front seat, putting his wallet and some other things, but not his money, in a place out of sight. He faltered a moment when he realized that she was watching.

"You want the truth, Ms. Worth?" he asked matter-of-factly. "Or do you want the usual bull we hand the tourists?"

"I don't want anything, Sergeant. I read the newspapers." She knew perfectly well what happened to targeted Americans in the Middle East, especially ones who had the misfortune of being identified as military personnel. And, since she was going to be with him on this outing to the marketplace, hiding his military ID was fine with her. She supposed that the nondescript nature of the car he was going to drive had to do with the need to be inconspicuous, too.

He looked at her thoughtfully, but he didn't say anything. He took her first to get some money changed into local currency, embarrassing her half to death because he suggested—a bit high-handedly, Annemarie thought—that she go to the rest room while they were in the bank.

"I don't need to!" she insisted.

"Go anyway," he told her. "There are no sanitation facilities in a Kharani market."

She went. And when they got to the marketplace, she discovered that he was right. There were no sanitation facilities—but there was everything else.

Now, *this* is what I was expecting Kharan to look like, she thought as he led the way down a narrow side street to a kind of "no-man's-land" that lay between million-dollar Western oil industries and the ancient past. There were shops at every turn, a hubbub of sight and sound and color. Peddlers, beggars, musicians, holy men, street urchins, sailors, and an endless parade of women, draped all in black except for their eyes and carrying urns, or woven baskets, or tied-up bundles on their heads. She could smell tobacco smoke, oranges, hot candle wax—and something else. A waft of sea air from time to time, because they were close to the harbor on the Red Sea. She could see the wares—so many things for sale—Coca-Cola, oriental daggers, opium pipes, and, yes, camel saddles. She saw pottery and brass, silk and linen, dates and figs and almonds. And amid all of that, she suddenly realized that nearly everyone around her was staring at her, particularly the men.

She glanced at David Gannon.

"It's because your face is uncovered," he explained quietly, and she nodded, wondering why no one stared at the bare faces of the dancing girls who swayed and clapped just a bit farther on.

She asked, and David grinned.

"Those are ladies of the evening, Ms. Worth."

"Oh," she said demurely, making his grin broaden.

"Hey," he said, and she looked up at him.

"You've got a beautiful face, Ms. Worth," he said. "I'm glad you don't have to cover it."

With that, he walked off, leaving her there not knowing quite what to do. Was that a compliment—or a pass? Was she supposed to ignore it—or say thank you?

Apparently, he didn't think she was supposed to do anything. He waited until she caught up with him.

"You smell nice, too," he advised her immediately, his eyes traveling over her so-called "beautiful" face. He ended his inspection with a little wink and a waggling of the eyebrows.

"Will you stop that!"

"What?" he asked innocently.

"Giving me the business," she said, using his own phrase.

"Why? I kind of like giving you the business, Ms. Worth."

"I'm supposed to be shopping and sightseeing. I want to keep to the plan."

"Oh, yes," he remembered. "The plan. I want you to pay attention, Ms. Worth, because I'm going to tell you what the plan is."

"Oh, Lord. Logistics again," she complained. "Don't you ever do anything by chance?"

"Never," he said. "Now here's what we're going to do. We walk through the market a couple of times so you can see what they've got. Then you pick what you want, and I'll haggle, okay?"

"What if I see something I want the first time through?" she inquired.

"It'll never happen," he assured her.

"How do you know?"

"I got sisters," he said over his shoulder.

Annemarie stood for a moment trying to decide if she and the female sex had been insulted. They had, but not overtly enough for her to risk being left here alone.

"Come on, Ms. Worth," he said, beckoning her to follow. He didn't have to tell her twice. "So," he said as they walked along. "Where are you from?"

"Virginia," she said, thinking that the question sounded safe enough. "Near Meadows of Dan, in the Blue Ridge Mountains. And you? No, wait. Let me see if I can guess . . ."

"Guess away," he said. "And don't let the accent fool you."

"Oh, I won't. I'm really good at accents. Okay. Here's my guess—" She paused dramatically. "Picayune, Mississippi," she teased.

He laughed out loud. "Wrong! Go ahead, let's have guess number two."

"Okay." She grinned up at him, noting with some surprise that whether he was giving her the business or not, she was enjoying herself immensely. "Cuthbert, Alabama."

"Wrong again, Ms. Worth. This is your last guess." He reached out to put his hand on her shoulder to guide her through a group of men arguing over a goat. His hand was warm and firm and not at all unpleasant through the beige linen jacket she was wearing.

He took his hand down as soon as they were through the crowd. "Go ahead," he prompted.

"The Bronx," she said, serious now, and he looked down at her, his eyes once again probing hers for something she wasn't sure she had.

"Damn, Ms. Worth," he said, his teasing grin firmly in place. "Like I said, they don't get much by you, do they? Come on over here," he said, taking her by the elbow until they got where they were going—a stone building that housed an upright water wheel. The wheel was being powered by a camel that trod around and around in a circle, making the wheel and its pottery jugs dip into a large basin of water.

"Why are the camel's eyes covered?" Annemarie asked.

"He's wearing blinders like that so he won't see what he's doing. It's too damn monotonous walking around in a circle—" He stopped, apparently because Annemarie was frowning.

"Is that the truth?" she asked suspiciously.

"I swear," he said, holding up his right hand. "Now I want you to see the mosque—Ninth Century."

They worked their way on through the market. Annemarie watched several old men in gray robes and red felt skullcaps, smoking and solving the world's problems as they rested on benches along the way. They reminded her of the old men at the Exxon station at home.

She saw more women, the edges of their head coverings pulled together just under the nose to haphazardly hide their faces. One of the women, whose hands were full, efficiently held hers together with her teeth. Annemarie watched in fascination, thinking that women would always find a way to do what they had to do no matter what dress codes were imposed upon them.

She glanced at David, finding that she had his full attention. She looked at him quizzically, thinking that perhaps she'd just committed some social blunder in watching the women the way she had, but he didn't say anything. He continued on through the crowd and the noise, pausing once at an ocher-colored wall that didn't seem to belong to anything.

"Roman," he said to her, pointing at the wall, and she nodded, looking up the full height of it.

The street was widening, and they were approaching a huge pair of double doors in the façade of an extremely old-looking building. The heavy doors were made of carved cedar, and David strained to open them.

"Are you sure this is all right?" Annemarie asked a little worriedly.

"It's all right. The mosque is open to the curious and to the faithful. We fall in there somewhere..." He managed to get the door open, and other people came inside with them. The entrance opened into a huge courtyard with an arched gallery all around. Their footsteps echoed loudly on the tightly packed stone paving.

"Come over here. I want you to see this," David said, leading her to what looked to her like the footing of a Roman column. "So what do you think that is, Ms. Worth?"

She peered at it, into it. "A hole?" she said, suggesting the obvious.

"No, it's not a 'hole,'" he said. "It's more than that. Now look at it close."

She looked. It still looked like a hole.

"Not from way over there, Ms. Worth—even if it were a hole, it's not that kind of hole." He caught her hand, pulling so that she would kneel down beside him. She noted that his fingers were warm and strong and a little rough-textured. "Now look," he instructed.

She looked. She could see water. "It *looks* like that kind of hole," she advised him, and he caught her hand again.

"Here. Touch this—"

All around the marble lip of the hole there were deep, nonsymmetrical grooves, and he placed her fingers into one. It felt cool and smooth as glass, and his warm hand covered hers longer than was required.

"I give up," Annemarie said. "I don't know what this is." She tried to avoid looking into his eyes.

"It's a well," he said, taking his hand away. "These places were cut into the sides here by the ropes hauling up the water. This whole courtyard is a cistern. Can you imagine how many centuries of drawing water it would take to wear the marble like that? When the United States didn't even exist, these people were drawing up their water."

Annemarie reached to touch the grooves again, thinking about what David Gannon was telling her. The antiquity of this land was obviously a subject that interested him, and he'd taken the time to learn about it— not just because his duty assignment was here, she thought, but because he was truly interested. She appreciated that, and she was glad that she'd come with him. No travel agency guide would make her literally touch the past the way he had.

They made a quick trip around the mosque, then he took her back into the marketplace, standing close to her while she watched a fish auction where customers bid on behalf of the big hotels or just for the family dinner. She watched a potter working his wheel, feeling a pang of homesickness. She was a Blue Ridge mountain girl at heart, and seeing this familiar mountain craft here made her remember it.

"Sergeant Gannon?" she said, and he leaned down to hear her over the wheel and the general raucousness around them. "Haggle for that bowl, will you?"

"Which one?"

"That blue-gray one."

David Gannon seemed to have a more than adequate command of the language, Bronx accent or not. The haggling took a while, but he finally made the purchase. "You know, this isn't the best he has," he said when he handed the bowl to her.

"I don't care," she answered. "Sometimes—"

"What?" he asked when she didn't go on, leaning down again. She could smell his masculine scent, feel the heat from his body. His arm just barely brushed against hers, and when she looked upward, she was lost in the blue of his eyes.

She shrugged to minimize the reason she wanted this particular bowl. "Sometimes—at home—the mountains are this color."

She braced herself for some remark, thinking that he wouldn't understand, but he smiled and pointed out a new direction for her to take.

"Right here," he said when she would have gone on by the place where he wanted to stop. The stall was empty for all intents and purposes—nothing but an old man in the same kind of gray robe she'd seen earlier and the red felt skullcap, and a few bottles, some empty, some filled.

"Ms. Worth," David Gannon said, putting both hands

on her shoulders. "I want you to stand right here and be good. No matter what happens—I don't want you to get crazy. Okay?"

"No," she assured him, but it didn't seem to matter. He said something to the old man in the stall, then leaned down to give an exaggerated sniff between her neck and shoulder. Annemarie would have protested but her attention was taken by the old man, who proceeded to imitate the sniff on her other side. Annemarie jumped as if she'd been shot.

"Stand still!" David Gannon said. "Let the master work—"

"What are you doing!" Annemarie cried when the old man continued to sniff.

"You'll see," David said. Annemarie was more than afraid she would.

"Sergeant Gannon—"

"Shhhhhh!" he hissed at her.

The old man went back into the stall, opening several small phials, then coming back to sniff her one more time. He took down a bottle with a glass stopper, filling it with minute amounts from the phials until it suited him. He said something to Annemarie, holding the glass stopper in her direction. David took her hand and offered it to him, totally disregarding her wishes in the matter. She watched warily as the man dipped the stopper into the bottle, shook once, then wiped the tip of it on the back of her hand.

"Smell," David said.

She sniffed carefully. It was a very close imitation of the scent she wore.

"This is my favorite perfume," she said incredulously, and David grinned, fishing some money out of his pocket and paying the bobbing impromptu perfumer.

"For you," he said, giving her the bottle.

She started to protest, but didn't. "Thank you," she told him instead, more than pleased. She looked back at the old man. "I am impressed!"

"I thought you might be. There's probably not a perfume in the world that old guy can't make up on the spot."

She took another whiff of the bottle. "It's lovely—I think it's better than the original," she decided.

He smiled down at her. "Just a token of my thankfulness, Ms. Worth."

"What—*another* one?" She still had the two cookies in her skirt pocket.

"Yes, ma'am," he assured her. "Believe me, Ms. Worth. Nobody delivers a can of cookies the way you do."

She laughed and walked on with him, catching sight of herself in a mirrorlike sheet of brass near a forge. She stared at her reflection for a moment, surprised at how relaxed and happy she looked. She was wearing a no-nonsense beige linen suit, but she'd worn a sapphire blue silk blouse with it that was more becoming than she realized. Her brown hair was in its usual knot at the nape of her neck, but it was coming loose, framing her face in wispy tendrils.

David Gannon was watching her, and she pretended suddenly that she was interested in a brass something-or-other nearby.

"Unless you have a camel, Ms. Worth, you don't need that," he whispered.

She gave him a hard look and put the brass thing down, leaving him standing and walking on to the next stall. He came along after her, grinning from ear to ear.

"If you think I'm asking what that thing is for, you're mistaken," she assured him.

"I'd love to tell you.

"I just bet you would."

She made the mistake of looking up at him, and they both laughed.

"Come on, Ms. Worth. Buy your stuff so I can show you one of the most fantastic sunsets in the world." As he took her arm to guide her, she felt a delicious shiver at the contact.

She made her purchases quickly—it was hard to do otherwise when David Gannon had decided that now one was going to be speedy. Then he hurried her back to the place they'd parked the car—only he wouldn't let her get in until he'd made a meticulous inspection of the motor and the underside. Annemarie understood this precaution, too, and she didn't ask any questions.

"We're going to the Red Sea," he said when he was satisfied that no one had tampered with the car. And he whipped out into the frenetic every-man-for-himself flow of vehicles as if it were nothing. "You can open your eyes now, Ms. Worth," he added.

It was a short trip, but snarled traffic made progress slow. Annemarie passed the time trying to decide why she was suddenly so sensitized to David Gannon's presence. The inside of a car that was not moving seemed incredibly small somehow. She was much more aware of him here than she had been in the marketplace, and Lord knows, she'd been aware of him there. Everything about him exuded masculinity—the way his hair grew on the back of his neck, the timbre of his voice, his hands. She had never liked pudgy hands; David Gannon's hands were lean and strong-looking. He had capable hands, hands that could carefully feed a child or

handle an automatic weapon or make love to a woman.
He would know how to touch a woman. She knew it,
just by being with him. She knew it the same way the
nurse, Karen, knew it. He'd know when he needed to
be gentle and when he didn't. The mere thought of what
it would be like with him made her close her eyes.

"You okay?" he asked.

"Oh, yes, I'm fine," she said quickly.

"It's not too hot for you, is it? You could take off
your jacket."

"No, no. I'm—fine."

The conversation lagged, and she tried watching the
cars around her instead—a limousine with dark, one-
way windows, a red Renault packed full of European-
looking children, a small truck with six young
men—students, she thought, in the back. The young
men had the same route and destination in mind as she
and David. She saw them several times along the way,
and they were already walking around on the shore of
the Red Sea when she and David arrived. They had
musical instruments—something with strings, and a
drum, and something that sounded like an oboe. The
tune they played was upbeat and lively, and Annemarie
asked David about it as they got out of the car.

"I can't make out the words," he said, taking her
hand to help her over the rough ground.

"Sounds happy enough," Annemarie said, but she
was thinking how much she liked the feel of his fingers
clasped around hers.

"Well, you can't always tell about music here,"
David said. "Sad or happy, the tempo is usually the
same." He let go of her hand. "If you were going to be
here longer, I'd show you the flashlight fish—that is, if
you can dive."

"I can't," she answered. "What are flashlight fish?"

"They have little places in their eyes that glow in the dark. They hang around the reefs not too far from the surface. When you're in a school of them it's like— floating among the stars. It's really beautiful . . ."

Annemarie smiled, thinking how fortunate he was to have experienced all the things he had.

"I've never heard of flashlight fish."

"Neither had anybody else around here until about twenty years ago. Until then nobody knew they were in this part of the Red Sea."

"How do you know all these things?" Annemarie asked. "Flashlight fish and ancient marble wells . . ."

"Because I'm nosy as hell," he answered, and she laughed. "Been that way since I was a kid. You wouldn't believe the things I want to find out about you—what are you looking for?"

"Two pebbles," she said, pretending that she didn't hear the part about his wanting to find out things about her. She just didn't know what he meant when he said things like that. Nothing? Everything? She wasn't offended. He sounded more honest than crude. If she were sophisticated and worldly, she'd straighten up, look at him suggestively and say, "Like what?"

But not being sophisticated or worldly, she kept looking for rocks.

"Ms. Worth," he advised her, "you're knee deep in pebbles."

"I know, but these are for Naomi and Ruby Chandler."

"Who are they?"

"My surrogate mothers," she said absently. "They were my mother's best friends. When she died, they both sort of took over the job. Anyway, I know they'd love a pebble from the Red Sea, but if one pebble is bigger or not as interesting as the other, I'll get reproachful looks for the rest of my life."

"You know, Ms. Worth," he said, coming closer to help her look. "You've got problems other people can't even imagine—what with trying to get rid of cookie cans and finding matching rocks . . ."

"Don't make fun of me, Sergeant. A problem is a problem if you're the one who has to live with it."

"I'd never make fun of you, Ms. Worth. Here," he said, holding his hand over hers. She opened her palm and he dropped two stones into it. They were identical. "How's that?"

"Perfect," she answered. She put them into her skirt pocket, the one without the cookies.

"Now look that way," he said, turning her around. She stood in front of him, facing the Red Sea and the first rays of a brilliant sunset. He kept his hands on her shoulders.

"It's hard to believe," she said, looking out over the water.

"What is?" he asked.

"This place," she answered. "It's in the Bible. And it's here—really here." She was acutely aware of his hands on her shoulders, acutely aware that with just the barest movement on her part she could lean against him.

What is the matter with me?

She shouldn't be feeling the things she was feeling, and she certainly shouldn't be standing here considering doing something about them.

But she didn't move away. She stood perfectly still, watching the gold and purple and orange of the sunset intensify, listening to him talk and feeling his warm hands resting on her shoulders. The wind was picking up, and she turned her face into it, the same sea air that had tantalized her from time to time in the marketplace. Several people with cameras walked past them, and the student-musicians were closer, still playing their music with its driving, repetitive beat. The ones without instruments clapped their hands loudly.

"What do you do for a living, Ms. Worth?" Sergeant Gannon asked abruptly, lowering his head a bit so she could hear him. She looked back over her shoulder to answer him. Their eyes met and held, and their faces were very close—too close for both of them. They moved apart.

"No, let me guess," he said, looking out over the water, his hands resting on his narrow hips. "Schoolteacher."

"No," Annemarie assured him.

"No?"

"No," she repeated.

"Librarian?"

"No, I'm not a librarian—why would you think I was a librarian?"

"Because you're innocent," he said matter-of-factly. "Like somebody who's spent all her time with little kids or books . . ."

"I am not—" *Innocent*, she was going to say. She'd been married and divorced; she'd made a man she loved so unhappy he'd sent her away from him. But she never got the chance to say it. She felt David tense. He suddenly grabbed her by the forearm, slinging her around behind him.

"Go!" he hissed at her. "Run!"

She never got the chance to do that, either.

CHAPTER

Three

ANNEMARIE WAS TERRIFIED. She was lying in the back of a speeding truck with David Gannon, jammed together in as little space as possible near the cab and covered over with a piece of canvas. The canvas reeked of gasoline; she could hardly breathe. Her wrists had been taped behind her with duct tape; and her shoulders felt as if they were being wrenched from her body. Every bump, every sway of the truck, exacerbated the pain.

She'd thought they were students on holiday, playing their music, singing . . .

She couldn't breathe!

"Be—still—"

She stiffened. The words were whispered against her ear. She hadn't thought Sergeant Gannon was conscious. They hadn't taken him easily. They'd hurt him —oh, they'd hurt him . . .

She gave a small whimper of despair.

"Listen to me! Listen!"

Annemarie could hear him. She just couldn't do what he wanted. She was trembling, and she pressed her face into his shoulder to stop it.

"If—they—know—they'll—kill—me—" he whispered. "Understand—"

No, no, she didn't understand! She didn't understand anything!

"Listen!" The whisper was desperate this time. "Don't—lie. Tell the truth—but not all of it. If—they ask—why—you're in Kharan. Tell the truth—I'm a friend—you came to see me—but do not—do *not*— say where. Don't call me—Sergeant. If they—know— they'll kill me—"

Now she understood. This was what hiding his wallet under the car seat was all about.

Don't say anything. Don't say anything!

She ordered the thought into the chaos of her mind, elaborating it into *Tell the truth. Don't call him Sergeant—oh, God!*

The ride seemed to take hours. Her shoulders hurt so. She was terrified that the truck would stop, and terrified that it wouldn't.

The truck was slowing, and her heart began to pound in her ears.

"Be—brave—" David whispered as the canvas was jerked off them.

Annemarie was dragged to her feet, pushed off the tailgate of the truck. She landed on the hard ground on her knees, the burning scrapes momentarily overriding the pain in her wrists and arms and shoulders. It was so

dark. One of the young men was yelling at her, screaming—they were always screaming, waving their guns,
seeming to be near hysteria over this thing they'd ac-
complished. She tried to get up and couldn't—she had
no idea if that was what he wanted her to do. Her legs
wouldn't hold her. She was bent forward, her head near
the ground, straining against the tape around her wrists
in an effort to get up again.

She didn't make it, and he grabbed her by the hair.

David intervened then, with one Arab word that
made her captor furious. He flew at David, screaming in
Arabic, threatening him with the butt of his rifle, and
finally kicking him hard. David continued to speak in
Arabic, his words strained and broken from the pain.
The young man kicked David again, sending him
sprawling on his face.

David kept on talking, and Annemarie cried out,
"Please!"

The young man turned on her, rifle butt raised, and
she braced herself for the blow. But another captor intervened, apparently the one in authority, and she was
jerked to her feet by her elbow. Two of them dragged
her along the ground, winding downward into what felt
like a large crater in the earth. She kept stumbling. She
could hear them bringing David along behind her.

This is it, she kept thinking. *I'm never going home
again.*

She was never going to see the people she loved—
her father, Naomi and Ruby, her lifetime friend, Russell. And Grayson—what would he feel when he heard
that the woman who had once been his wife was dead?
And poor Joe. He'd never get over this. His wife had
been killed in an auto accident in this country, and now
her—

They reached the bottom of the crater, and they were climbing up again. Annemarie strained to see. There seemed to be narrow doorways cut in the side of the crater just in front of her.

With no warning, they shoved her through one of them into the darkness.

I'm so cold!

She couldn't see. She strained to make out something in the place. Maybe it was better that she couldn't see, she thought. She closed her eyes, feeling the hot tears spill down her cheeks. She was lying on the ground, her hands still taped behind her back. She tried to wriggle her fingers, making a soft sound at the pain that slight movement caused.

"Stop crying," David said quietly in the darkness, making her jump. She hadn't known he was in here—when did they put him in here?

She took a long, deep breath. "No," she answered, her voice husky and hardly recognizable. Crying was the only comfort she had, and she wasn't going to let go of it.

"Then come over here and cry."

She didn't hesitate, rolling over, forcing herself to her painful knees.

"The other side," he said when she moved closer to him. She couldn't see him, and she had to sit on the ground and extend one foot to locate his legs.

"If you're going to cry, you may as well keep me warm while you're doing it," he said as she crawled over him. She lost her balance and fell into him, making him cry out in pain.

"I'm sorry—I'm sorry—" she whispered.

"It's—okay—"

"It's not okay! They hurt you—what did you say to them?"

"Oh, nothing much . . ."

"Don't be cute, Gannon!" she cried, trying not to sob. "I can't stand this if you're going to be—*cute!* And don't you lie to me, either. I mean it!"

"Hey—Ms. Worth. Take it easy, will you?"

"And don't talk to me like that, either!"

"Ms. Worth," he said tiredly. "Like what?"

"Like I'm being silly or unreasonable because I'm upset. I've got plenty to be upset about and you know it!"

"Ms. Worth," he said again. "I'm in pain—and I'm freezing to death. Give me another chance, okay?"

"You're being cute again!"

"No, no—I'm not. Just—move closer to me."

He *was* cold. He was shivering. She, at least, had her suit jacket, but David was only wearing a T-shirt and jeans. He was sitting up, his back against the wall of whatever they were in. She moved closer to him, trying not to fall into him again.

"Lean against me," he said. "Put your legs over mine."

She leaned against his chest, but she couldn't manage bringing her legs up without toppling over.

"Wait—wait—" he said, because she'd hurt him again. "Now—"

She leaned into him, this time bringing only one leg over his. That seemed to work all right, and she put her head down on his chest. She could hear his heart beating.

"Tell me what you think," she said when he'd stopped shivering so much.

She expected him to put her off again, but he didn't.

"I think they're amateurs."

"Is that good or bad?"

"Both—maybe—"

"Why?"

"They're scared. I don't think they've ever done anything like this before. They don't have much—self-control. It's hard to predict what a man with a gun will do when he's scared."

"You mean one of them might kill us in panic," she said quietly.

"Yes."

"What did you say to them?" she asked again.

"It was a religious quote. I . . . wanted to see which he put first—his revolution or his religion. And I didn't want him to hurt you. I don't know if I got it all right—but he understood. I got places all over me where he understood . . ."

"David, don't. Don't—" she whispered. He was being cute again, and he was doing it for her. She simply couldn't bear it.

"Hey—you're not crying again, are you?"

"None of your business!" she snapped. "Tell me about the quote."

"It's kind of a—loophole."

"A loophole?"

"Yeah. It says that men's souls are inclined to covet things—but if a man is kind to women, if he fears to wrong them, God will know him—God will be well-acquainted with what he does."

"Sounds like a good deal to me."

"I thought we weren't going to be cute," he chided.

"That's not being cute. That's the *truth*."

"Ms. Worth?"

"What?"

"I like it when you call me David. What can I call you?"

"Ms. Worth," Annemarie said. Lord, she thought. This cute business is catching.

"No, really. What's your name?"

"Annemarie," she said. "All one name—no middle name."

"Annemarie. That's nice. It suits you."

"Oh, sure. All we librarians and schoolteachers are named Annemarie—"

"Hey. Hey—you're not crying again, are you?"

"Yes, I am. All in all, Gannon, this has really been one *hell* of a day, and you know what's really bad? I'm starving. My hands are tied. And I've got two of Teresa's cookies in my pocket..."

"Sabah Il-khair"

Annemarie's eyes flew open. Had she been asleep? How could she possibly sleep?

"Sabah In-nur," David said in return, his voice wary.

The sun must be up, Annemarie thought. She could see the man plainly. He was older, not one of the ones who had brought them here. She looked around her. They were in a room—not a cave, a niche that had been cut into rock.

"You speak our language very well," the man said to David. He was dressed in Western clothes—a white shirt and khaki pants. "Why is it you speak our language so well? What is it you do in our country?"

"I teach handicapped children how to feed themselves," David said.

Ah, Annemarie thought. This is what David meant by "telling the truth."

The man abruptly clapped his hands together, and two other men came into the room. Annemarie could feel the fear rising in her. No, not fear. Fear was too tame a word for what she was feeling. It was more like raw panic. They came straight to her, lifting her to her feet and leading her out. She managed one last look at David before they forced her through the door. His eyes held hers for a split second, telling her the same thing he'd whispered last night.

Be brave —

"Where the hell have you been?" David said — as if she'd stayed away deliberately and could have done something about coming back sooner.

"I've been answering questions."

"Are you all right?"

She looked at him. He wasn't asking what he meant. Had she told them he was in the United States Marines and were they coming to kill him was what he meant.

"Are you?" he asked again. This time she nodded, sitting down heavily on the ground across from him. Her hands had been untaped, and she noted that his hands were free as well. The only difference was that he was now wearing leg irons. Leg irons and Nike running shoes. What incongruity.

"What kind of questions?"

She looked up at him. She was so tired. She hadn't given David away, and the effort left her exhausted. "The same four or five. Am I with the CIA? What am I doing in their country? What are you doing in their country? What is the plan we were sent here to carry out? Am I a relative of the President?" She put her face into her hands for a moment. "I did what you said," she said in barely a whisper. "I told the truth. They know a lot about Charlie now. It—makes them very angry. They want to hear about some kind of plot to take over this country; I talk about visiting a hospital to feed one of their abandoned children . . ."

"Did they feed you?"

"A little. You?"

"No. You still got the cookies on you?"

"Yes—but—hold out your hand."

"What?" he asked, doing what she asked. She aligned her hand over his and shook her sleeve. Three pieces of bread and two chunks of fig fell out.

David grinned. "What is this?"

"Your lunch—listen, if you don't want it—" she said, making a grab for it.

"I want it!" he assured her, wolfing the bread down. He went a little slower on the pieces of fig. "How did you get by with this?"

"It wasn't too hard. I ate with my cheek propped on my hand. I was afraid to try anything big. So. What's new?" She was looking directly into his eyes when she asked him.

"Nothing," he said, looking away.

"David, please. Don't do that. I can take it. When I was a little girl my mother told me she'd never worry about me because I was a realist. I'll do better if I know."

He shifted his position, making the leg irons clank.

"Please," she said again, and he looked up at her.

"I still think they're amateurs," he said.

"Why?"

"They aren't keeping us separated, for one thing. We could hatch up any kind of story we wanted to."

"That doesn't matter if they don't plan to believe it

anyway, does it?" she said tiredly. She stretched out on the hard ground with her back to him.

"No, I guess not. I also think they put the religion ahead of the revolution, and I want you to listen to me —are you listening?"

"I'm listening."

"I want you to be very careful not to offend them— are you listening?"

"I'm listening, for god's sake!" She rolled over so that she was facing him.

"Okay. They believe that a person's head is the most holy part of the body, understand?"

"No," she said truthfully.

"It goes in descending order—the soles of the feet are the least holy. Whatever you do, don't sit with the bottoms of your feet toward any of them."

She looked into his eyes. "Are you serious?"

"Annemarie," he said. "You and I are up a very smelly creek—without a paddle. I'm very serious. It's the same way with the left hand. You're not left-handed are you? Don't take anything they offer you or give them anything with your left hand. These bastards are about as wired as you can get—and I don't want you to do anything—*anything*—that's going to send them over the edge. Understand—"

She didn't answer. *This is crazy. This can't be real,* her mind kept insisting, but she was here. Her wrists were raw from duct tape, and for hours, a hysterical Arab had demanded to know if she were a relative of the President of the United States. Annemarie in Wonderland, she thought crazily. She looked around sharply at a noise. Two of them were coming in again.

"My turn," David said, and she looked at him in alarm.

"Don't worry, sweetheart," he said in a very good imitation of Humphrey Bogart. "Just keep your pecker up—"

He winked at her as he went out, and she didn't know whether to laugh or cry. He was being cute again, damn him.

The questionings continued—always separately. She and David passed the time in between sessions with questions of their own—sitting across from each other in the small niche. They got little to eat, and nothing to keep warm with but each other. At least I get fed more often and I'm not in leg irons, Annemarie thought, and she supposed she had David's religious quote to thank for that. She continued to drop bits of pieces of whatever she could into her sleeve for him.

"You never did tell me what you did for a living," David reminded her.

"You were going to guess," she said, because she didn't feel like talking. One became very resistant to having to give information after a while.

"I used both my guesses—what do you do?"

"How do you know I do anything?"

"You act like a woman who does something."

"Just what is that supposed to mean?"

"Now, there you go, Worth. Flying off the handle. It doesn't mean anything. It means you act like a woman who does something, that's all. Women who do something for a living, they got this real streak of—" Annemarie's eyebrows raised a fraction at the word "—in them—"

"We do not!" she said indignantly.

"Do, too," he insisted. "You got to. People would run all over you if you didn't."

"Men, you mean."

"Men—women—whatever. So what do you do?"

"I run a restaurant."

He laughed. It made her mad.

"What is so funny about that!"

"Oh, I don't know. You wear a little apron, I bet, don't you?"

She didn't answer.

"God, you do! Don't you? Tell the truth, Worth."

"Yes, I wear an apron! It's that kind of restaurant!"

"Now, don't get mad at me—"

"I am not mad."

"Sure you are. Know how I know? No contractions. You said *am not*. You're hacked, all right. So what could I get to eat in this restaurant?"

She didn't answer.

"Come on, Annemarie. Don't be mad at me. Tell me what's on the menu. I may want to come by there sometime."

"I am starving to death, Gannon. I don't want to talk about food—"

"Make an exception. Go on. Tell me—please."

She couldn't see him in the dark. He'd had a very long session of questioning today, and she'd thought they'd hurt him again. He wouldn't say when she'd asked him. And he was making her talk to keep her from worrying about it, she suddenly realized.

She cleared her throat. "We—do two meals a day. Breakfast seven to eleven-thirty. Family style twelve to nine."

"What's family style?"

"A traditional mountain meal. If you lived on a farm

and you had the preacher for Sunday dinner, this is what you'd have—" And she proceeded to torture them both with a vivid description.

"Worth! Hey—"

"Gannon, will you leave me alone! And quit kicking me every time you say something!"

"I have to kick you. You ignore me if I don't. I want you to talk to me. Tell me about the Blue Ridge Mountains."

"I've told you about the Blue Ridge Mountains. I've told you about the restaurant, I've told you about the flame azalea, I've told you about the mountain laurel—"

"And the rhododendron—" he supplied helpfully.

"Exactly. There's nothing else to tell."

"Tell me about Naomi and Ruby."

"They're big—and they cook. At the restaurant. Now leave me alone."

"Tell me some more of their mountain sayings."

"David!" Annemarie said in exasperation.

"Go on. Tell me."

She was never going to get a moment's peace if she didn't. "Okay! One time I wanted to wear nail polish— loud red nail polish. I was thirteen. Ruby said I couldn't. I said I was going to anyway. She said I wasn't. I said I was. Then she put her hands on her hips and said, 'Well, we'll just *see* which way the pig went with the butter!'"

David laughed out loud, his infectious laughter making her laugh with him. "What the hell does that mean?"

"I don't know—it means you don't wear the nail polish!"

"And what did Naomi do—no, wait, I know. She

didn't say anything, because she doesn't talk much—
but she was so upset she got the hiccups, right?"

"Right." Lord, Annemarie was thinking. If this kept
up, he'd know as much about her life as she did.

"Okay, Gannon. It's your turn. You talk."

"About what?"

"About when *you* were a little kid."

"You don't want to hear it. Me being a little kid in
the Bronx isn't like you being a little kid in the mountains."

"Go on. Tell me."

He stared at her for a moment. "Okay," he said,
looking into her eyes. "My old man cut out when I was
sixteen. He just couldn't take it anymore, so he left
us—my mom, three brothers, two sisters, and me. No
money. No food in the house. He didn't care. My mom
wouldn't let me quit school—so I got odd jobs. You
know how hard it is to feed seven people on odd jobs? I
worked hard—it didn't do any good. I needed money
—bad. I knew a way to get it, but I got caught. I was
looking at felony larceny when I was seventeen years
old. The parish priest put a good word in for me, because he knew my family situation—and the cop who
could have busted me, he knew, too. He scared the hell
out of me, and he took me home and let me get a good
dose of what it was like to make my mother cry—and
he let me off."

"Go on," Annemarie said when he stopped.

"I . . . wasn't sorry—I was just sorry I got caught. I
was tough, see. I had to get money for the family, so I
did what I had to do. It wasn't *my* fault it just happened
to be against the law, too."

"So what did you do?"

"I was on my way to bust number two. This old street wino turned me around. His name was Archie. He was a World War Two vet—a marine. I went to a Catholic school. He used to come down there to the kitchen at lunchtime for a handout. He'd tell us guys all about his glory days, about storming the beaches in Iwo Jima —stuff like that. Anyway, he told me I had to get myself together. He said I was trying to punish my old man by doing stuff I knew was against the law—but the only person I was hurting was me—and the people who loved me. He said I ought to join the marines, because they'd give me something worth doing—make me find out who I am. I think he even talked to my mom, because she brought it up, my enlisting. I couldn't stand to see the hurt look in her eyes anymore, so I went. And here I am—a big success," he added, holding up one foot to show off his leg iron. "And you can get the pity out of your eyes."

"This isn't pity, Gannon." It was respect—tinged with admiration.

He looked away, and he didn't say anything.

"So where's your father now?" Annemarie asked, because she was just as nosy as he had once confessed to being.

"Home in The Bronx. He came back a few years ago. If we work really hard at it, we can just about manage being in the same room together—for a while."

Annemarie didn't comment on that, thinking how difficult it must be for the both of them.

"So what else do you want to know?" David asked.

"Why? Do you want to try to shock me some more?"

"I'm not trying to shock you."

"Yes, you are. But that's all right—whatever gets you by."

He grinned his slow, mischievous grin. "You want me to tell you about the love of my life?" he offered.

"Go ahead," she said, but she didn't mean it. Of course, he must have one—he was too handsome and personable not to. She just didn't want to hear about it.

"Okay," he said, still grinning, and he launched in to a lengthy, poignant description of—his uncle Salvatore's '59 Harley.

"You got a boyfriend, Ms. Worth?"

"Yes," she answered. There was just the barest flicker of something in his eyes—as if he hadn't expected that answer.

He recovered quickly. "Yeah? What's his name?"

"Russell Chandler."

"So what does this—Russell do? Is he a preacher or something like that?"

"No, he's not a preacher. Why would you think he's a preacher?"

"You just seem like somebody who would hang out with a preacher, I guess. So what does he do?"

"He sells mountain real estate."

"Yeah? You and Russell—you getting married?"

"No."

"No? Why not?"

"I've been married," she said evenly, thinking it was his turn to be shocked for a change. The straight-laced little restaurant owner who ought to hang out with a preacher had been married.

And this new turn of events definitely interested him. "Your husband—did he die or something?"

"Or something."

"What?"

"None of your business."

"What's that got to do with anything?" He poked the side of her foot with his. "So tell me. What happened to him?"

"We—Grayson Barkley and I—got divorced."

"Damn, Ms. Worth," he said incredulously.

"So how come you're not marrying Russell?"

"He hasn't asked me."

"What—is he crazy?"

Annemarie laughed. David Gannon could be very charming sometimes.

And then again.

"Worth—hey!"

"What!"

"Play Twenty Questions with me."

"No."

"Why not?"

"Because your questions are too earthy, that's why not."

"Earthy? My questions are *earthy?* Hey—don't I spell anything I think'll make your eyebrows go up?"

"It doesn't help," she assured him.

"It's only words, Worth—" He kicked her foot again. "Hey, did you hear that? 'Words, Worth.' Pretty cute."

"Quit kicking me!"

"You have to quit letting words get you all pushed out of shape like you do. I mean, what are they—an arrangement of letters."

"They might be an arrangement of letters in The Bronx. In Meadows of Dan, they'll get your mouth washed out with soap."

* * *

"So how old are you, Ms. Worth?"

She looked at him hard. He was wearing his Dead End Kid grin.

"I am in my thirties," she said loftily.

"Yeah? Me, too. I don't think I'm going to get out of them."

She looked at him with such alarm that he reached out to touch her, his hand warm and firm on her arm. It was a kind of unspoken agreement between them. At night, they slept together to keep warm. In the day, they rarely touched.

"That's not what I meant, Ms. Worth. I meant I was going to be like Jack Benny—I'm not going to go past thirty-nine. I didn't mean to scare you."

But she was scared. She was scared all the time—except during these conversations he insisted they get into.

"Ms. Worth? What's wrong? What's *wrong!*"

Annemarie could hear him—perfectly. She just couldn't seem to answer him.

"Where are you going!" he yelled at her.

"I have to get out of here," she murmured. "Let—go —David—"

"God, you're burning up with fever—come over here—come on—"

"You don't understand. I have to get out—I have to get *out!*"

"Annemarie!" he yelled at her, wrapping his arms around her to keep her still. "Stop it! I'm going to let you go now—"

He did, and she tried to run.

"David, please! Please! I have to go—I don't like it here—"

"I know," he whispered, holding her tight, brushing her hair back out of her eyes. "Not now—not now, Annie. You have to lie down now."

"Lie down?"

"Yes. Right now."

"David—I feel so bad."

"I know. Come over here. What are you looking for?"

"Teresa's cookies. I don't feel like eating. I want you to have them."

"We ate them already, Annie. A long time ago."

"We did?"

"Yes—lie down. Take it easy, okay?"

"Okay—okay. I—hurt, David."

"Where?"

"Everywhere. Am I going to die?"

"No, you're not going to die."

"Yes, I am. I'm going to be just like Lady Elizabeth . . ."

"Annie, don't talk crazy, okay? I don't like it when you talk crazy."

"No—no, you don't understand. Her diary's in the Carroll County Library. She was my great—great—aunt. She didn't want to leave the mountains either. She—died. Out West, on the frontier. David, promise me! Please! If I die, promise you'll take me home—"

"Annie, you're not going to die."

"Promise me! You'll put me somewhere where you can find me, won't you? And then when you can—I want you to take me home. Don't leave me here, David!"

"No, no, I won't."

"You promise?"

"I promise."

"Good. Good—then. Lady Elizabeth's husband brought her home—after she died. I'm like her, David. She couldn't live away from the mountains, and I couldn't either. Grayson—Grayson took me away. I loved him so—but I couldn't—stay there, don't you see? I tried so *hard,* but it made him angry. If I loved him, I shouldn't have to *try.* Go home to your hillbillies, Annemarie! Go home! David, I'm so cold!"

She could feel his arms wrapped around her, feeling him rocking her as if she were a child.

"He married the wrong one of us," Annemarie murmured.

"Who?"

"Grayson."

"Annie, let's don't talk about Grayson anymore," David said tiredly. "The man was a sonofabitch. Try to sleep."

"No, he just married the wrong one of us. He should have married my sister Susan. Susan is—so beautiful. You wouldn't believe how beautiful she is. And she hates living in the mountains—he could have been happy with Susan. Or my sister Charity. She's smart, David. She would have known what to do. Charity is smart and Susan is beautiful. And I'm stuck in the middle. I'm not anything—except I can run a restaurant like nobody's business."

"I bet you can," David whispered.

"I like it, you know? I really like it. All kinds of people come in—all kinds. That's why I know you're from Picayune, Mississippi."

He laughed softly, his arms tightening around her.

"I love talking to all those people—is anybody looking for us, do you think?"

"Sure they are."

"David?"

"What?"

"You are such a liar."

"Annie?"

"What?"

"How do you feel?"

"I feel better."

"Are you sure?"

"Yes—I'm sure."

"We still have to test."

"Test?"

"Yeah—answer this: What planet are you on?"

Annemarie looked around the stone walls of the niche. "Damned if I know," she assured him, and they both giggled like children.

"Gannon?"

"What, Annemarie?"

"When I was sick—did I tell you about Grayson?"

"Everything but his shoe size, Annemarie."

"Oh," she said, wondering when it was he'd started calling her by her first name. She looked at him carefully. He was losing weight. She couldn't hide enough of her own ration up her sleeve to keep him fed.

"What is it, Annemarie?" he asked, apparently because of her scrutiny.

"I was just wondering . . ."

"What?"

"Are you married?"

"Nope."

"Why not?"

"She wouldn't marry me. She didn't want to be a camp follower."

"A—camp follower?"

"That's what she said. She didn't want to be dragged all over the world with me. From what you said about you and Grayson, you can understand that, I guess."

Annemarie looked at him thoughtfully. She could understand it well enough. She'd hated having to go from city to city with Grayson while he tried to find an upwardly mobile executive lifestyle that suited him. She'd been miserable living in treeless, urban concrete away from her beloved mountains, so miserable she'd let it ruin her marriage. And now, having experienced such wrenching homesickness, she had nothing but empathy for anyone who had to be in a situation that might be similar. Usually. Ordinarily, she would have been feeling sorry for this woman who wasn't interested in camp following. This time she wasn't; she was feeling sorry for David.

"What was her name?" Annemarie asked, knowing from the closed expression David was wearing she probably shouldn't.

"Gina. Her name was Gina. She was my high school sweetheart. She was the first girl I ever made love with, and I was crazy about her. She wasn't so crazy about me—not with a military career and three brothers, a mother, and two sisters who were used to having me take care of them. She told me to forget it, and I thought it would kill me. It didn't. I have known and been fond of a lot of women since then, but I'm not married now because I never met one I cared about enough to marry, okay?"

"Okay, okay!" Annemarie tried to hold back a question, but it wouldn't be held. "What about Karen?"

"Karen who?"

"The nurse at American Hospital—the one who painted the Mickey Mouse oasis. She's in love with you, you know."

"Where in the hell did you get that information?"

Annemarie quietly held up both forefingers, rotating her wrists inward, and pointed to her two eyes.

"Knock it off, Annemarie," David said. "Tell me about your dad."

"I thought you wanted me to knock it off."

"I want you to knock it off about Karen. You can tell me about your dad. Why don't you talk about him?"

Annemarie didn't answer. She'd had a very different relationship with her father from the one he'd had with his, and she just hadn't brought it up.

"Go on. Tell me. Your mother died when you were twelve, right?"

She nodded absently.

"And?" he said pointedly.

She sighed. "And . . . my dad is a very . . . kind man. He's funny. He likes to joke around a lot. The restaurant on the Blue Ridge Parkway was the dream of his life. He always thought Joe would take it over, but he got me instead. Joe hated it. I didn't. Technically, Dad retired, but he still comes to the restaurant every day—and he goes fishing when he feels like it. He likes to keep Naomi and Ruby stirred up all the time."

"Why is that?"

"Oh, he was kind of . . . wild when he was young."

"Wild for Meadows of Dan, or wild for the rest of the world?"

"I'm going to ignore that," Annemarie said, and he grinned.

"Go on."

"Naomi and Ruby were two of the great host of people who advised my mother not to marry him. They still think he's going to do something awful after all these years—and he just loves making sure they do. His latest thing really has them going."

"What's that?"

"Well, this retired man from England bought some mountain property near the restaurant—his only daughter lived in Roanoke, and he wanted to be near his grandchildren. Anyway, he started something called the Calder Valley Mouse Club, American Branch."

"God, what is that?"

"I don't know. It's very private—men only—by invitation only. Naomi and Ruby can't find out what they do there—I think they think naked women jump out of cakes or something. It makes them *crazy*—Daddy makes sure of that."

David was smiling. "Your mom and dad—they had a happy marriage?"

Annemarie nodded. "They loved each other, and all us kids knew it." She stopped talking, suddenly overwhelmed with memories and with the reality of her situation now. Her eyes were welling, and she looked away.

"Worth—hey—" David said, reaching out to put his hand on her shoulder. "Don't do that. I didn't mean to make you sad."

She gave him an apologetic, wobbly smile and tried to wipe the tears away. She couldn't wipe fast enough.

"Hey," he said again. "I thought you weren't going to bawl anymore."

"I lied," she managed, abruptly reaching for him. He

hesitated for an instant—because it wasn't cold or dark, because she wasn't raving with fever, and they still had their unspoken, no-touching agreement.

But then he wrapped his arms around her, comforting her with one whispered word: "Annie . . ."

Something was happening. The food ration was cut, and the questioning intensified—for David. He was taken out of the niche more and more often. This time he was so quiet when he returned, sitting against the wall with his knees draw up and his eyes closed. When she couldn't stand it anymore, she asked him if he was all right.

He turned away from her. "Leave me alone, Ms. Worth."

They began to take David out in the middle of the night. It was as if they had consulted someone about the best way to wear a captive down, and they were now employing what they'd learned. David said little, and what he did say left her more worried and anxious.

"You know what they've got in this part of the world, Ms. Worth?"

Why was she "Ms. Worth" again? Annemarie wondered.

"No. What?"

"Hate. Centuries and centuries of it. It's so . . . refined. So . . . pure. They feed off it, Ms. Worth."

"David—"

But he was shutting her out, sitting with his knees up and his eyes closed. And he'd taken to quietly singing to himself, a song she recognized, one that gave her gooseflesh. Phil Collins's eerie "In The Air Tonight."

*   *   *

It had been hours and hours since they'd taken David out. Annemarie lay on the hard ground, listening. She couldn't hear anything—no voices, no movement outside the niche. She moved closer to the opening.

Still nothing.

She lay on the ground, watching a shaft of sunlight track across the opening.

Wait, Annemarie. All you have to do is wait. You can do that.

She waited. The shaft of light moved. She placed her fingers just outside the edge of that beam of light, and she waited until it reached them. Again and again.

David!

I can't stand this anymore, she thought. She sat up and crawled to the opening, squinting against the brightness as she peered outside.

Nothing. No one.

She was going to have to go out; there was no other way.

She stood in the doorway for a moment to shore up her courage.

"Well," she whispered. "We'll just *see* which way the pig went with the butter—"

She stepped into the light.

CHAPTER

Four

ANNEMARIE STOOD VERY still, listening, her eyes aching from the bright sunlight. She could hear nothing, see no one. This place—this primitive dwelling place with many rooms cut into the sides of a crater in the earth—yielded nothing. She walked cautiously along the narrow ledge that led from one doorway to another. She was afraid to call out. She stepped on some loose rocks and they tumbled down into the crater, the noise echoing loudly around her. She held her breath.

Nothing.

She moved on, trying to be quiet.

Clink!

Annemarie whirled around at the sound, holding her breath again, listening intently.

Nothing.

She waited, then moved on around the ledge, peering into each doorway as she came to it. The ground was littered now with the evidence of their captors having been here—stepped-on cigarette butts, orange peels, and a crushed Coke can. The sun beat down on her head.

Clink!

The sound came again, sharply this time, making her jump.

"David?" she called softly.

"What?" he answered calmly, his voice echoing around her.

"Where are you?"

"In here."

"Where?"

"Here!"

Her knees nearly buckled with relief when she saw his hand appear briefly out a doorway below her. She scrambled over the rocks to get to it, finding him doing what she would have expected him to be doing—working on logistics. He was trying to get out of the leg irons, hitting a weakened link with a rock he had in one hand. His other hand he kept pressed close to his side.

Annemarie dropped to her knees beside him.

"You okay?" he said without looking up from the chain he was battering.

"No, I'm not okay—I thought you were dead!"

He glanced at her. His face was bruised, and one eye was swollen shut. "Nope," he said unnecessarily. "We've got to get out of here, Worth. Go look and see what you can find—see if they've left any food."

She didn't move.

"Well, go on," he said. "We've got to get out of here before they come back."

That was enough to spur her to get up again. "Where did they go?"

"Damned if I know. It looks like the ballgame's over, but we're not going to wait around here to see—damn, this thing!" he said in frustration over the leg irons. She looked back at him once before she went outside, closing her eyes in relief. He was all right, thank God.

She didn't take the time to explore her feelings any further, noting only that David Gannon's safety was vitally important to her.

She couldn't find much in the way of supplies—a half-eaten orange and some dates that had been dropped on the ground. When she returned, David was still beating the leg-iron chain with a rock. He was pale and sweating, and he'd made no progress at all.

"I can't get the damn thing off," he told her. "What did you find?"

She showed him what little she had, wondering why he was avoiding her eyes. "Not much."

"They left a half canteen of water—"

"David?"

"What?" he asked, working on the leg irons again.

"You want to tell me what's on your mind?"

"Getting the hell out of here, Worth."

"Don't do that!" she cried. "You're in pain, and you're talking at me, not to me. What is it?"

He almost smiled, but his face was grave when he finally looked up.

"I'm in chains, Annie. I think I've got some broken ribs. You're in better shape than I am. We've got a better chance if you take the water and walk it out alone."

She stared back at him, determined not to let him see how much this calmly stated, matter-of-fact suggestion upset her. "What—" she began, but her voice broke, and she started again. "What is—the plan?" She knew he must have one. She'd listen to it carefully, and then she'd tell him what he could do with it.

"Our friends always came and went in that direction —south. I think if you go at night—if you walk in that direction you'll likely run into somebody."

"Them, for instance."

"No—you know what the truck looks like. And you can see the lights or the dust from any kind of vehicle from a long way off. They aren't going to be able to sneak up on you. I think you'll run into a highway eventually. They came and went too quickly for us to be very far out."

"We're talking rough terrain, no road until then, and in the dark, though, aren't we?"

"Yes."

"I suppose you've had desert-survival training—how to keep from meandering in circles and what's edible and what's not—things like that?"

"Yes, but—"

"I've had training in how to quilt and crochet—oh, and I've got a degree in business administration. It comes in really handy at the restaurant, but it hasn't done me a lot of good lately. Now, while I'm out there with all my experience—surviving in the desert—what —" She had to stop because her voice was rising. She took a deep breath. "What is it exactly that you're going to be doing?"

"I'll be waiting here."

"Waiting," she repeated. "Without water. For what?"

"For you to send somebody back for me." He was avoiding her eyes again. "I'm hoping you'll hurry."

"Don't be cute!" she cried, and he reached out to take both her hands. Her fists were clenched, and he made her open them, sliding his fingers in between hers. She looked down at their interlocked fingers, loving the feel of his warm hands even in the middle of all this.

"You said you wanted me to tell you the truth. Well, here it is—" He paused, and she looked up at him. "I think you can make it. I don't think I can. You understand?"

She nodded.

"Good. I'm counting on you to do it. I'll give you a crash course in—"

"There's just one thing," she interrupted.

"What?"

"I'm not going to do it. I'm not taking the water and leaving you here. If I did make it to a highway, I might not be able to find this place again. If it were easy to find, they wouldn't have used it. Listening to you now, I just realized something about you—and Hershel. Your job is to protect American lives and property, and you see yourselves as expendable. If I had brought a bomb or something into the embassy that day, your job would have been to stop me or to go up with me, wouldn't it?"

He didn't answer her.

"You're not—expendable to me. I'm not brave. My perseverance isn't what it should be—Grayson could tell you about that. A person like me needs a lot of moral support, so if we're going out of here, we're going together. I don't care if you are in chains. I don't care if you have to take itty-bitty steps from here to— Cairo. I don't care if I have to drag you by your leg irons. I'm not going anywhere without you. We go together, or we don't go at all."

"Annemarie—"

"No! And you're not going to make me do it, Gannon."

He tried. He talked to her, reasoned with her, swore at her until they were both near tears. She finally had to escape from him, going blindly out of the niche and sitting on the ground on the ledge outside. She could hear him coming slowly after her.

David, I can't go without you! an inner voice pleaded.

"Annemarie—" he said. He had to hold on to the doorway to stay upright.

"No," she said stubbornly, trying not to cry. "No! No!"

He sighed. "Okay," he said finally. "You win."

It was a painful victory. She could hardly bear watching him struggle along, and she finally had to do something about it, sliding her arm around his waist on his good side, hooking her fingers in his belt loops on his bad side so she wouldn't forget and touch his ribs. He leaned on her heavily, but the going was easier. They could see the glow of lights from a city or town, and they kept walking.

It was cold in the desert at night.

"We have to find—some shade," David said, his breathing shallow and gasping from the exertion and the pain and heat of the sun.

The best they could do was a narrow outcropping of rock that the two of them could barely sit under. David fitted himself painfully under it first, and then Annemarie followed, taking off her jacket and draping it over both their heads. Dozing, not talking, and hiding David from the sun, she waited for the night to come again.

*   *   *

David heard it first, and he prodded her to listen.

"What?" she kept saying, because she heard nothing.

"Listen!" he said again.

This time she heard it. The flapping noise of a helicopter. She scrambled to her feet, running into the open, waving her jacket into the air. The helicopter was low and moving at a right angle from her, too fast and too far away.

All the energy seemed to drain from her, and she sank down on her knees, her arms wrapped around her, her head bowed. It was no use. They were not going to get out. Never...

She lifted her head. The flapping noise was getting louder. She shaded her eyes.

"David!" she cried.

It was coming back. Incredibly, it was coming back! She stood up again, waving her jacket, still yelling for David. The helicopter was hovering now—she could see the Aramco emblem on the side. She dropped her jacket, running to help David get up. They stood arm in arm, hiding their faces from the whipped-up sand as it came lower to land, David's unshaven face rasping against her cheek.

"That's my brother, Joe!" she yelled at him when the first man climbed out of the helicopter's open door. Joe was running toward her, several other men in Aramco jumpsuits following behind him. She reached toward her brother with her free hand, but she didn't let go of David. She held on to David's hand as long as she could, until the men were taking him away from her, and Joe was lifting her off her feet.

"Annemarie! Thank God!" he was yelling at her. "Are you okay?"

"Hi, Joe," she said, as if she were at home in the Virginia mountains and he'd just dropped in. "What's new?"

"Are you all right!" he demanded, still yelling. Cuteness in a crisis didn't work on him, either.

"I've been better, Joe," she told him truthfully. "David—Sergeant Gannon—" She turned to see what they were doing to him.

He was being put on a stretcher, and Joe was urging her along with him. He lifted her up into the helicopter, handing her over to another man in an Aramco jumpsuit, who made her sit down immediately. She was covered in a blanket, and she hadn't realized how dirty and ragged she was until she saw the shock in her brother's eyes.

He abruptly hugged her to him anyway.

"Are the girls all right?" she asked, sagging against him.

"Yeah, they're fine—God, I've been so worried! Are you sure you're okay?"

"We need to give her some fluids, Joe," one of the men in jumpsuits said. Annemarie thought he meant something to drink, but he had a plastic bag of intravenous fluids in his hand.

The man made her lie down, starting the fluids expertly in a vein in her forearm. "Sergeant Gannon—?" she asked him.

"He's going to be on his butt for a while, but he's okay."

They were bringing David on board, and she reached out to touch his hand briefly as his stretcher passed. He gave her a thumbs-up signal and a weak grin.

She took in little of the flight, nothing of their admission to American Hospital. She woke in a light, airy room with a bedraggled Joe at her bedside, thinking how much he was beginning to resemble their father.

"You look worse than I do," she told him.

He grinned. "No, I don't."

"Do you think I could get anything to eat around here?" She was starving.

Joe told her she had slept thirteen hours. She wanted to get up, and she wanted to see David.

"I don't think they'll let you see him," Joe said. "He's military. He has to be debriefed."

"He's all right, isn't he?"

"They tell me he's doing fine."

"Then why can't I see him? I was there. I know what happened."

"Annemarie, there's something else . . ."

"What?"

"This—the hostage taking—it didn't happen."

She gaped at him.

"What do you mean it didn't happen!"

"Not officially. Ever since this group—whoever they are—made their demands, I've had State Department people all over me. Dad and the folks back home don't know anything about it. I had to tell him you were going to visit here for a while—because I'd decided if you'd just wait, I could wind up things here and come home with you. Then I had to say your passport was stolen and we had to wait for a replacement—oh, and you've had the flu. That will take care of your . . . looking the way you do."

"Thanks a lot," she said, and he grinned. "Why couldn't you say anything? How long have I been gone?"

"Kharan is one of our few allies in the oil cartel; the government couldn't afford an—incident is how I understand it. And, Annemarie, you were missing twenty-six days."

Twenty-six days. So. She was expendable, too.

"Unofficially, they did everything they could, honey. And Aramco. When we got the word that you'd been set free in the desert, Aramco put out helicopters to help look for you. The official word for the hospital staff here is that you were on a trip with one of those safari groups and you got lost for a few days. Sergeant Gannon went looking for you."

"Didn't anybody wonder why he was in leg irons?" This was crazy!

"He wasn't—by then."

She closed her eyes. "I'm going to be glad to get home."

Except for leaving David.

She opened her eyes again. She shouldn't be thinking things like that. She looked at her brother and tried to push the thought aside.

"Well, that's another thing," he said.

"Don't tell me they aren't going to let me go home!"

"No, you can go as soon as you're able. But they have—requests."

"What kind of requests!"

"Honey, I don't know—don't worry about it now. In a couple of days, you and the girls and I are going home. Let me go tell somebody you're hungry..."

Annemarie recovered rapidly. She was interviewed endlessly by embassy people, and she was still waiting to see David. She thought about him constantly, but no one could tell her anything about him. It puzzled her that he hadn't at least sent her some kind of word, a chocolate chip cookie—*something*. She stayed in the hospital for five days—very much against her own wishes, and yet another representative from the State Department came to see her on the morning she was to be discharged.

He was a somber-looking man wearing a dark gray suit who introduced himself as Mr. Beam and noted politely that she was looking well.

"Thank you," she said. She thought this man was more important than the others, and she waited for the "requests" Joe had warned her about.

"Sergeant Gannon has told us that you were very brave," he said next.

"I was a sniveling basket case," she said matter-of-factly, and Mr. Beam's somberness faded for a moment into a smile. "I would have fallen apart completely if it hadn't been for Da—Sergeant Gannon. Is he all right? I haven't been allowed to see him."

"He's doing very well, Ms. Worth. He has had some fractured ribs, some lung congestion, I believe, but you have no cause to worry. I saw him just this morning. Ms. Worth—" he said, and clearly the smiling was over. "Your government appreciates the fact that you have—suffered—on its behalf. You have been through a great deal, and unfortunately, it is my task to ask you to prolong it—"

"My brother has told me some things," Annemarie interrupted, wanting to get whatever this was finished. She was determined to see David before she left this place. "Kharan is an ally in the Mideast oil cartel. You don't want to rock the boat."

"Yes. It's very important, Ms. Worth, or I wouldn't be here. It is imperative that we keep this thing under wraps. Americans are tired of being targeted, Ms. Worth—and rightly so. We can't afford a—cause, if you will, at this time—"

"You think *I* could become a cause?" Annemarie said.

He smiled again. "With the right press man. Teddy Roosevelt is very popular these days."

"I beg your pardon?"

"I was alluding to a Hollywood movie version of Teddy Roosevelt's sending the marines to fetch an American woman who had been kidnapped and held for ransom in this part of the world—but then, you had your marine with you, didn't you? Let me just say that any notoriety at this point—when the cartel is just about to meet again—could cause widespread economic repercussions. We ask that you not give out any information about your ordeal to the media, that you not speak of it to anyone—not even to your family. You are an American citizen, Ms. Worth. Your government can't order you to comply, we can only request your help. Do you understand?"

"Yes, I understand," she answered. This was the same as her not being upset because Hershel had thought she was carrying a bomb.

"I also have this for you," he said, handing her a card. "This is the name of a therapist in your vicinity. He has had experience in helping Americans who have been in your situation to. . . . readjust. It may be difficult for you at first, particularly since we've asked you not to use one of your primary support groups—your family. We're not unmindful of what a difficult thing we're asking you to do—"

"Ms. Worth," one of the nurses said, rapping gently on the door and pushing it open. "Your brother is waiting downstairs. He says to tell you you have to come right now or you'll miss the plane—and he's double-parked."

"Thank you," Annemarie said, gathering up her purse.

"I'll walk out with you," Mr. Beam said.

But Annemarie wasn't leaving just then—whether Joe was double parked or not. She had something else to do first. She walked out into the hallway, Mr. Beam not far behind. The nurse's station was crowded with various hospital personnel.

"I'd like to see Sergeant Gannon before I leave," she said to the nurse in charge. The nurse glanced at Mr. Beam.

"No, I'm sorry, Ms. Worth. You can't."

"Why not?" Annemarie asked. Again the nurse glanced at Mr. Beam.

"His medical condition is—"

"I know what his medical condition is," Annemarie said, surprising herself with her forceful tone. "I'm catching a plane in forty-five minutes. I want to see him. Now." She caught a glimpse of Joe as he got off the elevator.

"Annemarie?" he said. "Didn't anybody tell you I was waiting? I've left the girls in the car—what's going on?"

"I want to see David," she said, knowing her voice was rising but unable to do anything about it.

"David," Joe repeated as if he'd never heard of him. He glanced from her to the nurse and back again.

"Look!" Annemarie said. "Don't you start with me, too! I want to see Sergeant David Gannon. I don't care if he hasn't been debriefed! I don't care if he's conscious or unconscious! I want to see him. I'm not leaving here until I do!"

"Annemarie—we have to catch the plane," Joe said,

taking her by the arm. She was embarrassing him, but she couldn't help that.

"Don't any of you understand? He's my friend! I'm not going out of here without seeing him!" She jerked her arm out of her brother's grasp.

No, they probably didn't understand. The hospital staff thought she was some addleheaded tourist who'd wandered off from her safari group in the desert. Even Joe didn't seem to understand that David Gannon was much more than just the man she was with when she was rescued. She and David had been together for twenty-six days. They'd taken care of each other. She couldn't have made it without him, and she had to see him!

"Mr. Beam," she said, turning to him. "The nurse here keeps looking at you. Do I get in to see David—or don't I? And before you answer me, please remember what we talked about just now. Whether or not you get what you want depends on my getting what I want— right now!"

"Good God, Annemarie," Joe said under his breath.

"Joe, be quiet!" she hissed at him.

"This man is from the State Department," he reminded her.

"And I help pay his salary! Mr. Beam? What's it going to be? Do I see Sergeant Gannon or don't I?"

Mr. Beam stared at her a long moment and then smiled. "Down that corridor," he said. "Turn left. He's in the last room on the right."

"Thank you," Annemarie said.

"Ms. Worth!" Mr. Beam called after her. "May I report that you've given me your word?"

"Yes, Mr. Beam," she said over her shoulder, and she kept walking, leaving the nurses' station in a buzz and Joe worrying about her sanity. She couldn't help that now. She had to see David.

When she reached his room, she hesitated outside the closed door.

What if there had been some good reason for her not being able to see him? she thought suddenly. What if he'd asked not to be bothered by mindlessly grateful tourists or something?

No, he wouldn't do that. She took a deep breath and smoothed her hair back into its knot, then she rapped lightly on the door.

"Yeah? Come in," David said on the other side of it.

He sounded fine, and Annemarie pushed the door open.

"Annie!" he cried when he saw her, but the enthusiasm of his greeting did nothing to change the fact that he wasn't alone. Karen was with him, sitting on his bed, her legs folded under her tailor-fashion. She and David were eating ice cream.

"Damn, Ms. Worth, if you don't clean up good," he said, looking her over. She was wearing yet another no-nonsense linen suit, this one yellow with a white silk blouse. He was never going to see her when she didn't look as if she were about to lead a group of children or catalog a book. And she didn't feel as if she "cleaned up good." She suddenly felt like Susan and Charity Worth's plain and not-so-smart sister.

Even so, she was smart enough to know when three was a crowd. She could see it on Karen's face, feel it in David's too-cheerful welcome. And Lord, he was so handsome! He'd cleaned up nicely himself, bruised face or not. She'd forgotten how good-looking he was. He was clean-shaven again, and his blue eyes—she couldn't think straight if she looked into his eyes.

"Come over here—I'll give you a bite," he said, holding a spoonful of ice cream toward her, still trying to be hospitable. She made herself smile.

"No, thanks. Hello, Karen . . ."

Karen waved a few fingers at her, and clearly felt no compunction about staying.

"It's homemade, Annie," David said, still trying to share his ice cream with her. "Karen tells me Charlie sent it. I owe you a bite for all those pieces of figs. Come here. Come here . . ."

She went—because she was too ill-at-ease not to. She was feeling too many things at once—sadness because she was leaving, embarrassment at having interrupted something between the two of them, jealousy because Karen was here in the first place.

"Good," she said around the spoonful David fed her. "Peach."

"Nectarine," Karen said.

"So pull up a chair," David said.

"No—no, I haven't the time. Joe's waiting for me. I . . . just wanted to say thanks for—everything." She forced herself to smile again. "So—" She gave an awkward shrug and backed toward the door. "Good-bye. I won't forget what you did for me."

"I didn't do anything," he protested, but he was still being polite.

"Well—I think you did," Annemarie said, opening the door. "If you're ever in the Blue Ridge, stop by the restaurant. Russell and I will show you the sights. Milepost 179—"

She looked into his eyes again, realizing that if she didn't get out of here, she'd cry. She didn't know what she'd expected, seeing David again, but this wasn't it.

She gave him a small wave and fled, running headlong into Joe, who was pacing worriedly outside.

"Annemarie—the plane!"

"I'm ready," she told him, but it wasn't true. She wasn't ready. She wasn't ready at all. She didn't want to leave here. No—she didn't want to leave David. It was all she could do not to go back into his room and tell him, Karen or no Karen.

She briefly closed her eyes and took a deep breath, forcing herself to walk away.

"I can't *believe,*" Joe complained on the way out, "you actually blackmailed a government official!"

CHAPTER

Five

ANNEMARIE COULDN'T BELIEVE she'd done it either, any more than she could believe that she was so bereft at leaving that she wept quietly on the plane for hours.

What is the matter with me? she chided herself.

She was going home to her beloved mountains. *Home*. To the place she, like Lady Elizabeth, had never wanted to leave. But her mind was filled with only one thought: David.

She sat next to the window on the plane, holding on to Joe's hand for comfort, trying to put up a brave front for her nieces and the flight attendants, pleading air sickness as an excuse for her ravaged face.

She was better by the time she reached New York. Quieter, at any rate, not so tearful. She was simply going to have to put all this behind her. It was over. She

81

and David Gannon were really strangers, regardless of
their ordeal. He was supposed to protect American lives
and property abroad, and she had been the living,
breathing personification of his job—a job that ended
once they were in the hospital in Kharan. They had
nothing in common but an event that both of them
wanted only to forget.

Intellectually, she understood all these things, and
she tried to get back into the routine of her life. Because
Joe and the girls had come with her, she had no difficulty explaining her prolonged stay to her father. But
Russell was another matter. She had known him since
they were both children. They had no real romantic interest in each other; they were just friends who went out
together to keep his mother and Naomi and Ruby and
the rest of the ladies in the church choir from match-
making. She and Russell had an "understanding" sup-
posedly, but it was more a protective convenience than a
reality—or it had been until now. Her unexpectedly
long absence seemed to have had a profound effect on
Russell's feelings about maintaining the status quo of
their relationship. He'd suddenly turned amorous, and
he'd announced while she'd fended him off one night
that he desperately wanted to marry her.

Annemarie handled it the same way she would have
handled it if they had been ten and he'd come up with
some equally hairbrained suggestion. She told him in no
uncertain terms exactly what she thought of it.

Russell was undaunted. He continued to try to kiss
her every chance he got, and he continued to propose,
vowing to "wear her down" until she saw the sense of
the alliance as clearly as he did. They were compatible,
he insisted. They had known each other for years, so
they both knew what they were getting. Everyone

thought they were going to marry sooner or later anyway—so they might as well do it, and by God, he'd
missed her. It was at this point that his passions usually
got the best of him, driving her once to stave him off
with a sound whack over the head with a rolled-up Sunday newspaper she happened to have handy.

She liked Russell. She had always liked him—but it
was David Gannon who filled her mind night and day.
She had nightmares that he was hurt, that he needed her
but she couldn't get to him. In the daytime, she couldn't
concentrate, leaving her father in a bind more than once
at the restaurant because she couldn't seem to work a
cash register anymore.

She went to see the therapist in Roanoke. He listened
attentively to her as she recited the sequence of events
from the hostage-taking, to the scene she'd made at the
hospital when she thought she wasn't going to be allowed to see David, to her constant thoughts about him
now.

The therapist was very matter-of-fact, almost routine. She had, he explained in his soft, comforting
voice, known what it was like to be in the hands of
madmen, to totally lose control of one's fate, to fear
death, and to strive every minute of every day not to do
anything that would cause harm to the other hostage.
And now, for all intents and purposes, she was in love
with him—but only temporarily, he qualified. Because
of the emotional trauma she'd suffered, she was experiencing a kind of lateral Stockholm Syndrome. She had
become attached to her fellow victim instead of her captor. It was a symptom—just as the sleeplessness and the
nightmares and the inability to concentrate were symp-
toms. She mustn't be alarmed at what she was feeling.

And she was to rest assured that all these things would take care of themselves in time.

In time.

She believed what the therapist told her, and she tried to look at her "emotional bonding" realistically. She understood the cause, and time would effect the cure. She did understand; it was just that she was so . . . lonely. She had always had a sense of aloneness, even when she was a little girl, and that had come from her being born in between two outstanding sisters, she thought.

But that feeling wasn't the same as what she felt now. Now was worse, so much worse, the feeling of isolation even more acute than when Grayson had sent her away from him. She missed the intimacy she'd shared with David Gannon. Sometimes she woke up in the mornings expecting him to be there—and, Lord, she *wanted* him to be there. She wanted to feel his arms around her again. She wanted him to tell her she'd be all right. She wanted—more.

The nightmares sometimes gave way to erotic dreams, dreams in which David loved her, made love to her.

But she always woke up bereft and alone.

In time, she kept reminding herself. *In time*. She waited—one month, then another, and another. Russell calmed down somewhat—after she'd promised she'd at least think about his proposal, and she progressed to the point where she could make change again at the cash register. But she still didn't sleep well, and she still missed David. She was trying so hard to forget about him, and one Sunday afternoon in the middle of June she realized how little progress she was making.

She looked up from the cash register, and her heart stopped. A man who looked like David Gannon was crossing the parking area outside. He hesitated for a moment, apparently trying to decide whether he was going to come into the Milepost 179 Gift Shop or into the restaurant.

Please, please! she thought, realizing at that moment that she hadn't been waiting to get over this. She'd been waiting—praying—to see David again.

"Annemarie," her father said at her elbow, and she dragged her eyes away from the man outside. "You want to take this gentleman's money so he can get back to seeing the beauties of the Blue Ridge Parkway?"

She looked at her father and the customer who was trying to pay his check, then left them both standing as she hurried across the crowded dining room to the screen door. The man who looked like David was about to go back in the direction he'd come.

"David!" she called as she pushed the screen door open, letting it bang against the outer wall before it slammed closed. "David!"

The man stopped walking.

Oh, Lord, it *was* David!

He turned around, searching for the location of her voice, finally seeing her standing on the restaurant porch. She hesitated for a moment, then stepped off the porch to walk toward him, her heart pounding in her ears.

Lord, she thought. Don't let me cry. He hates crying. He looked fine, and he didn't say anything as she approached. He was wearing jeans and a T-shirt again. The wind ruffled his dark hair, and his piercingly blue eyes searched her face.

"Hello, beautiful," he said when she reached him, the barest of smiles playing at the corner of his mouth.

"Hello, yourself," she said, her voice so strained she

hardly recognized it. It was all she could do not to fling
herself at him, and the best he could do was a very tame
"Hello, beautiful?"

He continued to stare at her, and the silence lengthened. They were in full view of a goodly portion of the
thousands of people who drove along the parkway on
any given summer Sunday, not to mention her father
and the restaurant staff—all of whom thought she was
on the verge of an engagement to Russell.

"How have you been?" she asked.

"Hey—I'm fine," he said. "I'm great." She knew
immediately that it wasn't true.

"Are you?" she couldn't keep from asking.

He smiled to fool her. "Annie, would I lie to you?
This is the Marine Corps' finest here. I'm *okay*—" His
eyes met hers, but then he abruptly looked away.

Oh, David, she thought.

"Sometimes I don't sleep so good," he admitted,
looking back at her. "You're . . . doing okay." It was
more a statement than a question.

"Yes, fine," she said too quickly.

"Liar," he said softly.

"David—"

"Look, Annie," he interrupted. "I could have written
you a letter, but I wanted to see for myself—how you
were doing. And I'm starving to death—so what do you
think of that?" He grinned his endearing Dead-End-Kid
grin for her.

"I think you'd better come inside and let us feed
you," she said, smiling. She linked her arm through his,
pretending that she could touch him and it would mean
nothing. "Country cooking," she said, trying not to
think about the warmth of his muscular arm or the way

her heart was still pounding. "All you can eat. It's on the house."

"You still got big Naomi and Ruby in the kitchen?"

"Still," she told him.

"You married to Russell yet?"

"No."

"Hot damn," David commented as he held the screen door open for her. "I'm on a roll today. A free dinner—and the best-looking woman in Virginia's still single."

Annemarie laughed and took him on inside. He was "giving her the business," just like he always did.

She bypassed her all-too-interested father at the cash register, leading David through the maze of diners to a small table by the window so he could see the mountain ridges. She left him there with the menu, the sunlight shining through the windowpanes and lighting up his dark hair. He'd let his hair grow a bit longer than she remembered, and it was very becoming, she thought, knowing that the only thing that mattered to her was that he was here; she didn't care what he looked like.

"Who's that?" her father asked immediately.

"David Gannon. He's an embassy guard—the detachment commander, actually, in Kharan."

"Hmm," her father said. He readjusted his mesh Red Man Chewing Tobacco ball cap. Annemarie gave him a furtive look. She wasn't about to comment on his . . . noncomment. Her father could know more without knowing and say more without saying than anybody she'd ever met. And the mere fact that she was now in her thirties did nothing to keep him from poking his nose in where it wasn't wanted. She would have thought that he'd been annoyed enough with Naomi and Ruby's inquisitiveness over the years to show a little restraint himself, but that didn't seem to be the case.

She glanced across the dining room at David, who was inundated suddenly with college-age waitresses who recognized a blatantly sexy male when they saw one. He looked up at her from the menu, waggling his eyebrows at her because of all the attention he was getting. Annemarie couldn't keep from smiling.

"Russell know about him?" her father asked innocently.

"There's nothing to know, Daddy," she said with a patience she didn't feel.

"Does he know about Russell?" her father persisted, still trying to find out something.

"Yes, he knows about Russell," she said testily, losing her patience.

"Hmmm," her father said again. "My hip's bothering me, Annemarie. I got to sit down for a while."

"Fine," she said, and she meant it—until she realized that her father intended to sit with David. "Daddy!" she whispered in his direction, but he didn't hear her— or he was ignoring her the way he always accused her of doing to him. "Deafness by design" he called it, and unless she was very mistaken, her kindly old father was suffering from a bad case of the same ailment. She watched anxiously as David stood up to shake her father's hand. She knew exactly what he was doing. If he couldn't find out from her how this stranger knew her so well and what he was doing here, he'd just have to check it out himself.

Annemarie's attention was taken by several women who wanted to pay for their meals, and she gave one of them too much change. She had to muddle through the counting again, and all the while, her father and David talked.

What am I so worried about? she asked herself.

David certainly wasn't going to tell her father anything about Kharan he wasn't supposed to know. And he was here now because she'd *invited* him to come here. There was no reason why her father couldn't know that, for heaven's sake. She'd met David in Kharan, she'd issued the invitation, he'd taken her up on it, and that was all it was to it. Except that her hands were shaking. Except that her father must have asked her a hundred times of late why she hadn't said yes to Russell.

Well, there you are, Daddy, she thought, looking at them still talking. He's the reason.

She finished at the cash register, swiftly scanning the dining room for another customer ready to leave. There were none at the moment, and she walked back to David's table, pulling a nearby chair around and sitting so she could see if anyone else wanted to pay.

"Are you talking his ear off, Daddy?" she asked, her eyes meeting David's briefly, then darting away. It unsettled her so to look at him, and yet she didn't want to do anything else. "How's the food?" she asked him, saying the first inane thing that came into her mind.

"Great," he said from among the homemade biscuits, country ham, four vegetables, fried chicken, and strawberry preserves that were Naomi and Ruby's specialties. "I'm trying to save room for some of Ruby's cobbler."

"You know about Ruby's cobbler?" Mr. Worth asked, his tone suggesting that there was a great deal more here than met the eye.

"Annemarie told me about it."

Her father didn't say "Hmmm," but he might as well have. "Annemarie, did you know David's got a 1959 mint condition Harley motorcycle?" Whatever suspicions her father had, clearly he was trying to verify them.

She didn't answer.

"You remember, Annie," David prompted. "Red and white—with a couple hundred pounds of chrome. Two saddlebags. Belonged to my uncle Salvatore. Looks like it was made out of Coupe de Ville—"

"I remember!" she said a bit testily. She looked from one to the other. They both grinned.

"My father is a frustrated Hell's Angel," she said, wondering how in the world the two of them made the jump from "Hello, I'm Annemarie's father" to motorcycles.

"You never told me anything about that," David said with enough reproach in his voice to suggest that they were supposed to have discussed *everything,* and he was a little miffed at the omission. "You're a biker, Mr. Worth?"

"Me?" her father said. "Never got the chance. Didn't have the money before I was married—and after, it just didn't seem like the kind of thing a man with a wife and four babies ought to be doing."

"Especially with Naomi and Ruby watching him every minute," Annemarie said. "He was afraid they'd both have a stroke."

Her father grinned. "Well . . . they are kind of high strung, daughter. I reckon I did them a favor."

David laughed, his eyes holding Annemarie's as long as she would allow it.

What are you doing her? she wanted to ask him.

"What brings you to these parts?" her father said for her—much to her dismay.

"A little R&R—maybe some fishing," David said, holding up his iced-tea glass to a young waitress who was dying to pour him a refill. "And I've got some personal business to take care of." He glanced at Annemarie.

"Well," she said abruptly, "I've got to get busy. David, enjoy your meal. Daddy, you come help me." She got up quickly, greatly relieved that, for once, her father did what she wanted and came with her.

Her relief was short-lived.

"Russell know about him?" he asked again.

"Daddy, I told you. There is nothing to know."

"You're not the 'personal business,' are you?"

"Daddy!" she said in exasperation. She was saved by a rush of customers who wanted to pay and be on their way. She and her father both worked the cash register. Unable to keep her mind off David, Annemarie kept losing her train of thought. She was suddenly as inept with the cash drawer as she'd been when she'd first returned from Kharan.

She kept glancing at David, because she knew she'd likely never see him again. She could tell that word of his arrival had spread to the kitchen. Both Naomi and Ruby stood wedged in the kitchen doorway. Russell would know within the hour that Annemarie had run down some handsome stranger in the parking lot and had brought him inside for a free ham and chicken dinner.

She sighed and took another customer's money. Russell was going to demand that she explain the unexplainable.

"You all right, daughter?" her father asked. She could feel his worry. He'd had to ask that same question more than once in the last few months.

"Yes, Daddy, I am fine," she assured him. He went to bus tables because more cars were coming into the parking lot.

Annemarie glanced in David's direction again. His table was empty. He was waiting at the end of the line at the cash register.

"The meal was great," he said when it was his turn. "I want to ask you something, Annie."

"What?" she asked, shuffling through receipts to keep some distance between them.

"Does your dad know what happened to us in Kharan?"

She looked up at him. She hadn't expected that question. "No," she said. "They asked me not to tell anyone."

David seemed about to comment but he didn't, dropping several bills on the counter.

She left the money lying. "No, it's on the house," she said. "It's the least I can do for you—"

"No, Annie," he said quietly. "It's not." He picked up the money and pressed it into her hand. "Mr. Worth!" he suddenly called to her father. "You want to take a spin, Mr. Worth?"

Her father's face lit up in a way she hadn't seen since Ruby and Naomi had made the mistake of telling him the women's choir thought he was the most eligible widower in the valley.

"You bet, David!" he yelled across the dining room, busing tables completely forgotten. And he came on the run. "Hot dang, a '59 Harley!" he said to Annemarie in passing.

"Daddy—" she called, but he'd gone deaf again. She looked down at the crumpled money in her hand.

CHAPTER

Six

ANNEMARIE HAD BEEN treated to the sight of her grinning father flying past the front windows of the restaurant on a red, white, and chrome monster motorcycle—holding on to his Red Man Chewing Tobacco hat for dear life.

Now she was beginning to think that that was the last she was ever going to see of him. He hadn't returned when it was time to close the restaurant, and she'd gone on home—not finding him there, either. She paced about the house, toying with the idea of calling the sheriff's department to report him missing.

Lord, this was crazy! Her father should be here worrying about *her* flying around with David Gannon on a motorcycle—not the other way around! And on top of that, she'd had to renege on a dinner invitation with

93

Russell and his mother because her father wasn't around to cover for her at the restaurant.

Annemarie kept walking out onto the front porch to listen for a motorcycle motor. She heard nothing coming up the long, winding drive to the Worth place on the ridge. She listened harder, identifying an occasional whippoorwill. And crickets.

And two male voices singing the chorus of "I'll Fly Away!"

"Will you listen to that?" she whispered, stepping off the porch to peer down the dark road, finally seeing two silhouettes coming toward the house—more or less. The singing grew louder, and Annemarie went back inside to wait, picking up a *Life* magazine and thumbing through it so that she wouldn't look like that was what she was doing.

"Dammit all!" she said out loud as the singing drew nearer. She slammed the magazine down. It was after midnight, and she had every right to stand on the porch with her arms folded. Who had been worried half to death? Whose dinner plans had been ruined? Who'd been left to close the restaurant alone?

The singing continued into the yard—only to stop abruptly when David and her father saw her standing on the top step.

"Evenin', daughter," her father said politely. His Red Man hat was on backward.

"Good evening, father," Annemarie said, her voice soft and quiet enough to strike fear in the hearts of AWOL detachment commanders and frustrated bikers alike. Her eyes cut to David, who promptly grinned.

"What have you done to my father?" she demanded, torn between wanting to return the grin and wanting to punch him in the nose. Whatever made him think he could do this?

"Who, me?" David asked, hard pressed to keep her father upright. He sounded just like Hershel at the embassy.

"Yes, you! He's drunk! Where did you take him!"

"I didn't take *him* anywhere, Now, listen, Annie. It's the other way around here. For an old guy, your father—"

"Who're you calling old?" Mr. Worth demanded.

"You, sir," David said respectfully.

"Oh. Carry on then."

"See, Annie, we rode around—and your dad took us to the mouse club."

"Mickey's?" she said sarcastically.

"No, not Mickey's," David said, hiking her father up a little higher to get a better grip. "The place where the naked women are supposed to jump out of the cake. The . . . what's the name of that place, Joe?"

David had definitely gotten her father's attention with the part about the naked women. "I don't believe, son," Mr. Worth said with as much dignity as he could muster, "that you and I were at the same *place*—"

"No, no," David tried to explain. "Annemarie—and Ruby and Naomi—*think* they've got naked women there."

Her father frowned. "Well, why didn't you say so," he chided, putting his head down on David's shoulder.

"So what's the name of it?" David asked him again.

"The name of what?"

"The mouse place!"

"Oh. The . . . Calder Valley Mouse Club, American Branch!" her father roused up enough to say.

"Right," David agreed. "The English guy's place.

Joe wanted him to see the Harley. And then he wanted
Joe to see his new mouse stock—white with black spots
and flower ears—"

"Tulip ears, David. *Tulip,*" her father corrected.

"Right, sir. See, Annemarie, at the mouse club they
grow . . . mice. And there were a bunch of musicians
there. And somebody had a jug. See, we were riding
along the parkway and your dad said, 'You know anything about mice, David?' And I said, 'Hell, yes, sir.
Where I grew up, rats were domesticated animals.'
Then he said, 'Turn here—' How mad are you, Annie?"
he asked abruptly.

"Do you two know what time it is?" she cried.

They looked at each other, apparently to see if either
of them had that information.

"You tell us, daughter," her father suggested politely,
and she rolled her eyes upward in exasperation.

"Honestly!" she said, coming down the steps to take
her father's other arm. "I have been worried to death! I
didn't know what happened to you—for all I knew
you'd ridden off a mountain somewhere! Daddy, let's
get you inside. There are such things as telephones, you
know. Honestly!" she said again. She stopped abruptly
halfway up the porch steps. "Why are you on foot?" she
demanded.

"I *told* you she'd notice," Annemarie's father said,
and both men burst out laughing.

"You've wrecked the motorcycle, haven't you?" she
cried.

"It's not too bad, is it, Joe?" David said earnestly.

"Noooooo," her father assured her.

"The two of you are disgusting! Riding a motorcycle
when you're too drunk to walk!"

"Now, now, Annie," David said. "We got more sense

than that—" He grinned. "Between the two of us," he added to head off any exception she might take to that statement. "It was *before* we ran aground. The fiddler —Uncle Charlie—brought us home. You know, that guy can really play a fiddle. I never heard that kind of playing in all the places I've been. The music was like —it made me feel like I was homesick and missed Christmas and everybody forgot my birthday all at the same time. You know?"

Annemarie knew, but she wasn't going to let herself be sidetracked.

"See, Annie, Uncle Charlie brought us home, and we thought—your dad and I—we thought we ought to walk it from the road up here so we could—"

"Sober up," she finished for him.

David grinned again. He was so damn handsome! She frowned to keep a grip on her righteous indignation. She cared about him so, and she'd missed him. Every day. Every single day since she'd left him in the hospital in Kharan.

"Well, yes," he admitted.

"And did it work?" she asked, trying hard not to return his mischievous grin.

"Oh, heck, yes," her father observed.

"Well, I'm certainly glad to hear it. It's going to make things so much nicer for you in the morning. Good night, David," she said as they maneuvered her father through the front door. "I can manage from here. I hope you have a nice vacation in the Blue Ridge. We don't want to keep you."

"He's staying here," her father said, rousing up again.

"No, he isn't." She didn't trust herself to stay in the same house with David. He didn't know how she felt about him, and she didn't know how much longer she was going to be able to hide it.

"This is my house, daughter," Mr. Worth said firmly.

"Sorry, Daddy, but you've been overruled. He can't stay."

She avoided David's eyes as she tried to direct her father into the front hall and toward the stairs. David seemed not the least bit interested in leaving, regardless of her good night, and he continued to help her father along. There was not enough room for all three of them to go up the staircase, and Annemarie squeezed him out.

"This way, Daddy," she said. "Daddy, he can't stay here," she whispered to him as they climbed the steps.

"Why not?" her father asked. If he was going to have to take back an invitation, clearly he intended to know why.

"He just—can't!"

"He is *your* friend, Annemarie," he reminded her. "And after this... very... fine evening, he is also mine. "David—" he called over his shoulder as they reached the top of the stairs. "You sleep on the couch. Tomorrow we fix the Harley!"

"Yes, sir," David called.

He was waiting at the bottom of the stairs when Annemarie came back down. She stopped before she reached the bottom step, and he smiled up at her.

"You know that was a pretty good comeback, Annie."

"What was?"

"*Mickey's* Mouse Club. I always knew you could think on your feet, though. I'm... alive today because of it."

Annemarie tried to push by him, but his arm shot out to keep her there.

"You're not sleeping either," he said. "Your dad told me. He says you walk around at night. He says sometimes he can see your footprints in the damp ground—"

"David, please," she said, trying to get by him again. But he wouldn't move. He was so close. She could feel the heat from his body, feel that his gaze traveled over her face. She was afraid to look at him.

"You don't owe me a thing, Annie," he said quietly. "If anything, it's the other way around. I don't want to worry you . . . or upset you. I just wanted to say that I—" He stopped, and she dared to look at him. She longed to touch him, to see for herself that he was all right.

He smiled. "Be seeing you, Annie."

He turned to go.

"You're leaving?" she asked, unable to keep from saying it. *I* can't stand this, she thought. She was afraid for him to stay, and she couldn't bear for him to go.

"I have to go get the Harley. Uncle Charlie's going to pick me up on the road. He went on down to the store to get some chewing tobacco."

"Oh," she said. She wanted to know what his plans were—he always had a plan—but she didn't ask. They stood awkwardly at the foot of the stairs.

"Well," he said finally, "I guess I'd better get going. Charlie's a nice old guy. I don't want to keep him waiting."

She walked with him to the door, going out onto the porch with him.

"The motorcycle's not too bad?" she asked, knowing she was doing it to keep him there longer. She was behaving like the girl in an old mountain ballad, "The

Wagoner's Lad." The wagoner's lad was leaving, and the mountain girl who loved him tried to delay him: His horses are hungry, his wagon needs greasing—anything to keep him as long as she can.

"Not bad," David said. "Mostly it's just getting the mud out of the tailpipe. You were right—your dad is a frustrated Hell's Angel."

Annemarie laughed. The night was quiet around them except for the crickets and the whippoorwills. The stars were out, and she would hear the wind in the tall pines.

"Annie," David said. She could just make out his face on the dark porch. "Come here," he whispered, and her heart gave a great leap. Incredibly, she went, letting him put his arms around her. She pressed her face into his shoulder, holding on to him in a desperate grip while he gently stroked her hair. He smelled of the outdoors —of moonlit rides on a '59 Harley and home-brewed mountain whiskey and tobacco smoke. And he smelled like David. It was like coming home again.

"It's been a long time since I did this," he said against her ear, and she pushed herself out of his arms. He didn't understand how vulnerable she was, or that she hadn't recovered from what had happened to them in Kharan. She was still emotionally attached to him. She had to be strong to keep from being foolish.

"Annie—"

"David, I'm . . . very glad to see you, but we're not in Kharan now. Everything is all right."

"Is it?"

"Yes."

He caught her by the arm to keep her from leaving. "Then don't look at me like that, Annemarie."

"Like what?"

"Like—'David, help me.' And at the same time, 'David, you have to go.'"

"I don't do that."

"Yes, you do."

"David, good night!"

She left him standing on the porch, closing the front door firmly and turning the lock. She hurried upstairs to her bedroom and sat on the edge of the bed in the dark. Her mind was in a panic. She was dead tired, but she knew she wouldn't sleep. She sighed and put her hands to her face for a moment. She hadn't known that her father knew about her sleeplessness, or that she prowled around at night.

Oh, David, it's not working. Time was supposed to take care of her infatuation with him, and it hadn't. She wanted to go to him so badly, just to be with him, to have him tell her in that cocky way he had that she wasn't to cry—everything was going to be all right. He could make her believe it. He'd done it in Kharan; he could do it here.

She gave another long sigh. David didn't know how glad she was to see him. He didn't know she wanted—

I don't even know what I want, she thought.

"Liar," she whispered immediately, echoing David's earlier response. She wanted everything, anything. She wanted to be his lover. She wanted to be anything he'd let her be. Hot tears welled in her eyes, then spilled down her cheeks. Twice she got up and walked to the bedroom door—but she didn't open it. She couldn't give in to her passion for David—it wasn't real. It was a symptom, and it wasn't going to last. It was ironic really. All her life she'd wanted to feel about someone the way she felt about him. She understood him, admired and respected him, *loved* him, regardless of what the therapist said.

But she was a realist. If David had come here, it must be because he was suffering an emotional attachment, too. She couldn't encourage him. These feelings were only temporary. And even if they weren't, his life was foreign embassies and the Marine Corps; hers was a restaurant in the Blue Ridge. She had never in her life looked out over these mountains and wished herself someplace else. She had tried to deny that basic truth about herself once before, and she and Grayson both had suffered for it. She couldn't—wouldn't—make that mistake again.

She took a deep breath and wiped her eyes. The realist part of her knew and understood all that. But deep down inside, some other part of her clearly hadn't listened.

CHAPTER

Seven

ANNEMARIE FELL ASLEEP just before dawn. She hadn't set her alarm, and she overslept. It left her short-tempered and edgy and in a hurry to get out of the house and away from her father's inquisitive looks — which he managed only too well, hangover or not.

But coming to the restaurant was no better. They were late opening because Annemarie had the key, and she had to wade through the unabashed interest of not one but two stout cooks to unlock the restaurant door. Ruby and Naomi were wearing their usual cooking garb — nearly identical flowered dresses with big white aprons, regulation hairnets, and Jordache pink satin running shoes. And as usual, Ruby was doing the talking.

103

"You are so deep, Annemarie," she said as soon as Annemarie got out of her car.

She didn't comment. It was safer than pretending she didn't know what Ruby meant. This inquisition was her own fault. She had shared all the important events in her life with the two of them, and they felt no more constraint about poking around in her private business than her father did.

"How come you didn't tell us about the motorcycle fellow," Ruby persisted as Annemarie unlocked the door.

"Ruby—Naomi—now hear this! I didn't mention him, because there was really nothing to mention. I met him on the trip to Kharan. He is one of any number of people I met along the way. All right?"

"Well, me and Naomi don't think he's 'any number,' do we, Naomi?" Ruby said.

"No," Naomi said—a long speech for her. She was from the Georgia branch of the Chandlers, who never talked.

"To my way of thinking," Ruby said pointedly, "when some outlander comes riding up on one of them machines and you up and give him a free dinner—and then he takes your daddy off to who knows where, well, call it peculiar, Annemarie, but people wonder about things like that."

Annemarie tried not to grin. She was tired, but she still knew who the "people" were—these two. "So," she said on the way inside. "What did you tell Russell?"

Ruby and Naomi exchanged approximately the same look as David and her father when she noticed they were minus a motorcycle.

"I know you told him something."

"Told him if he'd quit fiddle-fumping around and

married you, he wouldn't be having to worry about no Black Jack David now," Naomi said in spite of her non-talkative nature. Annemarie smiled at the analogy. "Black Jack David" was one of Uncle Charlie's best fiddle tunes, one about a sweet-talking stranger who enticed a woman away from her warm feather bed to lje at his side on the cold ground.

"He's not a Black Jack David," Annemarie said. "He doesn't steal women from their loved ones and run off with them."

"That's what you think," Ruby said. "Me and Naomi know one when we see one."

Annemarie had no doubts whatsoever about that. "Go cook, will you!" she said, looking around at the sound of a motorcycle in the parking lot. She went immediately to the front windows to see, her heart pounding again. David was already at the front door. She turned around to head him off. The last thing she needed was him coming inside and Naomi and Ruby listening to everything he said.

But the two cooks were right behind her. Nothing was going to keep them from missing anything today. "Lord," Annemarie muttered under her breath. "I'm surrounded."

"Good morning!" David called across the dining room. "Ruby—Naomi—" he said to acknowledge their presence. It took them both by surprise, and it was a good guess on his part. Annemarie couldn't keep from smiling. The cooks might not know anything about him, but he certainly knew about them.

"So," David said. "Are you ready to go?" He didn't seem to mind at all that they had a rapt, two-member audience.

"Go?" Annemarie said blankly.

"Yeah. You're not still mad at me, are you?"

"I wasn't *mad*—"

David raised both eyebrows, and she couldn't keep from smiling. He looked so nice this morning—just showered and shaved and smelling of Ivory soap.

"Don't be mad at me, Annie. Your dad's going to cover for you so you can show me the sights "

"My dad," Annemarie said pointedly, "is still recovering from the hangover you got him into."

"Annie, will you quit blaming me for that? I told you. At the Mouse Club they had—" He stopped, glancing at Naomi and Ruby. They were hanging on his every word. He cleared his throat and tried not to look as mischievous as Annemarie knew he was. "At the Mouse Club—" he started again, "they had a jug— well, actually it was a jar. A canning jar—"

"I know about the packaging," she assured him, heading for the cash register Everybody in the place followed her.

"You promised you'd take me sightseeing, Annie "

"No, I didn't," she lied.

"Yeah, you did. In the hospital in Kharan. When they said you couldn't see me and you pitched a fit—"

Oh, Lord, Annemarie thought. He knows about that.

"You told me then, Annie, if I was ever in the Blue Ridge, to stop by—and you'd show me the sights. And—" he added, giving her his best grin, "—here I am. We forget the part about Russell coming along, too."

"David," she said, trying not to notice how incredibly blue his eyes were against the pale blue of the T-shirt he was wearing this morning. "I'm very busy today and—"

"Your dad's coming in."

"When I left my dad," she said significantly, "he was complaining because the cat walked too heavy."

"Now, don't give me all this grief, Annemarie. I need the R&R. Your dad says you could use a little rest yourself. I want you to come along with me."

"I have too much to do!" she said again. "I can't just walk off and leave everything." She suddenly remembered Ruby and Naomi. "Will you two go cook!"

"You aren't upset because I put my arms around you, are you?" That question put an end to any hope Annemarie had of getting some privacy.

"This is not the place to talk about this," she insisted, trying to make him remember with her eyes that Naomi and Ruby were hearing every word. He didn't remember.

"I want to be with you today, Annemarie."

"We're running late already. The crowd from the campgrounds will be here soon. I overslept—" She was babbling like an idiot.

"I'll wait," he assured her. "And I'll help."

"You can't help!" she cried in dismay. Having him close to her was *not* going to help.

"Sure I can. Here comes your dad."

Amazingly enough, her father had arrived. He was a little less than his usual chipper self, but even so, he was much better than when she'd left him complaining about the heavy-footed cat And his Red Man hat was pointed in the right direction. He waved in passing, motioning for Ruby and Naomi to come out to the kitchen with him. They didn't go.

"That's it!" Annemarie said, throwing up her hands. "David, let's go—it's the only way I'll ever get anybody into the kitchen."

"You got it," David said, taking her by the arm. "You're going to love that Harley."

"Coffeepots first," she told him. "Harleys later—or didn't I just hear you volunteer for KP?"

"You heard me—point me to it."

Oddly enough, he seemed to know quite a lot about restaurant kitchens and giant coffeepots.

"What?" he said, looking up to find Annemarie watching him.

"You've done this before," she accused him.

"Yes, ma'am. You got to know all kind of things if you're going to guard an embassy." He reached out to pat her cheek. It left her addled and blushing because Naomi and Ruby *and* her father were watching.

She escaped into the dining room with the silverware and glasses. She could hear Ruby laughing from time to time at some comment David made, and then, surprisingly, quiet Naomi.

"What are the three of you laughing about in there?" Annemarie asked him later.

"You," he said, grinning. "All the dopey stuff you did when you were a little kid."

She frowned, and his grin broadened. He was giving her the business again—she hoped.

The morning crowds from the campgrounds arrived, and it was nearly eleven before the dining room began to clear. At some point amid the clatter of dishes and conversation, she made a decision. She was going to take David sightseeing. There was no reason why she couldn't do that. She knew the dangers; she could handle it. And he might as well see firsthand how different her life was from his.

"Have you seen David?" she called to her father, who was rolling a carpet sweeper around.

"Out on the back porch."

She found him sitting on the porch steps, staring out across the blue-hazed mountain ridges that stood one behind the other as far as the eye could see. Clouds moved eastward over the range, some of them seeming to snag on the mountainsides. The view was beautiful from here; it pleased her that he seemed to appreciate it.

"What do you think?" she said, nodding in the direction he was looking.

"It's not like any place I've ever been. It's rugged— but in a quiet, peaceful sort of way. I can see why you love it."

She sat down beside him. She had given up wearing her hair so severely, and it blew about her face. David reached up once to take a strand out of her eyes, catching it carefully behind her ear. The tender gesture made her knees weak and her belly warm. She looked away from him.

"Are you ready for some lunch now?" she said, to keep her composure.

"Not unless we can pack it and take it with us," he answered. He stood up, catching her hand and pulling her up with him. "Are we going sightseeing?"

"We are."

"Good. I got this plan, see."

"Oh, Lord," she said ominously.

He draped his arm around her shoulders. "We take the Harley," he elaborated, "and—"

"Can't," Annemarie interrupted, loving the feel of being this close to him in spite of her resolve to keep her distance. "It's against the law of the Blue Ridge Parkway—no littering, no commercial vehicles, no motorcycle riding in a dress."

"I never wear dresses," he assured her as they passed her father.

"Now, there's a good thing for a father to know," Mr. Worth observed dryly. "You going with David, daughter?"

"Yes, Daddy," she said over her shoulder.

"Now, son, you watch yourself. Annemarie here is the only one of my babies who ever wanted to go with me when I went looking at motorcycles."

"He means I was the only one he could take along who wouldn't tell on him," Annemarie explained, and David laughed.

"Forget the lunch," he said when she turned toward the kitchen. "I want to get you out of here before a couple of tour groups pull in and you think you have to stay and help feed them."

"I wouldn't do that."

"The hell you wouldn't," he said, and she laughed. "Come on—come on—Annie, I'm telling you you're going to love this motorcycle."

"We're not really going on the motorcycle, are we?"

"Sure we are. Why not?"

"I'm wearing a dress," she reminded him as he pulled her along with him outside.

"Yes, you are," he said appreciatively. "Don't worry about the dress, Annemarie. You've got great legs. Did I ever tell you you had great legs?"

She thought for a moment. She'd seen him check them out in the reflection in the office window at the embassy that time, but he'd never actually *said*. "No. Never."

"I didn't? Well, I'll tell you now. I like your legs, Annemarie."

She grinned. "Yes, I know."

"You know?"

She told him about the time at the embassy.

He laughed out loud. "You saw me do that? I'm surprised you went anywhere with me."

"So am I," she said dryly.

He grinned, catching her around her neck and giving her a token sock on the jaw.

"Now, look at that," he said, making her stand where she would have the best view of the bike. "Have you ever seen anything like that in your life?" His warm hands caressed her shoulders, and the Harley glistened in the sun. It was a beautiful machine, all right, one lovingly kept and cared for.

"I'm—speechless," she declared.

"Now, this is *class*, Annie. Some of the cars they make these days aren't as big as this thing. There's nothing to worry about."

"I . . don't know," she said doubtfully, just to tease. She wasn't afraid, not at all—at least not of the '59 Harley. "You won't jump ditches or anything like that, will you?"

"No. I had enough of that last night with your dad." Abruptly, he lifted her off the ground, making her squeal as he set her on the seat. She was wearing a loose-fitting white cotton dress with a dropped waist, and even though the skirt was full and long, she still showed a lot of thigh. She didn't miss David's appreciative look. He knew she'd seen him, and he tried to look innocent. He was too full of himself to manage it.

"Caught me again," he confessed, making her laugh.

She had to hold on to his shoulders, and she remembered immediately the muscular feel of his body. She remembered, too, the times she'd looked with a certain envy at the bikers' women on the parkway, who rode close to their men like this. Annemarie Worth never did anything like that—poor Ruby and Naomi must be going crazy.

"At last!" David said as he kicked the starter, yelling over the motor noise.

She gave him an inquisitive look.

"I thought I was going to have to steal you—like Black Jack David!"

"They didn't give you a hard time, did they?" Annemarie asked. They had stopped at a small stone church on the secondary road that ran parallel to the parkway. It was becoming apparent that David was the one who was directing the sightseeing, and that he only wanted to find the places she'd told him about in Kharan. They were walking in the tall grass in the churchyard. David took her by the hand to help her over the low stone wall around the cemetery. The sun was bright; she had to squint to look at him. "Did Ruby and Naomi give you a hard time?" she persisted.

"No, I asked for it. They wanted to know what I was doing here—and I told them. Lady Elizabeth," he read off one of the headstones, clearly surprised. "There really is a Lady Elizabeth!"

"Did I tell you about her?" She didn't remember it.

"Yeah—when you were sick. You thought you were going to die far away from home like she did. You made me promise I'd bring you back here—the way her husband brought her."

Annemarie leaned down for a moment to flick a grasshopper off her skirt, a bit disconcerted because she hadn't realized the extent of her ravings, and because she was afraid to ask what he'd told Naomi and Ruby.

"Does anybody know what he was like—her husband?" he asked.

"Not much. He was ambitious, I guess, or he wouldn't have wanted to go out West looking for gold. He used to write in her diary sometimes—things like 'My wife is sweet and little and I love her.'"

When she looked up again, she found David staring at her. "What?" she asked, regretting it immediately. She wasn't sure she wanted to know why he was looking at her so intently.

"I want to ask you something. I want to know if you know why I'm here."

She moved away from him toward the shade of an oak tree to keep from answering. She had a very good idea why he was here; she just wasn't sure she wanted to tell him. He joined her under the tree, coming to stand very close to her, assaulting her senses with his clean, masculine smell. She sighed and looked up at him.

"Talk to me, not at me," he said, recalling her own complaint the day their captors abandoned them.

She lost her nerve.

"Go on," he prompted. She didn't, and he poked her with his elbow.

"Go on," he said again. "You can tell me."

She was just going to have to do it, she decided. "I think you're here because you're suffering from the same thing I am."

"And what's that?"

"Kharan." Again she moved away from him, this time toward the stone wall, picking her way through the tall grass and being carefully respectful of where she stepped in the old cemetery. She could hear him following behind her. "I'm told that we're emotionally bonded, you and I," she said over her shoulder. "Or I'm bonded to you, anyway."

He caught her by the arm to keep her from walking any farther. "You know, this is kind of like that pig and the butter thing Ruby said. I'm not sure I know what we're talking about. Who says you're—we're—bonded."

"The therapist I went to see after I got back. Mr. Beam from the State Department recommended him. I went because of that . . . scene I made at the hospital when they wouldn't let me see you. I've never done anything like that in my life. I knew something was wrong with me. The therapist said it was a symptom of the emotional trauma. Because of what we went through together in Kharan. Since you've come all this way, I think you must be having some trouble, too. But you don't have to worry," she added because he was frowning. "It goes away. It's kind of like men who fight together in a war, I guess. They think their buddies are going to be their best friends all their lives, but then the war ends and they never see them again—never want to, really."

She glanced at him. He looked so perplexed; she could feel how hard he was trying to understand her. "It's just something that happens to people who share a crisis. They bond—emotionally—why are you looking at me like that!" she said in exasperation.

"Because I don't know what the hell you're talking about!"

"I'm talking about the—Stockholm Syndrome. A lateral Stockholm Syndrome."

"Stockholm Syndrome, I know. Lateral Stockholm Syndrome, maybe. What does either of them have to do with you and me?"

"It's what happened to us. It's why I don't sleep at night. It's why I think about you all the time—" She broke off. She hadn't meant to say that.

"You . . . think about me all the time?" he said carefully, as if he knew perfectly well what she said, but he just wanted to make sure—and she had damn well better not try to get out of it.

She looked him straight in the eye. "Yes."

"And you think I'm here because we're emotionally attached to each other—because of the emotional trauma, right?"

"Right," she said, relieved that he was finally getting it.

"And I don't have to worry because this is just a passing phase, right?"

"Right," she said again.

He considered this for a moment, his arms folded over his chest. "You want to know why *I* think I'm here?"

"No," she said because he was taking her by the hand.

"Why not?" he asked, pulling her closer.

"I just don't—"

"You're not afraid of me, are you?"

"No," she said worriedly, because he was taking her other hand.

"Well, that's good, because you might not like this if you were. I want you to do something for me."

"What?" she said, still worried. He had both her hands, but he wasn't making her come any closer. She looked down, trying to angle her feet so that she didn't stumble over him.

"I want you to put your arms around me," he said quietly, and she looked up at him. He was serious.

There was no mischief in his eyes, no teasing smile, only that desperate, haunted look she saw on her own face when the sleeplessness and nightmares were too bad.

"David—" she said, taking her hands out of his and reaching for him. He made a quiet "oh" sound as she put her arms around him, pressing his face into her neck. They stood in the old cemetery, holding each other, ignoring a car full of tourists that was slowly driving by.

"I'm so tired, Annie."

"I know," she whispered, turning her face to his. He hesitated, and then his mouth sought hers. She lost all sense of caution, parting her lips for him, tasting, savoring. His kiss was everything she'd thought it would be, so warm and so pleasurable. This was the kiss they *hadn't* shared on the banks of the Red Sea.

His hands slid over her body, pressing her into him, cupping a breast. She could feel the hard male part of him against her, feel the heat of her own desire uncoiling. She forgot where she was. There was nothing but David and this urgent hunger she had for him. She couldn't get close enough to him. She wanted him to touch her, to fill her with his maleness, to love her...

It was he who finally broke away, his breathing harsh and warm against her ear. They were both trembling.

"Annie," he whispered, trying to kiss her again, but she pushed out of his arms. What was the matter with her? She couldn't do this!

"No," she protested, moving away from him, standing with her arms folded over her breasts. Good Lord, she thought. She wasn't just emotionally attached; she was sexually enthralled as well.

"Annie—"

"Don't call me Annie. Nobody calls me that."

"I do," he said mildly. He reached out to touch her, but she stepped sharply away. "We're going to have to talk about this—"

She was still shaken by her response. He could have taken her right here. She had been only too willing for him to do just that. "No," she said stubbornly.

"Yes!" he insisted. "I understand about the emotional bonding thing. But if I think I'm crazy about you, and you think it's some kind of psychiatric condition, we've got a lot to talk about. Did you tell the therapist how it was with us *before* we were taken hostage?"

"I don't know what you mean."

"You do know what I mean. We were getting into something before it happened, Annemarie, and you know it. You think I go chasing after every woman who comes into the embassy the way I chased after you?"

"How should I know?" she cried.

"Well, I don't. I liked you. I liked you the first five minutes I met you. You were so sweet and pretty with that tin of cookies under your arm—and, God, you smelled good!" He smiled at her, and she couldn't keep from smiling back. She was so tired suddenly. He reached to take her into his arms again, and this time she didn't resist. She rested her head on his shoulder.

"I should have left you alone that day," he said quietly. "If I had—" His arms abruptly tightened around her. "I'm . . . so sorry, Annie. I just wanted to be with you. I wanted to impress you with how much I knew about Kharan. I wanted you to see how old and beautiful it is. I wanted you to remember me. I was supposed to protect you, and I couldn't. I was supposed to know, to *see* something like that coming, and I didn't."

"David, don't. Don't—" She didn't blame him for anything. How could he think that?

"I'm here for one reason, Annemarie. I'm here because you are. I—need to be with you. I want us to pick up where we left off—as if the bad things in Kharan hadn't happened."

"It's not going to work, David."

"Why not?"

"Because we're too different!"

He held her away from him so he could see her face "You mean because I'm a street punk in the military and you think you're another Lady Elizabeth." The remark was close enough to the truth to make her angry.

"I've been through this before, David!"

"Yeah? Well, there's one thing you ought to know by now, Annemarie. I'm not Grayson!"

No, she thought. He wasn't Grayson. She cared more about him in the short time she'd known him than she'd ever cared about Grayson Barkley. But that didn't change anything. She was still afraid.

"I like my life here," she said. and he gave a long sigh. He walked a few feet away from her, looking out across the cemetery, his hands resting on his hips. She let her eyes travel over him lovingly, noting as she did how pleasing he was to her. She loved the way he looked, but there was more to it than that. She admired his physical self, but she loved his humanness. She had seen him strong and weak, brave and afraid. The kind of person he was on the inside was no secret to her. The realization came that she was standing at a crossroads. She had two choices, one with David for as far as they could go together, and one without him. Both roads were hard.

"Hey," he said, looking around at her. "Let's call a

truce, okay? We just take it easy, and we don't get into any heavy stuff. We can just be together for a while. You show me around the mountains, and I'll . . . try to keep my hands off you. What do you say?"

She couldn't keep from smiling. This was her David. No matter how crazy things were, he always had a plan.

CHAPTER

Eight

THEY WERE GOING sightseeing. It was the sensible thing to do. Except that when David was helping her get back on the Harley, he abruptly let go of her and walked away.

"What's wrong?" she asked.

"Nothing," he said, his voice sounding a bit strange. She gave him a worried glance, thinking he might be ill. "Stay there!" he barked when she was about to get off the motorcycle.

"What's wrong?" she said again, not understanding at all.

He half-smiled and shook his head. "Married before or not, you don't know much about men, do you?"

She frowned. "What has that got to do with anything? Are you sick or what?"

"Or what, Annemarie. Or what." He was grinning openly now. "I'm . . . still aroused. I can't help it. You do that to me. You have for quite some time now— since—oh, you accused me of using you for show and tell with Hershel at the embassy. Holding you—kissing you and nothing else isn't easy." His grin widened. "So what do you think of that?"

She was still frowning. He could ask her the damnedest questions sometimes. "I don't know," she said in all truthfulness, and he laughed out loud, throwing his head back. "And you can quit—giving me the business, Gannon. You know I don't know what to say to something like that, and you do it on purpose!"

He was grinning and nodding. "You are so cute when you think I'm talking dirty."

"I didn't—I don't—" She gave up because he was laughing again. She sat awkwardly on the motorcycle and tried to think of some snappy comeback that would put him in his place. Absolutely nothing came to mind. "Can we go now?" she asked pointedly.

"If you insist," he said. "Somehow I don't think you've got the proper sympathy for my physical discomfort here."

"Maybe not," she allowed, unable to keep from laughing herself now. "But don't explain it to me, okay?"

He gave her a quick bear hug and climbed on the motorcycle, and aroused or not, made her lock her arms around his waist before they rode away. Annemarie was beginning to see the appeal of traveling the parkway on a bike. Riding under the great trees and in and out of the dappled shade, past the manicured grass along the sides of the road, the split-rail fences, the flame azalea that were beginning to bloom, gave her a new perspective of a place she'd seen nearly every day of her life.

But it wasn't just this free-spirited, two-wheeled approach that caused it. It was seeing a place she loved through David's eyes. She took him to all the standard tourist overlooks so he could see the panoramic views that stretched into North Carolina. She took him to the Mayberry Trading Post so he could poke around an antique general store and strike up a conversation with the old men who sat on benches in the shade outside and puzzled over the outlanders' fascination for the mundane. And she took him home, showing him all around the Worth place, letting him see firsthand the ingenuity of her forbears.

He walked from one outbuilding to another, making a guess about what they were for, then letting her explain their purpose. He recognized the spring house that was once the Worth family refrigerator easily, but was completely baffled by the smoke house where freshly butchered hams were put to be salted, then smoked, to preserve them.

"Some people just used salt, or salt and pepper— maybe borax," she explained. "Now Great-Grandmother Worth used salt. molasses, black pepper, and red pepper. People would come from miles around to trade for one of her hams. She'd put green hickory and oak chips in that wash pot there and set them on fire. You had to keep the smoke billowing for several days—until the hams got a brown crust. It must have smelled wonderful around here—" She stopped because he was looking at her so fondly. "Moving right along," she said, leading the way to what she hoped were other places of interest.

"Now, this I know," he said as they passed the relic privy. "Latrine, right?"

"Right," she said, laughing. She let herself look into his eyes, marveling a bit that he really seemed to want to do this. She walked on to a gnarled apple tree. "This is where I used to skin the cat," she said, placing her hand on a heavy branch.

"Did you smoke him, too?"

"I didn't mean it literally, Gannon."

"Well, thank God for that. I was beginning to think life in the Bronx wasn't so bad after all."

They ended the tour in the Worth kitchen, raiding the refrigerator, laughing together in an easy comaraderie that was well-laced with the undercurrent of sexual desire. They ate at their leisure—leftover ham and cold fried chicken, potato salad, pickled beets, apple pie—both of them remembering the time when they'd made do with hard bread and pieces of dates and figs. Stuffed and drowsy, David headed for the hammock in the backyard, making Annemarie come along with him. He had no reservations at all about lying down in the thing and pulling her in with him.

"Now, this isn't what you think," he said explained hurriedly. "We're going to take a nap. It's not like we haven't slept together before. If you can't trust *me* as a hammock partner, now who can you trust? I'm sleepy—and I'll sleep a lot better with you here." With that, he hung one leg over the side to give the hammock a push, rocking them precariously and not letting her up.

She found almost immediately that she didn't want to get up. She was entirely comfortable in David's arms. The hammock swayed gently, and she closed her eyes, sensing the dappling of sunlight through the trees against her eyelids as she moved back and forth. She listened contentedly to the leaves rustling overhead, the buzzing of a bee. David sighed heavily, pressing a chaste kiss on her forehead, and she settled closer to him, languishing in his heady, masculine scent, then draping her arm across his chest. Never in a million years when she'd slept on the ground in captivity with this man did she think she'd be home again, with him, like this.

"To sleep," he murmured. "Perchance *not* to dream."

Annemarie opened her eyes, not knowing what had awakened her. The shadows were longer, the breeze cooler. She closed her eyes, but the sound came again —the discreet "Psssssst!"

"Sorry, daughter," her father whispered because David was still sleeping soundly. "I thought you'd want to know in case you want to do anything about it."

"What?" she whispered back.

"Russell was here."

"Russell?" Lord, she'd forgotten all about Russell. "When?"

"Just now."

"He didn't—" Annemarie stopped, not knowing quite how to phrase the question—which was ridiculous. Here she was lying in the backyard hammock asleep with a man none of her family and friends had even heard of until yesterday. It didn't matter what she *said*, for pete's sake.

"He was standing about where I am," her father said, still whispering.

"Oh, Lord!"

"I don't mean to put my nose in, daughter, but I reckon maybe you owe him some kind of explanation."

And what was she supposed to tell him? Russell, it's

not as bad as it looks—it's worse? If only Russell hadn't changed so when she'd gotten back from Kharan. If only they were still just childhood friends, and he hadn't gotten this crazy notion that he wanted to marry her. Russell Chandler was a good man; she didn't want to hurt him. She reached for her father's hand so he could help her up.

"Annie," David murmured, stirring restlessly.

"It's all right," she said to him. "Go back to sleep." She reached to gently touch his cheek, then straightened up to find her father watching. She didn't say anything. She could feel his concern, but she couldn't say anything that would assuage it. She was concerned herself.

David sat up abruptly. "Hello, Joe," he said to her father. "What's going on?"

"Russell seen you and Annemarie sleeping out here," her father said point blank.

"So where is he now? Gone to get his gun?" David rubbed his eyes and tried to wake up.

"Wouldn't surprise me—Annemarie ain't told nobody much about you."

"Then I guess—"

"Hold it!" Annemarie interrupted. "If you two don't mind, I'll handle this." She had no idea how, but she certainly wasn't going to stand there listening to David and her father hashing this whole thing out.

"You want me to talk to him?" David called as she went back toward the house.

"No, I don't!"

"Son, son," her father chided. "Annemarie's independent, just like her mama. You got to watch questions like that."

But David wasn't taking advice. He followed Annemarie into the house.

"Annie," he said as he caught up with her. "Does Russell know about me?"

"No, he doesn't know about you. What could I tell him?"

"The truth," he suggested.

"And what is that?"

She left him standing in the kitchen and tried calling Russell at the real-estate office and at his mother's. No one admitted knowing his whereabouts. She hung up the phone. David was sitting at the kitchen table—waiting.

"I can't find him," she said, sitting down at the table with him. She could feel his eyes on her.

"What are you going to tell him, Annie?"

She looked at him, then sighed. "He says he wants to marry me, David."

"Yeah? Old Russell finally got around to it—popping the question."

Annemarie didn't comment on that remark. It was the truth, but somehow, the way David said it, it made Russell sound extremely trifling.

They stared at each other across the table.

"I don't want to hurt him," she said quietly. "He's my friend. He was my friend when I was six and afraid of the dark. He was my friend when Grayson sent me packing."

"In that case, I guess you'd better look for him. I think I know what he's feeling. I'll . . . hang around here with your dad."

She looked into his eyes, grateful that he understood and that he wasn't going to add to her confusion.

"But there's just one thing—" He reached across the table to take her hand. "Don't come back betrothed or anything like that, okay?"

She smiled, and he squeezed her fingers.

"And don't let old Russell give you hell about what I'm doing here."

"He wouldn't do that."

David looked at her thoughtfully, his fingers caressing hers. "Yes, he would. It's like I said. You don't know much about men."

She was about to reply to that, but he grinned and reached out to playfully pinch her cheek.

"You handle Russell. I'll be out here with your dad."

She continued to sit at the kitchen table, watching David as he crossed the back porch and sat down on the steps with her father. Her father made room for him, and they fell into an easy conversation that she couldn't hear, but that required her father to point out something about the old barn. More about mountain homesteading, she thought. It was a good thing David was "nosy." By the time he left, he'd know more about curing hams and the like than any city boy needed to know.

By the time he left.

She didn't want to think about his leaving. It pleased her so that he was here. This old place held all the memories of her lifetime, and yet David didn't seem to be an outsider at all. To her, he belonged in the same way that everything around her belonged. And he seemed perfectly at ease in her home and with her family—even the hard-won Naomi and Ruby, who had likely told him to his face that he was a "Black Jack David."

She looked at him now, sitting and talking quietly with her father, the rapport between them obvious. Lord, she didn't want him to go, and she hadn't even asked him how long he was staying.

She gave a long sigh and turned her thoughts to the problem at hand—Russell. He was her friend; she would have preferred that he not have found her sleeping in the arms of another man. But they weren't formally engaged. She'd told him plainly that she didn't want to marry him—a hundred times. And she did *not* have to explain her behavior to him unless she chose to do so. She sighed again and shook her head. Who was she kidding? She couldn't explain, even if she wanted to. She didn't know herself beyond the proverbial bottom line: She wanted to be with David. She wanted to be with him even if they were both still emotionally traumatized, even if nothing could come of it because he loved the military life and she was happily rooted here.

You ought to know by now, Annemarie, I'm not Grayson!

No. He wasn't Grayson—but she was still afraid.

What was she going to do?

She had no idea. Her method of problem-solving was to cope with the present. She wasn't like David. She never had a plan.

She got up from the table and went outside, smiling at her father, who suddenly stood up and repositioned his Red Man hat. "I . . . got to see a man about a horse," he announced. He could be the soul of discretion if he wanted to be, Annemarie thought wryly.

She waited until the back door slammed before she sat down on the steps. David gave her an inquisitive look, then put his arm around her. She leaned against him, wanting him to keep her close.

"I don't want to look for Russell," she whispered. "I want to stay with you."

He grinned his familiar Dead-End-Kid grin. "Yeah?"

"Yeah," she assured him. "Hey—" she said, using his favorite salutation.

"Annemarie?"

She looked around sharply at the sound of Russell's voice. He was standing at the end of the porch. He was subtly handsome despite the grim look he was wearing, and he was as fair-haired as David was dark. Russell always dressed for success; he never seemed to need a haircut or a shave, and he had on one of his tailored suits—summer-weight khaki with a light blue shirt and a blue and yellow striped tie. He looked the successful land broker he was.

Annemarie stayed where she was—in the circle of David's arm. If she should feel guilty, she couldn't seem to manage it, and she wasn't going to pretend otherwise. She could feel David tense as the two men took stock of each other like rival warriors who were about to do battle.

"Russell," she said without apology, "I'd like you to meet David Gannon."

"This is not David Gannon!" Russell exploded, jabbing the air in David's direction with his forefinger. "You know who that is? That's Grayson all over again —all flash and no substance. Didn't you learn anything? How stupid can you be, Annemarie!"

"Hey—" David said, standing up. "Don't talk to her like that!"

"You stay out of this! How I talk to her is none of your business! You think because you went out drinking with her daddy you're going to fit right in here, don't you? Well, you're not! Annemarie, what is the matter with you! Grayson, at least, had a little class about him —but this guy! He runs around on a motorcycle, for godsake! Where did you pick up this trash?"

Annemarie had been holding on to David's pants leg in a feeble attempt to referee, but he was off the porch steps, his fist shooting out to connect with Russell's lip.

Russell went sprawling in the grass; he came up spitting blood. Annemarie grabbed David's arm, hanging on for dear life to keep him from hitting Russell again. Russell was a real-estate salesman; he was no match for David Gannon—whether he deserved a punch in the mouth or not.

"What did you do that for!" she cried.

"What did I do it for?" David said incredulously. "Oh, I don't know, Annemarie. The guy calls you stupid and me trash. Call me peculiar! Hey, Russell," he said around her. "You got to watch what you say to us guys with no class—we're liable to clean your clock for you!"

Russell was on his feet, apparently with every intention of taking a swing of his own, and David was visibly delighted.

"David, stop it!" Annemarie screamed, still hanging on to his arm. "What is the matter with you!"

"What is the matter with *me?* Nothing! Not a damn thing!" He looked from her to Russell and back again. "Nothing that getting the hell out of here won't fix! Take care of your boyfriend there." He stalked away, and Russell would have gone after him if her father hadn't intervened.

"David!" Annemarie called after him, but he kept walking, and he didn't look back. He disappeared around the side of the house. She could hear the motorcycle start and then go winding down the long drive. "Lord," she said, looking around at Russell. He was still bleeding, and her father was arranging his bifocals so that he could assess the damage.

"Say the wrong thing, did you, Russell?" he inquired politely, trying not to grin.

Russell gave a concise but heartfelt opinion of

David's family tree. "Annemarie, if you get mixed up with him, you're going to regret it!"

"Russell, you don't know anything about this."

"Now, that's the truth! Who the hell is he!" He took the handkerchief her father offered him and dabbed at his lip.

"He's a marine, an embassy guard. I met him when I was in Kharan."

"I cannot *believe* this," Russell said. "He's the reason you stayed a damn month? He's the reason you were so different when you got back? You worry me, Annemarie. You really do. I stood around and watched you make the mistake of your life with Grayson. I'm not going to watch you do it this time, too!" He shoved the handkerchief back at her father and went stalking off in much the same manner as David.

Annemarie sighed, and her father grinned.

"Been . . . interesting, daughter," he said with a wink.

"Daddy, don't tease me—and don't ask me anything, okay?"

"Now, daughter, I'm not asking a thing. If I had any idea what was going on, it'd take all the fun out of it. You know, this puts me in mind of when I was courting your mama."

"Did you punch out somebody's lights, too?" she said morosely.

"Well . . . you could say that. See, when a man's in love with a woman and he don't know if she cares about him or not—and then here comes the man he's pretty sure has got the inside track—well, it don't do much for his disposition, especially if that man's going to shoot off his mouth the way Russell did."

"This isn't the same."

"Sure it is. David told me he loves you."

"Why did he tell you a thing like that!"

"'Cause he does, I guess. Now, why are you all upset about that?" he asked, trying to get her in line with his bifocals the same way he had Russell.

"Because he hasn't told *me*, that's why!"

"Well, daughter, why else did you think he was here?"

She couldn't answer that question.

"He told me last night he come here because he really cared for you. He said you left him high and dry in Kharan. You just took off for home all of a sudden, and you didn't give him the chance to say the things he wanted to say."

"I didn't give him a chance? Daddy, he was eating ice cream with another woman!"

She realized immediately how crazy that sounded, and when she dared to look at her father, he was grinning from ear to ear.

He worked hard to pull the grin in. "Ice cream, you say," he managed with a straight face, but the grin got away from him and they both burst out laughing.

"Daddy, I . . . just can't explain any of this, okay?"

He held up both hands. "I'm not asking—but I got one piece of fatherly advice."

"Daddy," she tried to interrupt. She didn't want or need *advice*.

"Do what's going to make you happy, daughter— and not what everybody else thinks you ought to do. Now, I know something about that, because Naomi and Ruby and half the county thought I was a Black Jack David, too. They thought I was going to ruin your mama's life—but she didn't care what they thought, she took a chance on me. And if I did ruin it, she never once let on to me about it. Now, I want you to do something for me."

"What?"

"I was supposed to work the church food booth tonight at the Fiddlers' Convention. I want you to do it."

"I can't do that, Daddy!" She had to be where David could find her—here or at the restaurant. Or she had to go find him.

"Well, you got to—my arthritis is killing me and they done switched things around so I'd be stuck in that booth with the two women that get on my nerves the worst in the world. I just can't take it. And David ain't going to come back here yet a while anyway. He's mad, daughter. And he's jealous because you took up for Russell the way you did."

"I didn't take up for Russell!"

"It sounded like you did to him. You just got to wait until he gets over it, so you might as well sell ham biscuits. I'll close the restaurant, and then I want to sit on the porch with my hot water bottle and my cat. If the wind's right, I'll be able to hear the fiddling from here." He patted her cheek, and turned to go back into the house. "If I see David, I'll tell him where you are."

She didn't want to sell ham biscuits. But she followed her father into the house anyway, torn between wanting to find David and doing her daughterly duty. Her father asked very little of her—and he was probably right. David wasn't going to come around until he got over being angry.

She took a long shower and changed clothes, putting on a cotton skirt and blouse in a bold flower print of deep blue, lavender, and pink. The material was soft and clinging. She'd intended to wear it for David. She sighed and went downstairs, letting her father drive her to the restaurant and dreading having to go there every step of the way. It would be a miracle if Naomi and Ruby hadn't already heard about the fight between David and Russell—Russell wasn't the type to keep his grievances to himself, and he would certainly see Naomi and Ruby as allies. She'd gotten off lightly with her usually inquisitive father; she wouldn't be so lucky with the cooks.

They were both waiting—and worse, *they* were the two women who would get on her father's nerves in the food booth. She had thought he meant some of the choir members who had decided he was such an eligible widower. But Naomi and Ruby, both of them avid lovers of mountain music, had gotten one of the church women who did back-up kitchen duty for them to finish the evening cooking. Not only was Annemarie going to have to face them at the restaurant, she was going to have them at her elbow all night at the Fiddlers' Convention as well.

"Thanks a lot, Daddy," she hissed at him. She loved Naomi and Ruby, but she did *not* need this.

"You're young, daughter. You can take it."

She wasn't so sure. She was worried about David— particularly if her father was right and he'd thought she was siding with Russell. She began to load pan after pan of the foil-wrapped ham biscuits that the restaurant had donated to the church booth. Both Naomi and Ruby watched her walk back and forth to her car, but neither of them said anything.

"Will you two just say it!" Annemarie exclaimed in exasperation when she couldn't stand the silence any longer.

Ruby rearranged her hairnet; it was all the invitation she needed.

"Where's Russell?" she asked.

"I don't know."

Naomi and Ruby exchanged looks. Annemarie couldn't count the times she'd seen them do that, silently verify with a glance that, yes, our Annemarie is up to something.

"You ain't taking him along with you to the fiddling?"

"No, I'm not taking him along to the fiddling. Russell shot off his big mouth, David punched him for it, and I'm selling ham biscuits. I don't know where Russell is. I don't know where David is. I'm not sure how it came about, but they're both mad at *me*. And if I did find them, I don't think either one of them would talk to me. Are there any questions?" She looked from one of them to the other.

"Well, not right now," Ruby said airily. "But I reckon we'll think of one directly."

Annemarie had no doubts about that. She drove the two of them and enough ham biscuits to feed an army to Blue Ridge Lodge, a ski resort that made ends meet in the summer by hosting outdoor craft and music shows. The Fiddlers' Convention began just before sundown, and the asphalt parking area was crowded with locals and tourists alike, most of the "outlanders" coming from the campgrounds on and near the parkway.

The competitions for the fiddlers were held on a wooden stage at the edge of the parking lot, and Annemarie could hear the music before she got out of the car. People filled the bleachers that had been set up, or sat in lawn chairs, or spread blankets on the grass. And they were all hungry. The local churches, the scout troops, and several women's clubs all had booths of some kind —desserts, hot dogs and hamburgers, ice cream and soft drinks. There were long lines at all the booths, and people began queuing up before Annemarie and Naomi and Ruby could get set up for business, some of them cloggers who clicked and stomped their practice steps on the asphalt while they were waiting. Annemarie was grateful for the rush—it kept Ruby from thinking of any more questions, and it kept *her* from thinking of David.

"Russell's here," Ruby announced.

"Fine," Annemarie said, and she kept working.

"He's talking to David," Ruby said a little later.

"Oh, Lord," Annemarie said, looking up sharply as another fiddler played his best tune. It was Uncle Charlie. No one could wring the melancholy out of a minor chord the way he could. He was playing a song that wasn't one of his usual competition tunes. He was playing "Black Jack David."

Annemarie scanned the crowd. "Where are they?"

"Standing over yonder by them pine trees—where the path goes down to the gazebo. Go see about him, Annemarie."

Go see about him?

"Me and Naomi...think he's right handsome," Ruby said. "Your David."

Annemarie didn't take time to digest the incredible nature of that remark. She shoved the biscuits she was holding into Ruby's hands, seeing David standing just at the edge of the lighted area at the far end of the food booths. Russell was with him, all right, and he was doing all the talking. She didn't hesitate, all but running from the booth and into the crowd. She threaded her way among the spread-out blankets and lawn chairs, edging her way past a baby in a stroller. The infant caught her skirt in both its chubby fists. She bent down, tugging gently to get free, and when she straightened up again, both men were gone. She hesitated, standing on tiptoe to try to see which way they went. Both of them were tall enough for her to be able to spot them in the crowd. She finally saw Russell heading toward the back of the stage—alone.

She walked on until she reached the path. David must have gone this way. The noise of the crowds and the music began to fade as she followed the winding route downward into the trees. There was a cedar-log gazebo at the end of the path, but she could barely make it out this far from the lights. Annemarie shivered from a cool night breeze and kept walking. She could smell the rich, dank smell of the woods around her; she could hear the faint rumble of thunder down the mountain.

David was standing at the far side of the gazebo, leaning against the railing, his arms folded. The gazebo provided a spectacular view, and Annemarie could see the lights from the houses on the mountainside across from them, one of them likely her own house on the next ridge. There were paths and old wagon roads all through these mountains. One that branched off this one would eventually take her to her own back door. She stepped up into the gazebo, not knowing what to say.

"If you're looking for Russell, he's not here."

"I know that," she answered. They stared at each other in the darkness. The music was still loud enough to be heard, but it was punctuated with other twilight sounds—whippoorwills, crickets, tree frogs.

"I made an ass of myself, didn't I?" he said, turning away from her and propping both his hands on the railing. "You know why I hit Russell? I hit him because he wants you—because he'd been close to you all these years and I hate it. I'm in love with you, Annemarie, and it's got nothing to do with emotional trauma in

Kharan. It's because you're the person you are. I like the way your mind works, and I like to listen to you. I like the way you look and the way you smell—Lord, I like the way you smell "

He glanced at her. "I like the way your body feels against mine. I like the way you ... taste. I've never felt about a woman the way I feel about you. I think about what making love with you would be like. I think about it all the time. Sometimes, when you look at me, it's all I can do not to drag you off someplace. When you left me in Kharan, I cried like a little kid, did you know that? Big tough marine. Bawling like a baby."

He took her into his arms then, holding her tightly.

"I cried like a little kid, too," she whispered.

He moved his head so he could kiss her, and she forgot that he'd been angry She forgot everything but the feel of his warm mouth against hers. She could feel her response to him in the tightening of her breasts, in the first stirrings of passion deep inside her.

David . . .

He was trembling, his hands sliding low on her hips to bring her against the hard, urgent male part of him. She wanted him to touch her, and he reached downward, catching her skirt and pulling it up so he could caress her bare thigh. His fingers were warm and insistent against her skin. She pressed her face into his neck so she could take in his masculine scent—while his fingers touched, stroked, reached higher. She shifted her position to accommodate him, and his mouth found hers again, draining all resistance, all coherent thought from her. "Annie, Annie—I want you ..." he breathed against her ear.

Thunder rumbled overhead, and someone laughed on the path to the gazebo. They broke apart, both of them trembling with the desire that threatened to overwhelm them. She stood well away from him, trying to breathe quietly, trying to straighten her disheveled clothes. But David took her by the hand, pulling her along with him out of the gazebo and off the path. They stood in the deep shadows of the trees, wrapped in each other's arms again, hearing the first drops of rain hitting the leaves overhead. They held each other tightly, not kissing now, both of them afraid to begin again the passion they could not consummate.

She reached up to touch his cheek.

"Annie?" he whispered, asking without saying.

"Let's go," she said, taking him by the hand. She wanted to be with him—she was going to be with him and make love with him—*now*.

He was willing to be led along, to follow her blindly wherever she wanted to go. "Which way?" he said when they came to the fork in the path.

She showed him. The wind was picking up, and the fiddling, fainter now as they wound their way deep into the wood, suddenly stopped as the summer storm began in earnest. They had to wait, because they couldn't see the path anymore. David hugged her to him in the downpour; his mouth, only inches away, nipped at hers in quick, hungry bites. She was soaked to the skin, and he reached up to brush her hair out of her eyes.

The rain abruptly slackened; she stepped away from him, pulling him along with her.

"Aren't you going to ask where you're going?" she said over her shoulder.

"I don't care where I'm going, so long as it's with you—can you see the path?"

"Nope," she said, and he laughed.

"Well, what the hell." He lengthened his stride so he

could walk beside her. They were going upward now, zigzagging through the trees until they came abruptly into a grassy clearing on the mountainside. A cabin loomed wet and dark in the middle of it. Annemarie could smell the sweet scent of honeysuckle in the overgrown orchard farther up the slope.

"What's this?" David asked as she led the way.

"My place," she told him. "And Lady Elizabeth's."

"You didn't tell me about this in Kharan," he said as she searched under the stone step for the key.

"I didn't have it before the trip—at least not the way it is now." She unlocked the door and led the way inside. "I—needed something to do when I got back," she said in the darkness. *So I wouldn't think about you.* "Lady Elizabeth's husband built it for her, but then he got the gold fever or whatever it was that sent him west. Their relatives have lived in it over the years, but it was vacant for a long time. When I got back, I needed a place to—"

"Hide," he supplied quietly when she didn't go on.

"Yes." That was it exactly.

"The power's off," she said, flipping a wall switch ineffectually.

"Good," David said. He put his hands on her shoulders, and she savored his touch for a moment.

"We can have a fire," she said a little too brightly. "I'm freezing!" She fumbled in the dark to light several candles, bringing one to the hearth and placing it on one of the stones. "There's kindling ... and logs ..." She was rattling and she knew it, but she couldn't seem to stop.

David knelt in front of the fireplace, expertly laying

the kindling and lighting it. The damp room filled with the scent of burning wood.

"Not bad for a city boy," she said, but he didn't reply, waiting for the flames to blaze up before he put on the logs. Anxious and uncertain again, she roamed about the room, finally going to a small cedar chest and taking out two towels. She braced herself and turned around, watching David's wet T-shirt cling to his strong, muscular back as he set the logs on the burning kindling and replaced the screen.

"Here, you are," she said as if she were a hotel maid handing him a towel. He didn't take it. Instead, he caught her by the waist with both hands, keeping her from flitting off again.

"Annie, sit down," he said quietly. "Sit."

"David—"

"Sit!" he said, pulling her around so that she had no choice but to sit on the hearth rug facing him.

"What's the matter?" He took the towel out of her hands, but he dried her with it.

"Nothing," she said as he gently blotted her face. She didn't sound convincing, even to herself.

"Nothing," he repeated. He used the towel to dry her neck and arms. The blouse she was wearing clung wetly to her breasts. She was cold. Her nipples jutted sharply against the thin fabric, leaving nothing to the imagination. She could feel David looking at her, feel the rise of his desire and her own. She closed her eyes.

"You're . . . not afraid of me, are you?" He reached up to touch her face, and she pressed her cheek into his warm palm, placing her hand over his.

She gave a soft sigh and looked into his eyes. "No," she said truthfully.

"You know I wouldn't ever . . . hurt you or anything like that."

"Yes, I know." She tried to get up again.

"Annie, you're making me crazy here! Do you want me to leave?"

"No!" she said in alarm. That was the last thing she wanted.

"Well, then, help me here! Talk to me!"

"I . . . don't want you to go," she managed.

"And?"

"And . . ." she tried because he wanted her to.

He sighed heavily and looked around the sparsely furnished room. There was no sound but the rain on the roof and the crackling fire. She took the towel out of his hand, gently drying his face as he had done for her. He closed his eyes, suffering her ministrations, opening them again when she stopped. She met his frank gaze head on.

"I'm not afraid of *you.* I'm just . . . afraid."

"Of what?"

"I'm . . . not very good at . . . making love."

"Who told you that—Grayson?"

She didn't answer him.

"Annie, I love you. I want you—but if it's not right for you now, it's okay." He smiled mischievously. "Of course, I'll probably keel over right here and die," he teased, "but it's okay."

She couldn't keep from laughing, and she reached up to put her arms around his neck, pressing her forehead against his. She loved him so, and she could feel him waiting for her to decide. She leaned back to look at him. This was one decision she wasn't going to have difficulty making.

Slowly, she offered him her mouth, and she parted

her lips as he tenderly kissed her. His lips were cool and moist at first, and his breath came sweetly into her mouth. Then he made a soft, needy sound, a sound that left her shaken and weak and shamelessly pleased. She could feel the hunger in his kiss. His hands tangled in her wet hair. He was pushing her backward on the hearth rug, but she resisted, wrapping her arms around him to stay upright.

"Come to bed with me," she whispered into his ear. "David . . ."

She managed to get to her knees, and he followed, his arms sliding around her waist as she stood up. He pressed his face against her belly, as if he savored the feel and the scent of her body. He moved his head lower, pressing a kiss into the *v* between her thighs. She gave a sharp intake of breath at the feel of his lips through the thin cloth.

Then he stood up, following her to the narrow stairway that led to the loft and Lady Elizabeth's antique rope bed. Annemarie had salvaged it from the family attic, replacing the ropes and making her own goose-down pillow and rye straw mattress. The bed was made up in muslin sheets and covered over with a crazy quilt that had belonged to her mother. David gave her no time to arrange a place for them, no time to be shy, to have second thoughts.

"No," he said gruffly when she would have moved away from him to light a candle by the bed. He took both her hands, placing them around his neck, his mouth again covering hers. The rain beat against the tin roof overhead, and she could feel him against her, hard and wanting.

Too many sensations. His kisses on her neck and shoulder, his hands on her breasts. She wanted to prolong this, to remember always, but she was bare to the waist somehow, and David's warm mouth was where his hands had been. She gave a low, guttural sound of pleasure at his hungry tugging, and she slid her hands into his hair to keep him there when he would have hesitated. She didn't want him to stop, and he didn't, elaborating his thoroughness with teeth and lips and tongue.

Too many sensations. Her body naked and unashamed—cold, then warm as his body covered hers, her body yielding under his beloved male one, the hoarse sound of her name as he brought her hand downward and she touched him.

Satin smoothness, silky liquid, hard and wanting and strong—

I love you, David. She was still afraid to say it, but she would make him feel it. She would make him know.

"You're so beautiful," he whispered, looking into her eyes, kissing her mouth, her cheeks. "I want to be inside you, Annie—I want to feel you around me . . ." His hand moved over her breasts, her belly, lingering, moving again. She jumped when he touched the insides of her thighs.

"No—no," he protested urgently, still whispering. "I won't hurt you, Annie—you know that, don't you? I want to touch you. Let me . . ."

Too many sensations. A rainy summer night and the sweet scent of honeysuckle and rye straw ticking; soft, warm kisses moving downward over her, gently probing fingers that left her heated and wet.

Soft . . . warm . . . kisses, unrestrained, loving, coaxing. Her body arched in wanton pleasure when he pressed his mouth against her in that most intimate kiss of all, a pleasure she'd never dreamed existed, a pleasure that wouldn't let her stay quiet.

He was a relentless lover, driving her unselfishly to the brink, but not letting her go over until he was deep inside her. He filled her perfectly, wonderfully, and he hesitated, watching her eyes as he gave his first deep thrust. She whimpered in pleasure, and he stopped.

"Did I hurt you?"

"No. No," she whispered, locking her arms around him, rising to meet him so he'd know how truly wonderful the hard male feel of him was.

"Yes—oh!" he said, his voice soft and urgent against her ear. "Like that—love me—Annie!"

I love you, David.

Had she said it? She didn't know. He was losing control, as was she, and she had but one last coherent thought: *Everything I am, my love, I give to you.*

CHAPTER

Nine

"WHERE ARE YOU going?" David said in the darkness.

"Nowhere. I—"

"Don't go anywhere, Annie, please. Please—" He took her into his arms again, holding her close, spoon fashion, and pulling the quilt around them. The tears she'd wanted to hide from him overwhelmed her, spilling downward, wetting her cheeks.

"I should have said that to you in Kharan, at the hospital," he said.

"That I didn't want you to go. I wanted to—God, I wanted to. But you were so different. I thought maybe I was wrong. Maybe you didn't care anything about me now that we were safe. You looked like a librarian again, and you were acting as though you were double-parked."

"I was double-parked," she said, her voice sounding

147

remarkably calm, and she could feel him smile in the dark. "I'd just blackmailed Mr. Beam into letting me see you—Joe was having a fit because he thought we were going to miss the plane."

"Blackmail, huh? I was ... wondering why you didn't come to see me." He kissed her softly on the ear, and his hands cupped her breasts.

"You didn't come to see me, either."

"I couldn't. They—Beam—was afraid the bastards would try to finish me off before I could give them all the information I had. And that somebody would spill the beans about the hostage-taking. I didn't go any-where. I didn't talk to anybody."

"Except Karen."

He laughed, hugging her tightly. "Ms. Worth, I'm surprised at you. You're not jealous—are you?"

He sounded so wistful that she turned to him. A hot, wet tear slid out of the corner of her eye and dropped on his arm.

"Hey—" he said, trying to see her face, but she wouldn't let him. She pressed against him, wrapping her arms around him and holding him tight.

"Yes, I'm jealous," she confessed, crying still. "What do you think of that?"

"Hey," he whispered. "What are you crying for?" He kissed her cheek and her neck, and then her cheek again.

"I don't know," she said miserably.

"Yeah, well, I've been there," he said with a sigh. "I told you—it was when you left me in Kharan. But the big tough marine can't go around crying over something he can't even name. Got to get back in shape, go right back to the front line, show everybody Gannon's on top of it—everything is A-OK."

He sighed. "Except that it wasn't. I thought I was

going crazy. I couldn't concentrate enough to read a damn newspaper or fill out a form. I couldn't sleep—the dreams were too bad. I kept thinking you were calling me. And when I was awake, I thought about you—the way you looked that day at the Red Sea. You were so . . . innocent. When we were kidnapped, I thought: She doesn't know, not really. She doesn't know this kind of mindless hatred exists—and these bastards are going to teach her. I nearly went crazy when they'd take you out of the niche. I couldn't help you. I didn't know what they'd do to make you say what they wanted to hear—if you'd slipped just once and called me Sergeant Gannon the way you had all that day, I'd be dead now—"

"David, don't. Please . . ."

"I want you to know that I won't ever forget what you did for me."

"I'm not brave, David. We were lucky." She wiped at her tears with the backs of her hands, then kissed him softly on the lips and sat up.

"Annie—" he protested, and she lowered her head, silencing him with another kiss.

"I need some light. I want to look," she said, getting up from the bed to light the candle he'd given her no time to light earlier. She put it on the table by the bed, then found another, lighting it from the first one and placing it on the table as well.

"What are you going to look at?" David said with interest, the smallest of smiles playing at the corner of his mouth.

"You, Gannon."

The smile broadened.

"You hurried me," she explained matter-of-factly. "I didn't get the chance before." She came back to bed,

resting on her knees beside him and grasping the top
edge of the quilt to pull it down.

"Annemarie," he protested, and in the dim candlelight, she could swear he was blushing.

"What?" she asked, raising both eyebrows, her hand
still on the quilt. "David, will you let go? It's just me.
You're a man of the world. You can handle this—
surely." She tried to pull the quilt again.

"Annie, listen. I'm—shy!"

"That'll be the day," she assured him, still pulling.

"Annie!" He was laughing now, and she tried to
wrest the quilt away from him, kissing him, tickling
him, whatever it took.

Abruptly, he released the quilt. "Go ahead," he said,
his voice filled with mischief. "Have your way with me."

"Right," she said, flinging the quilt aside. She was
still on her knees, and he lifted his arm so that she could
move closer to him. His fingers stroked lightly over her
bare hip.

"So now what?" he asked interestedly.

"I told you. I want to look. Maybe touch."

"Touch?" he asked, and she tried not to smile at how
hopeful he sounded.

"Maybe kiss," she suggested.

"Now you're talking!"

"I thought you were shy?"

"Some parts of me are. Some aren't," he assured her.

"I'll remember that."

She inspected him slowly, lovingly, letting her eyes
travel over him from head to toe. David Gannon was an
extraordinarily beautiful man. She reached out to touch
the light matting of dark hair that began just at his neck,
trailing her fingers downward over his chest. He was not
nearly so hairy as one might suppose—just enough, she

thought. She watched her hand move languidly over the trail of dark hair to his abdomen, watched the ridges of muscle contract at her touch, heard his soft intake of breath. Her fingers trailed back to the flat male nipples, the swirl of dark hair that grew around them. She bent her head to kiss him there, to lightly outline each nipple with her tongue.

His eyes closed. He made a random movement with his hand, then let it fall back on the bed.

She shifted her position, moving her hands over his thighs in long, sensuous strokes, her thumbs sliding inward to almost but not quite touch the male part of him that had begun to reawaken. She wanted to memorize every part of him. She had to remember everything about him. Circumstances were wrong for them, and it was only a matter of time before it was over and he'd be gone. She was like Cinderella, and the clock was fast approaching midnight.

She switched to his forearms, stroking, feeling his strength there, moving upward to his well-developed shoulders, letting her fingertips come down his chest and brush lightly over his nipples again.

"I . . . always wanted to do this," she whispered candidly.

"I always wanted you to," he answered, his eyes closing in total submission.

She bent her head to gently trail her kisses over his chest. So many scars.

"What happened to you?" she asked, lifting her head.

He sighed. "Embassy bombing in Beirut. Street fights in the Bronx. Our friends in Kharan—don't stop."

She smiled, then began again, loving the scent and the taste of his skin. He gave a soft murmur of pleasure, and she lifted her head again to look at him. She loved him so! His eyes held hers for a moment, then narrowed.

"No," he said, grabbing her by both shoulders and bringing her to him. "I know what you're doing, Annemarie. I'm not going to let you do it. You're telling me good-bye. I can feel it. To you, I'm already gone."

"It's not going to work with us. You know it's not..." But his mouth came down on hers, hurting, pressing her lips hard against her teeth. He wouldn't stop—and after a moment, she didn't want him to.

"I love you," he said fiercely. "You belong to me. I'm not letting you go. I need you, Annie—and you need me. You don't have to say it. I don't care if you never say it!"

He rolled her onto her back, pulling her legs around him. She felt him enter, quick and hard. He gave a long moan of primitive pleasure, of possession, thrusting deep. She was his, *his,* and he made her feel it with his every stroke. Desire and possession and love all one, driving away her doubts and fears. They were burned, consumed in the heat of bodies joined. She belonged to him, and he to her, their need of each other soaring upward until the pleasure overcame the needing, then burst and spread, red-hot, through her body.

She whispered his name, couldn't keep from whispering it, over and over. She heard his anguished cry of release from far away, and he shuddered against her, fell slack. She held him tightly, stroking his brow and his back. They were both drenched in sweat. He lifted his head to look at her, to kiss her above her breasts, to stare at her with incredibly sad eyes.

He lay his head back down. "It'll work with us if we want it to."

Annemarie closed her eyes tightly, feeling the tears

squeeze past her eyelids. "No—" she whispered. God, she wanted to believe it! But she knew better.

He rolled away from her and sat up on the side of the bed, looking for his jeans and putting them on.

"David," she said, reaching for him, but he caught her hand before she could touch him and put it purposefully aside. "You know about Grayson. You know how I feel about this," she cried, coming to her knees in the middle of the bed. "David—"

He didn't answer her, going down the narrow stairway to the room below. She came after him, dragging the quilt off the bed and wrapping it around her as she went. The fire was out, and he removed the firescreen, kneeling on the hearth to stir up the embers and put on another log. She hesitated only a moment, then went to him, kneeling beside him, opening the quilt to wrap it around them both. He held his body rigid, resisting the press of her breasts against his bare back and arm. She refused to be put off.

"Talk to me," she said.

"What do you want from me, Annemarie? I love you." He leaned away from her to continue with the fire. "But I can't give you guarantees. I can't promise you we'll last forever—even if I'd known you as long as Russell has, I couldn't promise you that. You find somebody you care about and you take your chances. It's nothing new—even Lady Elizabeth did it—that's how it is. Tell me what you want—you want me to give up the marines? You think I'm trash the way Russell does?"

"No!" she said sharply. "You know better than that!"

"Then *what?* Give me something I can deal with— you're like Gina, you don't want to be a camp follower either, is that it?"

"I live here. I love living here, and you know that. I don't want to be any place but here . . ."

"I'd give up the marines."

"No. You can't give up what you are, for godsake! It would make you miserable—believe me, I know. You're so good at what you do, and I'm proud of you for doing it. You volunteered for it, worked hard to get it—"

He stopped the flow of words with his fingertips. "I love you. I've told you why. And it's not some kind of syndrome. I *love* you. You believe me, don't you?"

She looked into his eyes. She wanted to believe it.

"Fine," he said when she didn't answer him. "So much for the voice of reason."

"I need more time."

"Time? Why, Annemarie? It's not going to change things. We've been together and we've been apart. If you don't know how you feel by now, you're never going to know. This is where you jump in with both feet—and the hell with what *might* happen."

"David—" She tried to put her arms around him again, but he moved away.

"We keep going around and around. Why are you doing this to us! Haven't we been through enough!" he said angrily.

"I told you I need more time!" Why couldn't he understand? She was afraid!

"You want time, Annemarie? Well, by God, you're going to get it! All the time you need. I'm leaving in two days. I'm going back to Kharan."

CHAPTER

Ten

"WHEN WERE YOU going to tell me that?" Annemarie said quietly. "Or weren't you? Were you just going to let me wake up two days from now and find you gone?"

"I was going to tell you."

"So tell me now." She kept trying to look into his eyes, but he wouldn't let her. This was like the time in Kharan when he'd decided that she would take what little water they had and walk out alone.

"I have to go back," he said. He sat down cross-legged on the hearth rug, picking up a piece of bark and tossing it absently into the fire.

"Why?"

"Because I—couldn't handle it before. I went back on duty at the embassy as soon as they'd let me."

155

"They let you go right back into it after what you'd been through?" Annemarie said incredulously.

"I wanted to go back, Annemarie. I knew the right answers to give to get there."

"Why did you—give the right answers?"

It was raining harder, and she sat huddled in the quilt, staring at him. He still wouldn't meet her eyes.

"Because that's how it is. You want to get right back into it. It's the only way you can tell if you're okay."

"And were you? Okay?"

"No, I fell apart. I told you I couldn't concentrate. I couldn't sleep. I kept going over and over it in my mind—all the things I should have done and didn't. I was a good marine, and then I couldn't hack it. And for nothing. You know why we got away? They *were* a bunch of damned amateurs! They did it for the prince in the district. They'd heard him say just one time too many how much he hated Americans and how they were ruining his country. So they went out and got a couple hostages for him."

He made a wry grimace.

"But the prince makes all his money off the American oil companies, and it scared the hell out of him. That's why they let us go. He wouldn't take the little 'gift' they wanted to give them. He made them play nice and give their hostages back. It was all—a damn joke! God, it made me sick! A bunch of damned amateurs, and I didn't do anything!"

"What were you supposed to do, for godsake!" she cried. "It didn't feel like a joke to me. It felt real. I know they hurt you every day, but you survived. We both survived! What did you want? Did you want your picture hanging in the lobby of the embassy with one of those little brass plaques that says 'killed in the line of duty'?"

"Maybe. Maybe it's better than feeling like this—"

"David, don't go back there!"

"It's my job, Annie. I've still got six months of my tour of duty left. They sent me back here to the Marine Security Guard School in Quantico to get myself together, and it's helped. But I need to know I'm all right. I need to know that I can do the job I'm trained to do. I couldn't when I left Kharan. I couldn't even do the paperwork—I wouldn't have been worth a damn if those fanatical bastards had come at the embassy. I . . . wasn't going to see you until my tour of duty was up. I know I've made things harder for you, but I couldn't be in Quantico and not come here. I had to see you, be with you. Annie, it's not something I have to do just for me—it's for us . . ."

"For us?" she said incredulously. "And if you run into one of them in the marketplace one day? Where are *we* then?"

Something flickered in his eyes, something that made her heart go cold. The rain abruptly stopped.

"God," she whispered. "That's what you want, isn't it? You want to find them."

"I grew up on the streets, Annemarie. An eye for an eye is all I know. I can't help what I am. Please—don't make it any harder for me than it already is."

She gave a short laugh. "You're going back there looking for revenge, and you don't want *me* to make it any harder for *you.*"

"I thought you'd understand!"

"No, you didn't think I'd understand! If you had, you would have told me before now!"

"Will you . . . wait for me?"

She looked into his eyes and shook her head slowly.
"No."

"Annemarie—"

"No, David. You don't know how familiar this is to me,
having a man I care about tell me all our misery is for the
best. It's not going to work out for us and I can't—won't
—go through that kind of pain again. You go do whatever
you have to do, but we end it. Here and now."

She turned away from him and climbed the steps to
the loft. She dressed quickly in her still-damp clothes.
He was still sitting on the hearth rug when she came
back down. She said nothing to him, tossing him his
T-shirt and going to stand by the front window, leaning
her head against the cool, rain splattered glass. It was
nearly dawn. Out of the corner of her eye, she could see
him putting on his shirt and she turned her head to look
at him.

"I'm going now," he said. "I want you to know that I
meant what I said. I love you. I'm not going to give up
on us. I don't care what you say. I want you to know
that I'm never going to meet anybody in my life more
special to me than you are."

Her throat was burning and her eyes filled. He turned
abruptly and went out the door, letting it bang shut.

She waited, her arms wrapped tightly around her
body for comfort. The silence of the room was deafen-
ing. She waited . . .

"David!" she cried, flinging open the door. The sun
was just over the mountaintop, and the world had been
washed clean. She could smell the damp, woodsy smell
of the land around her and the sweetness of the honeysuckle in the orchard. Raindrops sparkled in the sunlight, and a wild rabbit crossed the yard with little or no
regard for the humans around him. David had reached

the path to the gazebo. He stopped once to turn and look back as if he were trying to etch this place in his memory. Then he was gone.

"David," she whispered, but it was too late. He had to go, and she had to stay, and that was the way it would always be with them.

Better to get it over with now, the realist part of her reasoned, but the part of her that loved David Gannon was breaking apart. She sat down on the wet doorstep. She hadn't even told him. He was her heart's desire, and she hadn't told him. She closed her eyes. She could still feel him inside her, still feel his wanting, open-mouthed kisses.

David . . .

He was gone. There was nothing she could do.

"Annemarie?"

She looked around sharply. Russell stood on one of the flagstones that led to the front door. She lifted her chin a bit under his intense gaze. She was an emotional mess, but she wasn't going to cower under his I-knew-it look.

"Are you . . . all right?"

"Yes," she said, her voice barely a whisper.

"Is he still here?"

"No."

"Are you sure you're all right?"

"Russell!" she said in exasperation.

"You don't look all right, Annemarie."

She didn't say anything. She looked as well as she could, considering. The silence lengthened. Annemarie could hear the mournful cry of a turtle dove somewhere nearby.

"Here," he said, handing her her purse. "I got it from Naomi and Ruby last night. I . . . had to drive them

home when you didn't . . . come back. I left your car at
your house. You hadn't come home . . . so I thought you
might be down here."

She glanced at him, taking a furtive wipe at her eyes.
"Thank you, Russell." He hadn't changed much over
the years. He still looked the same as when they were
children, tailored suits or not.

She suddenly remembered an incident from their
childhood. There had been a carnival on the school
grounds, a real carnival with a carousel of the most
beautifully carved horses she had ever seen. Their class
had been treated to a free ride, but there were not
enough horses. She hadn't gotten on the carousel fast
enough and she was left out. She could still remember
her disappointment, still remember her disbelief, then
her joy, because gallant Russell Chandler climbed down
from a shiny black galloping horse and motioned for her
to take the reins.

"How's your lip?" she said, trying to manage a
smile.

He shrugged. "Okay. I've . . . been thinking about
that. I shouldn't have said what I did—talked to you the
way I did. In his place, I would have punched me in the
mouth, too." He came closer, but he didn't sit down on
the wet step. "You know what I did? My whole life I
just kept thinking there would be plenty of time if I ever
wanted to do anything about you. I was thinking that
when I introduced you to my good friend, Grayson
Barkley. And I kept thinking that all these years right up
until the time you went to Kharan. When you came
back, you were . . different. It scared the hell out of
me, and I knew I had to do something. I realized now
that you weren't different—you were the same. The
same as when you'd fallen in love with Grayson." He

gave her a small, crooked smile. "I missed the boat again, didn't I?"

"Russell—" She didn't want to hurt him, and he was giving her no choice.

"Never mind," he said. "You know what Gannon told me last night? He said you were the best friend he'd ever had, and there wasn't a damn thing I could do about it. Well—that's kind of true for me, too. You're my friend, Annemarie. And if you want me to do anything for you, all you have to do is ask."

Her eyes were welling, and he gave her a quick hug, discreetly leaving before she cried again.

She sat by herself for a long time.

What would you think about all this, Lady Elizabeth? she asked her ancestor silently. That her descendant had no courage probably, Annemarie decided. That she should be brave enough to be with the man she loved the same way Lady Elizabeth herself had.

I'm doing the best I can, Lady E., she offered.

Eventually, she got herself together enough to go back to the house. Her father was sitting at the kitchen table drinking coffee.

"Where's David?" he asked immediately. Clearly, their being together last night was no secret.

"In harm's way, Daddy," she answered, pouring herself a cup of coffee from the old white enameled coffee-pot her father favored.

"Did he go back to Kharan?"

She looked at him in surprise.

"Yes," she said after a moment.

"I thought he might," Mr. Worth said. "He's got a lot of . . . bad feelings to get rid of."

Annemarie didn't answer. She took another sip of coffee to avoid her father's eyes.

"He told me what happened over there, Annemarie," he said quietly, and she looked up at him.

"He wasn't supposed to—"

"I asked him. I wanted to know what he was doing here. And I wanted to know why you weren't anything like yourself when you came back from over there. You're my middle baby girl, Annemarie. You're the one who went to all the motorcycle shops with me. You think I couldn't tell when there was a sorrow in your heart so big it was all you could do to stand up under it? David's not a man who'll lie to you. I was pretty hurt that you didn't see fit to say what happened yourself— oh, I know you weren't supposed to—David told me that, too. But I'm your daddy, and I just reckoned you'd come to me with that kind of trouble even if you were grown."

"I . . . wanted to, Daddy."

"I believe I could have made things easier for you, daughter."

She shook her head sadly. "You have to do it yourself."

"Like David does," her father said.

She didn't comment.

"What are you going to do about him?"

"Daddy, you don't understand about David and me."

"I understand the two of you have been through a mighty hard time—and you come out on the other side of it with a love for each other. A blind person can see that—even Naomi and Ruby can see it, and you know how bad they wanted you to marry Russell."

"Daddy—"

"If your David's gone in harm's way, Annemarie, you better get yourself and him straight on what you're feeling for each other. That's all I got to say about it.

Time won't hold still for you to make up your mind. And sometimes you don't get much time—me and your mama didn't get much. You don't want to live a life of regret."

"Regret can come no matter what you decide to do, Daddy."

"Yes, it can. But I've lived long enough to know that the regret that comes from not trying is ten times worse than the regret that comes from giving it your best shot —even if you fail."

"I'm—scared, Daddy," she admitted. "My track record's not so good." She tried to smile and didn't quite make it.

"You ain't the same girl and David ain't Grayson by a long shot—I don't care what Russell was spouting. And being scared is what life is, daughter. Wanting something awful bad and being scared." He got up from the table.

"I...do love him, Daddy," she said, because she hadn't told David and she needed to say it.

"I know it. And I'm not the one you ought to be telling," he retorted, thumping her on the head on his way out the way he used to do when she was little.

CHAPTER

Eleven

SHE WAS SO afraid something would happen to him. She started listening to newscasts and haunting the mailbox. But no letters came from Kharan.

She grimly set about working in the restaurant in the days that followed. She went out with Russell occasionally, and she avoided all of Ruby and Naomi's questions. The summer stretched out ahead of her, hot days filled with hungry travelers and no word from David. She toyed with the idea of trying to contact Mr. Beam, of going to Kharan herself, knowing all the while that she couldn't do either of those things. David had had no alternative other than the one he'd chosen, and neither did she. She had told him that their relationship was ended, and now she had to make herself believe it.

The days grew shorter, and the leaves began to turn.

165

Impossibly, October was gone, and it was time to close the restaurant. Annemarie had always been like a schoolchild about that—glad of its closing and equally glad to open it up again. But this year she dreaded not having the hectic days at the restaurant to fill her time.

If she could just see him. She could be happy with that, she told herself, knowing all the while it wasn't so. She couldn't see him and not want to touch him, to put her arms around him, to make love.

She woke up every morning with the same thought: How am I going to stand this?

And she stood it because she had no choice.

On a cold Saturday the first weekend in December, Annemarie took Ruby and Naomi on their annual jaunt to Roanoke to do their Christmas shopping. They returned to the Worth house tired and late, laden with packages and finding Annemarie's somewhat harassed father cooking in the kitchen.

"It's about time you got back here," he said testily, but no one paid any attention particularly.

"Smells pretty good, Joe," Ruby said, "for a body that can't cook worth a hoot—Annemarie, you got my package there."

"No, I don't," she said. "That's not yours."

"Yes, it is. I said for you to hold it when I had to find that dime for Naomi at the Cookie Factory—well, don't open it!" Ruby cried in alarm. "It might be your Christmas."

"Ruby, how am I going to know if it's mine or not if I don't open it?"

"Annemarie—" her father tried to interrupt.

"Let me look," Ruby said.

"Nothing doing. I know you, Ruby. You'd do anything to get to see a Christmas present early—wouldn't she, Naomi?"

"Yes," Naomi said, succinct as ever.

"No such a thing," Ruby said, highly insulted. "I never—"

"Annemarie," her father said.

"I'll just take my package," Ruby decided.

"You will not! Ruby, shame on you!" Annemarie laughed, trying to hang on to the bag. "You are the biggest kid—will you quit!"

"Annemarie!" Mr. Worth yelled.

"Daddy, *what?"* she yelled back, clutching the mystery package tightly to keep Ruby from peeking.

"Try to tell a woman something she wants to hear and you can't get a word in any which way you try," he muttered. "David's here!"

She let go of the package, nearly sending Ruby sprawling.

"Daddy—where—?"

"I sent him down to Lady Elizabeth's place to wait."

Annemarie didn't listen to any more. She was out the back door and running.

"Annemarie, get your coat on!" Ruby yelled after her.

"Let her alone, Ruby! She ain't studying no dang *coat."*

Annemarie kept running, past the old barn and the smoke house, past the split-rail fencing that bordered the yard, and the sour wood grove with her father's beehives. She took the narrow path that led down the slope toward Lady Elizabeth's cabin.

The sun was bright, but it gave no warmth. She shivered and kept going, her breath coming out in white clouds. There was no scent of honeysuckle here now, only the barren trees and dead grasses of winter.

She came to the clearing that surrounded the cabin. A thin spiral of smoke came from the chimney. David opened the door before she reached it. He was dressed in civilian clothes—a light gray suit with a white shirt and a deep blue tie. He wore a blue silk handkerchief of the same shade in his breast pocket, and just those subtle touches of blue made his eyes incredible.

She had stopped dead. He looked relaxed and rested —and so damned handsome!

"Say something," he prompted. The sound of his voice made her knees weak, made her heart pound.

"You look like—Russell," she managed, and he threw back his head to laugh. It had been so long since she'd heard him laugh.

"You know, I had it all worked out in my mind— what you'd say when you saw me. Believe me, that wasn't it. You're freezing—come in out of the cold." He stood back for her to come inside. She brushed up against him as he held the door open. That brief contact was her undoing. She turned and flung her arms around him before he could get the door closed. He held her for a moment, then reached up to take her arms from around his neck. "Annie," he whispered against her ear, his breath quick and warm, "we have to talk—"

It wasn't talk that he needed. She could feel him trembling. She could see the naked desire in his eyes. He didn't want to talk, and neither did she.

But he stepped firmly away from her. She had said the relationship was ended, and now she was going to have to live with it. The sun was streaming in the side window of the cabin. She could see the motes of dust floating in the bright light, feel a brief, transient warmth as she crossed the patches of sunlight on the floor. The fire in the fireplace burned brightly, and she went to stand there, holding her hands out to the warmth while she waited for David to say something.

"Annemarie," he said finally. His voice had a strained, almost husky quality.

She didn't look at him. She kept warming her hands. He came to stand close to her, reaching out to put his hand on her shoulder. At his warm touch, her heart began to pound again.

She still didn't look at him.

"Annemarie, are we still friends?" he asked quietly. He took his hand from her shoulder.

"Yes, of course," she said evenly, forcing herself to look at him.

"Are we still—lovers?" His eyes probed her for the answer, regardless of what she might say.

"David," she began, but the words left her. She reached blindly for him, but he backed away.

"No, don't, Annie," he said miserably. "If you touch me, we'll make love and we won't talk about the things we need to get settled."

She sat down abruptly on the raised hearth, her eyes on the floor. She was trembling. He sat down next to her, leaning forward, his elbows propped on his thighs, his head bowed.

"I've tried to do what you want," he said. "I didn't bother you. I've given you time—"

"Are you all right?" she interrupted. If he wouldn't let her touch him so she'd know, she'd have to ask.

"Depends on what you mean by 'all right.' Yes—I'm all right."

She had to look into his eyes to know whether or not she believed him. Abruptly, he stood up.

"Annie—" he said, looking down on her, his voice still strained.

"What?"

"If you'd just—God, this is killing me! Annie, I want you so *bad*—"

This time it was he who touched. She was in his arms. His hands were on her breasts. His mouth devoured hers as if he were starving. He let her feel it, all the longing, all the heartache of their separation. She was starving as well, and time meant nothing now. She couldn't feel it, didn't suffer from its passage. There was only David. She had been alone too long, and he was her heart's desire.

"I love you so!" she whispered against his ear.

"Do you?" There was such doubt, such pain in his voice.

"Yes," she promised. "Yes!" She pressed her face into his neck to keep from crying. But he was kissing her again, letting the kisses deepen, letting her know how much he needed her.

He broke away, his breathing quick and harsh, his hands shaking as he lifted her up to carry her to the loft. He put her down in the middle of Lady Elizabeth's bed, and she shivered in anticipation as she watched him tear at his clothes. He was so ready to make love.

"I love you," she whispered again, reaching out to touch his bare thigh as he came to her. In only moments, they were naked together, their bodies feverish with long denial. He pressed her against him, his hands moving over her, touching all the places that craved his touch. She gave a small whimper of pleasure as he suckled her breasts. He kissed her everywhere, wanting lover's kisses that made her weak with desire for him, that made her arch her body to receive the pleasure that only he had ever been able to give her.

"David," she murmured.

He was moving over her, quickly parting her thighs, pressing his hardness into her in a long thrust. "Oh, Annie!" he said, thrusting again. She rose to meet him, reaching for this closeness with the man she loved. They belonged to each other. They belonged together.

She let the passion take her. She gave in to her desire once and for all. She made love to him without the dread of parting. It was so exquisite, so consuming.

He began to kiss her lips. She looked into his eyes until that final, shattering moment of release. Wave after wave of pleasure. Her body diffuse with it, hot with it. She held him tightly, trembling, feeling him shudder against her in that last moment, feeling his warmth spilling inside her. She gave a soft, incredulous moan, lifting her head to press her lips against his forehead, his hair. He kissed her deeply, their bodies still joined. They lay quietly together, neither of them wanting this to end.

After a while, he said something, but she didn't understand it.

"What?" she asked, and he lifted his head to look at her.

"I said I can't believe how much I love you. It— hurts, you know?"

"Yes," she said. She knew. She tightened her arms around him, kissing his mouth and his eyes. "David, I missed you so much!" she said fiercely. She could feel him smile.

"Yeah, but are you going to marry me?"

She didn't say anything, and he moved to lie beside her, pulling the quilt over them both.

"I really know how to thrill you with a question, don't I?" he said quietly, keeping her in the circle of his arms and legs because the room was cold. "I'm desperate, Annemarie. You said you wanted to end it—and I don't want to let you go. I don't know what else to say to you to convince you. If all I'd wanted was to get into your pants, I'd have had all kinds of things to say to you. But I love you. I want to marry you. I want to spend my life with you. And I can't think of a damn thing to say that you don't already know."

"What about Kharan? I don't know about that."

He sighed. "I'm sleeping nights. I still have a nightmare now and then. I still have a need for personal revenge—but I can live with it. These months at the embassy, I did okay. I'm a suspicious bastard—you'd be in big trouble if you brought a cookie tin in the embassy now—but I'm not a basket case. And you?" he added politely, making her smile.

"About the same."

"The bad part is over, Annie. I can let go of it. *We* can let go of it. Time has taken care of it like the therapist said. But the love we have—the good that came out of all this—it's *alive.* We don't have to worry about it. We're just like everybody else. We make our pledge, and we take our chances." He suddenly hugged her tight. "Annie, it will work if we want it to—and I don't care what happened with Grayson! Take a chance with me, Annie—please."

"David, I want to--but I'm so afraid!"

"No—hey. You don't have to be afraid. I've got a plan," he advised her, making her smile again. "I do. Now, listen. See, after what we've been through, getting married is a piece of cake. And—now this is the good part—I've been assigned to Quantico, to the Ma-

rine Security Guard School. They want me to be an
instructor-adviser. They tell me I'm good at it—hell, I
am good at it. I can teach these new guys what they
need to know so they can handle themselves in a mess. I
can't keep them from being afraid, but I can make them
so damned good, they can control it—what?" he asked
because she chuckled.

"Nothing, Sergeant Gannon. I know you can do it.
Look what a job you did on me."

He laughed easily, happily. "You're the best damned
marine I ever served with, Ms. Worth. So, see—this is
how we'll work it. We get married, and I'll come here
every pass I get—in the summer. In the winter, when
the restaurant's closed, you come to Quantico and stay
with me."

"You make it sound so simple."

"It *is* simple. Annie, it'll work if we want it to. I'm
telling you!"

How she wanted to believe him!

"So what do you think of that?"

She looked into his eyes. She could see the love
there, but her mind swirled with a thousand "What-ifs."

This is where you jump in with both feet and you
don't worry about what *might* happen, she told herself.

"I think—David, help me," she said, clinging to
him, saying it out loud the way she'd wanted to say it
ever since that first day at the restaurant. "Help me—I
need you so!"

His strong hands stroked her back. "I'll help you,
Annie," he whispered. "You know I will."

Epilogue

AT SIX O'CLOCK on Christmas Eve, Annemarie arrived
at what everyone in the area called the Stone Church.
She could see the two parkway rangers who waited for
her on the front steps with the key. It was part of the
agreement for the use of the church that someone be
there to tend the fire they'd just built in the old potbellied stove—an agreement that wouldn't have been
granted at all if her father hadn't been a longtime fishing
buddy of the parkway ranger commander, and most of
the tombstones in the small cemetery outside hadn't
been marked with the name *Worth*. There had been no
congregation here, no ceremonies, for nearly a century.
But tonight, Annemarie thought, the windows would
reflect the soft glow of candlelight, and the altar would
be filled with red and white poinsettias. She had wanted

more than anything to be married here—even if the potbellied stove did stand in the middle of the center aisle.

She listened carefully to the instructions about the stove, holding her wedding dress aside so that she didn't brush against anything sooty. She smiled at the ranger's comment in the middle of the lecture on dampers:

"You're a beautiful bride, ma'am."

She was wearing a long, cream-colored muslin dress—Victorian-looking, with billowy sleeves and hand-crocheted lace. The muslin was as fine as woven silk, and Naomi and Ruby had spent hours intricately braiding her hair with daisies and baby's breath.

"Thank you," she said. "You'll both try to get by the restaurant for the reception, won't you?"

"I don't know if you'll want him there or not," he said, nodding at his partner. "Tommy eats like a pig."

"I heard that!" the other ranger called form the large bow window behind the altar. "You're going to have snow for your wedding, ma'am."

She looked out the window, recognizing the swirl of fine snowflakes as the start of something big.

The ranger who knew about potbellied stoves shook her hand. "Best wishes for a happy marriage, ma'am. Let's go, Tommy!"

She watched out the window after the rangers left, smiling a bit at Naomi and Ruby's fender-and-a-prayer arrival in a station wagon full of poinsettias.

"The groom ain't here," Ruby announced as soon as she hit the door. "We're late, it's going to snow—no, it *is* snowing—and the groom ain't here."

"He'll be here," Annemarie said placidly, surprised herself that these two hadn't been able to stampede her into a major attack of nerves. "I talked to him this morning."

"Your daddy wanted to wear brown shoes—brown, now—and I—Annemarie, don't you pick up any of them flowerpots. Some of them's still drippy. You'll get it on your dress."

She gave in about the poinsettias, standing back to let Naomi and Ruby rush back and forth.

"The groom ain't here." Ruby said on her fourth trip back from the station wagon, as if she hadn't already covered that. "What are you going to do if he don't make it in this weather? They ain't never going to let you have this church again. As it is, if the government finds out about it, I reckon there's one head ranger that'll be working in a dime store somewhere—what if David don't make it?"

"Then I'll live with him in sin," she said mildly.

"Now, that ain't funny, Annemarie," Ruby warned her. "That's how you got the Reverend Merriman to let you use the wedding music you wanted—I never heard tell of such a thing. Telling a preacher if you can't have what you want, you'll live in sin!"

She shrugged and tried to look contrite. It was a good thing Ruby didn't know about Mr. Beam.

"Hic!" Naomi ejected on cue.

"Now, see?" Ruby admonished her. "See what you done with that song of yours—you done give Naomi the hiccups!"

"Naomi, honey, drink some water," Annemarie said, making the best suggestion she could think of. She was *not* changing the wedding music.

People were beginning to arrive, and Annemarie moved to a small side room at the back of the church, looking out over the sanctuary before she closed the door. It was beautiful—quaint and old and beautiful. Lady Elizabeth had been married here.

Lady E. would approve of her wedding.

She stood quietly by herself in the small room, listening to the commotion of friends and relatives assembling for the occasion of her marriage.

Ruby suddenly flung the door open, and Annemarie expected the same announcement. The groom's not here.

"Russell's drunk," Ruby said instead. "He'd been hanging out at that Mouse Club place before he got here—and they all been drinking, Annemarie."

"Russell doesn't drink," Annemarie said, still refusing to be panicked. That was one good thing that had come out of her experience in Kharan, she supposed. This crisis, too, seemed tame.

"Yeah, well, you tell Russell that. Annemarie, he can't usher drunk—I don't know why you had him usher anyway."

"He asked if he could, Ruby," she said patiently. "David and I thought it was nice of him to do that."

"Well, I'm telling you, Annemarie. He's got his boutonniere pinned on his tie, he's putting people on the wrong side—"

"If he's not drunk enough to fall down or throw up, we won't worry about it."

"Annemarie—"

"Ruby, you fix his boutonniere."

"I'll do worse than that," she said as she closed the door.

The door promptly opened again. "Your daddy's got on them brown shoes!" she announced, as if she knew all the time he'd do just that and it was the straw that was going to break the camel's back.

"Daughter, my feet hurt," her father said, standing on tiptoe to talk over Ruby's shoulder. "I can't do nothing when my feet hurt—"

"Daddy, I don't care if you go barefooted," Annemarie said, trying not to laugh.

"Too cold for that," he advised her. "You know it's snowing?"

"Yes, Daddy."

"And your brother sent you a big bouquet of flowers. They come to the restaurant a while ago."

"That's good, Daddy," she said, and the door closed again.

There was more commotion—men's voices and heavy walking. Annemarie suspected that the marine contingent had arrived.

"You can't go in there, boy!" she heard Ruby bark on the other side of the door, but the door opened anyway.

"Ruby, you sound just like my DI," David said, bribing her with a kiss on the cheek. "See, I got to go in there, you sweet thing, you. I got to make sure I'm getting the right woman, don't I?"

"Oh, go on!" Ruby capitulated, as flustered as Annemarie had ever seen her.

David came in grinning, closing the door behind him and leaning against it like the fox who had just escaped a pack of hounds.

"Look at you," he said, holding his arms out to her. "My, but you're beautiful—"

"So are you," she assured him. He was born to wear marine dress-blues. He kissed her deeply, then again. "I love you, Annie," he whispered against her ear.

"I love you, too," she responded, smiling into his eyes.

"Have I got lipstick on me?" he asked, and she wiped

a smudge off with her fingertips. "I got my whole class with me—I told them it was a field trip on wedding decorum—you look so pretty!" he said again. "You got all that borrowed and blue stuff?"

"I've got it," she said, showing him a lace handkerchief borrowed from Naomi and the antique cameo pin that Ruby had given her on her sixteenth birthday. The "something new" were the pearl earrings David had given her.

"And what have you got that's blue—besides me?" he said, smiling down at her. "You wearing blue underwear?"

The door flew open again.

"Sergeant Gannon," Annemarie whispered demurely. "Whatever makes you think I'm wearing underwear?"

"Hey—wait, now—Annemarie—" he said, as she hurried him out the door, grinning from ear to ear because she had introduced a topic he definitely wanted to pursue.

"It's time, Annemarie!" Ruby said worriedly. "It's time!"

Yes, she thought. It was.

The wedding party assembled. And to the strains of the wedding music—a ballad rendered with talent and enthusiasm by Uncle Charlie and a rather laid-back Calder Valley Mouse Club, American Branch—Annemarie Worth took David Gannon by the hand.

> *Black Jack David come a-riding through the woods,*
> *He sang so loud and gaily,*
> *Made the hills around him ring,*
> *And he charmed the heart of a lady.*

Fire Under Heaven

Come go with me my lady-oh,
Come go with me, my honey,
I'll take you 'cross the deep blue sea,
You'll never want for money.

She pulled off her high-heeled shoes,
All made of Spanish leather,
She put on her low-heeled shoes,
And they rode off together.

Last night I lay in my warm feather bed,
Last night I was a high-born lady,
Tonight I'm happy on the cold, cold ground,
By the side of Black Jack David.

DILLON'S PROMISE
CINDA RICHARDS

AN AUTHORS GUILD BACKINPRINT.COM EDITION

For my Mama,

who made up stories for me
until I could make up my own

Author's Note

A silkie is an enchanted creature who lives in the depths of the sea. In the Scottish islands, it is said that silkies favor romantic alliances with humans, and that they sometimes discard their seal skins to live on the land, passing as mortal men.

The first time I heard the ballad, "The Great Silkie of Sule Skerry," I knew that I wanted to do my own version of the silkie legend.

1

SOMEONE WAS ON the roof. Thea Kearney stood listening intently, certain now of the faint scraping noise of metal against slate she heard above the eternal Orkney Island wind. She walked around the kitchen looking up, locating the disturbance just to the left of the chimney. She abruptly reached for her coat—Griffen's coat; it comforted her to wear it. She listened for a moment longer, then reassured herself that the baby quietly sleeping in the crib by the kitchen window had not been disturbed. Her hand rested briefly on the crib, feeling the warmth of a patch of sunlight on the wood, then reaching down to caress the pale, red-gold curls.

Hair like your father's . . .

The thought came unbidden, and she forced it aside, moving quickly to the back door. The door opened easily enough, regardless of the wind, because the old crofter's cottage had been built in a depression in the earth to shield it from the winter gales that blew in from the North Atlantic. Even on balmy days the wind was almost constant, and Thea braced herself to step away from the

1

protection of the cottage and its stone wall windbreaks so she could look onto the roof. The sun was in her eyes, and the wind whipped her skirt around her legs. The man didn't see her, continuing to work at fitting a missing piece of slate near the chimney, his shoulders hunched against the wind. He was wearing an army field jacket with the collar turned up and a wool fisherman's cap pulled low over his forehead.

Cupping her mouth with her hands so she could be heard, Thea called, "What are you doing?" not caring if the answer to her question was blatantly obvious. Poor manless widow or not, she wanted no stranger on her roof without her permission.

The man heard her—she could tell by his brief hesitation as he reached for a hammer—but he didn't look around.

She climbed higher on the slope that protected the house. "I asked what you're doing," she called, and he stopped working. She could sense more than hear his put-upon sigh, and she reached up to keep the wind from whipping her hair into her eyes.

"I'm fixing the roof," he called out, still not looking at her. His words were almost instantly snatched away by the wind. His accent was Orcadian, Thea thought; his tone was exaggeratedly patient. He shifted his position and went back to replacing the slate.

"I don't want the roof fixed," Thea called up to him. He didn't answer her, and he didn't stop working. "Did you hear me?" she yelled. "I don't want the roof fixed!"

The man looked at her then.

Dillon! she thought wildly as she recognized him, involuntarily taking a step backward. Even as far away as she was, she could feel the penetrating force of his eyes.

"I'm not doing it for you," he yelled back. "I'm doing it for Griffen." He looked away from her then, dismissing her while he continued his task, and her temper flared.

"Griffen doesn't need your help now, Dillon!" she yelled. He didn't stop working. "Did you hear me, Dillon?"

"I heard you, Thea," he answered, but he didn't stop chipping at the piece of slate.

Thea stood there a moment longer, still trying to keep her auburn hair from blowing into her eyes. Then she turned away, stumbling, nearly falling in her rush to get back into the house.

Dillon...

She slammed the door shut behind her and leaned against it, her heard pounding. What was he doing here? She didn't want him around. Surely he must know that. She took a long, deep breath and realized she was trembling. It was all she could do to keep from barring the door.

"Dillon, what are you doing here?" she said aloud, closing her eyes and trying to force herself to stay calm. She had never expected to see him again. She glanced at the blue delft clock on the kitchen mantel. She had less than forty minutes before the Orkney Island Tourist Office in Kirkwall sent her another B&B guest.

Her cottage was located on South Ronaldsay, on the outskirts of St. Margaret's Hope, and Griffen's love of modern conveniences had made it a much sought-after place now for bed and breakfast among the hikers, weekend archeologists, and bird watchers who found their way to the Orkney Islands from the Scottish mainland. She'd even had two ghost hunters from the BBC determined to photograph the dairymaid who purportedly wandered the isolated Kirkhouse passageways on the eastern side of South Ronaldsay, and a few botanists fascinated with the orchids that grew along the roadsides.

But it was the wrong time of year for orchids. The winter storms would begin soon, and that was likely the reason that Dillon Cameron felt such a pressing need to make repairs. Well, guests or no guests, she didn't want his belated concern about the missing slate on her roof.

She took off Griffen's coat and tried to think what to do, coming once again to the crib to look at her sleeping child. "I can't do anything," she whispered, pulling the white wool blanket more closely around Caitlin's small form. "I'll just wait it out until I know why he's here."

She looked up at the ceiling again, hearing him move around. At least she didn't have to worry about his staying here at the cottage as he had when Griffen was alive. The room was rented out. She hung Griffen's jacket on a peg by the back door. Caitlin would sleep for a little while yet, and she went upstairs to make a final check of the guest room.

The cottage was a series of stone cottages actually, though at first glance it seemed too long and haphazardly rambling to be a single structure. Each section turned this way and that according to the whimsy of its successive owners. Thea had no less than six outer doors, and because she couldn't hear knocking at any of them unless she happened to be in that part of the cottage, she had painted the door in the two-story mid-section of the cottage a bright red as a guide for her B&B guests.

The guest room was in order with all the little touches— a collection of Agatha Christie books, knitted afghans she'd bought from the local knitters' co-operative, and a high-backed rocking chair in front of a small stone fireplace. The fireplace worked if the guest felt inclined to have a peat fire in addition to the electrical heating, and the iron bed boasted pastel flannel sheets to keep out the dampness, and a heavy, crocheted bedspread she'd made herself. Thea's favorite place in the room was the window seat with its sweeping view of the fertile though treeless stretch to the sea. She had missed having trees at first, but now she didn't think she could live in a place where she couldn't always see the sea. She plumped a pillow that didn't need plumping and checked the small modern bathroom for fresh towels and Pear's soap before she returned downstairs.

She faltered a bit as she came into the kitchen; Dillon was sitting at the table, his cap and jacket hung on a peg beside Griffen's. Her body tense, Thea immediately looked at the baby, but Dillon wasn't disturbing Caitlin; his compelling eyes were fixed on Thea.

"How are you keeping, Thea?" he asked in that quaint way the Scottish had, standing up as she came a little closer.

"I'm fine, Dillon," she answered, unnerved because his formidable presence had always left her not knowing quite what to say or do. She looked at him gravely, once again trying to reconcile Dillon's reputation with the Dillon she knew. To Griffen, Dillon Cameron had been a wonderful friend and a bit of a rogue—two-thirds silkie, Griffen had called him, because he was the very devil with women and because he was more at home in the sea than any mere human had the right to be. She remembered the two of them teasing her that Dillon's mother had been a MacCodrum, one of the Scottish clans that considered itself descended from a deceived human's marriage to a silkie, the mythical sea creature who was sometimes a man and sometimes a seal and always irresistible to women.

No one knew better than Thea about Dillon Cameron's

irresistibility—Dillon, who had always been so quiet with her, who had rarely spoken to her out of Griffen's presence, and who had helped her make the arrangements for Griffen's funeral. That had been nineteen months ago, nearly two years since Griffen Kearney died three hundred feet down in a North Sea oil field southeast of the Orkney's, and even his best friend—The Great Silkie, Dillon Cameron—hadn't been able to save him.

"You've . . . changed the place," he said, looking at the white painted walls above the wainscoting.

He was a big man; his presence filled the narrow kitchen. He was clean-shaven and fair-haired, but he wore his hair much too long, and that, along with his expensively nonchalant clothes, made him look more like a nineteenth-century poet than one of the rowdy divers from the oil rig crews.

Thea stared at him across the room, feeling as she always did that Dillon had more money than he knew how to spend, and that he cared little if anything for the clothes and cars and women he bought with it. She supposed that when one made what amounted to two thousand dollars a week diving, one simply *had* to spend it on something—like the off-white cashmere fisherman's sweater and the baggy designer trousers he was wearing. And he *was* a bit of a poet, Thea suddenly remembered— no, he was more a collector than a writer, favoring obscure Anglo-Saxon verses and Celtic translations to modern poems.

"How much do I owe you for the roof?" she asked abruptly, knowing the question would offend him but wanting to establish a safe distance between them. She was not about to accept charity from this man. "I was in another part of the cottage, and I think you were up

there for a while before I heard you. I'll take your word
for whatever—"

"Thea, don't," he interrupted, his quiet regard so un-
settling that it made her shiver.

Caitlin was waking and fretful, and Thea turned away
from him. "I don't want you here, Dillon," she said as
she reached into the crib to take her child into her arms.
The baby was sleep-warm and cuddly, her joy and her
life.

"I thought you'd go back to America," he said, ignoring her preference as to his whereabouts.

"I'm sure you did," she answered. "You always thought
the way of life here would be too much for a — a *spoiled*
American. You've been expecting me to go since the day
I married Griffen."

"Why haven't you?" he persisted. "Your family is
there." His voice was deep and gritty with the "burred"
r's of the Scots accent. Thea didn't answer him, shifting
the baby protectively to her other arm. She tried to avoid
his eyes, but she couldn't. He walked closer.

"Griffen told me once that you loved the sea, Thea.
And you loved great trees, and you loved him. Two out
of three wasn't bad, he said. Now the sea is still here,
but Griffen's gone, and you'll never see a great tree in
this wind-scoured place. Are you not . . . lonesome here,
Thea?"

"No," she said stiffly. And if she were, she had no
intention of admitting it to him.

"The winters are stormy and long," he suggested, his
pale gray-blue eyes probing hers. Or were they green?
she wondered. He had eyes like the sea, always changing.

"I don't mind the storms," she said. "And I keep
busy."

"By taking strangers into Griffen's house?" he asked quietly.

Her temper flared again. How dare he criticize her for that? "I take them in because I have to."

"What have you done with Griffen's insurance money then?"

"There isn't any insurance money!" Thea snapped. "Most of it went to his father, with some in trust for his grandmother."

"Why would he do that? His dad will drink it all."

"How should I know? And it's really none of your business, Dillon." She wasn't about to discuss Griffen's uncharacteristic lack of planning for his widow. She had too much pride, and she had loved Griffen too much.

But Dillon wouldn't leave it alone. "You've enough to live on?"

Thea didn't answer him.

"You've enough to live on?" he repeated.

"Dillon—"

"Thea, answer me!"

"If I take in B&B's from the Tourist Office," she said sharply, and he gave a tired exhalation of breath.

"And work in the post office or the grocery store for Roddy Macnab," he said. "And trail around with the tour groups for the Tourist Office when they get American incomers here to see the archeological sites, and—oh, yes—you do typing for the local folk—I saw your notice on the bulletin board in Roddy's. Now, that surely must keep you busy. How do they pay you around here for that, Thea? Half-dozen eggs and a bucket of fish?"

"Sometimes," she said evenly. "I don't mind it."

"Don't you? It's a sad use of a college education, Thea. What were you in America? A public relations director? Wasn't that better than living here?"

She didn't answer him, putting Caitlin down to play with a pile of blocks on the kitchen floor.

"Why haven't you gone home?" he asked again.

"This is my home, Dillon. I like it here. I always have."

Dillon suddenly smiled.

"You find that funny?"

"No," he said, still smiling. "I was thinking of something Griffen said about the cairns. 'Everybody who comes here sees a cold pile of stones,' he said. 'My Thea sees the warm, living folk that brought them.'"

Thea turned abruptly away, feeling the sudden pang of Griffen's absence in a way she hadn't in a long time.

"I miss him, too, Thea," Dillon said, as if he sensed her pain, and she looked back at him, staring into his eyes, afraid suddenly of what he might say.

She turned her head sharply at the sound of a car, breathing a sigh of relief and blessing the Orkney tourist trade. She must have miscalculated the time—or the guest had come by plane instead of the ferry.

"You'll have to excuse me now, Dillon," she said. "That's my B&B from the Tourist Office."

"No," he said, catching her by the arm as she tried to get past him to the door. "I'm your paying guest."

She looked at him in alarm, panicked by the idea that he planned to stay. She pulled her arm free, panicked, too, by the memories his warm, firm touch evoked. "The girl at the Tourist Office said D. Smith—"

"I lied," he said.

"Dillon—" she said, trying again to reach the back door. She could see the woman getting out of the car. He wouldn't move.

"Don't you think I know you wouldn't rent to an incomer named D. Cameron?" he asked, ignoring the woman who now knocked on the red door.

"Dillon, will you let me get by?" Thea said sharply.

"There are things we have to settle, Thea."

"No," she said firmly. "You and I don't have anything to settle. Dillon, get out of my way!"

The woman knocked for the second time, and Dillon still refused to move.

"I think I'd better handle this," he said.

"Dillon . . ."

"She's followed me here, Thea. I suggest you let me handle it. She's a bit—impulsive."

Thea stared into his gray-green eyes, finally understanding. He was the rake she'd always heard he was after all, and this was one of his women. She moved aside to let him answer the door.

It surprised her that Dillon would arrange to have one of his notorious lovers' weekends here. She sighed and carried Caitlin to the kitchen sink, filling a small cup with water. "Here you are, baby face," she whispered, offering her several hit-or-miss sips. No, she thought suddenly. *Surprised* was the wrong word. The word for what she was feeling was *offended*.

She kept glancing at the back door, expecting Dillon to bring the woman inside. He didn't, and Thea couldn't keep from leaning closer to the window over the sink to see them, moving aside a string of red peppers she had drying there. They were standing near the back door, out of the wind, Dillon with his hands jammed into the pockets of his stylish corduroy trousers, the woman with her arms folded in an attitude of stubborn defiance. The woman was quite pretty, her platinum-blond hair worn in a straight but artfully mussed geometrical cut. Expensive clothes, Thea noted idly. She had the same fashionable slouchy-by-design look that Dillon had.

The woman suddenly put her fingertips to her forehead.

"Hmm," Thea said. "The classic your-failure-to-do-what-I-want-is-making-me-ill gesture." Thea doubted it would have any effect on Dillon Cameron.

Thea suddenly smiled at the baby. "And you and I had better get out of the window before we get caught. Spying like this," she said, nibbling a chubby fist, "is *very* tacky."

The baby chuckled, and despite her worry about Dillon, Thea grinned, marveling as always that a child conceived in such sorrow could be so merry.

Dillon and the woman walked by the kitchen window, away from the back door. Thea caught a glimpse of Dillon's face. He was angry, and he was having a hard time trying to control himself.

Thea moved to another window. "We'll be tacky just a little while longer," she whispered to the baby, who was bent on giving her a wet kiss on the cheek.

Dillon opened the car door for the woman, but she wouldn't get in.

"Will you look at that?" Thea murmured, straining to see. She suddenly leaned back to see the baby's face. "What are you doing here?" she teased. "You're too young for this. No more soap operas out the window for you."

The baby grinned at her silliness, and Thea forced herself to move away from the window. This was ridiculous. She didn't care in the least what Dillon Cameron was doing. She set Caitlin in the highchair, opened a jar of strained peaches, and poured some baby formula into a cup. She kept up a running chatter to hide the fact that she was much more interested in what was happening outside.

A car finally started, and Thea sighed, not with relief, but with resignation. She waited for Dillon to walk by the window, but he didn't, and she finally got up to see, discreetly pushing the curtain aside in one window, then another.

The car was gone, and so was Dillon.

Now what? she thought. She was fully aware of the irony of the situation. What a choice she'd had: Dillon alone, or Dillon with one of his women. And now there was no Dillon at all.

"You understand, don't you?" she said to the baby as she sat back down again with the jar of peaches. "He's not for us, baby face. He'd break our hearts." Thea gave another heavy sigh. "The trouble is, you'd like him— all of us women like him—and then where would we be? I don't know why he came back, and I don't know why he just left, and I don't know if we'll see him again, but other than that, everything is just . . . peachy." She scraped the bottom of the jar while Caitlin watched attentively. "So what do you think?"

The baby made a long "raspberry" sound, loud and juicy with peaches.

"My sentiments exactly." Thea laughed. "You know, you have your mother's crude American ways, child— yes, you do!"

She washed Caitlin's face and hands and then wandered through the house, taking the baby with her as she did household chores that didn't need doing. She wanted desperately not to think about Dillon Cameron. A lot of good that did her. Her mind went on of its own accord, considering all the possibilities. Dillon must have a car somewhere. He'd probably left it in St. Margaret's Hope and walked out to the cottage, taking the beach path so he could be ever near the sea. He was probably at the

hotel pub now—or at Roddy Macnab, the grocer's. Thea
smiled slightly, thinking of the quaint island custom of
identifying a man and his job all in one swoop. In Roddy's case it took some doing, since he was also the post,
the piper, the fisherman, the accordianist, and the fiddler.

Thea's smile faded. And she was more than a fool if
she thought Dillon Cameron would take a woman like
the one who was just here to a grocery store—post office
to buy fish or to hear the music. They might well be at
the hotel, but they wouldn't be in the pub.

She halfheartedly dusted the banister, remembering
something Dillon had once said. Orkney Islanders were
farmers with a boat, he'd told her, and Shetland Islanders
were fishermen with a piece of land to farm.

"And what are you, Dillon?" she'd asked, knowing
he was neither of those things. He had smiled his devilish
half-smile and not answered, but Thea knew. He was the
flame . . . and both she and the geometrical blonde were
card-carrying moths.

Thea bent down suddenly to kiss the top of the baby's
head.

"Is that fun?" she asked, getting the wide baby grin
she expected. "What a smile," she said admiringly, smiling herself at her child's joyful side-stepping from one
piece of furniture to another. Caitlin would be walking
soon. A strange concept, time, she thought. It passed so
quickly from milestone to milestone in a child's life, but
it lumbered along forever in this one afternoon while she
tried to decide what to do about Dillon Cameron.

If he's gone, I won't have to do anything.

But if he hadn't gone yet, she knew only too well
who was likely to be the one left crying in the end. Her.

She suddenly couldn't bear staying indoors any longer,
and she decided to take Caitlin outside while it was still

light. Night came early to the Orkneys in winter.

Dillon's question abruptly came to mind: *I thought you'd go back to America . . . why haven't you?*

I certainly didn't stay here because of him! she thought. All things considered, she hardly knew him, and what she did know made him an unlikely candidate for—

For what, Thea?

For another Griffen? He wasn't Griffen. He wasn't anything like Griffen Kearney. He was a sea-diving playboy, a devil-may-care womanizer, and he was the last thing she needed in her life. Why had he been so persistent about her reasons for staying? It couldn't matter to him. Their only link had been Griffen, and Griffen was gone.

"I don't need him," she whispered as the baby fretted over the interruption in their walking project. "Listen, baby face, it's either fresh air or listening to the sheep prices on the radio." *Or watching your mother cry?*

She bundled up both of them quickly and carried the baby outside. She paused briefly to breathe in the moist sea air, watching the gulls hang like kites in the strong wind. The baby was eager to get down, and Thea gave in to her ten-month-old's delight with ambulation, letting the small hands grip her forefingers as the chubby little legs high-stepped around the back of the cottage out of the wind.

"That's it," Thea declared when she couldn't walk bent over any longer. "No more prancing." She tried to stop and straighten up, but the little pre-walker in yellow corduroy pants strained forward. "No, no, please!" Thea begged, both of them laughing.

Her laughter faded, and she abruptly picked the baby up. "I'm sorry, little one," she whispered to her child, fighting a sudden urge to cry. Dillon hadn't directly mentioned the baby at all, and she found unexpectedly that she was as saddened by his indifference as she would have been wary of his questions.

I don't need you, Dillon.

She had worked hard at not needing him, at not needing anyone but her child. She was strong now, and she could handle Dillon Cameron. Whatever he was looking for he would have to find somewhere else.

2

THE BABY WENT to sleep peacefully for the night, leaving Thea nothing to do but worry and remember. She took a hot bath and put on a long blue flannel nightgown that smelled of the violent sachet she kept in her dresser drawers, draping an afghan over her shoulders like a shawl while she wandered through the rambling cottage.

Where is he? she thought as she looked from window to window for some sign of Dillon's return. But she didn't see the woman's car or whatever Dillon was driving these days, and it was too dark to see the beach path. She finally settled down before the fireplace in a downstairs room off the kitchen, a room she really had no name for since it was just like several others, but that the rest of the islanders called her parlor. She sat staring into the fire, savoring the acrid fragrance of burning peat.

A wind-scoured place, Dillon had called the island. It was certainly that. Wind-scoured and sea-wracked, it was nothing like the place near the South Carolina coast she had once called home. She had grown up in a small tobacco-growing community along secondary Highway

9, a quiet alternative backroad for thousands of people who flocked to the beach resorts every summer. As a girl she had stood on the sandy roadside, shaded by tall pines or by water oaks covered in Spanish moss, and she'd watched the lines of travelers caught by the one nuisance stoplight, wondering where they'd come from and to what posh motel in Myrtle Beach they'd go. In her family a vacation was canning tomatoes instead of suckering tobacco, and it was to these travelers, Thea supposed, that she owed her emigration to Scotland.

She hadn't intended to emigrate at first, of course; she had only wanted to travel, to actually see a new place instead of always standing by the side of the road watching other people go. She had been twenty-four years old before she could afford it. She had a job with a title— Developmental Director—for a small arts council, and the perpetual fund-raising and public relations that went with it often left her frazzled. The tour was called "The Wild Highlands of Scotland," and it promised crofters, lochs, solitary islands, and quiet moors. The peacefulness was appealing, and best of all, the cost was affordable. So, she kissed her parents, sister, and one maiden-lady aunt good-bye on a hot June morning, and she never came home again. She had gone to Scotland in search of a new adventure, but what she found was Griffen Michael Kearney, a red-bearded diver-extraordinaire for an offshore oil rig in the North Atlantic.

Thea found herself firmly entangled in Griffen's life in a matter of days, a life that included Dillon Cameron, the daring boyhood friend who had talked Griffen into becoming a diver in the first place. It rather surprised Thea that these opposite men were friends at all. Dillon had a reputation for fast cars and faster women, while Griffen manfully assumed responsibility for looking after his usually inebriate father and psychic grandmother, squirreling away what money he had left for his dream: a prime Orkney Island farm.

Griffen and Dillon had left the Orkneys because there was oil in the North Sea, and oil rig divers were fed the best and paid the most—and how the women's eyes did sparkle when they found out a man made his living *under* the sea.

Thea smiled to herself. She supposed her own eyes had done their share of sparkling, but it hadn't been Griffen's romantic-sounding job that had done it. It was Griffen himself, the kind and caring Scotsman she'd loved and married. She still loved him after six years of marriage and nearly two years of widowhood, but in a quiet, gentle way now.

She hadn't cried when the company officials came to tell her that Griffen had been killed. Emotionally, it was as if she had had a secret, windowless room, and she had gone into it and shut herself firmly away. Part of the activity surrounding Griffen's death she perceived, but for the most part she was shut away in the dark. She knew that Dillon had come to help her, just as she knew that Flora and Roddy Macnab were there and that most of St. Margaret's Hope would gather to comfort her as she struggled through the ordeal of saying good-bye to the man she loved.

Will you cry now, Thea?

She heard that question asked again and again in the lilting island accent she loved, the voices sometimes sounding strangely high-pitched to her American ears, something like that of a vaudeville Irish brogue.

But she hadn't been able to cry, not even with Flora Macnab's gentle coaxing, and Thea knew that her friends worried about it, about her "greeting without tears." They fretted over her with offers of tea and food, and all the while she hid in her secret room.

She was alone when the walls to that room began to crumble, alone except for Dillon.

She had been sitting before the fireplace that night, too, her mind numb and cold. She could hear the wind, always the wind, and Dillon moving quietly about. She kept seeing him out of the corner of her eye, moving restlessly from window to window like some wild thing hearing a call it couldn't answer.

"Will you take tea now?" he asked her suddenly, kneeling down by the rocking chair where she sat and stared at nothing. He'd removed the jacket to his expensive gray suit, and it lay carelessly tossed over the back of a chair with the vest and the maroon tie that had been so fashionably appropriate for the funeral service earlier. He was down to the blue silk dress shirt, the sleeves rolled up, and he was warm and alive and he smelled faintly of Drakkar Noir that some woman had probably bought him.

"Thea," he said, "I have some tea ready. Flora Macnab left it. It will make you sleep."

"I don't want to sleep," Thea said, looking away from his eyes, momentarily hating his warm aliveness and his concern.

"Thea . . ."

"Leave me alone, Dillon. Everyone else is gone. I'd like you to go, too."

She stood up abruptly, seeing that there was sand on the painted wood floor from the endless line of people who had trekked in and out. At that moment the most important thing in the world became the sweeping of sand. She went to the pantry off the kitchen and brought back a broom, beginning at the far side of the room and quietly sweeping the tracks of sand toward the opposite door.

"Thea, don't," Dillon said, taking the broom out of her hands. "Don't now. You'll make yourself ill."

Thea looked at him, incredulous that he could think it mattered if she became ill or not.

"Come drink your tea."

"I don't want any tea! I don't want anything!"

He hesitated, then went back toward the kitchen, taking the broom with him. She found suddenly that there was something she wanted after all.

"Dillon," she called after him, and he turned to look at her, his face so neutral, so controlled. "Tell me what happened."

Dillon moved to get a cup and pour the tea she'd told him she didn't want.

"Tell me, Dillon," she repeated, her voice brittle with unshed tears.

"Thea, you know what happened," he said wearily.

"I don't want the company version. I want to know what happened to Griffen. I want you to tell me." She wanted to know, too, why Dillon seemed so detached from it all. He's worse off than I am, she thought suddenly.

She could feel him bracing himself to humor her, but she didn't want to be humored. "How can I believe it if you don't tell me?" she asked quietly. "Will you leave me always listening for him to come home again?"

He took a long, deep breath, and he avoided her eyes. For all their lack of emotion, she knew he was hurting— just as she was—but she didn't care.

He set the steaming cup of tea down on the table.

"We . . . were out . . . Griffen and Sinclair and I," he began, but he didn't go on.

"And?" she insisted, moving to where she could see his face better. "Sinclair," she prompted like a child hearing a story for the thousandth time. "Sinclair is young."

"Yes," Dillon said, his voice soft and strained. "He's ... young. Do you know how it is at all, Thea? The long shifts—twenty or thirty days of getting into the diving bell and having to go down—and then coming up and having to stay in the pressure chamber. We ... live on top of each other. There's no room ... for privacy. We can go down, we can dive, but the sea and the gloom—the light doesn't shine very far, Thea, and everything still presses you down—closes you in. You're never away from it—that feeling of being closed in ..."

Thea looked away from him, watching the curl of steam rise from the cup of tea. The wind outside buffeted the cottage, straining through the cracks and crevices in a low, mournful sound.

"I ... didn't know how bad it was for Sinclair," Dillon said, and she looked back at him.

"No," she said, staring at him across the room. "You wouldn't, would you?"

"I ... don't know what you mean," he said carefully.

"I mean you were never afraid, were you, Dillon? You're The Great Silkie—half man and half seal. You weren't like Sinclair. Like Griffen."

"Griffen wasn't afraid," Dillon said, but Thea could hear the edge of doubt in his voice.

"He was. Griffen was a farmer, Dillon. All he wanted was his island land, and you showed him how to get the money for it. Go on. Tell me what happened."

He stared back at her, but she didn't waver. His sea-colored eyes searched hers for some way out.

"Please," she said finally, and he looked away.

"Dillon, please!"

"We were . . . clearing the way for the pipe," he said, looking back at her, giving her the recitation she demanded. "It kept getting caught. We had to cut a piece out and rejoin it. Sinclair was welding, but he . . . couldn't stand any more of it. Griffen was trying to hold on to him, to keep him from going up. Sinclair was mad to get to the surface. He couldn't come up without decompressing in the pressure chamber—he would have died of the bends. Griffen had him, but the boy still had the torch. He damaged Griffen's line."

"His air line," Thea said as if she would lay a trap for him, find some inconsistency, some lie that would mean Griffen wasn't dead after all.

"No," Dillon said in his strained monotone. "The hot-water line in Griffen's suit was nicked. The diving bell was—" He faltered, then looked directly into her eyes. "It's so cold down that far, Thea."

Thea understood what he didn't say. So cold—cold enough to freeze in a matter of minutes.

"You tried," she said.

"Thea, do we have to keep on with this?"

"You tried," she insisted because she realized now that there was something she hadn't been told. "You . . . just forgot all about Sinclair."

Dillon took a long time to answer. "No," he said finally.

"No?"

Dillon's eyes shifted away. "I didn't know Griffen was in trouble."

"You didn't know? Why didn't you know? How many times have the two of you told me you could nearly read each other's minds when you were out?"

"I didn't know! We were three hundred feet down— the both of us trying to hold on to that half-crazed boy! I didn't know!"

"But when you did know, you tried."

Dillon didn't answer.

"You tried," she repeated. "You didn't let Sinclair keep you from trying."

"Thea." There was such a plea in his voice, but she was past caring.

"You didn't do that, did you? Dillon, you didn't just let the sea take him—isn't that what they say around here? Sometimes you let the sea take its own—you don't interfere. You didn't just let Griffen freeze to death!"

"Ah, God, Thea!" Dillon cried, going blindly away from her toward the back door. She followed him, but he hadn't gone far, only to the alcove just inside the back entrance. He was standing in the shadows, the light from the kitchen shining on the lower half of his face.

"Dillon," she said quietly, and the wind hammered against the back door. "Tell me. Please. All of it."

"Thea, I can't." His voice was barely a whisper.

"You have to! There's no peace for either of us if you don't! Please, Dillon—please!" She waited what seemed an eternity for him to answer.

"I was going to have to choose," he said quietly. "Griffen knew that. I was the senior diver, and I was going to have to choose—" He stopped as his voice broke. "Griffen knew," he began again, his voice shaky. "I . . . couldn't bring them both into the diving bell. He knew I couldn't, and he—"

"Dillon, tell me!" she cried when he didn't go on.

"He made the decision for me, Thea! He wouldn't let go of Sinclair and let him kill himself trying to surface. It was my responsibility—mine! But he . . . wouldn't let the boy go up."

Yes, Thea thought sadly. Griffen would do that. Griffen with his rogues' gallery: an alcoholic father and a playboy friend; a fey grandmother and a foreign wife.

There was plenty of room for a terrified boy-diver.

She stood staring at Dillon, wanting to hate him. She couldn't do it. She understood now what Griffen had done—not only for Sinclair, but for Dillon, the man who had been his best friend all of his life. That's how much he'd loved Dillon.

"I'm so . . . sorry, Thea," Dillon said, his voice barely a whisper.

She could see a single tear running slowly from his shadowed eyes into the light. He was in such pain, and she reached out to touch him. He was Griffen's friend, and she couldn't help herself. She put her hand on his arm, and his shoulders sagged. He was holding her suddenly, the anguished sound he made against her ear releasing her own pent-up grief. They cried together in the shadows, his grief silent and intense, hers a pitiful sobbing that welled up as the walls to her secret room crumbled. Once, as she struggled for control, her lips brushed against his face, just grazing the corner of his mouth.

It was as if she had burned him. He stiffened, visibly shaken by the force of his response to her touch. Then his mouth was on hers, his arms around her so tightly that she thought he would crush her in two. She had never in her life known a passion so abrupt and so intense, and she did nothing to resist it. Dillon Cameron was warm and alive, and he was as close to Griffen as she would ever be again. Her secret room had been breached, and Dillon was the only place she had left to hide.

The next morning he was gone, leaving her no word of apology or regret or farewell, and she'd heard nothing from him until today.

"This is not doing anybody any good," she said abruptly, pulling her thoughts back into the present. "Least of all, me." She got up from the rocking chair, keeping the afghan around her, and went into the kitchen. She put water on to boil, more because she needed the company of a whistling copper kettle than because she wanted something hot to drink. She needed the ritual of making herself tea, needed to fill her mind with something besides Dillon Cameron. She didn't want to think about him. It was too painful, and it served no purpose except to leave her more confused—and ashamed.

And yet, she was waiting for him to come back to the cottage, and she knew it. She couldn't keep from looking out the window, knowing she'd be glad to see him however he arrived—on foot or in the red Porsche he used to drive or in the car with the geometrical blonde.

The kettle whistled sharply, and she poured the boiling water into the teapot, listening intently at a sudden, faint sound.

Nothing, she decided. It was so hard to tell in a house like this what was wind and rain or fretting baby.

Or Dillon.

Stop it! She had to stop this. For all she knew Dillon could be gone for another nineteen months. She waited for the tea to steep, then carried a cupful into the entryway with the red door, making sure it was locked, and then going past the stairs back into the parlor. She sat down by the fire again, sipping her tea and wishing she'd put sugar into it.

She abruptly got up again. She was not going to sit here and wait for Dillon Cameron. She banked the fire and turned off the downstairs lights, walking down the narrow hallway to the bedroom and the small room across from it where Caitlin slept.

She had forgotten her tea, and she turned back to get it, glancing into the softly lit nursery as she passed. She gave a small intake of breath, because Dillon was standing by the baby's crib, the fisherman's sweater and corduroy trousers now soaking wet and dripping puddles on the floor.

Thea quietly released the breath she was holding. "How did you get in here?" she asked, working hard to sound calm. She didn't ask what he was doing; she was too afraid to. It didn't seem to bother him in the least that he was wet, and Thea listened for the sound of a car, wondering what he'd done with his blond sidekick.

No, she thought. He hadn't come by car. He was too wet.

"Dillon?" she prompted, but he simply stood and stared at the sleeping baby, ignoring her question. "Dillon!" she said again.

He finally looked at her. "I . . . have a key," he said with effort.

"A key?" She never gave out a key. The Tourist Office didn't have one. She stared into his eyes, not knowing what to say. He was here now, and she had no idea what to do with him. She suddenly remembered one of her mother's axioms:

Be careful what you want, Thea—you might get it.

"Griffen . . . gave me a key," Dillon said finally. "She's very beautiful," he added, looking back at the baby. "Very . . . beautiful."

"Yes," Thea said, deciding to come closer. He was weaving slightly. "Dillon, are you all right?" Are you drunk, is what she meant, but she decided at the last moment to uphold the social amenities as long as she could. She was upset and worried, and she didn't want Caitlin awakened.

Dillon didn't answer her. Instead, he reached down to gently touch the baby's hair, his movements unsteady.

"Dillon, are you drunk?" she asked in spite of herself.

He gave her a sheepish grin and reached up awkwardly to scratch his left eyebrow. "I'm . . . a bit full, Thea," he admitted ruefully.

Well, fine, she thought, again trying to decide what to do with him. She was going to have to get him out of here first.

"You can be 'a bit full' someplace else, then," she said, taking him by the arm to lead him away from the baby.

"I . . . don't make a habit of it," he said defensively, taking a few steps. "We were drinking . . . Griffen's health tonight."

Thea frowned, not knowing whether this was alcoholic nonsense or if he actually had been drinking to Griffen's health. Probably so, she decided. They still had birthday suppers for Robert Burns here; why wouldn't they have some sort of belated toasting for Griffen?

"He wanted it," Dillon rambled on. "And, you know, a fine gathering it was, Thea. Singin' and dancin' and toasts to our Griffen—*Slàinte Mhòr, Mo Craid!*" he said loudly by way of demonstration. "Great health, my friend!"

"Dillon, will you be quiet!"

"No, I think not, Thea. There's no sense in that— not when you've been quiet enough for the both of us." He leaned toward her, and she frowned at the whisky fumes coming directly into her face. "I want my baby," he whispered, and she stiffened.

"Dillon, you're drunk."

"Aye," he agreed. "I am. But I still know, Thea. I know that wee baby girl is mine. What I don't know is how you could do it—how could you do that to me, Thea? How could you have my child and no' tell me?"

"Dillon, she's not—" Thea stopped. She was looking

directly into Dillon Cameron's sad eyes, and she couldn't tell the lie.

"Thank you for that, at least," he said. "You can't look me in the face and deny it."

"Dillon—" She tried to get him out of the room again.

"No, it wasn't denying that you did, was it, Thea? It was omitting. Lying by omission is still a sin, Thea."

"Dillon, please. Not now. You'll wake her."

"I'll wake her?" he asked loudly. "Shouldn't she know she has a dad after all?"

"Dillon, please!"

"What? What, Thea? Tell me what you want. Have you nothing to say to me? You don't want your money?"

Thea's temper flared. Clearly he'd been through this sort of thing before. *"My* money? Why? Is there some kind of standard fee you pay the women you think have had your illegitimate children for you?"

"Don't!" Dillon said, grabbing her by the shoulders. "You know that's no' true, and I know you don't mean it—"

"You don't know anything. Dillon, let me go!"

"I know that child is mine, Thea," he said, turning her sharply around so she was facing the crib. "She is so beautiful," he said again, his voice going soft. "My *dochter.* My ... sweet ... wee lady. Do you know that poem, Thea? Robbie Burns's promise to his—" He stopped, frowning.

"To his illegitimate daughter," Thea finished for him. "Yes, I know it. But you're not 'Robbie' Burns."

Dillon grinned. "No. I'm no' Robbie Burns, but I'm The Great Silkie, am I not? Isn't that what Griffen always said of me?" He was weaving again. "I'm The Great Silkie, Thea, and I've come to see my bairn!"

"Dillon, I'm about out of patience with you," Thea

said, trying a different tactic. He stumbled, and she tried to keep him upright, frowning at the look that suddenly crossed his face. "Dillon, you're not going to be sick, are you?" she asked worriedly.

"Never!" he assured her loudly, and he was grinning again.

"Dillon, will you be quiet!" she whispered fiercely, trying to start him walking again.

He suddenly leaned on her heavily. "Thea, you know, I'm no' feeling as well as I have."

"I'm not surprised," she answered, maneuvering him down the hall toward the kitchen.

"Where is it you're taking me? You'd not put me out in a gale?" he asked incredulously as he recognized their direction.

"This is not a gale, Dillon. It's just a little rain. A gale is when the wind blows the sea as flat as a tabletop, and the breakers crash against the rocks so hard you can't tell sea from sky."

"Aye," he told her. "You know, Thea, you're no' as thick as some Americans."

"Thank you," she said dryly, perfectly aware of The Ugly American image her countrymen sometimes had abroad. "It's very kind of you to say so."

"You're welcome, Thea. Thea? Don't put me out in the rain. I've no stomach for sleeping in a car."

"Silkies like the rain," she assured him. "Especially great ones." She wouldn't put him out into the rain, no matter how much she wanted to, but she couldn't resist teasing him.

"I'll catch cold," he promised her, his arm heavy over her shoulders. His wet sweater had ridden up, and Thea's hand grazed his bare back.

"Silkies don't catch cold—Dillon, could you pick up

your feet?" she asked, pivoting him around in the entry so that he faced the stairs.

"I can," he assured her, grinning again.

"Then do it!" she said in exasperation.

"I will!" he answered. "Thea?" he asked as they started up the stairs. "What kind of 'Thea' are you? Dorothea or Althea?"

"Just plain Thea, Dillon," she said to humor him, knowing that not answering him could mean a thirty-minute delay in getting him to the second floor.

"And what is its meaning?" he inquired, standing on one foot so long that Thea felt they were both going to tumble backward.

"It means, Dillon, that my Aunt Mary Ann read *Hedda Gabler.*"

He looked at her blankly. "No, Thea. Your name has to *mean* something."

"And what fascinating thing does 'Dillon' mean?"

He stopped trying to step up and frowned at her. "With the *i* and the *o* or the *y* and the *a?*"

"Surprise me."

"*I* and *o* means faithful and true—why are you laughing, Thea?"

"This is a joke, right?"

"Indeed, no, Thea," he said, clearly offended. "It's no joke. It's . . . what I am. Faithful and true—you're no' supposed to grin like that, Thea."

"Oh, sorry. So what's the other one—with the *y* and the *a?*"

"My name like that—and there's only the one *l*, you know—"

"I know."

"Like that it means—it's Old Welsh, you see—"

"You don't say." She tried to start him moving again.

"Aye. I *do* say, Thea. Did you no' just hear me?" he asked earnestly.

"Dillon, will you get on with it."

He frowned, clearly offended again. "It means from the sea."

"Well, then, you'd best be changing the way you spell your name, hadn't you?"

"Wait—wait!" he insisted when she tried to move them on up the stairs. "I'm thinking you've insulted me."

"Then you're not as drunk as I thought."

"Thea, Thea—I know! Anthea! 'To Anthea Who May Command Him Anything'!" he quoted loudly.

"Dillon, you're beginning to get on my nerves."

"Then why are you doing this for me?" he inquired, stopping dead on the stairs again.

"I'm not doing it for you," she said, repeating his own earlier remark. "I'm doing it for Griffen—*will* you step *up* before we both fall!"

"Aye! I will!"

"Then do it!"

He did—approximately.

"How was that then, Thea?" he wanted to know.

"That was wonderful. Do you think you could do it three more times?"

She finally heaved him into the guest room, all but forcing him in the direction she wanted him to go. Then he sat down on the bed before she wanted him to sit. "Dillon!" she snapped. She had met with the St. Margaret's Hope Knitters' Co-Operative nearly every Thursday of her entire pregnancy making the hand-crocheted spread, and Dillon Cameron was soaking wet and sitting on it.

"Give me your sweater," she said, abandoning the idea of moving him and trying something else instead.

"Why?" he asked, his voice muffled inside the sweater as she tried to pull it over his head. If she couldn't get the bedspread away from the wet, she'd have to get the wet away from the bedspread.

"Because, Dillon," she said sarcastically, "it's wet. Everything you have on is wet!"

He gave her a hurt look as she pulled the sweater free of his head. "I was only asking, Thea. It's raining out, you know," he added helpfully.

"I know, I know," she said, giving a short sigh. This was turning out to be more difficult than she'd planned. "I ought to leave you like this," she threatened as she went into the bathroom for a towel. "Let you catch a cold."

"Ah, no, lass. Silkies don't catch cold," he reminded her, missing the towel she threw at him. She tried not to look at his bare chest, tried not to acknowledge what a beautiful man he was—physically at any rate.

"How far are we going with this?" he asked politely when she bent down to unlace his muddy boots. And he had the audacity to grin.

"This is it!" she snapped, but Dillon, ever helpful, suddenly stood up, nearly treading on her fingers as he tried to undo the snap on his pants. The job was entirely too much for him.

"You are a complete idiot, Dillon," Thea said as she tried to straighten out the tangle of tight-cuffed pants stuck on muddy boots. "Will you sit down!" she cried, jerking one leg upward so he'd have to sit. She finally got his boots unlaced and off, and he fell back heavily on the bed.

"Dillon!" she said, still worried about the bedspread. She tried not to look at him again, tried not to remember.

"You're no' smiling, Thea," he said, his eyes closed.

She didn't answer him. "Roll over, Dillon," she said, trying to get the precious bedspread off the bed. She was too close to him for her own peace of mind. Her nostrils filled with his masculine scent: soap and sea air and whisky. Her hand brushed across his chest as she tried to move him, and she remembered suddenly the feel of it that night nearly two years ago, hard and muscular and wet with her tears. She forced the memory aside and gathered up the bedspread.

"You're no' smiling," he said again.

"To tell you the truth, Dillon," she said matter-of-factly, "I feel a lot more like crying."

He reached for her suddenly, catching her by the shoulders and holding on. She could feel his warm hands through the flannel nightgown. "No, Thea," he said urgently, his eyes probing hers. "There's nothing for you to be crying about." He awkwardly tried to caress her face.

"Dillon, don't."

"My beautiful Thea," he whispered.

"I'm not beautiful, and I'm not yours," she said, trying to dodge his hand.

"You are," he insisted. "Sweet . . . and beautiful . . . and mine. Don't be afraid of me, Thea."

"I'm not afraid, Dillon. I just want you to let go."

"You understand, don't you? You have to understand."

"No," she said truthfully. She didn't understand anything, except that once he'd let himself into this house, she should have gotten him out.

"You're mine, Thea. Griffen gave you to me."

"Griffen was *always* giving me to you. It was the worst threat he could think of."

"Thea."

"Dillon, go to sleep!" She caught both of his hands

in hers, pressing them against his bare chest as if she thought they'd stay there, but he reached for her immediately.

"Thea, we have to talk," he insisted, his eyes probing hers.

Talk? she thought crazily. How could they talk when he had such sad, beautiful eyes and when the touch of his strong male hands made her do nothing but remember? She slipped free of his grasp and fled the room, hearing him call her once as she reached the ground floor.

3

THEA WOKE TO the sound of voices in the kitchen, leaving her vaguely disoriented because they shouldn't have been there.

"Ah, no, lass," the male voice insisted. "Don't feed your poor old Da the porridge—he's not up to porridge this morning, lass. Wait, now—mmm—what—*fine* porridge it is, darlin'. Now you have a wee bit."

There was a brief silence, and then, "Da!" in the baby's high-pitched voice.

"What, lass?" the male voice said. "Will you be having a bit more now? That's my good girl."

Thea abruptly sat up, throwing her legs over the side of the bed. She didn't stop to hunt for her robe, bursting into the kitchen just as Dillon fed Caitlin another spoonful of oatmeal.

"Here's your mum now," he said to the baby. "Good morning, Thea. Did you have a good sleep?" he asked calmly.

"Did I—!" Thea cried, making him wince from the hangover he must have. He managed to feed the baby something from a cup. "What do you think you're doing?"

Dillon sighed. "Well," he said, wiping the baby's mouth with the towel he had thrown over his shoulder. "We're having breakfast, my daughter and I. There's some bacon fried up over there for you if you want a bacon sandwich, Thea."

"I don't want a bacon sandwich! What are you giving her?"

"Porridge," Dillon said. "Oatmeal," he clarified. "And some orange juice."

"She doesn't like oatmeal!"

Her adored only child promptly made a liar out of her by taking a big spoonful.

"Where did you get orange juice? There's no orange juice here!" Thea went on crazily because she was so upset.

"Well, Thea," Dillon said, still feeding the baby, "as long as you're so agitated, I might as well tell you— and don't yell anymore, all right?"

"I'm not agitated!" she cried in a voice that made her an even bigger liar and made him wince again. "Tell me what?"

"Well, we've been a few places," he said, visibly bracing himself for another outburst.

"We *who?*" Thea asked, her voice deadly. And she didn't miss the barest of grins that played at the corners of his mouth, despite his hangover.

"The lass here," he said, "and me. You didn't tell me her name," he reminded her.

"Never mind that! What places?" How dare he take her baby!

"To Roddy Macnab's."

"Roddy Macnab's!" Thea cried, as if it were a hotbed of wickedness instead of the post office–grocery store.

"Aye," Dillon said reasonably. "The little one here asked me to," he added.

"She *asked*—" Thea said, faltering as the ridiculousness of the statement penetrated. She glanced at the baby, who promptly grinned. Wherever they had been, the baby was none the worse for wear.

"Aye," Dillon assured her, his delivery still deadpan. "'I've nae orange juice, Da,' is how she put it, so we went to get it. What else could I do?"

He was all innocence, and Thea stared from one guilty party to the other, completely incredulous at Dillon Cameron's audacity. But she was losing the edge to her anger in the face of the two identical grins she was confronting. "She asked, you say," Thea repeated, trying to calm down—for the baby's sake, not for Dillon's probably aching head.

"Oh, aye," Dillon said. "In Gaelic."

"In—" Thea laughed in spite of herself, and she suspected that she'd just been the victim of the famous Cameron charm. His poor mother, she thought with both sympathy and admiration. It must have taken some doing to drag Dillon into manhood.

"I . . . see," Thea said. "It's a pity she didn't tell you her name while she was at it. In Gaelic."

Dillon was grinning openly now. It had been such a long time since she'd seen him really smile. She looked into his eyes. It was interesting the way the color seemed to keep changing. He was letting her look all she wanted, she suddenly realized, the eyes she found so interesting frankly amused.

Thea frowned. She didn't like being the source of his amusement.

"She couldn't tell me her name, Thea," Dillon said. "She says she'll no' choose sides. She'll no' do anything that will cause her mother hurt. She says only her mother can introduce us properly, if she would be so kind as to do that," he added, looking gravely into Thea's eyes.

She didn't answer, determined not to be manipulated any further.

"She knows who I am," Dillon offered in a few moments, and Thea's temper flared again.

"She doesn't know who you are," she said tersely.

"She calls me 'Da,'" he insisted.

"Da!" the baby said as if on cue.

"That isn't you. That's a—a non-specific *d* sound all babies make at this age."

"Da!" the baby said again, this time holding up both arms for Dillon to take her.

Dillon stood quietly, his face so carefully arranged that it made Thea angry all over again.

"Do you think, Thea, it would be all right if her ... non-specific *d* sound picked her up?"

"No!" Thea said.

"At least until you put on some clothes," he suggested, letting his eyes wander over her body.

Thea looked down at her blue flannel nightgown. It was hardly revealing, but Dillon's calling attention to it made it seem unbearably inappropriate.

"I'll be right back," she said. "And don't either of you go anywhere!"

Oh, Lord, she thought as she fled back into the downstairs bedroom, repeating it when she caught sight of herself in the dresser mirror. Her hair was long and naturally curly—unruly at best in this wet and windy climate—and the few hours of fitful, restless sleep she'd had had left her looking like an understudy for *The Bride of Frankenstein*.

But she couldn't worry about that. She had a much

more pressing problem: what to do about Dillon. Last night he'd had too much to drink. This morning he was sober and firmly entrenched in playing at being Caitlin's father. And she had no idea what to do about it. She didn't want to keep him away from Caitlin, but she didn't want Caitlin to learn to love him only to have him leave.

I don't want to learn to love him either, she thought suddenly. And she could—so easily. Dillon Cameron was dangerously male. A woman couldn't be in a room five minutes with him and not know that. And yet he had a lost and lonely air about him that made women want to cut him the biggest slice of cake and not put him out into the rain when he'd lifted one too many pints of ale.

And take him to her bed.

"Oh, God, what am I going to do?" she whispered, grabbing a comb and raking it through her hair, hitting snarl after snarl. "Thea, Thea," she said through gritted teeth. "No silkie, great or otherwise, will ever stalk you. You look like —a dandelion!"

She finally got her hair into some order by twining it into a long braid she let hang down her back. She put on a mauve-colored sweater—one the color auburn-haired people weren't supposed to wear, one her Aunt Mary Ann would wring her hands over.

Thea sighed, experiencing a pang of homesickness. But the homesickness never lasted in this severe, glorious land, and she dragged on her usual pair of jeans so Dillon wouldn't think she was going to any special trouble on his behalf. Then she promptly gave in to her vanity by putting on lip gloss. She wouldn't have done it, she noted ruefully, if she hadn't seen that sleek blonde Dillon had here yesterday. Certainly Thea wanted him to leave, but she didn't necessarily want him to flee in terror.

Dillon was eating bacon when she came back into the kitchen. And reading the *St. Margaret's Hope Free Press Weekly*. And holding the baby. He had porridge—oatmeal—in his hair.

"Dillon, we need to talk," she began as soon as she came into the kitchen.

"Aye," he said agreeably. His eyes traveled over her with interest, and the baby sat happily on his knee, kicking her legs and looking at him adoringly.

I knew she'd love him, Thea thought in dismay.

"There's a gale coming," Dillon said. "I got some groceries, too, while we were out, so you won't have to take the baby into the rain."

"You walked into Roddy Macnab's with my baby and you bought me groceries?" Thea said, her incredulity returning. Orange juice for a baby when she needed it was one thing, but stocking up on groceries was something else again.

Dillon glanced up at her absently while he adjusted the newspaper. "I did." Caitlin tried to poke an inquisitive finger into his mouth.

"Dillon, are you crazy?" The whole island was going to think he was keeping her! He couldn't go around buying her groceries!

"No, I don't think so," he said around the baby's finger. "Though I've done some things in my time that might make me suspect. Why?"

"Why! You know why! Flora and Roddy and the rest of the old men who hang out in there—what are they going to think? Half the village hangs out in there! You can't just go buying groceries with Caitlin in your arms!"

Dillon smiled. "Caitlin, is it?" he said, reaching up to caress the baby's hair. "My wee Katy," he added softly, already presuming to give the baby a pet name.

"She is not your 'wee Katy'! And you had no right to take her into Roddy Macnab's!"

"Thea, for godsake! Do you think for a minute Roddy and every other man, woman, and child on this island doesn't know how you got her? Griffen was on the oil rig nearly a month before he was killed. This is a tiny island, Thea. We've not had much to do over the centuries but watch each other's comings and goings, and we've amused ourselves for a long time now counting backwards from nine. I'm her dad, and they know it. And if they didn't know it, I'd tell them. As it is, Thea, I've missed an important part of her life, and it's going to take me a while to get over it!"

Thea barely heard him. They knew. Everyone here *knew*. "But—but Flora and the rest of them—they let me into the St. Margaret's Hope Knitters' Co-Operative," she said.

Dillon looked at her blankly. "Thea, what has that to do with anything?"

"Dillon, I can't knit!" Thea said in exasperation. "I crochet! Why would they do that—let me sit with them every Thursday—if they knew about Caitlin?"

"God," Dillon said, under his breath. "There's only one daft woman on the whole island and she's the mother of my child. Thea, they *like* you. They don't care if you can't knit. They don't even care if you're a rude American. And they certainly don't care that I'm your baby's father."

"Don't you start up on my citizenship, Dillon Cameron! I'm not rude! Oh, God," she said, wandering aimlessly around the kitchen.

"Thea, it's no' that bad," Dillon insisted.

"It is!"

"No, it isn't! Thea, will you stop pacing. Thea! I've come to marry you."

She stopped dead, staring at him as if he were surely out of his mind. "Be still, my beating heart," she said with as much sarcasm as she could muster. As if that would solve anything! She moved to the kitchen window, staring out toward the sea. Dillon was right: A gale was coming. She thought of Griffen. Always expect the wind and the rain, he'd told her about living here, and be grateful for the sunshine.

I haven't had much sunshine lately, Griffen.

"Thea?" Dillon said.

"What!"

"Do you think you might answer me at least? I've never proposed to a woman before. Marriage, Thea, *marriage,*" he added quickly, apparently because of the skeptical look on her face.

"Why?" she asked, turning toward him and folding her arms over her breasts.

"Why what?"

"Why on God's green earth would *you* want to marry *me?*"

"You know, Thea, I'm having some trouble knowing why you'd ask that—with you looking right at me and I've got Katy on my lap."

"Because I'm the only woman you know who's never asked you to get a haircut?" she asked, her sarcasm still intact. "And don't call her Katy!"

Dillon closed his eyes and gave a brief sigh, and Thea turned away from him, busying herself with straightening up the kitchen. But there was nothing to straighten. Dillon, apparently, was the most disciplined of cooks. Fried bacon and oatmeal, and no mess. She realized suddenly that he was standing behind her.

"Because you are the only woman who never nagged me about my hair," he said quietly.

"Because I don't *care* if you want to run around looking like Wild Bill Hickok or George Custer!" she cried in exasperation. "Dillon—" she started, looking into his eyes in spite of herself. She reached out to touch the baby, who promptly grinned from her secure perch in her father's arms. "Our being together shouldn't have happened. It's something I'm not proud of, but it did happen. Still, there's no reason to ruin both our lives because of it. I don't need you, Dillon. I don't want anything from you. If I had, I would have sent you word. You don't have to concern yourself—"

"Don't concern myself?" he interrupted. "She's mine, Thea."

"No, Dillon. She's *mine*. What do you want here?"

"I've said. I want to marry you."

"No, thank you. Now, why don't you just go back to Aberdeen or wherever you hang out when you're not diving. I'm sure there must be someone somewhere who would be just delighted to see you."

"I intend to 'hang out' here."

"I don't want you here!"

"Aye! I understand that plain enough!" He handed her the baby. "I want to stay here until my next shift." He crossed the kitchen to get his jacket off the peg by the door. "But I'm out for a time now, Thea. I'm angry with you, and I don't want to be saying something I can't take back."

"You're angry!"

"Aye, I am! A man doesn't like to be made to feel a fool when he offers marriage to a women who needs it!"

"Yes, well, next time you decide to propose, don't

bring your mistress along with you when you do it!"

Dillon started to say something and didn't—twice. "We'll talk later," he said, coming closer, his voice tight and controlled. He smiled at the baby, stooping to give her a kiss. "Good-bye, darlin'. And don't you go telling your mum where else we went."

"Dillon!" Thea called after him, breaking off as Caitlin began to cry. "Oh, Caitlin," she said, jiggling the baby up and down on her hip. "Don't cry, baby face. Things are bad enough without crying."

The baby wailed louder, reaching after her disappearing father, and Thea found herself moving from window to window to catch a glimpse of him.

"I'm not going to do this!" she said suddenly. She didn't care where he was going, damn him! And she didn't care if he never came back.

She spotted him on the beach path toward St. Margaret's Hope, seemingly unconcerned about the raw weather this morning, his long-legged strides taking him rapidly away.

"Caitlin, don't cry!" Thea admonished, close to crying herself. She'd done it now—made Dillon angry. And who knew what he'd do? She didn't know anything about Scottish laws, and she couldn't afford to go to court even if she did.

She patted the baby and tried to soothe her and paced the floor, finally sitting down heavily in one of the chairs at the kitchen table. The baby cried louder.

"Caitlin, please," Thea whispered, unable to restrain her own tears now. Dillon was angry. How dare he be angry! He wasn't the sort of man who would want to be shackled with the responsibility of a child—and a girl child at that. If anything, she had done him a kindness by not complicating his life or his finances so he could do what he did best: chase women and buy new cars.

"What's the matter with him, Caitlin?" Thea whispered. "He's making me crazy! He's here—and he's not here. Silkies—what good are they, baby face? They're never around when you need one. I knew he'd make us cry!"

They both continued to cry until they grew tired of it.

"Now, wait a minute," Thea said, sniffing hard and looking at her baby's face. "What is this 'Don't tell you mum where else we've been' stuff?"

"Da!" Caitlin said, grinning.

"Da, indeed," Thea murmured, wiping their tears away. As she set the baby back into the highchair, she glanced up, hearing knocking at the outside kitchen door and sighing heavily on her way to answer it. When she released the door latch, Dillon stood in the rain and stared at her.

She waited. So did he, his eyes traveling over her face in a way that made her even more edgy.

"I thought you were angry," she said finally.

He gave a short shrug and stared off into the distance. "I'm over it now," he said, looking back at her. He'd been gone all of three minutes.

Thea didn't move out of the doorway.

"I don't want you here, Dillon," she said yet another time.

"I know that," he answered gravely. He was getting wet, his long hair plastered to his head by the rain. His eyes were gray now, and they relentlessly searched hers. It was all she could do not to look away. "You've got my baby, Thea. I . . . don't know how you can expect me not to be here."

"Dillon, look. Why don't you just tell me what you

want? I really don't need anything from you. I release you from all moral, legal, and financial obligations."

"I don't want to be released, Thea! I want to get to know my daughter!"

"Why?" Thea asked evenly.

"What kind of daft question is that?"

"It's a question you'll have to answer before you're welcome here," Thea said quietly.

"Thea—" Dillon said. He hesitated, and she could feel him struggling for control. "Don't do this, Thea. Don't pretend there's nothing between us. You know it's only the guilt that's kept us apart—you doing your penance for what happened with me. We have Katy, but there's more than that. I've spent every day of the last nineteen months thinking of it, of us, Thea. We've been punished long enough—the both of us."

"Leave us alone now, Dillon," Thea said, trying to close the door. He caught hold of it to keep it from closing, and she stared at him, unwavering and implacable and yet knowing what he said was true. There was more between them than Caitlin.

"Thea?" he said, but she remained unmoved.

"Chlanna nan con thigibh an so is gheibh sibh feòil, Thea," he said softly in Gaelic.

"What is that?" Thea asked.

"The Cameron *sluagh-ghairm.* A Cameron says that before he goes into battle." Then he stepped back so she could close the door.

4

THEA WENT INTO St. Margaret's Hope after all, not because she needed anything, but because she was too upset to stay indoors and had to get out for a while before the storm imprisoned her—Dillon Cameron or no Dillon Cameron. She had no idea what he'd meant by the Gaelic battle slogan, except that he was going to give her more trouble and heartache than she already had. She was beginning to feel more like a fugitive than the island's fallen woman, and she constantly looked over her shoulder to see if Dillon was lurking about. But how could she successfully avoid him? She didn't even know what kind of car he was driving—if he was driving. She'd been too annoyed this morning about the grocery shopping to look.

"How did you get to Roddy's this morning, baby face?" she said, asking the only person she had handy who knew. "Porsche? BMW?" She got another inscrutable baby grin for an answer. "Cover for him to the end, don't you?" Thea complained.

"Da!" Caitlin said on the way out.

"Yes, I know," Thea said dryly.

The wind and rain were only moderate by Orkney Island standards, and she always kept the elderly white Volkswagen—another of Griffen's legacies she couldn't bear to let go—pulled up by the back door so Caitlin wouldn't get wet. The baby loved a trip of any kind, and Thea began to feel better, catching her improved spirits from her merry daughter. She cringed at the thought that Dillon had taken Caitlin so irresponsibly this morning, probably juggling her dangerously on his knee while he struggled with gear shifts and tried to comply with the British Empire's nerve-wracking habit of driving on the wrong side of the road.

Thea put the baby into her safety seat in the back of the Volkswagen, then climbed behind the wheel, slamming the door several times to make it close. When she tried to start the car, she realized her feet didn't begin to reach the brake and clutch.

Well, damn the man! she was careful to think instead of say with a budding linguist in the back seat. Dillon Cameron had the key to her car, too! "This is just great!" she said out loud. All she needed was Dillon roaming the island with her baby *and* her car.

"Bye-bye," Caitlin said as Thea drove the short distance to Roddy Macnab's. Thea made the trip carefully in spite of her aggravation, taking the time to scrutinize the cars parked in front of the hotel for a sporty, expensive one. Dillon did that sometimes—let the hotel keep his car out front when he didn't need it because the hotel owner thought it gave the place class. She saw no car that might have been Dillon's, and she drove on to Roddy's, parking easily because curbing in St. Margaret's Hope wasn't as defined as curbing in South Carolina. Sometimes the street simply extended to the foundation

of the buildings, and not parking on what was supposed
to be the sidewalk became entirely a matter of individual
judgment.

Roddy's was crowded as usual, impending gale or no
impending gale, because Roddy's was the island's central
intelligence agency. She could see the old Dunphy twins,
by profession fisherman and by disposition curmud-
geons, seated in straight chairs by the front windows.
She hoped they'd both be at odds with someone else or
with each other when she went in so she could get by
them without having to run the gauntlet of their con-
trariness.

"Here we go, baby face," she said, lifting Caitlin out
of her car seat.

Thea had always loved Roddy's, and she savored the
pungent smells it harbored: cheese and lemons and ancient, sagging wood flooring that had been oiled with a
sweeping compound that reminded her of her grammar
school days in South Carolina. She carried Caitlin inside
quickly, not stopping to read the notices in the front
windows as she would have on a finer day. And, while
she wasn't met with total silence precisely, she did note
a series of pauses in the various conversations when she
came in.

"Good morning, gentlemen," she said to the Dunphys
because they were both looking at her.

"Och, woman," Archie or Malcolm said—she could
never tell one from the other. "Do you no' know there's
a storm comin'? It's no *gude* morning, this!"

Thea closed the door behind her, trying not to smile.
All these years, and she'd never said the right thing to
a Dunphy yet. The air was thick with pipe smoke today,
and the smell of wet wool sweaters and caps.

"Are you out in this then, Thea?" Roddy called cheerfully. He was a burly man in his late sixties, given to political debates and long walks with his wife Flora and his mongrel dog and his rowan walking stick. His face and hands were weathered from having made his living on the sea in his pre-grocer, pre-postman days, and his white hair stuck out in random tufts around his ears because his ever-present golf hat seemed forever at odds with what his hair was doing. Thea gave a slight smile, appreciating as always the Gaelic penchant for stating the obvious.

"Yes, I'm out, Roddy," she answered, carefully scanning the place for Dillon. He wasn't in the store, and she wandered about, looking at the Sunblest bread she didn't really need and picking up a can of Bachelor's peas. At the sight of a large basket of onions sitting on the floor, Caitlin squirmed to get down. Wonderful things, onions—smooth, round, hairy, and rattling like paper all at the same time.

"Thea," Flora Macnab called, making her way from behind the cheese counter. "Let me give this little one a biscuit," she said, coming to take Caitlin. "Dillon wouldn't let her have one when she was in before because she hadn't had her breakfast. Out to check the lay of the land, are you?" she added in a whisper. Flora was tall and thin and nearly lost in the yellow plaid cotton dress she was wearing. She was English, not Scots, and she was quick to tell that to any incomer ignorant enough not to know the difference. Her manner was gruff but loving, and she'd seen Thea through Griffen's death and through childbirth, never once mentioning Dillon Cameron. Clearly she was dying to mention him now, though, and Thea had no intention of getting into that conversation.

"This is Flora, ducky," Flora whispered, "so don't

you go giving me that big hazel-eyed whatever-do-you-mean look? You've got Dillon Cameron all tied in knots, and the whole island's dying to hear what you're going to do about it—me included."

"Nothing," Thea said pointedly, putting down the can of peas.

"Good gracious, my hearing's going!" Flora announced, giving her left ear a few jerks. "I could have sworn you said 'Nothing.'"

"Flora," Thea said in exasperation, "don't start up with me now. I didn't come in here to talk about Dillon Cameron."

"Do you have any idea what a catch he is, my girl?" Flora asked.

"No," Thea assured her.

"And a hank, besides."

"Hunk, Flora, hunk."

"Hank, hunk. You know what I mean."

Thea was afraid she did.

The bell on top of the front door jingled, and every conversation in the place stopped.

"Criminey!" Flora whispered to Thea, who was afraid to look.

"It's not Dillon, is it?"

"Well, of course it's Dillon, silly. Who else do you know can stop a room the way he can? If that lad won't fair make a girl lie to her mother," Flora said in admiration. "And those thighs. Do you think it's all that diving around in the water that makes his thighs like that? Always did like a man with good thighs. The first time I saw those fine limbs of Roddy's, it was all over for him, I can tell you. Had him to the church so fast it fair put a draft up his kilt."

Thea fidgeted anxiously, torn between wanting to see

behind her and wanting to giggle about Roddy's kilt.

"Here you are again, lad!" Roddie boomed, ever observant. "Are you needing something, then?"

"No, Roddy," Dillon said. "I'm only looking about for someone."

Don't panic, Thea thought wildly. *He doesn't mean me.*

"Good morning to you again, ladies," Dillon called to the group of women by the front counter. They tittered like schoolgirls.

Dear God, Thea thought. *It doesn't matter if they're sixteen or sixty.*

"Dillon!" a woman's voice called. "Have you seen my Leon this morning?"

"Dillon had better watch that one," Flora whispered. "It's not her Leon she's hunting. It's a husband for that homely daughter of hers."

"Flora!" Thea said in exasperation. "He's not coming this way, is he?"

"Well, Thea, what do you think? You and Caitlin are here, aren't you? Come, my lovely," she crooned to Caitlin. "Let's go find you that biscuit and let your mother handle her own situations."

"Flora!" Thea hissed desperately—to no avail. Flora abandoned her.

Don't panic! Don't panic!

"Leon's down at the jetty, Miss Sarah," Dillon said.

Maybe he hasn't seen me.

Thea knelt to inspect the basket of onions at her feet.

"You don't need any of those," Dillon said above her head.

"How would you know what I need?" Thea snapped, more than annoyed because he'd caught her hiding and he knew it. She stood up quickly, knowing how the story would go: *Dillon no more than spoke to Thea Kearney, and she all but hid in the onion basket.*

"I looked," Dillon said in answer to her question. "Did I miss buying something for you this morning?"

"How the devil do I know?" Thea whispered. "I don't even know what you bought, and I want to pay you for whatever it was right now."

"Your money's no good with me, Thea."

"And I want the key to my house back!"

"You want me to give it to you now?" he asked, and Thea was aghast at his choice of words. The Dunphy twins were leaning out of their chairs, and two women on the other side of the bread rack got significantly taller.

"Dillon, they're listening!" Thea cried in a whisper.

He had the audacity to grin. "I'd be that surprised, Thea, if they weren't." He took a step closer, and she nearly bolted.

"Dillon, they're looking!"

"Aye, they are," he said matter-of-factly. "They want to see."

"There's nothing to see!"

"Oh, aye. But they don't know that. Can I do anything for you?"

"You can go away and leave me alone!"

"No, I'm not of the mind for going, Thea. Staying is more what I'm thinking."

God, she was going to kill the man! If she didn't die of embarrassment first. "You're doing this on purpose!"

"I'm not doing anything, Thea. Just standing here in Roddy's place talking to you. I like talking to you, Thea."

"Since when?"

"Oh, I always liked talking to you. If you don't put that onion down, Thea, you're going to have to buy it, you know," he warned her.

She looked down at the nearly mashed thing in her palm, her hand reeking of traumatized onion. When she looked up, Dillon was sauntering away in Flora and Caitlin's direction.

"Hello again, lass," he said to his daughter, who offered him a bit of the Crawford's cream cookie she had in her hand.

"Oh, Lord," Thea said under her breath, turning around to hide again. But there was no place to hide. The bell over the door jingled as Dillon finally went out—to lie in wait somewhere, no doubt.

Thea was faced with an entirely new problem. She could literally feel every pair of eyes in the place turn in her direction. She took a deep breath and picked up a jar of Rose's marmalade to go with the onion.

What the hell. If they know, they know.

"Roddy?" she called, turning around and walking, head up, to the counter. She looked everyone in the eye as she passed. "Has the post come?"

"Oh, aye, Thea. You've a nice parcel from America. I doubt it's your birthday parcel."

Thea smiled in spite of her agitation, knowing the Gaelic habit of saying "doubt" instead of "believe." Her present discomfort might just be worthwhile if she had a package from her family. She stood waiting at the counter. "Roddy?" she prompted when he made no move to get it.

"Aye?" he asked, eyebrows raised both at her and at the bruised onion he was about to bag for her.

"My package?"

Roddy looked at her blankly. "Dillon has it, lass," he said, as if she surely must know that but perhaps had momentarily forgotten.

"Dillon who?" Thea said evenly, hearing Flora give a half-suppressed yelp of appreciation in the background.

"Dillon Cameron, o' course," Roddy said, chuckling at the little joke he thought Thea was making.

"Why would you give Dillon Cameron *my* package?" she asked. She could feel the kibitzers perking up again.

"Well, Thea..." Roddy began, searching hard for a reason. "It's a wee bit hard to say. Flora!" he said in relief as she walked up with Caitlin. "Why is it I gave Thea's parcel to Dillon?" he asked, as if it were Flora's job to keep track of such things.

"Why?" Flora said thoughtfully. "Well, it's because you've no sense at all, Roddy Macnab. I said not to do it. I said our Thea is an American, and you don't go giving out an American woman's mail unless she says so. Didn't I say that?"

"Aye," Roddy said crabbily. "You said it, woman. But you said it with Dillon halfway down the road out there with Thea's parcel! Thea, you needn't worry Dillon won't bring it out to you."

"I don't want Dillon Cameron delivering my mail," Thea said, trying to hold on to her temper. "And I don't want him buying groceries on my behalf. And that's the absolute final and official word on the matter, all right?"

Roddy and Flora exchanged looks, Flora's glance filled with I-told-you-so.

"Shall I send one of the lads to fetch Dillon for you?" Roddy asked, trying to be helpful.

"No!" Thea cried. She took Caitlin out of Flora's arms, leaving her onion and her marmalade on the counter in her haste to get out.

"Well, what have I said?" Roddy muttered testily behind her as Flora tried to shush him.

Lord! Thea thought as she struggled to put Caitlin back into her seat. She sat for a moment behind the steering wheel.

"What am I going to do about this?" she said out loud.

She took a deep breath and started the car. She was simply going to have to sit down with Dillon and explain it to him: Yes, he was Caitlin's father, but he was not to fix her roof or buy her groceries or pick up her mail or anything else unless she asked him to do it!

"Da-da," Caitlin said happily from her perch in the back seat. "Da!"

Thea glanced out the side window in the direction that had Caitlin's undivided attention. Dillon was standing in the street, and Caitlin was already offering him a bit of her biscuit through the glass.

"Oh, Lord, it is Da," Thea said. She let out the clutch and drove away.

Coward, she kept thinking as the day wore on. She should have confronted him. She should have demanded her package from home, and she should have told him to take a flying leap, and *then* she should have driven away. But all she could manage was to cower in the cottage as the weather worsened—with the strains of "Wichita Lineman" going through her head yet!

Caitlin played quietly in the playpen–port-a-crib Thea kept by the window in the kitchen, and Thea stared out at the gray, bleak terrain, realizing suddenly the reason for the song in her head. The wind was making the power line that ran to the cottage sing.

She made a cursory check of the outside shortly before dark, tasting the salt on her lips from the mists that rose to cover the island as the wind drove the breakers against the rough shoreline. She wasn't afraid; she'd been through many gales in the years she'd lived on South Ronaldsay. She was just so . . . restless, and she knew perfectly well the reason for it: Dillon Cameron. She paced about the cottage and tried to sort through her feelings. She didn't dislike Dillon; she'd never disliked him. If anything, she'd always felt a little worried for him because, despite his reputation, he'd always seemed so alone.

The pacing didn't help. She kept walking into the nursery to watch Caitlin as she slept, and that didn't help either. It only called to mind that she had to do something to alleviate her uncertainty before her child suffered.

She heard a small sound from the direction of the kitchen, and she walked carefully into the hallway, uncertain if it was something other than the wind's capriciousness. Finally she determined it was knocking, low on the back door, and she turned on the outside light. Dillon stood on the doorstep about to kick the door again, drenched and windblown—and carrying her package. Thea unlocked the door and opened it, but she didn't welcome him, package or no package.

"Would it tax your incredible hospitality, Thea, if I were to come in out of the rain?" Dillon asked sardonically.

"Yes," she assured him, but she stood back to let him come inside. Her package was soaked, and Dillon mopped the rain off it as best he could with the inside of his jacket.

"Here," he said, giving her a smaller package first. It had the feel of a glass jar, but it smelled of onion.

Thea left him standing there, but he followed her into the kitchen, hooking his wet jacket on one of the pegs by the back door as he passed. The light overhead flickered, then steadied.

"Is Katy asleep?" he asked, and Thea fought down the urge to go a few more rounds with him about her child's correct name. She realized suddenly that she was going to have to humor him, at least until the novelty of his newfound parenthood wore off. She couldn't afford to antagonize him any more than she already had, simply because she didn't know how far he'd go. She'd just have to let him get this fatherhood business out of his system. She didn't expect it to take long. Babies cried and had to have their diapers changed, and Caitlin was teething. What he needed was a good dose of parenting, she decided, and then her life could get back to normal with the least amount of damage to her and Caitlin both.

"Thea, did you hear what I asked or are you just being rude?" Dillon said, breaking into her thoughts. She turned around to look at him, setting the marmalade and onion bag down on the drainboard of the sink.

"I'm being rude," she said evenly. There was no use lying about it. "She's asleep. She usually is by seven."

Dillon nodded, putting the package down on the kitchen table. He was wearing different clothes now, Thea couldn't help noticing—worn, tight-fitting jeans and a different off-white sweater. His muscular thighs strained the fabric of the jeans. He did have lovely thighs.

Watch it, Thea, she told herself. Here was the man who could totally disrupt her life, and she was checking out his thighs! To her dismay, he made himself at home and sat down at the table, moving the box he'd just brought to one side.

"I don't suppose you'd like tea?" she forced herself to ask. She was going to be civil if it killed her. He looked at her in surprise, and she abruptly busied herself with filling the copper kettle, her movements jerky from wanting him gone.

"I would," Dillon said, "now that you've learned to make it."

Thea looked sharply around at him.

"Griffen told me you nearly killed him learning," he said, and she smiled in spite of herself. She'd forgotten that.

"I did," she said, smiling still. "Either you could read through it or you could use it for ink. I thought I'd never hit the happy medium. I thought he was going to send me back to South Carolina—" She broke off, and her smile faded. The light overhead flickered again.

"Do you never talk about him to anyone, Thea?" Dillon asked, and she turned away, taking down a box of Tetley tea, finally shaking her head no because she knew he'd press her to answer.

"Why not?" he persisted. Thea avoided his eyes, but she could feel him looking at her, feel him studying her face. She gave a small, noncommittal shrug and moved to the window over the sink to stare out into the darkness.

"I should have taken you with me last night," Dillon said. "You Americans, you do it all wrong."

Thea turned around to face him. "What do we do wrong?" she said defensively.

"There's a time for grieving, Thea. And then there's a time for celebrating the life that's gone, for remembering the happy times and how much better you are for that person having been on this earth."

"Dillon, don't. I . . . I can't talk about Griffen with you."

"Who better than me, Thea?" he asked quietly.

She had no ready answer for that, and he didn't seem to expect one. She went on with her tea-making, leaving him to his silence and hiding in her own. The water hissed as the kettle began to heat, and the howling of the storm outside waxed and waned.

"Ta," he said when she finally handed him his cup of tea.

"You're welcome," she answered, and they had nothing to say to each other again. The kitchen had no "built-ins" like most American kitchens, and the gas stove was sandwiched between one large and one small primitive-looking blue cupboard that Thea had sanded smooth, but left "stressed" and un-refinished. She had a long wooden work table next to the sink and a butcher block she'd salvaged not from a butcher, but from a pastry store. She had strings of drying herbs in the end window instead of curtains, all the strings ending well above Caitlin's play-pen. She had little storage space, and because of the baby, nearly every utensil and pot she owned hung in some grouping on the walls. She would have given any-thing now for a drawer to straighten.

"I came out here because I was worried about you being alone," Dillon said abruptly.

"This isn't my first gale."

"No, it's *my* first gale—knowing you and Katy were here by yourselves."

"I thought you were out playing Royal Postman," Thea said, and Dillon smiled.

"That, too."

The baby began to cry in the other room.

"She's teething," Thea said, waiting a moment to see if this was a definite call or merely a shift from sleeping to waking and back to sleeping again. "Well, that's it. She doesn't sleep through the night very often now."

"Could I go get her, then?" Dillon asked respectfully as the crying continued.

"She'll be all wet," Thea hedged.

"My mother was a nanny, and I'm the oldest of six. I know what to do about that. Please."

Thea wavered, then capitulated, watching the door-way warily until he returned with a tearful but smiling baby girl who was obviously happy to see them both. Dillon sat down at the table with Caitlin to finish his tea. Apparently the tea was drinkable, regardless of Thea's brewing history. In desperation she sat down at the table with them, awkwardly fumbling with her own cup. Dillon, on the other hand, was completely at ease, soothing Caitlin as if he were indeed the oldest of six and watching Thea with such intensity that she abruptly got up from the table, knocking over her tea in the process. She hastily blotted up the spill with a kitchen towel, and all the while, Dillon watched.

The lights flickered again and stayed off.

"Uh-oh," Caitlin said. She'd been through this so many times with her mother, she obviously thought that was the appropriate remark, like "Bye-bye" when one made one's departure.

Dillon was delighted, chuckling and giving her a kiss. "'Uh-oh,' is it, lass?"

Thea felt her way through the darkness to the pantry to get the modern kerosene lamp her mother had sent her when she learned that Thea relied on candles and primitive kerosene lanterns when the power went out. Thea felt along the upper shelf until her fingers touched the brass base, taking it carefully down and colliding with Dillon when she came out of the pantry.

"Mind how you go in the dark, Thea," he said softly, his arm wrapping around her. The hard feel of his warm body, and the soap and man-smell that filled her nostrils made her knees weak, the sinking feeling frightening her because it had been so long since she'd felt it.

Oh, God, she thought. *It's the same.* She'd never felt like this with anyone but Dillon. It was as if her body remembered when her mind refused. She had loved Griffen, truly loved him, and yet her heart was pounding. Dillon was carrying Caitlin, and it was all Thea could do not to press her face into his broad chest so that he could keep her close, too.

But she couldn't do that. She had learned to get along

without help, and she had no one she could depend on but herself. She was not going to be another one of Dillon Cameron's women. The Great Silkie would have to fan the fires of gossip with someone else.

The blonde who was here yesterday came immediately to mind, and Thea pushed herself away from him. She lit the lamp and set it on the table, immediately noting the fact that the glow was bright enough for her to see Dillon's pensive face.

"Don't you have something to do?" Thea asked rudely when he was about to sit down with Caitlin again.

"Aye," he answered. "I'm doing it."

Thea sighed and began to clear away the teacups, again feeling Dillon's eyes on her every move. Caitlin babbled away, working on soothing her gums with a piece of Melba toast Thea handed her.

"She'll be happy in the highchair," Thea suggested, hoping he'd take the hint and leave.

"I want to hold her," Dillon answered, clearly hint-proof.

"You don't have to hold her."

"I *want* to hold her."

"Fine!" Thea snapped. "Hold her, then!"

And who's going to hold her when you're tired of it and gone?

"Thea, don't you care to open your birthday presents? The package I brought in," he added when she didn't respond. "Your birthday presents from America."

Thea stood awkwardly with a dishtowel in her hands. She didn't want to open it now with Dillon here. Her family was absolutely fanatical about birthdays, and she was afraid she might cry. And how did he know it was a birthday package in the first place?

"Griffen told me about the tradition," he said as if

he'd heard the question.

"Why on earth would he do that?"

"Conversation is the only thing that helps when you're stuck in the pressure chamber, Thea. Go ahead. I want to see if it's the same. Your mum will send you some of that South Carolina American food that makes you so happy—what is it called?"

"Grits," Thea said gravely.

"Aye, grits," Dillon answered with a slight smile. "Terrible name for—what is it again?"

"Corn," she said, momentarily forgetting that corn to her was oats to a Scotsman.

"Corn?"

"Not oats—maize—the inside of a kernel of corn," she said, seeing his confusion.

"Oh, aye. Griffen never liked it, did he?"

"No, thank heavens. That meant there was more for me—" Thea stopped, seeing how Dillon had drawn her into another exchange about Griffen.

"And your aunt," Dillon pressed on. "Mary Ann, her name is, but she glides her words together—May Rand she says her name is. May Rand has sent you undershirts with lace on them because she's afraid you'll catch pneumonia the way you did every winter when you were a wee lass in South Carolina. She doesn't know we're warmed by the Gulf Stream here, and she worries about the gales. Now, your little sister Tessa—Tessa's no' worried about your chest at all. She'll send you sexy night things. Griffen was always over fond of Tessa's presents."

Thea turned abruptly away and began to wipe off the kitchen stove, flustered from wondering exactly what else Griffen had told him.

"Open the package, Thea," Dillon said. "Katy and I

want to see what's come from America."

"Why? It sounds like you already know what's in it."

"Katy doesn't. Go on lass. Open your birthday gifts."

Thea hesitated, then threw down the dishtowel. Dillon shifted the package in her direction as she sat down across from him. The outer wrapping was spotted and crinkled from being in the rain, but Thea wasn't worried. Her mother had learned the art of sending packages overseas when all the men in the family were in World War II. Neither storms nor pestilence could breach her mother's brand of shipping—only the postal schedule. Try as she might, her packages never reached Thea on time, and this one was nearly two weeks late for Thea's thirty-second birthday.

Thea glanced at Dillon and Caitlin, noting again the similarity of their smiles. She gave a resigned sigh and began to dig at the folds on the end of the box, getting nowhere with bare fingers and finally accepting the pocket knife Dillon produced with difficulty from his tight jeans pocket.

Thea frowned to keep her mind off those jeans.

"Don't give up now," Dillon said as she began on the third layer, aluminum foil. She looked up from the pile of shredded paper to smile in spite of her determination to keep him at arm's length. What was it about this man that made a woman so . . . receptive?

She finally made it to the taped flaps of the actual cardboard box, and, using Dillon's knife again, she was at last able to peer inside.

"Here is is!" she said, producing several plastic-wrapped boxes. "Enriched white hominy quick-cook grits."

"It doesn't take much to make you happy, does it, Thea?" Dillon asked with a certain amount of admiration.

She made no comment, continuing to search among the packing for the rest of her birthday booty. "And my undershirts," she announced, bring out three sleeveless white vests. "Aunt Mary Ann does the lace herself," Thea found herself saying, as if Dillon Cameron would care about a thing like that.

"She does very fine tatting," he said, lifting one of the soft cotton-knit undershirts. "She'd make it into the Knitters' Co-Operative, right enough."

Flustered again, Thea took the shirt from his hand to put it aside. "And what's this?" she said, smiling at Caitlin. "It can't be mine," she said, reaching into the box. "I already have a baby girl." She produced the soft sculptured doll slowly, watching Caitlin's eyes widen. "See, baby face? A baby girl like you." She handed the yarn-haired moppet across the table to Dillon, watching quietly as he helped his daughter discover this wondrous new thing.

He's so good with her.

Dillon looked up as if he'd heard the thought, his eyes holding hers.

Be careful, Thea. You know what he is. He can't be domesticated.

"Thea?" Dillon said in a whisper. "Is this doll not a wee bit . . . homely?"

Thea grinned. "I understand they're all the rage, homely or not."

He turned the doll around to see its face. "If anyone had given my sisters a doll that looked like this, they'd still be crying. Thea," he said with the barest of smiles, "where's Tessa's gift?"

"She didn't send anything," Thea lied, feeling her cheeks flush and hoping that the light from the lamp was too subtle to show it.

"Ah, lass, now you're dancing away from the truth a bit. Go on. We want to see."

"Caitlin's too young," Thea hedged.

"I'm not," Dillon assured her, grinning as she frowned and tried to think of something clever to say. Absolutely nothing came to mind.

"Why won't you show me?" Dillon persisted, as if he weren't a near stranger.

"I can't," Thea said. "There's nothing to show. It's all . . . strings," she finished lamely.

Dillon laughed out loud, throwing his head back in delight, his easy laughter causing Caitlin to squeal and laugh with him. Thea sat frowning, waiting for their collective amusement to subside.

"Well, enough of this," she said abruptly, getting up from the table and gathering up papers and the box.

Dillon wouldn't let her take the box away. "Forget the 'strings,' then. What else have you got in there?"

"Nothing—a few letters, some books, some cassettes, music—" Thea stopped, knowing she was babbling like an embarrassed teenager.

"Show me. I want to see all of what's come from America."

Thea dumped out the box, mentally chiding herself for doing it. He couldn't possibly be interested, and she couldn't for the life of her think why he'd want to feign it, unless he wanted to pacify her so she wouldn't try to keep him away from Caitlin.

Dillon looked at the books carefully—two murder mysteries and one autobiobraphy of a female sex symbol—and he read everything there was to read on each cassette.

"Too bad the power's off," he said. "I like American music."

"I can't believe it!" Thea said. "You're actually admitting that there's something American you like?"

"I like many things that are American," he said, reaching to hand her the tapes back. "Corvettes, MacDonald's..." Their fingertips touched as he gave her the tapes. "You."

She frowned and didn't comment. She picked up the box again, noisily crumpling paper and trying not to look at him.

"Thea? Are you going to marry me?"

She laughed. "Dillon, Dillon, if I said yes, you'd keel over in a dead faint right here and now in the middle of the kitchen floor."

"Oh, aye," he admitted. "But when I revived, we'd go to the church, Thea."

"No, thank you, Dillon. I'm really not your type. What you need is one of those wholesome, fun-loving, soft drink, beer people."

"My God, what is that? A soft drink beer person?" He shifted Caitlin around so she could jump up and down in his lap.

"You see them on television—American television. They jump into mud puddles on purpose, and ride their bicycles off the dock and into the lake, and squirt each other with hoses—so you'll know what free spirits they are—and drink the right beverage. You need a woman like that, Dillon. Someone in keeping with your exuberant self."

"I'll admit to a certain rowdiness, Thea, but I've no' ridden my bicycle into the loch." He put Caitlin easily over his shoulder. "It sounds a bit odd if you don't mind my saying so."

"Oh, I don't mind," she answered. "But that seems a strange remark coming from the man who sang 'The

Quaker's Wife' *a capella* on Charlie platform—naked."
She glanced at him, and then back again because of his
stunned look.

"Who told you that?"

"Griffen, of course. Among other things."

"What other things?"

She tried not to grin. Incredibly, Dillon didn't like her
knowing about his escapades. She raised and lowered
her eyebrows once to annoy him. "We do not speak of
such things in the presence of children," she advised him.

"What other things!" he insisted, shifting Caitlin to
his other shoulder.

"Oh," she said airily, "probably all of them. The female fiddle-player from the Royal Highland Fiddlers—
and her mother. Oh, yes, and the little French bird watcher
you happened upon on—I forget which of the islands it
was—Burray? Now, there's a lusty story."

"God," Dillon said under his breath, and Thea looked
up from the bottle of formula she was about to pour.
"They don't call me The *Great* Silkie for naught, Thea,"
he said in his own defense.

"No," she said wryly. "I never for a moment thought
they did." She put the bottle of formula into a bowl of
hot water to take off the chill.

"Could I feed Katy?" he asked.

"Do you know how?"

"Aye, I told you. My mother was a nanny, and I'm
the oldest of six. Thea, I wish you wouldn't look at me
like that."

"Like what?"

"Like you think I'm on the wrong side of the law and
you expect Scotland Yard to bash the door in any second."

"Somebody's irate father, more likely," Thea said idly,
walking to the kitchen window to stare out at the darkness
again.

"I've lived a man's life, Thea, but no lass has ever been the worse for knowing me. Nor her father. Except—"

"Who?" she asked, handing him the bottle for Caitlin.

"I was going to say you," he said, looking down at his daughter. He was completely at ease feeding her. Perhaps he *was* the oldest of six—she couldn't remember Griffen ever saying—*or* he had other children.

"You don't despise me, do you, Thea?"

"Why would you think that?"

He gave an exasperated sigh. "You didn't tell me about her, Thea. I'm still trying to find out why."

Thea didn't comment, staring at her own reflection in the dark windowpanes instead.

"Do you blame me for Griffen's death?" he asked quietly.

"No," she said, looking around at him. She knew better than anyone how difficult that question must be to ask.

"What then? You think I'm a bounder who's no' fit to be Katy's dad?"

"Not that exactly."

"Well, what then!"

"Dillon, I thought you wouldn't care!" Thea said sharply. "And I just couldn't handle that, too!"

He didn't say anything for a moment, turning his attention to Caitlin again. "I want to thank you," he murmured without looking up.

"For what? For saying no to your gallant proposal of marriage?"

"No," he said pointedly. "For taking such good care of my daughter."

"She's my daughter, too, Dillon. Why wouldn't I take care of her?"

"You wouldn't have had to. Some women wouldn't."

"I wanted my child, Dillon."

"Aye. I only wanted you to know that I . . . I thank you. She's beautiful, and she's merry—like you. I like what you've named her, Thea. Caitlin. It's a fine Gaelic name and not one of those semi-abstract names like Misty Joy or April Dawn or the like."

"American names, you mean," Thea interrupted, and he grinned.

"Thea?"

"What, Dillon?"

"I had too much to drink last night. Was I . . . a beast or anything?"

"No more so than usual," she said dryly, glancing at Caitlin, who was on the edge of sleep.

"Well, that's something then, isn't it? I mean if you don't despise me and I wasn't a beast, then I was hoping you wouldn't send me away now that I'm sober and now there's a gale blowing. I've twelve days, Thea, until I go back diving. I want you to let me stay here. As your B&B guest. I'll abide by the same rules. I just want to get to know my baby. I want her to know who I am. She's my daughter, Thea. I want no bad feelings between us. Can you do that—let me stay?"

"Or what?" she asked quietly.

"I don't know what you're asking me," Dillon said.

"I want you to tell me what happens if I say no. I want to know the consequences if I tell you to go away and never come back again. I want to know the alternative."

This time he understood, and he didn't pretend otherwise. "If it comes to a legal battle," he said quietly, "here or in America, you know I can afford it."

Thea gave a small laugh. "Well done! Subtle but appropriately threatening."

"I've no wish to threaten you, Thea."

"Well, that's strange. I certainly *feel* threatened."

"She's my daughter," he said again.

"Yes, and you've got me with my back to the wall, don't you? Dillon, I don't want her learning to love you and then have you disappear."

"Thea, I have no intention of doing that."

"Not now, maybe."

"What is that supposed to mean?"

Thea didn't answer him.

"Thea, she's not some grand new toy I've found to amuse myself with until I find something better."

"Isn't she?"

"No!"

"I don't understand you, Dillon. She's not even a son!"

"She's my child, Thea! Do you think I care about that? What kind of man could see a beautiful wee lady like her and want something else? Thea—" He abruptly broke off, sighing heavily. "I don't understand you either, Thea," he said more quietly. "It's too bad I'm not a silkie. I'd have you bribed senseless by now. Wedded, too."

"Silkies seem to give themselves a lot of trouble," Thea observed, weary with trying to decide what to do.

"No trouble. Silkies have always seduced human women to the point of marrying if they have to. They have no problem getting out of it, you see, when love waxes cold. They change into seals again and disappear. It's only when there's a child that they get their come-uppance. I . . . I don't know what to do with you, Thea. A good silkie would have offered you a purse of gold at least by now."

"You did."

"Did I?" he said in surprise. "When?"

"Last night, when you were a bit stumble-footed."

"God, no wonder you look at me the way you do. You must have thought I was daft."

"No, I thought you had a regular fund to pay off the unlucky mothers of your unauthorized children."

Dillon stared into her eyes. "I don't have *children*, Thea. I have Katy. And I'm asking you to let me stay here."

She made no reply. Caitlin was sleeping soundly now, and she looked at her baby's lovely face.

I don't know what to do! She knew that now was the time for Dillon to grow tired of being a father, now while Caitlin was too young to understand. It was herself that she was worried about. She couldn't behave rationally with Dillon around. She was afraid of the consequences of having him here—she was already behaving like an idiot. When he was gone, she wanted him here, and when he was here, she wanted him gone. What if she became too emotionally involved with him? Dillon wouldn't want that, and it would be like losing Griffen all over again.

She breathed a long sigh. She was going to have to do it. For Caitlin. It was the only way to keep her from being hurt. The sooner Dillon tired of family life and went back to his fiddle-players and bird watchers and geometrical blondes, the better.

"You have twelve days?" she said abruptly, looking again into his eyes.

"Aye."

"And you'll abide by the same rules as any other guest?"

"I will," he answered.

"All right. You can stay. Until your next shift."

She had taken him by surprise, and it took a moment for him to recover.

"Good . . . good, then," he said. "You'll never repent it—letting me be here. Shall I put Katy in her bed then?" he asked politely, and Thea nodded, carrying the lamp along to light the way.

He was both efficient and gentle in tucking his child in for the night. Thea offered him the lamp to take upstairs when he'd finished.

"Ah, no. You keep it. A diver is used to mucking around in the dark." He paused in the hallway outside the nursery door. "You're no' afraid of the storm, are you?"

"No," Thea said too quickly. It wasn't the storm she suddenly feared. It was Dillon Cameron's intense look.

"Sleep well," he said softly, leaving her there holding the kerosene lamp.

Thea went into her own room, putting out the lamp and undressing quietly in the dark. The wind wailed around the eaves and rattled the windows, and Thea lay in her bed listening, as aware of Dillon's presence in the cottage as if he'd been lying beside her instead of being a floor away. She sighed and tried to find a position that was conducive to sleep, but sleep eluded her.

At some point Caitlin began to fret again, and Thea sat up on the side of the bed.

But the fretting diminished, then stopped, giving way to a softly singing baritone voice. Dillon had her.

Thea walked quietly to the nursery doorway. He was sitting in the rocking chair near the window. She could just make out Caitlin's small head resting on Dillon's shoulder while he rocked and quietly sang. She didn't recognize the song, only that it had the characteristic

melancholy of most Celtic songs, and that the words were
Gaelic.

"I'll take this turn," he said quietly when he saw her
in the doorway.

"You don't have to."

"I know that, Thea. I'm not sleeping—still on the oil
rig time, I think. You sleep. You haven't had a chance
to do that in a long time, have you?"

"No," she admitted.

"Sleep, then. If I need you, I'll call. Please, Thea,"
he added when she hesitated. "Let me do this for her."

"You're sure?"

"I'm sure, lass. Just let me sing to my *dochter,* will
you? I'm not much of a singer, but she doesn't seem to
mind it."

"She's not feverish or anything, is she?" Thea asked,
still uncertain.

"Come here, then," Dillon said, taking her hand as
she walked closer and pressing it gently against Caitlin's
forehead. "See?" he said, lifting her hand again but not
letting go. "She's cool and not fevering. She's only cranky
about her gums. You go and rest. I'll call if we need
you. I promise. I always keep my promises, Thea."

She took her hand away, still feeling the warmth of
his strong fingers in her palm. "The song you're singing,"
she abruptly asked. "What is it? A lullaby?"

"No, lass. It's no lullaby. It's . . . about a man and a
woman. It's about a . . . woman who says no and the man
who knows she doesn't mean it. He knows he'll melt
her anger between the night and the morning. He knows,
for all her pride, she'll follow anywhere he leads, and
he knows she'll lie with him, for all her firm farewells."

Thea could feel him smiling in the dark, and she went
blindly out of the room and back to her bed, listening

all the while to the soft words of Dillon's song. He had a fine singing voice, one that dragged up the longing and the sorrow of the haunting Celtic ballad he'd chosen for—

Not for Caitlin. For her. She lay in the dark, eyes open, her heart pounding. She could feel exactly what he meant for her to feel—the poignant need two people had for each other. She turned restlessly, closing her eyes tightly because she didn't want to feel it. She was all right alone. She *had* to be all right.

The song stopped, and she opened her eyes, listening intently. She heard him leave the nursery, and she held her breath as he passed her open bedroom door. Did he hesitate? She wasn't sure. Her heart was pounding.

His footsteps continued down the hall, and her heart lurched at another sound. The back door opening, and Dillon going out in the middle of a North Sea gale.

She was out of bed instantly, running barefooted into the nursery, panicked at what she might find.

He wouldn't take her!

He'd done it easily enough this morning.

Caitlin lay quietly sleeping in her crib, and Thea clung to the rail, trying to stop trembling.

What is he doing!

She just didn't understand. He worked so handily at getting her to let him stay here, just so he could leave. It made no sense at all to her. She moved restlessly to the window, but she couldn't see anything but blackness.

Dillon.

She abruptly looked around at the baby.

No woman's ever been the worse for knowing me, he'd said. That's it, Thea thought. The woman who had followed him here. She must still be on the island, at the hotel or some other B&B. If this was her first storm, she must be terrified. In her mind, Thea could see her waiting, panicked and alone. Dillon wouldn't leave her like that. He'd go to her. He'd tease her until she was laughing and not afraid anymore, and then he'd make love—

Stop it! What was the matter with her? She didn't care about any of that. Dillon Cameron was nothing to her or she to him, except for Caitlin. And she was going to have to remember that. She was going to have to stop letting him look into her eyes until it made her knees weak and her belly warm. She was going to have to do the things she'd said she'd do. She'd sit down and talk with him like a rational adult about his interfering in her life, and she'd get her blasted key back!

She gave a wry smile in the darkness. And that brought her to the things she wouldn't do. She wouldn't stop thinking about him, and she wouldn't sleep.

5

THEA HAD THE finely honed senses of a person who lived alone. So how did this keep happening? Granted it was raining and the wind was still high, but she hadn't heard Dillon come back, and here he was, asleep in the guest room in the middle of the afternoon.

"I have got to get that key back," she said under her breath. She had never thought of herself as having a fragile nervous system, but she was not going to be able to continue in her normally serene manner if she kept finding Dillon Cameron all over the place.

She stood in the doorway, shamelessly watching him sleep. He was lying on his stomach, his bare, muscular thigh poking out from under the cover. He was a sprawler, taking up most of the bed, and the sheet covered him only minimally. Quite clearly, he preferred sleeping in . . . nothing.

God, Thea, here you are looking at his thighs again. And anything else she could get a peek at. She was worse than Flora.

She left abruptly, chiding herself all the way down

the stairs. What was the matter with her? She had better things to do than to stand there drooling, for godsake! And that was exactly what she'd been doing: drooling. It was bad enough that she had to cope with his presence and with his insinuating his way into Caitlin's life—but, no, he had to be a prime specimen of virile Gaelic manhood, too.

She checked on Caitlin's napping, then went into the small laundry room off the kitchen to get an ever present basket of clean baby clothes to put away.

"Thea?" Dillon said from behind her.

Thea had never been a screamer, but the shriek she let fly in the shower of falling bibs and diapers was loud and long.

"Bloody hell!" Dillon shouted. "Thea, are you daft? You've scared the life out of me!"

"I scared *you!"* she shouted back at him. He was wearing jeans that were zipped but not buttoned—period—and he was barefooted and trying to give her back the laundry basket she'd thrown. She wouldn't take it. "Dillon, stop slinking around!"

"I'm no' slinking! I just came to see what you wanted. I didn't know I was in the house with a crazy woman!"

"I don't want anything!" she cried, jerking the laundry basket out of his hands and gathering up spilled baby clothes. She pushed by him, heading toward the kitchen with him right behind her.

"Well, you must want something, Thea! You came up to the room just now!"

"I didn't know you were in the room, you idiot! You didn't bother to let me know you'd come back!"

They glared at each other until Dillon sat down heavily at the kitchen table.

"I've had sharks tap me on the shoulder, and they've not scared me as bad as you did," he said reproachfully. "God! Why did you scream like that?"

"Why did you sneak up behind me like that!"

"I thought maybe you came to say I had a—a visitor!"

"Visitor? Another one of your women, you mean!"

"No, that's not what I mean—I meant my mother!"

Thea looked at him suspiciously, careful to keep her eyes off his bare chest. The last thing she needed here was Dillon's mother.

"Well, I have one, you know!" he said, clearly inspired by the look on her face.

"You could have fooled me," she said.

"And what is that supposed to mean?"

"People with mothers know how to behave," Thea snapped at him. "They don't go slinking around other people's houses! And why would your mother come *here?*"

"Because I'm here, Thea—and I wasn't slinking!"

"What do you call it then?"

"I call it coming down to see what the bloody hell you wanted! What are you doing?" he added.

"Listening to see if you woke Caitlin."

"I'm not the one who screeched!"

"Well, you're the one who's yelling his fool head off now!"

"I had the provocation!" he cried.

Thea abruptly grinned. His hair was all mussed. She really had scared him, and he was embarrassed by his un-silkie-like behavior.

"You think this is funny," he accused her.

"Not very," she lied, keeping her lips pursed so she wouldn't laugh.

Dillon got up from the table, and Thea tried not to look at his trim waist and his unbuttoned jeans *and* his bare chest.

"I've had my heart stopped, and you laugh at me. I make the best marriage proposal I know how to make, and you laugh at me. I've no' much practice at asking a woman to wed, Thea, but I'm thinking it's not supposed to be funny to her!"

"Dillon, what can I say?"

"You can say you'll help me!"

"Well, I'm not marrying you just because you think your mother's on her way."

"Very amusing, Thea. Indeed. I'm surprised you ever found the time to get to Scotland. It's amazing you weren't too busy watching those nitwit American television shows that turn your brain to mush and—"

"Nitwit *American?*" she asked, eyebrows raised. "'Benny Hill'!" she countered.

"'The Newlywed Game'!" he said, not to be outdone.

"'Doctor Who'!"

"'Doctor Who'?"

Clearly she'd wounded him to the quick with that one.

"You would stand there, Thea Kearney, and slur such an outstanding example of British television programming?"

"Now, Dillon," she said when he took a step toward her, "there's no reason to get hostile just because you make lousy marriage proposals."

"And what's wrong with my marriage proposals?"

"They stink, Dillon."

"I said I'd marry you!"

"Big deal! No woman wants to be a man's Fate Worse Than Death, Dillon."

"You're not that—exactly. You're a . . . fine woman."

"I know, I know, and you're just *dying* to marry me."

"I said I would!"

"Forget it, Dillon. I don't need any favors from you. I've done all right so far."

Dillon frowned. "What does that mean?"

"It means you're not the first man to dangle the promise of wedded bliss before the Widow Kearney."

"Just who else is dangling?" he asked indignantly. "The Dunphy twins?"

"Now, that was good, Dillon. The Dunphy twins. And we'd better stop while we're ahead here. The next thing you know we'll be into it about sacred cows like baseball and soccer. And then you'll make some crack about the way I make tea, at which point, sir, you will be out of here on your can, see?"

"Is that so, Thea?"

"It is."

Dillon looked her over thoughtfully. "You're no' big enough to put me anywhere on my can, Thea," he said softly.

"Cameron," Thea said with a soft sigh, "you're going to rue the day you ever said that."

"Am I, Thea?" he asked, clearly enjoying himself now.

"Oh, yes. You're an arrogant man, Cameron. You think all you have to do is lift your little finger. But, you see, I know something about you . . ."

"And what's that, Thea?" He was grinning because she was advancing slowly around the table.

"I know," she assured him, still advancing. "Griffen told me. And you are going to be *so* sorry." She was rolling up her shirt sleeves.

"All talk, Thea Kearney. All talk."

It occurred to her briefly that she probably shouldn't

be doing this. What the hell, she thought. He deserves it for embarrassing me to death in Roddy's. No woman had ever gotten the best of him, and it was high time.

She feigned a few assault moves while he chuckled at her feeble attempts. Finally, she rushed him in a halfhearted tackle as if she intended to bowl him over in the middle of the kitchen floor. He easily subdued her, catching her up in his strong arms and holding her against his bare chest.

"What was that you were saying, Thea Kearney?" he asked, infinitely sure of himself.

It was really a shame how easy this was going to be, she decided.

"I was saying, Dillon," she began quietly, arranging her face so that it was properly contrite. "I was saying ...that I know...where The Great Silkie is...*ticklish!*" she finished in a rush of flying fingers along his bare ribs.

The yelp he gave was more than worth her recent aggravation. He had her up off the floor, but she could still reach a vulnerable spot along his left side.

"Thea! God! Thea!" he cried, trying to get free of her tickling.

"What was it you were saying, Cameron?" she asked, resting for a moment, only to renew her onslaught when he was about to answer her.

"Thea—now—don't, you daft woman! Will you—!"

"No," she assured him, and he lifted her higher off the floor, leaning forward until he could dangle her precariously above the wooden planking.

"Now!" he cried. "You keep at it, and I'll drop you!"

"I don't mind," she said, wriggling the fingers he had clamped against his side with his elbow. He dropped her, but she wasn't about to be dumped alone. She hooked her foot behind his knee, sending him sprawling nearly on top of her. He was too quick for her to get into tickling position again, pinning her down with both hands above her head. They were both laughing, their faces close, until Dillon abruptly let her go, rolling over onto his back in the middle of the floor.

"Uncle," he said weakly, still trying to get his breath. He turned his head to look at her. "God, but you're a daft woman!" he said, breaking into laughter again, and Thea laughed with him, fully aware of how long it had been since she'd done anything this spontaneous and, well, *daft*.

"You've all the guile of the devil himself," Dillon said, reaching absently to brush a strand of her hair off her cheek. His fingers were warm and light and not at all unpleasant.

Thea abruptly sat up, but Dillon caught her arm when she tried to get to her feet. He was still smiling, a smile that showed only slightly around his mouth, but showed a great deal in his eyes.

"I haven't been put away that handily since I was a lad in school," he said.

"That's because Griffen kept your Achilles' heel a secret," she answered. She could hear the rain against the windows, and Dillon's long fingers tightened on her arm. He had beautiful hands. She remembered them suddenly, strong and comforting and trying to help her stop crying. She attempted to get up again, but Dillon came with her, and she only made it to her knees. He stood up first, helping her the rest of the way but not releasing her.

"Thea," he said, his compelling, soft Scots voice making her look into his eyes. "I would have come to you if I'd known," he said quietly. She tried to move away from him.

"You know that, don't you?" he insisted, his eyes gray now, as the stormy sea was gray, and searching hers. "You know I would have come if you'd wanted me."

"No," she said, shaking her head. She pulled free of his grasp. "I didn't know."

"Thea—"

"I have to see about Caitlin," she said, leaving him standing in the kitchen. She was going to have to stay away from him. She had no more resistance to his easy charm than the French bird watcher or the mother-daughter fiddle-players had, and the sooner she recognized that, the better off she'd be.

Caitlin was awake and side-stepping around her crib, looking up to grin as Thea came in, a grin that was all too familiar now. Strange, Thea thought, how she hadn't noticed long ago that their smiles were so much alike. But then, she hadn't seen them together before now.

"Caitlin, Caitlin," Thea crooned. "There she is, my baby face—oops! Somebody is wet here."

She dried the baby and put her into a clean pair of corduroy rompers—pink with a matching long-sleeved shirt—letting her down to make her own way along the hall into the kitchen. Crawling gave way to pulling herself up at a doorway to side-stepping—to absolute delight at the sight of the deep-voiced person who waited on his knees just outside the kitchen doorway, arms outstretched.

"Da!" she kept squealing as she made her way to him.

Dillon had put on a blue denim shirt without a collar, and it rode when he lifted Caitlin into the air. Thea forced herself not to look at his bare belly or the path of curling hair that disappeared into the waistband of his still unbuttoned jeans.

"Da's got you now, darlin'," Dillon said, laughing. He lowered her gently to kiss both her cheeks. "Where have you been? What shall we do until Mum's ready to feed us?"

"Us?" Thea inquired. "This is a B&B, Mr. Cameron."

"Oh, aye," Dillon said, grinning at Caitlin. "And we've only just woke up. We're wanting our breakfast, Thea."

"You don't say," she said, going into the kitchen. Dillon followed, carrying Caitlin.

"I'll tell you what we'd like," he went on, completely oblivious to her resistance and to the time of day. "We'd like stovie tatties, if you're of the mind to make them."

"I'm not of the mind," Thea assured him. She didn't run a restaurant, and she wasn't his personal chef.

"Did you hear that, lass?" he said to Caitlin. "She's no' of the mind. Thea, surely we can discuss this."

"Come here," she said, taking him by the arm and leading him into the hallway to a small framed sign. "Number seven."

Dillon scanned the list of rules. "Ah! Extra meals must be pre-arranged. Isn't that what we're doing?"

"Five minutes isn't pre-arranging, Cameron."

"Thea, I'm starving. There's a gale outside, and—"

"You didn't mind the gale last night," she answered, mentally kicking herself for doing it. The last thing she wanted was having him know that his leaving had worried her. "The gale is nearly over. They've even got the power back on. A little walk into St. Margaret's Hope will do you good."

"Thea, I had things to do last night."

"I'm sure you did," she said, avoiding his eyes.

"I had to get my clothes, Thea." She glanced up at

him, and he gave her a charming grin. "Thea, nobody in St. Margaret's Hope makes stovie tatties the way you do," he said, obviously desperate enough to try flattery.

She laughed. "Now, that's probably true. And you'll save yourself a lot of indigestion if you go on to the hotel."

"Thea, will you let a man starve? It's been a long time since I've eaten."

"You're breaking my heart, Cameron."

"I'm . . . willing to pay for it," he offered, his natural Scots parsimony losing out to his hunger. "You ask her," he whispered to Caitlin, who promptly gave him a wet kiss on the eyebrow. "See, Thea? I've been vouched for. Surely you can feed a man with that kind of endorsement." He smiled at Caitlin.

Thea tried not to grin. "Well . . ." She wavered. "I suppose I could make this one exception."

"Bless you, Thea. You're a fine, charitable woman."

"And you want to marry me," Thea said dryly.

"No, that was before I knew you screeched and threw things and took unfair advantage of a man's weaknesses."

"Ah, well, those are the breaks," Thea said philosophically.

"You needn't look so happy about it."

"If you think *I* look happy, you should take a gander at yourself in the mirror, Cameron."

"Take a gander?" he asked, frowning.

"Take a look. Don't you ever watch the cowboy movies?"

"Not lately," he said. "I did like rolling on the floor with you, Thea," he admitted.

"Now, there's a reason for marrying," she said, going back into the kitchen. Dillon followed right on her heels, totally violating her personal space. She stood frowning, with him at her elbow, because she'd moved the potatoes out of Caitlin's reach, and now with him so close, she couldn't remember where she'd put them.

"There have been worse reasons," Dillon said, moving aside so she could get to the bigger cupboard. "I keep wondering—" He stopped because Caitlin suddenly leaned to touch Thea's face.

"Ma-ma-ma," she said.

"That's me—all three syllables," Thea responded with a soft laugh. She loved this child so!

Caitlin kicked her legs and let her attention be taken by the fascinating flap on Dillon's shirt pocket.

"Are you not going to ask me what I'm wondering, Thea?"

"Lord, no," she assured him, bending down to check the other cupboard. "I'm liable to find myself engaged."

Dillon laughed. "I just don't understand you, Thea."

"That's because you think you're God's gift to women, Dillon. It never occurred to you that every woman you meet isn't dying to get you to the *kirk*."

"Well, I never thought I was the best laugh a woman ever had, if that's your meaning. Why don't you believe I'm serious?"

Thea found the potato bag on an out-of-reach shelf where she'd left it. "Because you're not serious. I screech and throw things and take unfair advantage, remember?"

"Would it help if I told you what a beautiful woman you are?"

"Nope. You've already done that," she said, squeezing by him with a handful of potatoes.

"Did I?" he asked incredulously.

"You were extraordinarily drunk at the time."

"I'm no' drunk now, Thea."

"No, but if I can believe a word you say, you're nearly delirious with hunger."

He didn't say anything, and she glanced up at him.

"I . . . think I'm going to like this," he said, his amused eyes holding hers.

"What?" she said, unable to keep from asking. And he was delighted with the question.

"Courting you, Thea Kearney," he said, grinning.

"I've told you, Dillon. I don't want to be courted."

"Even so," he said with a resigned sigh, "I'm courting."

"Must you?"

"Oh, aye. Could you have a care here, Thea? You're about to bruise my fragile self-esteem with that fervent enthusiasm of yours."

"You're a Scotsman, Dillon. I couldn't bruise your self-esteem with a sledge hammer."

He grinned. "Thea?"

"What!"

"You know how to make stovie tatties, don't you? You'd no' let me stand here starving and hopeful and then feed me the grits, would you?"

"I wouldn't feed the Prince of Wales himself my grits, and I'm not going to feed you anything if you don't get out of my way! Caitlin, my sweet," Thea said to her bouncing daughter, "take this man for a walk."

"Ah, a walk, is it!" Dillon growled, making Caitlin chuckle out loud. "Lead the way, darlin'."

He stayed out of the kitchen long enough for Thea to get the meat, potato, and onion dish done and on the table.

"You're not sitting down with me?" he asked when he saw only one place set.

"No. I don't eat with the guests. And it's a bit late in the day for breakfast for those of us who aren't out carousing all night."

Dillon stared at her, and again Thea could have kicked herself. It sounded as if she *cared* that he'd gone out last night. And she didn't, she assured herself. At all.

"I don't think I know what carousing is, Thea. Is that some kind of American thing?"

"I've told you, Dillon," she said, holding out her hands for Caitlin to come to her. "Don't press your luck at insulting my homeland."

"Could I keep Katy with me? I'd like to have her in the highchair by me if you don't mind."

Thea turned one hand palm up, giving him tacit permission.

"And don't call her Katy," she said over her shoulder on her way out.

"Caitlin to you, Katy to me," he said mildly.

Thea sighed, changing directions in the hallway because of a sharp knock on the back door. It was still raining, and Roddy and Flora waited to be let in.

"Counting noses, I see," Thea said as she opened the door, knowing the island custom of making sure all its residents weathered the storm. "Come in out of the rain."

Both of them were wearing their foul-weather gear, and Thea held Roddy's walking stick while he helped Flora out of her yellow mackintosh and her knee-high "Wellies."

"You and the bairn are all right then," Roddy said.

"Yes, fine. Would you like tea?"

"Of course we would," Flora said. "Roddy and I, old as we are, need a spot of tea if we're to carry on. Out in weather like this—" she complained further.

"And loving every minute of it," Thea finished for her, while Flora swatted the air in her direction and pretended to be annoyed.

"Is there any damage around the island?" Thea asked Roddy.

"None to speak, lass," Roddy said, taking his walking stick back and standing it in the corner. "And we've nearly everyone accounted for."

"You haven't seen Dillon, have you?" Flora asked. "He lifted a pint with Roddy sometime after midnight, but we've lost him since."

"He's here," Thea answered, hanging their wet rain garb on the pegs by the door.

"Oh?" Flora said, the corners of her mouth turning down. "He's here, is he? Now, there's a place we never considered," she added to Roddy, who tried not to grin.

"Flora, don't tease me. He's here as a B&B, just like any other guest."

"Well, not 'just,'" Flora said. "Where is he?"

"Having breakfast."

"Breakfast, is it?" Flora said, her interest definitely piqued by now.

"He was away all night," Thea found herself explaining. "He just woke up, all right?"

"Well, it's all right with me if it's all right with you, my girl," Flora said. "He's in the kitchen, is he?" She headed in that direction. "Here you are, you slippery devil! No, now don't get up on my behalf. Have your . . . breakfast, is it?"

"Can I give you some stovie tatties, Flora?" Dillon asked.

"Me? Good heavens, no, lad. I have to watch my girlish figure. Now, Roddy here'll sit down with you."

"Ah, no, I'm not asking Roddy. I'll have none left

for myself, and it was trouble enough talking Thea into
making them for me."

"Is that so?" Flora said with interest. She reached to
pat Caitlin. "It's a bit wet on the southern plains, Thea,"
she called as Thea set the kettle on the burner to heat.
Thea handed Roddy a place—whether Dillon wanted to
share or not—while Caitlin gave Flora her most charming baby smile.

"Come on, Caitlin," Thea said, getting her out of the
highchair. Flora followed them into the nursery.

"Not sleeping much, are you, my girl?" Flora said
immediately, handing her a dry diaper. Thea went on
quietly drying the baby, not wanting to talk about her
lack of sleep—and particularly not wanting to talk about
the reason for it.

"I think I understand," Flora said quietly.

"No, you don't."

"Why? Because I'm twice your age? Because you
think I don't know what it is to have some big, hardheaded Scotsman take a fancy to you? Oh, it's easy
enough if he's not serious about it all—and if you're not
scared witless of what you're getting into—but I was
scared, my girl. Damned scared. Roddy Macnab dug me
out of a bombed tea shop in the London Blitz. He had
his left arm still mending from Dunkirk—on light duty,
they called it—and there he was, digging hysterical
women out of tea shop rubble. He kept coming round to
see me in hospital afterwards, but I was near done for.
Lost my husband in Burma, my only child in the London
fires. I was ready to pack it in, I can tell you. But
Roddy—" She stopped, looking off into the distance as
if she could see him then. "Roddy wouldn't let me. Took
me out of hospital right over the matron's head, and he
brought me here. I've been here ever since, Thea, be-

cause there's no reasoning with a Scotsman when he sets his mind to something. Aren't you here because of that in Griffen?"

"Dillon isn't Griffen."

"No, my girl, he's not. He's a living breathing man who wants you, just the way Roddy wanted me. I only want you to know that no matter how muddled things seem, if he's determined and you want it, the whole of it can come right again."

"Flora—"

"Ah, my girl, you're all done in with this. Why don't you go for a little walk out on the beach path? The rain's going. I'll take Caitlin and get the tea ready. You'll feel the better for it."

Thea hesitated, then put her face into her hands for a moment. Flora was right. She was exhausted.

"It's the indecision that makes us so weary," Flora said kindly, and Thea managed a smile. She lifted Caitlin out of the crib and set her down to crawl.

"Flora, I just don't know why Dillon is doing this."

"He wants to marry you. You don't find a man like Dillon Cameron saying he does if he doesn't, I can tell you."

"Well, he took his own good time getting here!"

Flora frowned. "Took his own good time? Thea, you didn't *tell* him about Caitlin."

"He said everybody here knew."

"Well, of course we knew Dillon was her father likely. We didn't know you didn't *tell* him, my girl!"

"Then what is he doing here now?"

"Oh, well, that's simple enough. Roddy and I spilled the beans—and don't interrupt me till I get everything said. It was after Caitlin had the bronchitis last month. You were all worn out with taking care of her night and day with no help, and, well, Dillon is Roddy's . . . godson, I guess you'd call it. You know how they do hereabouts, working on the sea the way they do. A man asks a friend to take care of his family if something happens to him. Roddy didn't have a son of his own, so Ian Cameron gave Dillon to Roddy if ever he couldn't take care of him. You know what an old duffer my Roddy is. He expects that every man will do his duty and all that, and Dillon certainly wasn't. So we went down to Aberdeen to give him what for. Caught him at the—what is that place?—the heliport. Dillon was there in his orange suit they make them wear so they can find what's left of them if they fall into the sea. And there was Roddy about to bash his nose in for him—" Flora stopped.

"Well, go on!"

"Right," Flora assured her. "I wasn't sure for a minute there you wanted me to. Well, I was saying, Roddy was about to bash him, and then he sees that our Dillon doesn't know the first thing about Caitlin here. Thea, you should have seen the lad. It nearly broke my old heart, I can tell you. He just stood there, and then he had to walk off by himself for a bit. And the rest of the crew were yelling for him to get on the helicopter, but he was just standing. Finally I gave him that picture I had in my purse—the one of you and Caitlin sitting by the fire. He took it and he went—nearly thirty days with the shift and going through the decompressing—with all that on his mind. I'd say he got here pretty damn quick, for my money."

Thea bent down to keep Caitlin out of the diaper pail, her mind in a whirl.

I would have come if I'd known.

"Flora, I think I would like to go for a walk," she murmured.

"Go on, then. I'll hold the fort. Stay as long as you like."

Thea nodded, bending to give Caitlin a kiss. "Your mother needs this for her nerves," she whispered.

She went quickly down the hallway and past the kitchen door, hearing Dillon and Roddy quietly talking in Gaelic when she passed. Roddy, she thought with a sigh. The old dear would have punched Dillon on her behalf. She grabbed up Griffen's jacket, pulling it on as she went out the door and breaking into a run as soon as she was out of the yard.

The clouds were moving rapidly inland, and the last of the afternoon sun was shining through. Thea felt like a child let out of school, and she didn't stop running until she reached the rise of land that overlooked St. Margaret's Hope. She loved the sweeping view around her—St. Margaret's Hope with its quaint old houses turned gable end toward the sea, the sandy beach where the children had their Festival of the Horse in mid-August. The land and the sky and the water were all taking on the pink and lavender glow of the newly revealed sunset, and the constant cries of screaming sea birds rose above the relentless pounding of the waves. Her hair whipped around her face, and she turned her body into the wind, smelling the salt air, tasting it on her lips. She stood with her feet planted firmly on the rugged turf and breathed deeply, feeling this ancient place renew her strength. Griffen had been right. She had never seen the cold stone ruins of a long-dead people; she had always seen the people themselves, still warm and alive in Dillon and Flora and Roddy in this wild and beautiful place.

"It's no' like South Carolina, is it?" Dillon said behind her, and she whirled around to face him. "Now, let me say two things before you get angry, Thea. First, the

stovie tatties were grand, and second, I'm here over
Flora's dead body." He was looking into her eyes, and
he stopped talking as if he'd suddenly lost his train of
thought.

Thea didn't avoid his probing gaze. She stared back
at him, trying to see past The Great Silkie to the man
who seemed to love his baby daughter, the man who had
been her husband's best friend.

"You're no' going to say something like they say in
the American cowboy movies, are you?" he offered as
the silence between them grew awkward and heavy. He
gave her a small, tentative smile. "'This island's no' big
enough for the two of us,' or something like that?"

A gull screamed overhead, and Thea turned away from
him toward the sea. "I'm not going to say anything."

"I wanted to ask you a question," Dillon said, coming
closer. He stood beside her, their shoulders nearly touching. He wasn't wearing his jacket, and Thea could almost
feel his warmth through his blue denim shirt. In her mind,
she *could* feel it, knowing the texture of his skin and
how it felt and smelled and tasted.

"The trouble is, Dillon, you ask me the same two
questions."

"Such as?" he said a bit defensively.

"Will I marry you and why haven't I gone home."

"Why haven't you gone home?" he asked, and she
gave a small laugh.

"See?" she told him. "You need a bigger repertoire,
and you're beginning to sound like my mother and Aunt
Mary Ann."

"I want to know, Thea."

Thea glanced at him, feeling his worry without wanting to. If she felt sorry for him, she'd never be rid of
him, and she wanted that more than anything—for her

own self-preservation. She wanted him to tire of the domesticity she and Caitlin represented, so her life could go back to the way it was before he came . . . didn't she?

"I want to know," he said again, and she sighed.

"Dillon." She looked up at him, again meeting his eyes. She realized suddenly that she would always have to be wary of his questions, because she couldn't tell him anything but the truth when she looked into his beautiful eyes. "I'm afraid," she said simply. She gave a small shrug. "I have a strong family, Dillon. Close-knit. I love this island. I was married here; Caitlin was born here. It's my home now. But if I go to South Carolina, I'm afraid I'll never come back here again. I'll *think* that I will, but my family will love Caitlin and me and they'll absorb us, and everything here—my memories here—will become like a dream. I'll take Caitlin there later, when she's older, but not now while I'm—" *So alone,* she almost said. "Caitlin is a lucky little girl, and I want her to have the best of both places." She could feel him looking at her, and she turned toward him, staring into his eyes.

"Sometimes . . . you look at me with such reproach," he said.

"If I do, it's myself I'm reproaching, not you."

"Because we went to bed together?"

She hadn't expected such candor, and she didn't know what to say.

"When that happened, Thea, you were near mad with grief. I . . . knew how much you needed me to be Griffen. And I needed—"

He didn't go on, and Thea caught his arm when he would have walked away from her. "What?" she asked, her fingers digging into the hard muscles under his shirt sleeve.

"I couldn't save him for you, Thea. I needed your forgiveness."

He was standing close to her, too close, she realized, and she let go of his arm.

"I know how you loved him, Thea," he said quietly, reaching out to put his hand on her shoulder. Then his arms went around her, and she leaned into him, clutching the front of his shirt, desperately needing to be close to him. His hand slid up to rest against her face. She loved the warm feel of it, loved being with him like this. There was passion there, underneath it all, but there was more. She needed him more than just sexually; she needed his friendship. She needed *him*.

He suddenly held her away from him. "You still wear his jacket," he said, his face grave. He released her and headed down the path toward St. Margaret's Hope.

"I want you, Thea," he called back to her. "But I won't be Griffen for you ever again. I'm done with feeling guilty. When you lie with me, it'll be because you want Dillon Cameron."

6

When you lie with me. When, not *if.*

Dillon Cameron's arrogance was an open declaration of war as far as Thea was concerned, and he'd done well to announce his Cameron battle cry when he first came back. The battles were all verbal, all of them precipitated by Dillon's questions:

"Thea, do you have a lover?"

"Why don't you go down to Roddy's and ask?"

"They don't know. Do you?"

"Dillon, where and how do you think I'd get a lover they don't know about?"

"The oil rig crews come in for the *ceilidhs*, don't they, Thea?"

"Yes, Dillon, they do, but what makes you think I'm not sick to death of oil men?"

Or:

"Thea, why don't you marry me?"

"Dillon, how many women have you lived with in the last year?"

"What has that got to do with anything?"

"How many?"

"Two! Sometimes I stay with my mother and my sister Bronwyn in Aberdeen."

"And what about the geometrical blonde?"

"What the bloody hell is a 'geometrical blonde'!"

"The woman who followed you here, Dillon!"

"Thea, *that* was my sister Bronwyn!"

"Sure it was, Dillon—all the way here from Aberdeen!"

And yet he continued to court her, not with expensive gifts, but with a great willingness to spend time with their daughter and to take care of household repairs. He annoyed Thea endlessly when Caitlin was asleep with his relentless quest for something to fix. The truth was that excepting slate roofs, and with the muscle of the St. Margaret's Hope Knitters' Co-Operative on occasion, she didn't *need* anything repaired. In desperation she remembered that the kitchen sink was sometimes known to leak. Dillon had only three days left before his next shift, and one would have thought she had given him a million dollars.

He was lying in the middle of the kitchen floor with Caitlin trying to sit on him, his head under the sink.

He said something completely unintelligible.

"What?" Thea asked, bending down so she could hear, wary of doing it because she'd become so sexually aware of him lately. Even in their worst arguments, she wanted to touch him, hold him, make love.

"Was that somebody at the door?" he asked, and she tried not to look at him. *God, he's one hundred per cent "hank."*

"No," she said, going desperately on about her business.

It was approximately five minutes before he asked again.

"No!" she said testily, wondering if he was expecting his geometrical blonde supposed-to-be sister.

Someone promptly knocked. *"That* is somebody at the door," she advised him, going to see. Two redheaded little boys waited on the doorstep.

"This is for you, Mrs. Kearney," the spokesman of the two said, hitching his pants up and holding out his hand to give her something.

"I get to say it, Trevor," the other little boy whispered.

"Get on with it then," Trevor admonished.

The second boy, obviously a born speechmaker, cleared his throat. Twice. "These are—" He broke off and frowned. "Well, give her 'em," he whispered urgently to Trevor, who was daydreaming. Trevor promptly aligned his fist over Thea's wary palm, letting a stream of smooth, slightly translucent beach pebbles trickle down. "These are 'The Mermaid's Tears,'" the speechmaker began again. "A token of . . . of my sorrow at our soon parting." He stopped abruptly, searching his memory for the rest of it and scratching his head to help it along.

Thea smiled. She could tell the exact second he remembered.

"This is . . . a jewel . . . a jewel . . ." he repeated while he looked for it. Trevor had it in his pocket. "This is a jewel . . . from my kingdom in the sea . . . a token of my . . . joy at your being," he announced, and Thea held out her hand again. This time she received a seashell, iridescent with mother-of-pearl and delicately formed in the approximate shape of a human ear.

"Thank you *very* much," the speechmaker concluded, giving a short bow.

"From Dillon Patrick Cameron," Trevor prompted in a whisper.

"Aye!" the speechmaker conceded, giving another bow.

Thea stood grinning, watching them bound down the

road out of sight. She took the pebbles and the seashell inside, stepping over Dillon's long legs to drop the pebbles into the bottom half of an old cut-glass candy dish she kept on an open shelf with the jars of pasta. In was a perfect container for the "tears," and Thea stood holding the seashell, trying not to smile at Dillon's studied nonchalance under the kitchen sink.

Now what was he up to?

She was more than annoyed with herself for being so susceptible to his questionable unpretentiousness, wondering how many other women had fallen for the old single-perfect-rose and the fistful-of-hand-picked-violets ruse.

Only this time it was a seashell and beach pebbles. And she loved them.

"Thank you," she said, bending down to see his face.

"You're welcome," came the muffled reply.

"I like them," she offered.

"Aye," he answered, sliding out from under the sink. "No, darlin'," he said to Caitlin, who was about to teethe on one of his wrenches. He took the wrench away, giving it to Thea to hold. "Did they do all right, then? My representatives?"

"They were remarkable," Thea said. "Words fail me. The shell is beautiful."

"It's a *Haliotis,* an ear shell," he said, his eyes probing hers. "You find them when you dive around the Channel Islands. It's very beautiful in the sea, Thea. You'd like it, I think."

He kept staring at her. Thea wanted to look away, but she couldn't. His eyes traveled over her face, her breasts, not offensively, but lovingly, as if he wanted to touch her and knew that he couldn't, so he was making do with the next best thing.

"Thea, will you go to the *ceilidh* with me this evening," he said unexpectedly.

She looked away. "I'm already going."

"With someone else you mean?" The question sounded neutral enough, but there was a slight frown between his eyebrows.

"Not exactly. I have kitchen duty. I'm on the food committee."

"You're taking Katy?"

"Of course," she said, trying to decide if he approved or disapproved.

"I'll look after her when you get there."

Thea laughed. A *ceilidh* was a community gathering with dancing and singing and food and plenty of "wee drops" to keep everyone merry. She couldn't imagine Dillon Cameron going to one and babysitting.

"And what's so funny about that, if you don't mind saying?"

"I don't mind saying. I was just thinking that she'd cramp your style. You're the reason every woman on the island goes to these things, aren't you?"

"I wouldn't know about that," he said, annoyed. "I would still like to see you there," he added carefully.

"Fine. I'll be there," she said indifferently. She glanced at him.

"God, you make me angry!" He took the wrench she was still holding and slid back under the sink. "You think I don't know you want to go with me?"

Thea moved away, pretending she didn't hear.

"I know you heard me, Thea," he said more loudly. "You know we'd have a good time together, and you do want to go. But you have to keep at it, don't you. Who's it for, Thea? The Knitters' Co-Operative? Griffen? I don't know why you want to keep the both of us miserable!"

"I'm not miserable!"

"No?"

"No!"

"Happy is what you are, then?"

"I was until a few days ago," she said significantly.

"And will be again, no doubt, when I'm on an oil rig in the middle of the North Sea."

"Something like that."

"Well, you've only the forty-eight hours to wait, Thea. Go on with your bloody food committee. Pick yourself out a nice American from the oil crews that'll be there if it suits you."

"I usually do," she lied, and she glanced at Caitlin, who had been quietly placing wooden blocks in the middle of Dillon's chest. Her eyes were wide and solemn and afraid.

My poor baby, she thought, holding out her hands for Caitlin to come to her. The response was immediate as Caitlin used Dillon for leverage, then reached for a kitchen chair to hold on to as she side-stepped the distance to her mother.

Thea left Dillon muttering under the sink.

He finally went to the *ceilidh* without her—at least she assumed he was going. He didn't say, slamming the back door hard as he went out.

What is the matter with me? Thea kept thinking. She had wanted to go with him. She'd wanted more than that, if she were honest with herself. In her strong moments— when Dillon was nowhere around—she could see every-thing clearly and know the reasons she shouldn't become involved. But when he was here, she simply wanted to be with him. She wanted to sleep with him and wake up with him and raise their daughter with him. She wanted to be the object of his desire, the woman he thought about night and day the way she thought about him. She wanted to be more than just the mother of his child.

I want him.

There it was. The truth. And she felt no guilt, because whatever she was feeling now never would have flourished if Griffen had lived.

She put Caitlin on the nursery floor, sitting down with her and helping her sort through her pull toys and stacking games and finally settle for the red caboose toy box they were kept in. It was a fascinating game, taking all the toys out and then dropping them all back in again. Wonderfully noisy.

Dillon.

He was so beautiful. He was dangerously wild, yet he was thoughtful and kind. Thea had thought she could be happy being the only woman he'd ever met who had said no to him—surely there must be some prestige in that. But she wasn't happy. She was just like any other woman who let herself become involved with Dillon Cameron: willing to take whatever he would give.

Thea spent too much time getting ready for the *ceilidh*. She didn't have many choices in her wardrobe, but she kept trying out combinations of what she had.

"I'm not going to do this," she said finally. She was simply going to be what she was, a reasonably attractive thirty-two-year-old American woman. She picked up a black, mid–calf-length wool skirt and one of the hand-knit wool sweaters she'd bought from the Co-Operative, done in horizontally striped earth tones in the Fair Isle pattern. She put on black stockings that stayed up without garters, a pair of low-heeled black shoes, then tied back her unruly hair with a copper-colored satin ribbon.

She had good skin that needed no makeup, but she did some extra work on her hazel eyes with a dark green kohl shadow, smudging it until her eyes looked large and sultry.

"This is the best I've got to offer, Cameron," she said aloud. "I don't look too bad, and I smell good."

She dressed Caitlin in a white hand-knit sweater-smock with small embroidered pink roses over the yoke, white tights with rows of ruffles over her bottom, and black patent leather shoes that buckled.

"What a pretty girl," Thea said admiringly, brushing Caitlin's curling red-gold hair while she looked at herself in the mirror. "What will Da say?"

Don't do that, Thea abruptly admonished herself. No matter how much she wanted Dillon Cameron, she couldn't teach Caitlin to expect him to be around.

Thea put Caitlin into the stroller—the pushchair, the islanders called it—and walked the distance to the community hall–hotel ballroom, taking the long way over the road to accommodate the stroller. For once the wind was a little less than whipping and she walked slowly, making sure Caitlin's knit hat was tied securely and watching the changing colors of the land and sea around her as the sun began to set.

Flora met her at the front door—an ominous sign in Thea's estimation. "The two of you had words, did you?" Flora said immediately.

"What makes you think that?" Thea replied, trying not to scan the hall for Dillon's whereabouts.

"What makes me think that?" Flora repeated. Then she gave an exaggerated shrug. "Oh, I don't know, my girl. Call me psychic."

"Flora—"

"What I'm wondering, Thea, is are you thinking with all your cylinders? Dillon Cameron is a proud man. He won't be letting you spit in his eye forever. Now, do you want him or don't you?"

"I . . . don't know."

"Liar," Flora said good-naturedly. "A week ago you'd have laid my ears back with a resounding no. Well, let me take this beautiful child for you so you can do your stint in the kitchen. We'll stroll around and tell her Da who's here—in case he's wondering or anything." Flora already had the stroller, and Thea was about to protest.

But she leaned down to give Caitlin a kiss instead. She didn't want to protest, dammitall. She wanted Dillon to know she was here. She walked on toward the kitchen, encountering Roddy on the way.

"Och, you're lovely this evening, lass," he said to her as he passed.

"Thank you, Roddy."

He was headed for the stage, where the band was tuning up and waiting for their chief accordianist and fiddler. The group had two accordians actually, as well as a guitar and a set of drums. Thea had never liked accordian music until she came to the Orkneys. She had always thought of the instrument in terms of "Lady of Spain" in some early television talent show, and she hadn't known its capacity for wringing the melancholy out of a haunting Celtic tune.

She had arrived late, and the place was filled with locals and the oil men from Flotta terminal. A sudden whoop came from the dance floor as the band broke into a song Thea recognized as "Thunderhead." It was filled with unresolved minor chords and made her think of pagan dances in the moonlight, summer solstices, and fertility rites amid stark, upright stones. She could feel the floor jarring rhythmically as she started her kitchen duty, making sure the food dishes stayed filled so that the crowd got enough to eat for the price of their ticket.

The kitchen was hot, and Thea opened the back door to get a draft through, filling a plate with "Black Bun" and then going to stand in the kitchen doorway.

She spotted Dillon at the opposite end of the hall and watched him fondly as he moved through the crowd. He was so arresting, standing head and shoulders above nearly everyone there. He shook hands with the old men and teased the old women. She saw him stop Trevor and his speechmaking friend from running rampant through the crowd, and she smiled, wondering how much Dillon and Griffen had been like those two at that age.

A young woman with red—stoplight red—hair and a short pink dress the likes of which Thea hadn't seen in a decade, caught Dillon by his arm, hugging him hard and pulling him with her toward the outside door. He went without hesitation, and Thea hastily went back to filling food plates.

It ought to feel better being right, she thought. Dillon Cameron loved the women, and they loved him right back. Why couldn't she get that through her head? The music changed to a quiet waltz that drew the older women out in search of dance partners.

"Thea?" Dillon said close behind her.

He had come in the back door. How handsome he looked. He was wearing gray flannel trousers, a brown and gray plaid shirt with a gray tie, and black loafers. His long hair was mussed, and he had lipstick on his chin.

Thea gave him a small, crooked smile. "Ah, yes," she said wryly, wiping the lipstick off with her fingertips. "Yet another sister."

"That's the *same* sister," he said. "She's come all the way from Aberdeen to talk me out of my car."

"Right," Thea said agreeably, raising and lowering her eyebrows once.

"Thea, that's Bronwyn. She wants my car while I'm on the oil rig. She'd rather drive a red Porsche than a Toyota. Thea, that's *Bronwyn*. She's always changing herself around. You never know what you'll see. I half expect her to turn up with her head shaved sometime."

"Dillon, if she's your sister, why don't I ever get to meet her? She's Caitlin's aunt, and she's been here twice."

Dillon sighed. "Because," he said patiently, "she's incredibly rude. She only wants my car to dash about in, and once she talks me out of it, she's done with me. It's the way she is, charming and balmy. My mother thinks it's because she read that American pediatrician's baby book all the time she was carrying Bronwyn. It's the only reason she can think of that Bronwyn's no' like the rest of us. The lass has got a terrible wild streak."

"And you don't?"

Dillon gave her a "Who me?" look. "Indeed, no, Thea," he said. "I'm no' wild at all."

Thea looked into his eyes, trying not to grin and feeling her knees weaken perceptibly at the tender look she saw there, but still trying to decide if she was annoyed enough to comment on his remark about the *American* pediatrician.

No, she decided. She didn't want to fight with him anymore about anything. She just wanted to be with him—or to look at him if that wasn't possible.

"I've seen our lovely daughter," Dillon said, smiling. "She's force-feeding the Dunphys some raisins."

Thea returned the smile in spite of her resolve not to let him draw her into a better mood. She wanted to reach out and brush back the strand of reddish-blonde hair that had fallen over his forehead, but she didn't do it, looking down quickly to reposition a platter of jelly cake slices. She looked back up at him, letting her eyes stare deeply into his. They were alone in the kitchen now, and unless she was gravely mistaken, he was about to put his arms around her.

No! she thought wildly. She had to be strong for Caitlin. She couldn't weaken, couldn't let herself give in to what was nothing but unadulterated lust because he had beautiful thighs and beautiful, kissable lips. He needed to shave again. In her mind she could *feel* the stubble of his beard against her tender skin.

No! she thought again. She had to get away from him before she became like all his other conquests.

Dillon caught her arm when she tried to move away, pulling her against him and holding her fast. "I've never danced with you," he said gravely, and he was taking her out onto the dance floor, his grip like iron in case she had any further notions of escape.

The song was called "The Sapling," a quiet tender ballad, about what she had no idea. She was too addled to comprehend lyrics. There was nothing but the sensation of being pressed against Dillon's hard male body, feeling his warm hand on her back sliding lower to press her even closer so she could feel how much he wanted her. He was trembling slightly, and he wanted her to know that she was the reason for it. His breath came soft and warm against her temple, as soft and warm as the gentle kiss he placed there. She leaned into him as her knees weakened, knowing how they must look to the people around them.

Like lovers.

Forty-eight hours, she thought, holding on to the back of his shirt. Forty-eight hours and he'd be gone for nearly a month . . . or forever.

"Thea," he whispered. Nothing else, only her name, his arms tightening around her.

The song ended, and Thea stepped abruptly away from him while she still could. She headed blindly for the kitchen, feeling Dillon just behind her. The lights in the hall went low, and Roddy stepped up to the microphone.

"'The Great Silkie,'" he announced quietly, and there were soft sighs of approval all around the dance floor.

Roddy waited a moment longer for the room to settle down, and Thea stopped when she reached the kitchen doorway. Dillon came to stand close to her. She turned her head slightly to look at him, and Roddy began to sing without accompaniment, his fine, slightly stressed baritone voice rising in the hall.

"Do you know the song, Thea?" Dillon whispered, leaning toward her, his arm touching hers. She didn't move away, and she shook her head.

"The human woman weeps for her bairn," he whispered, lowering his head to whisper the translation of the Gaelic-English word mixture of the ancient ballad. "Her child is beautiful . . . *'Ba lily wean,'* she says . . . but she knows nothing of her baby's father . . . where he comes from or where he goes . . .

"But she wakes one night to find him at her bedside . . . she fears him . . . so fierce-looking he is . . ."

Roddy's song flowed over everyone in the hall as Dillon continued to whisper the meaning of the words, his voice soft and caressing against her ear.

"He is The Great Silkie, he tells her . . . a man on the land but a silkie in the sea. He's come for his baby, but she'll no' part with it. He . . . pleads with her . . . he offers her a purse of gold and wondrous riches . . . but she repents her love for him.

"He had no' but one other thing to offer her . . . he

will tell her the future if she will give him his child . . .
but with no promise as to whether it is happy or sad . . .

"This she cannot resist. He tells her of the fine human
husband she'll have . . . and—"

"Go on," Thea whispered, staring into Dillon's eyes.

"The Great Silkie will die of love for her," he said
quietly. His eyes searched hers. Thea was aware of the
loud applause around her, but she couldn't look away.
Dillon had her by the hand, pulling her along with him
into the kitchen and out the back door. She followed him
blindly into the dark alley. The wind was cool on her
face, and she could smell the sea, hear it lapping against
the sea wall and the jetty pylons nearby. Dillon still had
her by the hand, taking her into the deep shadows of the
row of buildings.

"Caitlin," Thea protested.

"Flora has her," he said gruffly. He stopped walking,
turning to stare at her in the dim light. He reached up to
gently touch her cheek, and she closed her eyes at the
power of his touch, flinging herself into his arms as his
mouth came down on hers.

There was no gentleness in him, and Thea wanted
none. His hands tangled in her hair.

It's been so long, she kept thinking. *So long since
I've held him.*

She was hungry, as desperate as he. She strained against
him, returning kiss for kiss, letting out a sigh of intense
pleasure when his hand cupped her breast. She kissed
his lips, his eyes, his lips again.

"Dillon," she whispered, and the kiss deepened, his
tongue exploring the deep recesses of her mouth.

His hands reached up, clamping down on her shoulders and holding her away from him, his breath coming

in quick, harsh gasps. But then he was holding her again, lifting her off the ground. She could feel the hardness of his arousal against her belly, and he pressed his face against her neck.

He was trembling. "I have to stop," he whispered urgently. "If I don't, I'll take you right here."

Thea heard him, understood, but her arms slid around his neck as she sought to kiss him again.

"My love, don't," he whispered, setting her down on the ground and loosening her arms from around his neck. She stayed where he put her, letting him step away from her. She said nothing, devouring him with her eyes.

"We have to go back inside," he said, and she nodded numbly, knowing that when he reached out to her, he only meant to straighten her sweater and smooth her hair. But she was drunk with the power she had over him. She stood mutely, head bowed, suffering his ministrations for the sake of propriety. It was only when she looked up at him again that he groaned and his arms went around her, his mouth coming down hard on hers.

"What are you doing to me?" he said shakily, pressing his lips against her neck.

"Nothing," she whispered into his ear. "You won't let me."

He laughed softly in the darkness, and Thea laughed with him, breaking the spell of their urgency. Dillon lifted her up off the ground again, making her squeal in alarm as he whirled her around.

"You are so good for me, Thea," he said, hugging her to him, then quickly letting her go.

"Am I? I had the feeling I was rather like a curse sent to end your carefree bachelor days."

"You say that—not me. Go inside now before I live up to my grand reputation."

"Now, that sounds interesting," she teased.

"Thea, I mean it!"

"That's easy for you to say. I'm the one who has to face the kitchen committee."

"Thea, go inside. I mean it," he said again.

"Do you?"

"No," he said with a groan. "Yes!" he insisted, but he kissed her again anyway.

"Are you always this decisive?" she asked, reaching up to smooth his hair in the same way he'd done for her.

"You'll see 'decisive' before this night is over," he warned her, turning her around and giving her a gentle whack on her backside. "Go on, woman, and stop having your fun with me."

She looked reluctantly toward the kitchen door, hesitating and looking back at him once before she went inside.

I want more from you than fun, Dillon Cameron. I want everything you are, and I mean to have it.

7

THEY WALKED HOME together in the dark, Dillon carrying Caitlin, letting her sleep on his shoulder with his jacket thrown over her to keep her out of the wind.

"Another storm coming," Dillon offered, and Thea said nothing, pushing the rattling, empty stroller along the paved road. She glanced at him from time to time, unsure of him suddenly because of his silence.

She still longed for him, but she supposed he didn't want her to lead him past the point of no return. If she did, he might really feel obligated to marry her. And if that *wasn't* the way he felt, surely he could manage to say more to her than that succinct weather forecast.

The wind whipped his long hair about his face, and there was no moonlight, no stars. The light from the street lamps became more and more dim as they reached the outskirts of St. Margaret's Hope. Thea fumbled in her coat pocket for a small flashlight she'd brought along. She could hear strains of music now and then from the *ceilidh,* but the wind gave it a strange ethereal sound. A

114

dog howled somewhere behind them, making her feel lonely and cold. She wanted to reach out and take Dillon's arm, but she didn't do it.

Oh, God, she thought in dismay. She didn't know what to say to him if he was having second thoughts, so she didn't say anything.

She stopped to fold up the stroller as they reached the cottage yard. Dillon took it away from her.

"I'll carry it," he said.

"You've got Caitlin."

"I *said* I'll carry it for you."

"Fine! Carry it! But I didn't need any help!"

"Help? Or help from me?" he asked, standing the stroller against the back door while he fumbled in his trouser pocket for the key he wasn't supposed to have in the first place. He pushed the door open for her, and she picked up the stroller on her way inside, causing him to give a sharp sigh of annoyance in the dark hall.

She didn't turn on a light, and he went on to the nursery with Caitlin, completely sure of himself in the dark.

Thea took the time to put the stroller away, entering the nursery as Dillon gently put the baby in her crib. He moved back to make room for her to tuck Caitlin in, his body brushing up against hers.

Thea closed her eyes at the warmth of his nearness, his dangerous sexuality and the masculine scent that was his alone making her knees weak. She thought he was about to say something, but he left the room without speaking.

When she had Caitlin dry and secure for the night, she walked back through the dark house, wondering why Dillon hadn't bothered to turn on a light. She could just make out his silhouette at the end window in the kitchen.

"Don't turn on the light," he said without turning around.

"Dillon, what—"

"Thea, have I kept my word to you? About staying here with you and Katy? You've no cause for complaint that I've no' been keeping your rules?"

"Dillon—"

"Thea, answer me!"

"I've . . . no complaints," she said. "You've kept your word."

"Aye. I've kept it, and you've no' known the times I've meant to break it. The first night I was here, Thea, I had to go out into a gale because I didn't think I could be here and no' . . . touch you. I've watched you sleep-ing—did you know that? I had to be close to you, Thea, and you'd no' have me anywhere near in the light of day, except as Katy's dad. I think about you all the time— about making love with you. I . . . can't keep my word anymore, Thea. I can't stay here tonight and no' . . . be with you." He gave a sharp sigh. "Thea, tell me. Do you want me to stay or go? I'll no' stay another night here without you in my arms, lass. There's no going back now."

Thea stared at him across the dark room. She wanted him; she had no illusions about that. And to have him, for tonight at least, all she had to do was say so. Her heart began to pound. He was right. They'd been in each other's arms tonight, and there was no going back.

"Stay," she said simply, hardly recognizing the sound of her own voice. He covered the distance between them, reaching for her in the dark. She went willingly, joyfully, clinging to him as if he might somehow disappear. She lifted her mouth to his, giving a soft moan at the first brush of his lips against hers. And she was afraid sud-

denly, feeling the uncertainty any woman would feel in
the arms of a man she knew would ultimately hurt her.
He was the flame, and she was the all too flammable
moth, and she said what all moths say: *Just this once.*

"You want me then?" he whispered against her ear,
and she knew what he was saying. *I'm not Griffen.*

"I want you, Dillon," she whispered back to him, her
arms tightening around him. Oh, she loved the feel of
him under her hands, his muscular, hard body that was
so unlike her own. The rough stubble of his beard
scratched her face as she sought to kiss him. She loved
the way he tasted, her mouth opening for him, accepting,
returning the insistent probing of his tongue. She was
melting with desire for him; she could feel it, feel its hot
core spreading outward from the very center of her being.
She was drunk with wanting him.

"Dillon," she whispered for no other reason than to
hear the sound of his name. He smelled so good to her.

He lifted her up off the floor, carrying her through
the dark house and into the downstairs bedroom. She
covered his face in quick, wanting kisses as he bent
slowly to place her in the middle of the bed, following
her down to lie beside her, then on top of her, his strong
hands cradling her face so that he could kiss her mouth,
her eyes, and her mouth again. He was trembling with
desire, his warm hands shaking as he slid them up under
her sweater to cup her aching breasts. She held his hands
there as he gently squeezed, giving a soft "Ah" sound
as his thumbs brought her nipples to hard, tight peaks.

Unexpectedly, he moved away from her, sitting up
and pulling her into an upright position with him. He
reached to turn on a small lamp on the table by the bed,
filling the area immediately around them in a warm glow.
The corners of the room were in deep shadow, and he

looked at her as if he expected her to protest about the light. She didn't; she wanted to see him, and she reached to cup his face so that she could kiss him wherever she liked. He sat quietly, suffering her exquisite worship until she softly pressed her lips, then her tongue against the corner of his mouth. He moaned then, pulling her closer, pulling her legs around him so they sat face to face. His urgent hands fumbled for the bottom edge of her sweater, tugging it swiftly over her head and tossing it aside. She lost the copper-colored ribbon inside the sweater, and her hair fell over her shoulders.

Dillon smiled, hooking a finger in the V-neck of her undershirt. "May Rand's handiwork," he said, his hands cupping her breasts again. The cotton-knit fabric clung to the outline of her still hard nipples. "What a beautiful woman you are, Thea Kearney," he said, his eyes dark with passion, heavy-lidded and intense in his inspection of her body. She felt no shyness, savoring his obvious pleasure. He lowered his head to kiss her neck and shoulder, lingering to outline each moist kiss with his tongue. She tried to sit quietly, her head arching back as she felt the hot circles both on her skin and somewhere deep inside.

Dillon was growing more impatient, tugging at the hook on the waistband on her skirt. She began to unbutton his shirt, and together they removed both of the restricting garments. Thea was down to her thigh-top black stockings and her wide-legged tap pants that her sensuous sister Tessa had sent her on some occasion she was now too addled to recall. Dillon was stroking the bare skin of her thighs above the stockings, sliding his fingers into the legs of the tap pants, seeking whatever would give her pleasure. She rested her hands on his bare shoulders, again trying to stay quiet under his touch, but the game of advance and retreat he was playing was more than she could bear. She needed to touch him, needed to share this place he had taken her where there was only pleasure.

But Dillon ignored her seeking hands, his fingers continuing to stroke the soft insides of her thighs, continuing to slide into the wide-legged, silky white pants.

She nearly cried out in protest when he suddenly stopped, but he had to be rid of his own clothes now.

"Bloody hell," he muttered, working feverishly to get out of his trousers and shorts, and Thea chuckled softly. He came back to her on the bed, throwing her pillows to the floor as he pulled down the pristine white counterpane Thea had on her bed. He moved her onto the sheets, taking away the tap pants and the undershirt, and Thea was suddenly bombarded with sensations: cool, crisp sheets; warm, rough man-thighs that separated hers; cool dry air on her breasts, then warm, moist lips and tongue. The window was partially open, and she could smell the sea, smell the clean scent of Dillon's hair as he suckled her. In her restlessness, she lifted her head to kiss his forehead, burying her hands in his long hair to keep him at her breast, reveling in this newest burst of pleasure he was giving her. His hands, his mouth were everywhere until she whimpered with readiness. Then he was holding himself above her, kneeling between her thighs, his hands sliding under her to lift her higher so she could receive him.

"Thea," he said, his voice gruff with passion. "Don't close your eyes. Look at me."

She opened her eyes as he asked, and he lowered his head slowly toward hers. "Look at me," he said again, his mouth hovering just above hers. "I want you to see who I am—your *leman*—your lover."

Thea stared into his eyes, her breath coming in quick

gasps as his mouth found hers. The kiss was one of possession, and she gave a soft cry under its onslaught. She could feel his male hardness pressing, and she was desperate to have him inside her.

"Look at me," he commanded again, and she thought she would faint from the pleasure of his slow advance. "Is it me you want?"

"Yes," she whispered, caught in the intensity of his eyes. He *was* The Great Silkie come to possess her.

"Tell me, Thea," he urged with his words and with his body.

"Oh!" she whispered, letting out the long breath she was holding as he withdrew.

"Tell me!" he insisted.

"I want *you!*" she said, her voice shaky with passion.

"Who?" he demanded, beginning his slow penetration again.

"Dillon!" she responded, lifting her hips to receive him. "I want you, Dillon."

"Aye!" he whispered against her ear, his thrust slow and deep and hard. "Dillon—your lover—your *husband!*"

Thea opened her eyes to find him looking at her, his face no longer stormy with passion. She reached out to lightly outline his lips with her fingertips, her body sated and heavy. She was too incredulous to speak.

Never—never like this with anyone but him.

He caught her hand as she touched his mouth, his eyes probing hers. He began to kiss each fingertip, and she watched with half-closed eyes, feeling the gentle suction he applied to her fingers echoing in a restless sensation at the base of her spine. His eyes were dark and inscrutable, and Thea's breath caught. He couldn't be ready to—

He pressed a kiss into her palm, his teeth nipping the soft flesh, his tongue darting out to soothe it. He tasted the soft skin between each of her fingers, and she abruptly reached for him, sliding against him, to kiss him, to hold him.

"Are you ready for me?" he whispered, his mouth, his kisses everywhere. She felt as if he were devouring her.

"Yes, yes," she whispered urgently, craving his possession as if it had never happened before. She was burning, on fire with wanting him. She couldn't kiss him enough. She tasted his skin, let him feel the sharpness of her teeth in her need to be taken. *Dear God*, she thought. *All he has to do is look at me*.

But she wasn't alone in her need. Dillon was no less hungry than she. His body joined with hers in the frenzy of that need, his desire as consuming as her own.

"Thea," he said against her ear. "My—beautiful—Thea—"

Her fingernails scratched him, digging into his back, and she was lost in this exquisite quest she was driven to complete. He belonged to her, and she told him so, hissing her ownership against his ear. "You—are—*mine!*" she cried at the moment of her release.

8

THEA MOVED QUIETLY to reach another of the pillows Dillon had flung onto the floor. He was asleep, lying on his back, naked and sated and so awesomely male. She turned onto her side, propping herself up on the pillows so she could inspect him at her leisure.

Dillon.

She was torn between the need to weep and the need to satisfy the rise of desire she felt just looking at him.

Just this once, she thought sadly. You've fixed yourself up now, Thea, old girl. Just look at him.

She bit her lower lip. She could be happy forever just looking at him. Her eyes traveled over him, head to toe. His body was so . . . appealing to her—the rough hairiness of his chest and belly and thighs, the satinlike smoothness of his maleness. She abruptly smiled. She was as besotted with Dillon Cameron as Queen Victoria had been with Prince Albert. She gave a long sigh, remembering Dillon's voice.

". . . your husband . . ."

"Thea, what is it?" Dillon asked, his eyes still closed. He turned his head to look at her.

"I . . . think you're beautiful," she said simply, and he smiled.

"No more beautiful than you are to me."

"I wish I didn't," she explained further, looking up at the ceiling.

"I know. You wish I kicked dogs and little old ladies and had snaggled teeth and a wart on the end of my nose."

"I'd probably *still* think you were beautiful," she said morosely. "Oh, hell!"

She moved off the pillows and into his arms, pressing a small kiss on his chest. He reached up to stroke her hair.

"You're so damned arrogant," she continued as he kissed her forehead.

"You're a spoiled American."

"I never liked you," she insisted.

"Never," he agreed.

"I'm lying."

"Aye, I know." He laughed, his amusement running into a sharp yelp when she pinched him.

She abruptly hid her face in his neck. "I don't know what to do with you."

"I have some grand ideas about that," he said devilishly, stroking her bare back.

"I'm serious, Dillon!"

"So am I," he said, grinning. "I have always fancied making love to a woman wearing nothing but her black stockings."

Thea hastily looked down. "This is awful!" she said, not because of the stockings, but because he'd had her too addled to notice.

"Aye!" Dillon said, grabbing her up tighter and rolling her on top of him, nipping her shoulder and neck and jaw with delicious little bites that gave her goose bumps. He gave her a squeeze. "You're awful," he said, gently kissing her on the mouth. "And so am I." He kissed her again, this time longer. "But can we make a beautiful bairn together or no'?" He covered her face with kisses, making her laugh and cling to him.

"If we don't stop this, we're going to have a whole houseful of bairns."

"I don't mind," he said, lifting her chin so that he could look into her eyes.

"People will talk," she whispered.

"Let them."

His smile faded, leaving only the hungry look in his eyes. His hands were sliding upward along her rib cage. He bent his head to kiss one breast, and then the other, letting his tongue make slow, deliberate circles until each nipple peaked.

He stopped, glancing up from his maddening exploration of her body. "Shall I show you my grand idea now, Thea?" he asked, and she was lost again.

She was no longer sated; she was starving, famished for the taste and the feel of him. She nuzzled his neck, relearning his delicious scent. She bit his lower lip, lifting her head to look at him, her hair wild, her hazel eyes locked with his gray-green ones.

"No," she whispered. "This time it's *my* grand idea."

Thea came awake immediately, gently disentangling herself from Dillon's possessive embrace. Caitlin was crying, and she hunted among the debris of discarded pillows and fallen counterpane for something to put on. She found Dillon's brown plaid shirt first, and she put that on, glancing at him as she buttoned it. The shirt came down to her thighs, covering the tops of the black stockings she still wore. It smelled of his scent, and she crossed her arms over her breasts, feeling as if it were his arms and not hers. Her mind presented her with a kaleidoscope of the night's events as she crossed the hall to the nursery: Dillon, his face contorted with the pleasure she was giving him; Dillon, satisfied and incredulous.

She pushed all of it aside when she reached the nursery door, putting it away like some secret treasure she'd hoarded to take out and savor later, miser that she was.

"Poor Caitlin," she said as she came to the crib. "Poor baby face." A tearful Caitlin hung over the side of the railing, arms outstretched. "Caitlin, Caitlin," Thea crooned, reaching for a dry diaper in her usual first-things-first approach.

"You know what?" Thea asked, putting the rail down and placing Caitlin on her back. "One of these days all those teeth will be in, and you and Mama will sleep all night."

Caitlin's skin was warm but not feverish, Thea noted on her mother's checklist, fastening the dry diaper and lifting her out of the crib.

"We'll talk about this a little bit," Thea promised softly. "And we'll find you something to make the gums feel better. And then it's back to sleep for this baby girl."

She took Caitlin into her arms, holding her close and savoring her sweet baby-smell, her heart suddenly filled to bursting for her daughter—Dillon's daughter.

"I love you even when you're teething," she whispered to their fretting child, walking around the room in an effort to comfort Caitlin, who still cried.

She glanced up to see a disheveled Dillon standing in the nursery doorway. He had on his shorts—period—and he was the very picture of the tortured male.

"Teeth?" he asked, frowning.

"Mmm," Thea acknowledged. When he'd first come back to the cottage, she would have given anything for this kind of episode—something that would annoy him into oblivion. Now all she felt was anxiety. Dillon wasn't a man to have his nights interrupted by anything except the things *he* chose, whether it be hedonistic pleasure or singing quiet ballads to a wakeful child.

"I forgot to tell you, Thea—" he said, disappearing.

Puzzled, Thea sat down with Caitlin in the rocking chair, watching the door for his return—not that she expected him to. But he came back with a folded washcloth, one that had been soaked with water and frozen.

"Here," he mumbled, still in a zombielike state. "Frozen flannel. I put this in the freezer for her. Works as well as anything. Let her bite that—it's nothing but water and cloth, Thea," he added a bit testily, and she grinned.

"How come you know about this and I don't?" she asked, taking the washcloth.

"My mother was a nanny, and I—"

"Am the oldest of six," she finished with him.

"Aye. Shall I take this watch, Thea?"

"No, I'm awake; you're not. The next one is yours."

He nodded sleepily, bending to kiss Caitlin on top of her head and Thea approximately on the eyebrow. Then he stood for a moment, rubbing one eye.

He was incredibly handsome, and Thea let her gaze wander over his fine, strong body. It seemed to occur to him that he couldn't sleep standing there, and he shuffled away toward the door.

"Love your outfit," he mumbled on his way out.

Thea laughed quietly, and Caitlin accepted the icy comfort her father had devised for her with only token protest, finding that the cloth soothed better than her or her mother's fingers. Thea sat rocking calmly as Caitlin verged on falling asleep.

"I love your Da," Thea suddenly whispered, kissing her soft cheek. "I love him, and you're the first to know."

Love. It was true. She did love him. And she'd just spent an incredible time showing him—without ever mentioning the word. The moth had made it through the fire all right this time, but had somehow gotten an incredible case of cold feet when it came to telling him how she felt. She remembered one of Tessa's letters, her sardonic humor in saying that when she was tired of a man, she didn't make the usual, face-saving speech about his deserving better. She simply told him she loved him and wanted to marry him—and stood back so she wouldn't be trampled in his exit.

Thea sighed. Perhaps that was all she had needed to do with Dillon all along: agree to marry him to have him gone.

But she didn't want him to go now. Truthfully, she had never wanted him gone. She wanted a fairy tale, one where the impossible came out all right.

Dillon was sleeping soundly when she returned to bed. Thea stripped off his shirt and the black stockings, switched off the lamp, and slid in beside him. She pulled the sheet over them both, and he stirred briefly to fit his body to hers spoon fashion, his breath warm against her neck and one hand cupping her breast.

The wind had risen, and Thea could hear the first drops of rain against the windowpanes. Sheltered and warm in Dillon's arms, she immediately fell asleep, dreaming at some point of a bright, sunny day on the beach at St. Margaret's Hope. August, she somehow knew—The Festival of the Horse, and all the village children gathered on the beach with their miniature plows making furrows in the sand.

And ... Griffen ... standing with his hands resting on his hips, smiling and happy. Thea's eyes traveled over him in disbelief. He was wearing a striped rugby shirt and a pair of white shorts, ready for a game of football with Dillon and the men in the village. He smiled broadly, his blue eyes merry, and Thea reached to touch the beloved, red-bearded face. But he shook his head slowly, blowing her a kiss and turning away. The sun disappeared, and he began to run up the beach.

"Griffen!" she called to him. "Griffen!" She needed to talk to him, needed to tell him that she wasn't alone anymore. Dillon was here now.

She couldn't catch him. Her legs were too heavy. She ran and ran, getting nowhere.

You must run twice as fast, the queen in *Alice in Wonderland* said, *just to stay in place.*

"Griffen!" she called, desperate to find him on the crowded beach.

Then she felt his arms around her, his warm kiss on her neck.

Here you are, she thought, laughing at her worry.

"Oh, Griffen."

9

THEA CAME AWAKE INSTANTLY, knowing what she'd done. Dillon stiffened against her; then he let her go and sat up on the side of the bed.

"Dillon," she said, reaching out to touch his bare shoulder. "I didn't—"

He shrugged her hand away. "It's all right, Thea," he said, his voice deadly quiet.

"Dillon, I was dreaming," she tried to explain, touching him again. "I thought you were Griffen."

"Aye," he said, and he stood up, searching for his clothes.

"Dillon, I was dreaming!"

"That's worse, isn't it?" he said in that maddeningly quiet voice. "Awake, it's deliberate. Asleep, it's what you really want and feel."

He found his shorts and put them on. "I'll check on Caitlin," he said on his way out of the room.

"Dillon!" she said, coming to her knees in the middle of the bed. She couldn't bear that hurt look in his eyes, and nothing she said could take it away.

129

"Leave it alone now, Thea."

She could hear him going into the nursery, then into the kitchen. The radio came on, and she could hear him switching stations until he found the weather forecast.

She got up, dressing quickly in jeans and a yellow T-shirt, but by the time she had her clothes on, Caitlin was awake and Dillon had gone upstairs.

He had his duffel bag when he came back down. He was wearing his tailored corduroy trousers again and the cashmere fisherman's sweater, that casual town-and-country look he wore so well and that was bound to turn heads in Aberdeen or wherever he happened to go. He set his bag down in the hallway at the foot of the stairs and came into the kitchen.

"Da!" Caitlin cried, making a beeline for his knees, kitchen chair to kitchen chair, until she reached them. He bent to pick her up.

"I . . . have to leave, Thea. If I don't go ahead of the storm, I won't get back in time."

Thea nodded, trying to look busy with a dishtowel and a handful of spoons that weren't even wet, her lips pressed firmly together so she wouldn't cry.

"Thea?"

"What?" She didn't dare look at him.

"Will you do something for me? I've . . . said too much to Bronwyn."

She made the mistake of looking at him, and her eyes welled with tears.

He gave a short sigh before he went on. "Bronwyn's told my mother about Katy. That was the reason she came here the other day. She thought she'd better say what she'd done if she was ever going to talk me out of my car again.

"I didn't mean for my mother to know about Katy yet—for any of them to know—because I didn't want you upset by the Camerons before I—" He sighed again, and Thea stared at him solemnly. "But they do know it, and if my mother should come here, would you treat her kindly?"

Thea turned away from him.

"She's volunteering these days at the Oxford Home for Infirm Children in Iverness. I don't expect her to get away here, but you've got the only Cameron grandchild, Thea."

"What do you think I'd do to her, Dillon?"

He suddenly smiled. "You'd no' tickle her, would you?"

Thea laughed in spite of his sad face, in spite of the burning ache in her throat and behind her eyes. "No, I wouldn't tickle her. I think I could promise you that."

"Ah. Good then." His smile faded. "Let me give you this wee one back again." He moved to hand Caitlin over just as she was about to put her head on his shoulder. "Ah, lass," Dillon whispered to her. "Don't make it any harder on your old Da than it is. Off you go to your mum." He shifted her into Thea's arms, reaching out to caress the back of her head as Thea took her.

"Thea," Dillon said abruptly. "You'd no' go back to America and not tell me, would you? I . . . think about that—diving and being stuck in the pressure chamber, not being able to come out." He shrugged. "When I come out again, I wouldn't want to just find you gone."

"I have no plans to travel," Thea said, her eyes probing his.

He nodded. "Well, I guess it's good-bye for a time, Thea. You won't be getting married before I get back, will you?" he teased, clearly trying to hide his pain at going.

"I have no plans for that either."

"Well," he said again, bending to kiss Caitlin gently

on the cheek. "Good-bye, lass." His eyes met Thea's as he straightened up. She lifted her mouth to his. His kiss was gentle and caring and filled with farewell, and his arms slid around her and Caitlin both.

"Dillon," Thea said, clutching the back of his sweater with her free hand. He let go of her, put on his jacket, and gave Caitlin one last caress before he picked up his duffel bag. "We have to talk, Dillon."

"I've told you, Thea," he said. "I'll no' be Griffen for you ever again."

"Dillon," she said again as he reached the back door. "Mind how you go," she said softly, using his own quaint expression to tell him that she wanted him back safe.

He opened the back door. "Oh, aye, lass," he said, smiling sadly. "I'll have to. It's the only thing you've ever asked me to do for you."

In her mind's eye she went with him, watching him as long as she could out the window, still holding Caitlin. The wind whipped at his hair and clothes, and he walked leaning into it with his duffel bag over his shoulder. He turned and looked back once at the last possible moment he could still see them at the window.

I love you, Dillon.

Why hadn't she said it, for godsake?

Because I'm so afraid.

She was totally unprepared for the desolation she felt, and Caitlin didn't help, cruising from chair to chair and wall to wall, looking expectantly everywhere she knew to look. But he wasn't hiding anywhere.

"Da!" she kept calling until Thea was ready to cry.

They had a late breakfast, and Thea tried to keep her occupied until the afternoon so that she wouldn't keep looking.

But Caitlin was a trusting child, filled with blind faith. She kept turning her head at some sound the wind made, hoping against hope that it might not be the wind at all, but her beloved "Da."

"Just look at us," Thea said. "And he's not even off the island yet."

When she put Caitlin down for her afternoon nap, someone knocked on the back door—two someones, actually—Dillon's junior messenger service in yellow rain gear. She hardly recognized them under their hats, and Trevor, she thought, importantly handed her a small envelope. She took it, staring at her name written on the front. Dillon's handwriting.

She looked up from the envelope, realizing that the messengers still waited.

"What is it?" she asked.

"Have you any cookies, Mrs. Kearney?" Trevor asked.

"Why?" Thea teased. "Do you want to give me some?"

"Ah, no," Trevor said. "It's cookie weather today, my dad says."

"He's absolutely right," Thea said. "Could I interest you gentlemen in squashed flies?"

"Oh, aye," they said in unison. She brought the raisin cookies out, hurrying the boys on their way before the storm got any worse.

She took Dillon's letter into the kitchen, sitting down at the table to open it. It wasn't a letter at all. It was one of the poems he'd collected:

> O Western wind, when wilt thou blow
> That the small rain down can rain?
> Christ, that my love were in my arms,
> And I in my bed again!

"Dillon," she whispered, the tears she'd held back so long sliding down her face. She had no idea what he meant for her to see in the poem. That he forgave her for calling him Griffen? That he wanted to be with her but couldn't say it? That he loved her?

No.

There had been no mention of love from either of them. She sighed and stared at nothing, rereading the poem from time to time just to reassure herself that he'd cared enough to send it, whatever it was supposed to mean.

She looked down at the poem again. "From Dillon Patrick Cameron," she whispered, smiling at last.

Someone was knocking at the back door again, and Thea went to see, sighing heavily and forgetting that she was red-eyed from crying. It was Flora Macnab with a bulging cardboard box tied up with string.

"Flora," Thea said, opening the door to let her and the wind and rain in. "Are you trying to get blown out to sea or what?"

Flora shoved the box into Thea's hands while she took off her mackintosh. The box was filled with notebooks, school composition books from the looks of them.

"Well, don't just stand there, my girl," Flora said. "I've come to hire you to—" She broke off, looking hard at Thea's red eyes.

"You've come to find out what's going on with Dillon and me," Thea said. "And we both know it." She carried the box Flora had given her into the kitchen, setting it down on the kitchen table and picking up the poem Dillon had sent while Flora tried to read it.

"Since you're the one who brought it up," Flora said, "what have you done this time?"

"This time?" Thea said defensively.

"You know what I mean. I saw Dillon today."

"What was wrong with him today?" Thea asked quietly.

"Nothing you could see if you didn't know him. I happen to know him, my girl. I have since he was a lad and he and Griffen tagged after Roddy and the lobster traps. I haven't seen him look the way he did this morning since the day Griffen died."

"Flora, what have you brought me?" Thea interrupted, tapping her fingers on the box.

"What, this?" Flora said, frowning and unwilling to be distracted. "Oh," she said airily, "this is my World War Two file. I want you to type up my memoirs."

"You do not."

"Thea, I've just said so. And there's some heady stuff in there, mind you. I may make a fortune."

"Don't tell me," Thea said dryly. "'Flora and the RAF'?"

"Well, I wouldn't go that far, though there are a few passages that will pop your ears for you. I've been meaning to get them typed, and you need something to do until Dillon gets back. He is coming back, isn't he?"

Thea would have laughed at how skillfully Flora had gotten around to what she wanted to know—if she hadn't felt so much like crying.

"Isn't he?" Flora persisted. "You need some tea, my girl," she decided when Thea didn't answer, and she promptly set about making it, as comfortable in Thea's kitchen from their years of friendship as she was in her own. She left off any further interrogation until she'd set a cup of steaming tea under Thea's nose.

"Well?" she inquired. "What have you done?"

Thea toyed with her cup. "Something stupid," she answered.

136   **Cinda Richards**

"That goes without saying," Flora commented. "I'll have to hear the specifics if I'm to give an opinion," she added pointedly.

"Did I say I wanted an opinion?"

"Well, of course you do. Why else am I out running around in this kind of weather, as old as I am?"

"You want your memoirs typed?" Thea suggested, and Flora gave a sharp laugh, clasping her hands together in appreciation.

"Touché, my girl. You caught me on that one. Thea, I only thought you might want to talk."

"I don't."

"You haven't your own mother here, so I might as well have a hand—"

"It feels like *two* hands," Thea complained.

"Thea, what have you done?"

"I called him by the wrong name!" Thea said in exasperation.

Flora leaned back and frowned. "You called him Griffen, you mean," she decided, quick as ever. "Well, that's not too bad unless—I don't suppose you picked the worst possible time to do it?"

Thea didn't answer.

"Oh, my sainted aunt, Thea!" Flora said.

"I said it was stupid!"

"Yes, and how are you going to make amends for it is what I'm wondering."

"I'm not going to make amends. I think it's probably for the best that it happened. It's better that he's out of my life now before it gets any worse."

"Thea, the lad is not a disease, for all your making him sound like one."

"He is for me! He'd never be happy here."

"Now, how the devil do you know that? Why don't

you just let Roddy have a go at finding out when his shift ends? Then you could meet him at the heliport in Aberdeen when he comes in off the oil rig. I'd keep Caitlin for you."

"Flora, will you stay out of this?"

"Not unless you insist—and then I'd have to mull it over," she said matter-of-factly.

"I insist! All right?"

"Still running scared, are you?"

"Flora, please!"

"Who's to say he's not scared, too, my girl? Can't be easy for him to find out he's a father—and your being Griffen's wife."

"If I'd had my way, he wouldn't have found out," Thea said pointedly.

"Yes, well," Flora said, picking a piece of lint off her baggy sweater. "I have a feeling you're not all that sorry he did."

"Not now, but what will I do when Caitlin's older, and he's off chasing some French bird watcher?"

Flora grinned. "Heard about that one, did you?"

"I'm serious, Flora."

"I know you are," Flora said, finishing the last of her tea. "Well, I'm off. I can see I'm no good to you here. And I do want my memoirs typed," she added as she got up from the table. "I'll even pay you the going rate. Been meaning to say something to you about it for ages. The truth is, you're about the only person I'd have do it. There's a lot of personal things in them, things I don't want just anybody hashing about. So you see, it was a legitimate trip after all—and don't you go saying something that will make me sorry I've just spilled my guts the way I have," she said testily.

Thea walked with her to the door, helping her get her

mackintosh and her Wellingtons on again.

"If you need an ear, I'm it," Flora said, snapping the chin strap on her rain hat. "Dillon is a good lad, Thea. He's worth the trouble, and he's—"

"Got manly thighs," Thea finished for her.

"I'm sure I hadn't noticed," Flora said demurely, making Thea grin.

She stood watching in the doorway until Flora disappeared down the beach path. Dillon's sad face suddenly same to mind. God, she wanted to go to Aberdeen. She wanted to be with him, to put her arms around him. Nothing she could say would make him think that she hadn't used him, hadn't been pretending that he was Griffen, but if she could just . . . hold him.

Thea took the poem out of her pocket to look at it again, closing her eyes as the poignant plea struck home. It was what she wanted, too: to be in her bed in her love's arms. The only problem was that she didn't trust him enough to marry him, and she didn't want to have an affair.

She suddenly smiled. Except when he was anywhere near her—asleep or awake or standing right in front of her with the button on his jeans unbuttoned and his shirt off.

She shook her head, determined to set about trying to survive.

If she hadn't been so determined to keep Dillon off her mind, she might have noticed the decline in her health before it was too stormy to do anything about it. It was simply that she hadn't been ill in so long, and she didn't immediately recognize the heaviness of mind and limb that made everything she did a chore, or the deep aching tightness in her chest that made her want to cough.

She couldn't sleep that night, and it was only after

she made an early morning trek outside in the rain to secure a flapping window that she realized that her Aunt Mary had been right to send her the undershirts.

Pneumonia, she thought incredulously. She was supposed to have outgrown it.

She was wet to the skin from closing the window, and she couldn't get warm. Her skin was hot and dry, and yet she was freezing. Her head ached, but she managed to feed Caitlin. She couldn't let her out to roam the house as she usually did because she simply had no strength to keep up with her. She seemed to lose track of time, relying on Caitlin's fretfulness to mark the need for meals. She couldn't manage much in the way of food for herself—saltines and milk, orange juice and water.

Her chest hurt so, and once, she woke up to find that she'd been asleep at the kitchen table without remembering how she came to be there. Caitlin was crying. Thea made her way to the nursery, holding on to the wall.

"I need help," she murmured, but the storm was coming. No, it was already here. She could hear the wind howling around the eaves. Roddy and Flora would come when the gale blew through. Surely, she could hold up until then. *If I could just lie down. No, no, I can't lie down. Caitlin is crying.*

Thea found the baby wet and hungry, her crib sheet and covers all tossed on the floor.

"Poor baby face," Thea said. "Had you given up hope? What time do you think it is?" she asked, trying to smile. Something was the matter with her voice.

She struggled to put the baby into a dry diaper and clean clothes, summoning all her strength to lift her out of the crib. "Don't worry," Thea said as they made their way down the hallway. "We'll make it—I think."

She managed to get Caitlin into the port-a-crib. "Don't

worry," she said again. "Now, this is the menu, baby girl. A bottle of formula or a bottle of formula. How does that sound?" She had to stop for a fit of coughing, but she was able to keep her word about the menu, because she rested every few minutes. It was so hard to breathe.

Caitlin finished the bottle rapidly and was still hungry.

"Caitlin," Thea tried to croon, but her throat hurt and her voice was too faint. She held on to the cupboard door while she got down a jar of baby food—cereal and bananas—she kept for emergencies like trips with the Tourist Office tour groups or visits with Flora and the Knitters' Co-Operative. She felt the current situation qualified, but she couldn't get the lid off.

"Oh!" she said in exasperation, trying to get her breath. She had to sit down in a kitchen chair and hold on to the rail of the port-a-crib, while Caitlin cried. "Don't cry, darling—oh!" Thea dropped the jar of baby food, and it rolled away from her under the cupboard. She sat staring at the place where it had disappeared, not knowing how to get it.

Thea took a deep, painful breath before she tried, realizing then that the noisy rattling sound she was hearing came from her. She clutched the crib rail and tried to reach the jar with her foot. On the third try she just managed to touch it. Caitlin was still crying, and Thea cried with her.

"Thea?" someone said. "Thea!"

She reached blindly for the familiar voice, feeling the strong arms go around her. "I can't get . . . the . . . lid off . . . Dillon."

"What?" he asked, trying to see her face.

"The lid—oh!"

"God, Thea, what's wrong with you?" He was brushing her hair out of her face, trying to keep her sitting upright in the chair. "You're burning with fever!"

"When you wanted . . . to . . . help me," she managed between laborious breaths, "and . . . I said . . . no . . . I was wondering, Dillon . . . do you . . . "

"What, love?" he asked as she let her head fall onto his shoulder. "What?"

"Do you . . . give rainchecks?"

"Thea," he whispered against her ear. "Be still now. I'll help you."

"I . . . didn't get my . . . undershirts in time . . . Dillon. Please . . . feed Caitlin. She's . . . so hungry . . . "

"Shh! Don't talk." He strained to reach a box of teething biscuits on the cupboard shelf without having to let go of her, finally managing to get it and give one to Caitlin.

"Now, lass," he crooned to the baby. "You, too. Don't cry now. Take your biscuit for Da." He patted her back and kissed her check to settle her down. "That's my wee lass. What a fine girl you are." He waited until Caitlin was quietly eating.

"I should have . . . thought of . . . that," Thea managed as Dillon lifted her up off the chair.

"Don't talk!" he said gruffly, carrying her toward the bedroom. And he promptly asked her a question. "You've seen the doctor, then?"

"No. The storm—"

"God!" he said against her ear.

"What are you . . . doing here?" she managed to ask.

"I missed the ferry *and* the plane. The storm came in before I could get out of Kirkwall."

"How did you get over . . . the causeway?"

"Thea, don't talk anymore," he insisted, putting her down on the bed. She was too tired to move, too weak to help him when he pulled the covers out from under her. She had another coughing fit, and she fought to sit up. Dillon dragged the pillows in to a pile to prop her up so she could breathe more easily.

"One pillow under each arm," she whispered. It was all coming back to her. How to be ill with pneumonia. He put the pillows where she wanted, and she felt better having her arms propped up, but it was exhausting to try to tell him. He brushed her hair gently back from her face, and she closed her eyes. When she opened them again, he was putting a blanket over her.

"I'm going to see about Katy, and then I'll be right back."

Thea nodded, but he seemed gone hardly any time at all. She opened her eyes to the noise he made bringing the port-a-crib into the room.

"Katy's fed and she's dry and she's asleep," he said. "I'm going to put her in here with you so she can see you if she wakes up, but don't get up unless you have to. There's a bottle of juice here that should keep her happy, if she's no' studying the effect of gravity on the downward motion of dropped objects again today. Thea, do you hear me?"

She nodded.

"I have to go into St. Margaret's Hope. The weather's too bad to take Katy with me. I'll be back as soon as I can."

He came and went a few times, finally bringing Caitlin and laying her gently in the crib.

"Try to sleep while she's sleeping," he whispered, sitting down for a moment on the side of the bed. "Thea, are you warm enough?"

"Yes," she managed.

Sleep. That sounded wonderful.

"Caitlin?"

"She's sleeping, love. Don't worry. I'll be back soon."

Dillon was a man of his word. Thea again felt as if she'd only just closed her eyes.

"I don't like the sound of this," someone said. Dillon was in the room, along with the village doctor, John Lewis-Shaw.

Thea smiled. Lewis-Shaw had always reminded her of a Scots Captain Kangaroo, and he looked at the moment as if he'd been caught in a very wet whirlwind, white mustache and all.

"You . . . look awful," she told him. "You make house calls?"

"So do you, and yes. It's the American doctors who have to have everything brought to them. Besides that—" He glanced at Dillon. "It's rather difficult not to make one when one is being dragged along by one's shirtfront. Let's have a listen to you. Dillon, you take yourself elsewhere."

"I have pneumonia," Thea advised the doctor.

"Do you mind if I decide? Sit up."

"Just trying to . . . save you . . . some time."

"Don't talk," he said, listening with the stethoscope over her back. "Say ninety-nine."

"Make up your mind," Thea said testily.

"Close enough. My dear Thea, you have pneumonia."

"What a diagnostician," Thea said, but the effort left her exhausted. She flopped back against the pillows.

"You'll have to go in hospital, straightaway to Kirkwall."

"No, no, John. No hospital. I have to be here . . . with . . . Caitlin."

"You are in no condition to look after her, Thea."

"I can do it!"

"Thea . . ."

"No hospital, John. I won't go."

"John," Dillon said in the doorway. "She can't be taken till the gale's blown through. I'll be here. You can tell me what to do."

"You're no' a nurse, Dillon Cameron."

"No, but I know enough to know it's no good for her to be as upset as you've gotten her. I'll take care of her, John."

The doctor looked from one of them to the other. "Thea, you're very ill. You know that."

She managed a smile. "I've been through it before."

He gave a sharp sigh and rubbed a small spot between his eyes. "Let me see what I can do. I'll talk to Dillon a bit. You rest now."

Dillon came close to the bed to briefly squeeze her hand, and Thea closed her eyes, letting go of her anxiety. Dillon was here. He'd take care of her and Caitlin both. When she opened her eyes again, Dillon was sitting by the bed in a rocking chair, and the crib was gone.

"What do you need, love?"

"Caitlin?"

"She's fine. Asleep for the night, I think. She had peas and carrots for her supper, and strained meat—that stuff tastes awful, by the way. And she ate half my potato. Then she wrecked the kitchen with the pots and pans you let her play with. She had her bath—God, she loves the water. She'll be ready for a wet suit by the time she's three. Then we stood in the doorway and waved good night to you—I offered Dream Angus a crown to bring her a sweet dream, and that's the whole of it." He was grinning.

"What did . . . Lewis-Shaw tell you . . . when I couldn't hear?"

"To make sure you had your medicine on time, to feed you lots of liquids, and to let him know if your fever goes up or if you start talking daft. I said that would be the devil to tell—Thea *always* talks daft."

She gave a short, painful laugh. "Thank you, Dillon," she whispered, holding out her hand to him. His fingers were warm and strong.

"Ah, it's nothing, lass. I owe you a bit of coddling. You put me to bed when I couldn't walk, didn't you? Go on to sleep now, love."

"Dillon?"

"Thea, don't talk. Sleep."

"I . . . like the poem."

He smiled. "Early sixteenth-century anonymous. My favorite kind."

"You . . . don't see the cold . . . words. You see the warm hand . . . that wrote them."

He smiled at her analogy, and she closed her eyes, sliding easily into a long sleep that was broken only by Dillon with her medicine or whatever drink he thought she should have. He held her upright for her coughing fits, and he monitored her trips to the bathroom with maddening diligence, keeping her posted on their daughter and the progress of the storm. Once she woke to find him quietly sleeping on the bed with her.

Finally, Thea opened her eyes to a room full of sunlight, not knowing what day it was. She was ravenously hungry, and she could hear voices in the kitchen, Caitlin's among them. She took a deep breath. It was painful, but not agonizingly so. She tried to sit up on the side of the bed just as Dillon came in.

"Thea, what are you doing?" he demanded, and whatever it was, he was determined she wasn't going to do it.

"I feel awful."

"Then lie back!"

"Not that kind of awful, Dillon. I need a bath, and I'm starving, and I want to see my baby. Who's here?" she asked abruptly because of the giggles that came from the kitchen.

"Flora and my mother."

Thea stopped trying to sit. "Your mother?" she said in alarm.

"Aye. She came over on the ferry this morning."

"Why? You said she wouldn't—"

"I asked her to come. I have to go on to the oil rig, and you're to rest."

"Dillon, I can't rest with your mother here!"

"You don't know my mother. You'll rest right enough," he said ominously. "Let me get her then. I want the two of you to meet."

"Dillon, don't you dare!" she cried with as much breath as she could spare. She toyed with the idea of making an escape while he was gone, but he didn't go anywhere.

"Mother!" he yelled from where he was. "Will you come in here?"

"I'm going to strangle you!" Thea whispered frantically.

"Now I know you're better," he said, grinning. "You even look better, Thea."

"I look like hell. I can't see you mother looking like—"

"Och, she's awake, is she?" a woman said in the doorway.

Kindly was the first word that came to Thea's mind in regard to Dillon's mother. She *looked* like someone's nanny. She was wearing a tweed skirt and a white blouse and sensible shoes. She had on a white apron, and she was so calm and neat and efficient-looking that it was all Thea could do not to throw the covers over her head and hide.

"Mother, this is Thea," Dillon said. "Thea, my mother, Maggie Cameron." To Thea's horror, he left the room with no further attempt to help in a situation that was awkward at best.

"So, lass," Mrs. Cameron said, "it's about time we met."

Thea nodded, completely at a loss for words. This was Dillon's mother, for heaven's sake, and he'd run like the rat he was.

"I . . . don't know what to say," Thea admitted. "You've seen Caitlin, I guess."

"Aye," Mrs. Cameron said. "She a beautiful bairn, Thea."

Thea nodded again and gave a long sigh. The silence lengthened. "Why do I have the feeling that Dillon does this to you all the time?"

"Does what, lass?"

"Finds some poor, sick creature for you to look after."

"Well, he was one for bringing home things when he was a lad, but he's not done that in a long while now. I had just about given up hope of his ever doing it again— bringing someone home. But now he's brought me to you, and that's just grand. Caitlin reminds me of him, you know. Something about the way she holds her head when she's up to deciding what you're about. And she's got his smile, o' course. And her lovely hair—your curls and his color."

"Yes," Thea said, for some reason feeling a terrific urge to cry.

"You mustn't be angry with him, Thea," Mrs. Cameron said gently. "For springing me on you the way he's done. It's just that he had no choice, you see, if he was to keep you out of hospital. Impertinent, he was, but our Dillon was never one for stepping aside for the proper way of doing things."

"Like me and Caitlin," Thea said.

"I wasn't thinking of that, Thea. It only matters to me that he's been so full of sorrow and now he's happy again. You're the cause of that, you and his bairn. Now," Mrs. Cameron said, smiling, "are you hungry for your breakfast? What could you be eating?"

"Everything," Thea said, and Mrs. Cameron laughed.

"I'd best be off to the kitchen, then."

"Mrs. Cameron," Thea said when she reached the door.

"Maggie, please, Thea."

"Maggie. What kind of things did Dillon bring home when he was a boy?"

Maggie Cameron smiled at the question. "Oh, half dozen generic dogs and cats, as I recall. And Griffen always when his dad was in a rage and tippling. And a gray seal left for dead by a fisherman when it mangled his nets. It's taken a bit of stamina to mother Dillon these thirty-five years."

Thea grinned. "I've admired you for it."

"Ah, lass," Maggie Cameron said with a twinkle in her eye. "It was a dirty job, but *somebody* had to do it."

"We're you talking about me?" Dillon wanted to know.

"Certainly not," Thea answered. "We were talking about the devaluation of the pound."

He was smiling, standing in the doorway with his hands on his hips and looking entirely handsome. Her eyes traveled over him lovingly. He'd been so good to her.

"I'm to help you with your bath," he said, his smile going mischievous.

"No way," Thea said, giving a soft sigh and closing her eyes. As much as she needed a bath, *that* was out of the question.

"Why not?"

"Your mother's here?" Thea suggested.

"Oh, aye. It was her idea."

Thea opened her eyes, and Dillon laughed.

"And we'd best be at it," he said. "If breakfast comes and I've no' done my assignment, there'll be hell to pay."

He wouldn't hear any of her protests, running the shower and carrying her into the bathroom.

"I can walk," she insisted.

"Oh, aye. I just like to carry you."

"Go outside," she said when he put her down.

"Thea, you've no secrets from me."

"I'm not talking about secrets. I'm talking about the basic need for privacy—Oh, my God!" she said when she caught a glimpse of herself in the mirror. "Dillon, go away. *Please*. I didn't know I looked so bad."

"You don't."

"Dillon, go away!"

"Thea, you've been ill. I like *who* you are, you daft woman. Illness or health or needing a bath doesn't change that."

"Dillon . . ."

"All right! But you're not to close the door, and if you feel weak, you're to call me. And if I don't like the sound of things, I'm coming in, understand?"

"Yes! Good-bye!"

Thea felt well enough to wash her hair, and she took a severe chastising from Dillon for it. He made her sit on the side of the bed while he worked at toweling her hair dry.

"Dillon!" she said, finally reaching up to catch his wrists. "Enough!"

He let the towel slide off her hair and onto her neck so he could see her face. Unexpectedly, he knelt down by the bed, his arms going around her waist, his face pressed against her breasts.

"Thea," he whispered, "I was so worried about you."

"I was worried about you, too," she answered, sliding her fingers into his hair. "We didn't part friends, did we?"

He leaned back to look at her, his eyes searching hers. Clearly, he didn't want to talk about that. He abruptly grinned.

"Thea, there's one *wee* thing you should know about." He held his thumb and forefinger apart to show her just how "wee."

"What?" she said warily.

He gave her a charming grin.

"What?" she asked again.

"You're no' to screech or anything when I tell you—"

"Dillon . . ."

"My mother thinks we're married."

"She what!" Thea yelled, and Dillon pounced on her, clamping his hand over her mouth and hugging her tightly to him, his shoulders shaking with laughter. No wonder Maggie Cameron had sent him in here to help her with a bath!

"Shh! Now, Thea," Dillon whispered in her ear. "Now, we can't be loud with this. I'll take my hand away, and you'll be quiet. Promise. You'll not yell again, all right? Promise?"

Thea hesitated, then nodded. He took his hand down, and she promptly hit him over the head with a pillow instead.

"You *lied* to your mother! Dillon, are you crazy?"

"No, no, now, Thea, I've not lied," he said, dodging another pillow. He caught her arms, tumbling her back onto the bed and lying down with her. "Don't go throwing any more pillows, love, or I'll never get this said." He was still laughing.

"You lied to her!"

"Thea, I've no' lied to my mother since she wanted to know what skinny, long-haired lad it was that broke Biddy McIntyre's front window with his football. It's the Scottish marriage laws."

"What Scottish marriage laws!"

"Shh!" he hissed at her. "Thea, you're no' well enough for all this."

"Well, it's a fine time for you to think of that now! What marriage laws?"

"Scotland has some strange laws," he began.

"There are a lot of things in Scotland that are strange," she said pointedly, and he grinned.

"It's called an irregular marriage, Thea. It's a—a simple contract with no formalities. A lad has to be over fourteen and the lass over twelve. One of the ways you can have that kind of marriage is to live together in the appearance of marriage—establishing consistent repute of marriage, it's called."

"You are a B&B guest!" Thea pointed out in a whisper.

"Well, who's going to believe that, Thea?" he said, trying not to grin. "I'm The Great Silkie, you know, and

I've been living here with my child and my child's mother. What else would she think?"

"Well, you can just tell her—"

"The breakfast is coming," he announced in a whisper, kissing her on the nose. He got up, pulling her into a sitting position and smoothing her hair.

"Dillon!"

"Thea, if you want her to know, *you'll* have to do it."

Thea had her breakfast with Dillon and Caitlin both on the bed with her—along with Flora.

"Well, my girl," Flora said. "You certainly went the hard way about to keep from having to type my memoirs. Felling better now, are we?"

"Much better," Thea answered, glancing up from her bowl of grits to find her "irregular husband" looking at her in that way he had that made her knees weak—or weaker, as the case may be. He let Caitlin feed him a bit of toast, smiling as she went back to turning the pages in the baby-proof book he'd given her.

"I was thinking," Flora said, and Dillon's mother called her loudly from the kitchen. "I was thinking," Flora started again.

"Flora!" Maggie Cameron said in the doorway.

"My sainted aunt, Maggie, what?" Flora said. "Why is it I feel that hook contraption they use in the theater is about to yank me out of here? I'm coming, Mag. Don't have to have a house fall on me, you know."

"No, I didn't know," Maggie Cameron assured her. "If you're no' needing a house to fall, it's the first time."

"Is that so?" Flora said on the way out.

"It is," Maggie answered, and Thea laughed.

"They like each other, don't they?" she said.

"Aye, they've been friends for years. Thea, I have to

go soon." His hand caressed her knee through the covers.

"How soon?" she asked quietly.

He gave a small shrug. "Now."

"Oh."

"Would you meet me in Aberdeen when my shift is done—if you're well and Katy's fine?"

She stared into his eyes, afraid again. But she pushed the fear aside. *If you want,* she started to say, but that sounded too passive. Passive was the last thing she felt about Dillon Cameron.

"Yes," she said instead, and he grinned.

"That'll be grand, Thea. There's one other thing I want to make sure you know before I go."

"Oh, Dillon, please," she said in mock alarm. "I'm not well enough to take any more announcements."

He hesitated, looking down as he still caressed her knee.

"What is it?" Thea asked, and he looked back up at her. Caitlin babbled softly over the pages in her book.

"I love you, lass. Hush now," he said when she was about to protest, reaching out to touch her lips with his fingertips. "It's no' a thing I say easily, Thea, and I don't want us to get into a contest here with you trying to show me I don't mean it and me trying to prove I do. You have my heart, and that's the truth of it."

He got up from the bed before she could comment, picking up Caitlin. "Let's go see what Gran is doing. I'll kiss Mummy for you. Wave good-bye."

"Bye-bye," Caitlin said, grinning and kicking vigorously.

"And a wave," Dillon said.

She mimicked her father's waving.

"That's my lass. I'll be right back," he said to Thea.

He returned quickly, taking the breakfast tray away

so he could put his arms around her.

"When you come to Aberdeen, we'll talk about things. And while I'm gone, you'll rest and you won't fret."

Thea shook her head yes and then no. She gave him a hard hug. "And you'll be careful." She pressed a small kiss on his neck in case she was still germy. And, like thousands of island women before her, she released the man she loved into the care of his mistress, the sea.

10

THEA'S RECOVERY WAS RAPID. She could hardly do otherwise with John Lewis-Shaw, Maggie Cameron, *and* Flora overseeing her progress. She rested as prescribed, ate only the most nourishing foods, and stayed indoors away from the "October drenching" the islands took this time of year, playing with Caitlin and thinking of nothing but Dillon Cameron.

Maggie stayed ten days, tearfully leaving for Iverness and her duties at the children's home when Thea had been officially declared well. Thea gave her a handful of pictures of Caitlin and a sincere invitation to visit again. She truly liked Maggie Cameron—liked her enough not to tell her the truth about that strange irregular marriage. Thea had enjoyed Maggie's company in the cottage, loving her stories of Dillon's childhood and of her wild "Lucy and Ethel" escapades over the years with Flora. The cottage was noticeably empty after she left, for both Thea and Caitlin.

Thea spent the rest of the time before she left for Aberdeen getting stronger and continuing to think—not about whether she had done the right thing in giving in to her feelings about Dillon, but about whether she could have done otherwise.

No, she decided. For better or worse, she was committed to see where their relationship would end. He loved Caitlin, of that she was sure. He even might have meant it when he'd said he loved her as well. The problem with Dillon was how he defined the word *love*. Was there some unspoke qualifications like "as much as I can" or "while I'm here" attached to it?

She missed him terribly. She tried to think if she'd missed Griffen as much. Yes, she decided, but differently. Everything with Dillon—living together, fighting, making love—was different and beyond comparisons.

She planned to fly from Kirkwall to Aberdeen. She could have ferried the Volkswagen to the mainland and then driven the distance into Aberdeen, but she didn't trust its aged motor or her newfound health. She toyed with the idea of bringing Caitlin, then decided against it, taking Flora up on her offer to "nanny" because the time had come to see Dillon with no distractions and no purpose other than to decide where the two of them would go from here.

She left Kirkwall on a bleak, gray morning, expecting the flight to be cancelled at any moment because of the weather. But the rain held off until she was well on her way, and she arrived in Aberdeen in a wind-whipped downpour.

She waited anxiously in the heliport terminal, watching out the rain-splattered windows as the crews came and went, regardless of the weather.

Please, she kept thinking. *Just let him get off the rig and be here.* She had no prayers beyond that, just that she could be with him again.

She finally saw him, walking in the middle of a group of oil riggers who had just arrived, all of them dressed in the standard orange flight suits. Dillon's too-long hair whipped about in the wind as he scanned the windows looking for her. Her heart lurched when she knew that he'd found her. She was wearing a soft dark green wool dress she knew was becoming, but in this kind of weather, she'd had to cram her hair into a forties-look roll at the nape of her neck to keep from looking like a wild woman, and now she worried that she might look too matronly and severe. She nervously pulled the belt on her raincoat tighter and tried not to think of all the other more sophisticated women who must have waited for Dillon in the past.

I shouldn't have come, she thought in a panic when she saw Dillon's grave face. Although she expected him to be reserved in front of his associates, that reservation didn't help her attack of butterflies one bit.

Dillon walked purposefully toward her, carrying his duffel bag.

"Hello," he said when he reached her. Period.

"Dillon," one of the men in the group called, "don't forget to see Oliver before you go."

Dillon didn't answer. His eyes were smiling, Thea decided, but not much else.

"Hello," she responded, her heart pounding with his nearness. She wanted to touch him, but only loose women did that sort of thing in front of a man's cronies.

"Dillon, did you hear me?" the man insisted.

"He heard you, he heard you," another, clearly American, voice declared. "Dammitall, Clyde, can't you see the man's working?"

The group moved on in a ripple of laughter.

"I don't suppose an old rat-hat diver like you would

need a little help?" the American inquired as he passed.

"Thank you, no, Barry," Dillon said without looking at him. "But I'll be remembering you asked that the next time the pipe's hung on the stinger."

Barry laughed and went his way, and Dillon took her by the arm.

"You have a suitcase?"

"No, everything's in here," Thea answered, showing him the large purse she was carrying.

Dillon looked at it doubtfully, then smiled. "Come along with me up to Oliver's office," he said, walking her rapidly toward the elevators where the rest of his group was already waiting. Dillon guided her on through them toward the stairs.

"Don't go in there with that man, ma'am," the American said ominously as Dillon held open the stairwell door, a small rascally smile playing at the corner of his mouth.

Thea went into the stairwell to Barry's better-than-average rendition of "The Theme From *Jaws*."

"Up or down?" Thea said, trying not to laugh.

"Neither," Dillon answered, throwing down his duffel bag and catching her wrist to pull her into his arms, his mouth hungry and hard on hers. The kiss left her breathless.

"Thea," he whispered, "kiss me." He hugged her fiercely as if he couldn't quite believe she was here. "Look what you're doing to me. You've got me trembling like a fresh-laced lad."

A sudden burst of whistles and applause came from outside the stairwell door. "We see you, Dillon!"

"Bloody hell," he said under his breath; then he grinned. "Let them spy. Kiss me again, lass."

Thea did so gladly, until she was trembling as well.

"You look lovely," Dillon said. "You're all right?" He

cupped her face with his hands to kiss her again.

"I'm fine," she said, looking deeply into his eyes.

"And Katy?"

"She misses you."

"Let's get this out of the way with Oliver, then," he said, reaching for the duffel bag. "No," he suddenly decided. "You've been ill. I can't go dragging you up these stairs."

Thea made a noise of protest as he was about to open the stairwell door again. "I can handle the stairs better than I can handle the oil riggers," she said, laughing.

Dillon grinned. "You're right. We'll go slowly."

He found her a place to wait in the hallway, dragging her a straight chair from one of the secretaries while he went to see Oliver. Thea hadn't remembered the name, but she did recognize his face when he came out. He was one of the company officials who had come to St. Margaret's Hope when Griffen died.

"Mrs. Kearney," he said, recognizing her immediately. "What a lovely adornment you are to this dreary place. I'll keep Dillon only a moment."

Oliver was a man of his word, and Dillon summoned a taxi for the trip to his Aberdeen "flat," because Bronwyn still had his car. The rain was coming down hard, and he took Thea's hand in the taxi, intertwining his fingers with hers.

"Slow down here," he said, leaning forward to get the driver's attention.

"This is no' the street, man," the driver said over his shoulder.

"I want her to see the trees," Dillon said, giving Thea's hand a squeeze. "She admires a good tree, you see."

"Oh, aye," the driver said, clearly not seeing at all. "Druid, is she?"

Thea and Dillon put their heads together to laugh, his

arm going around her to keep her close in the damp, cold cab. Dillon's apartment was in a long granite building that followed the curves of a winding, shady street, and they ran hand in hand through the rain and into the entry, still laughing about the cabbie's appraisal of Thea's tree fetish.

"You could have told him about my pine-filled history in South Carolina," Thea said.

"Ah, no, lass," Dillon teased. "He'd already heard your American accent. That was explanation enough for him."

"Is that so?" she said, waiting for him to unlock the door.

"It is," Dillon assured her. He held the door open, and to Thea's surprise, a fire burned in the small fireplace in the living room.

"How in the world did you manage this?" Thea asked, walking toward it.

"Oliver arranged it with my landlady just now. I didn't want you coming into a cold flat in this weather when you've been ill."

She smiled at him. "Thank you, Dillon," she said, touched by his concern.

The telephone rang in the other room, and Dillon went to answer it. Thea stood awkwardly for a moment, looking around the apartment, then took off her raincoat. It was too wet to put down, and she carried it toward what she supposed was the kitchen, finding a coat rack by the back door and hanging her coat there.

The kitchen was small and immaculate, with no clutter anywhere. Apparently the discipline Dillon had to have to live in a cramped pressure chamber carried over into his private life. A place for everything, and everything in its place. She had never really appreciated that cliché until now.

She could make tea, she decided, wondering as she filled the kettle how many other women had stood here and done the same thing for him.

She pushed the thought aside. It was something both she and Dillon were going to have to do if they were to last together: keep their ghosts in the past, where they belonged.

She chuckled softly. She could hear Dillon on the telephone having a row with Bronwyn about his car. Apparently she considered possession nine-tenths of the law.

"Thea?" Dillon called in a few minutes.

"In here," she answered, looking around as he came through the doorway. He had taken off the orange flight suit, and he was wearing jeans and a white T-shirt, his long hair combed back from his face. He was so incredibly handsome as he walked toward her, and as much as she welcomed his presence, as much as she wanted the feel of his strong arms around her, she turned away, busying herself with the tea, her body shivery as she anticipated his touch.

He didn't disappoint her, gently touching her shoulder, his fingers warm and firm through the wool dress. He reached around her to cut off the burner, turning her so that he could lightly touch her face with his fingertips.

"Let me hold you," he whispered, and she went immediately into his arms, loving the soft moan he gave as she pressed her body into his. "I've missed you, Thea," he said, his voice soft against her ear. "Every night, every day." His cheek nuzzled hers. "You feel so good to me. I don't want tea now. I don't want anything but you." His hands slid upward into her hair, raking it free of pins so that it tumbled on her shoulders. "I want you," he murmured, beginning to kiss her neck. "Don't make me wait."

Thea's hands were already moving over his broad back, tugging for the bottom edge of his T-shirt so she could touch his bare skin. She pressed her face into his shoulder, weak with wanting him.

"I'm going to take you to bed," Dillon whispered, placing kisses one after the other on her neck and ear and jaw. She could feel her breasts contract and grow heavy just from the sound of his voice, aching for the feel of his hands and mouth. "I'm going to make love to you." His hands slid down her back to press her hips into his. She could feel him, hard and male and urgent against her belly.

"Thea," he whispered, and she gave a long sigh.

It was as if her sigh had been the signal he was waiting for. He abruptly picked her up, carrying her into his bedroom and placing her on the bed. She could see the fire burning in the other room, hear the rain against the windows. Dillon worked at the buttons on her dress with trembling fingers, dropping soft, warm kisses on her shoulders, then the rise of her breasts as he took the dress away.

She wasn't wearing Aunt Mary Ann's undershirt. She was wearing a pale pink teddy she'd bought in Kirkwall that revealed far more than it concealed, and she'd bought it just for him.

"Beautiful," he said appreciatively, his hands flowing over her body in long strokes. Her nipples were hard and jutting against the lace of the teddy, and he kissed one breast and then the other through the lace. "God, do you know how sexy this is?" he asked, lifting his head to look at her.

"Yes," she whispered, smiling into his eyes. "Some of us don't have jewels from the sea and purses of gold to offer."

He laughed softly, kissing her breasts again, making her head arch back and her eyes close. His hands slid into the legs of the teddy. "You're wearing it for me then?" he whispered. "And you're glad to see me. You are, aren't you?" he insisted. His kisses were becoming hard and possessive. "Aren't you?" he demanded. "Aren't you?" he repeated, his voice gone hopeful and tinged with doubt.

"Dillon," Thea whispered. "Yes, for you." She loved the pleased look that came into his eyes. "I love you, Dillon."

She was still looking into his eyes, and she hadn't known she was going to say it.

"Thea," he said, hugging her fiercely to him. "You mean it? You wouldn't tell me a lie?"

He leaned back to look at her, and there was such worry on his face that she reached out for him again. "I love you, Dillon."

She released him so he could get rid of his T-shirt and jeans, and she smiled at the thought that he had done a little preparing himself. He wore no underwear.

Thea took off the teddy, standing up so that he could see her, loving the hungry look in his eyes. Then she went to him quickly, holding on to his shoulders as he tumbled her into his bed.

His possession was swift and deep and caused him to moan.

"Thea, you feel so good around me. So good," he whispered. His arms braced his weight, and his long hair fell forward, lit by the lamplight into a golden halo. He stared into her eyes, biting his lip for control as he began to move. She moaned at the powerful feel of him inside her, letting a soft cry escape as the pleasure he was giving her intensified. She could hear the storm outside, feel the storm within, and she knew that she was whispering his name as if he and the pleasure had become one, as if his name were some ancient invocation to call up this forbidden feeling. She was both driven and consumed by it, desperate for it, needing both to possess and to share, her only reality her relentless need of this man.

"I love you, Dillon," she whispered, soaring higher than she had ever been. She could hear him, the low, guttural sound he made now with every thrust, and locking her legs around him, she felt the pleasure burst and diffuse into a fiery sensation a thousand times better than she'd ever experienced before. Then, hesitating in the joy of release, the two of them began the slow plummet to earth again.

"Are you cold, Thea?" Dillon murmured, his voice muffled into her neck, their bodies sated at last.

"Yes," she said. "No!"

He lifted his head to look at her. "Yes—no?" he asked, smiling.

"I don't want you to move," she murmured, eyes closed. "Ever..." She locked her arms around him to keep him, and he chuckled, lowering his head to kiss her breasts.

"In that case, we'd better marry tonight." He abruptly gave her a hard squeeze. "Oh, I love you, lass! You're going to have to marry me—to save me if nothing else."

"Save you?"

"Oh, aye," he said, giving a mischievous grin. "I've been a real bastard these last two months. It's a wonder some of the lads haven't pitched me off the rig. Marry me, Thea. A regular marriage in the *kirk* with Roddy piping and Flora and my mother bawling their eyes out. I'll cherish you—you and our Katy. You know that, Thea."

"Dillon," she whispered, cupping his face in her hands so that she could kiss him gently.

"You're the only person I've ever wanted to come home to, lass," he said simply. "I want to belong to you, and I want you to belong to me. We'll have a grand time," he said, warming to the subject as if he'd given it a great deal of thought. "Christmas is coming, and—"

"You want to marry me because Christmas is coming?"

"No, you daft woman. I want to marry you because I love you. Christmas is extra. I want to know you're waiting for me. I want to see Katy learn to walk. I want to roll on the floor with you and fight with you . . . and make up with you."

He stopped, staring into her eyes, the barest hint of a smile playing at the corner of his mouth. "You're no' to look at me like that," he warned, making a slow rotation with his hips.

"Like what?" she asked innocently, already feeling her desire rising with his.

"You know what. Like you have something for me, and maybe you'll give it to me, and maybe you won't. Maybe I'll have to take it," he said, his thrust long and hard.

"Can you?" she challenged, suddenly clinging to his shoulders and letting out the long breath she was holding.

"Aye!" he said, showing her exactly what he meant. "I can—oh!" he gasped as she returned his thrust. "Thea!"

And they were lost again in the wonder of their togetherness.

"I thought we were going to sleep." Thea murmured, lying in his arms.

"Aye, we were," Dillon answered. He stroked her

hair and planted a kiss on her forehead. "But I'm dying of hunger." He abruptly sat up, pulling her with him. "Come on, we'll go somewhere and celebrate." He stood up, dragging her out of bed.

"What are we celebrating?"

"Getting married. You said you'd marry me."

"Did I? Strange, I don't remember a word of it."

"You and I don't always talk with words, Thea," he said, taking her along with him. Thea smiled. It was true. They didn't.

He hurried her into the shower, joining her in what must have been the most acrobatic bathing Thea had ever had in her life.

"Where would you like to go?" he asked when they were dressed again.

"I want a big hamburger and french fries—and lots of onion. Mustard. And dill pickles. Tomato," she added, talking herself into a major hunger attack.

"We can't celebrate with mince and chips," Dillon said.

"I can," Thea said. "I haven't had that in ages."

"Well, I'll have to find it for you, won't I?" Dillon said with a resigned sigh. "I don't want you going home to America to get it."

It was still raining, and he took her to a small place near the heliport called Little Houston that catered to the oil boom's influx of Americans. The place was crowded and noisy with country-western music blaring from a jukebox and an ongoing game of billiards in one corner. Dillon found them a booth by the window, and Thea watched the rainy street while he went to get the flagrantly American food she craved.

"Hey, you're Mrs. Kearney, aren't you?" someone said, and Thea looked up at one of the oil rig crew she'd seen in the heliport. Barry, she remembered, the one who had teased Dillon so and had hummed "The Theme from *Jaws*."

"Yes," Thea said, and he nodded.

"Mrs. Kearney . . ." he said slowly, and she realized that he was less than sober. "I knew Griffen," he offered. "Good man, Griffen. Dillon's a good man, too, though. Ain't a diver on the rig that don't feel better knowing Dillon Cameron's going down with them. He ain't scared . . . I mean he ain't scared of *nothing!* He tell you Oliver wants him testing the helium system? He—" Barry stopped and looked out the window. "Sure does rain a lot here, don't it? Sometimes I can't tell the difference between being on land and being down in the North Sea." He shrugged and rotated his shoulders, causing the beer to slosh out of the can he was holding. Thea glanced at his T-shirt slogan: RAT-HAT DIVER.

"Helium's good for diving," he said abruptly, looking back at her. "Might be dangerous, though. I mean, they know what nitrogen does to you—the bends, the Rapture of the Deep, and all that sh—crap." He grinned, drinking the beer he held so lovingly, showing her the can as if it would be of great interest to her. "Can't stand that warm stuff they have over here. I got to have it ice cold. I was just wondering, Mrs. Kearney . . ." He belched. "I was just wondering what you're going to do if Dillon—" He stopped as Dillon walked up.

"Barry," Dillon said, his voice a bit guarded.

"Hey, Dillon," Barry said, giving him a somewhat sheepish grin. "I was just talking to Mrs. Kearney a little bit here. How are you doing, boy?"

"I'm fine, Barry. Is there something you're wanting?"

Barry grinned wider. "Aw, no," he assured Dillon,

but then he glanced at Thea. "Well, hell, yeah, there is."
He looked at Thea again. "She's a pretty woman, ain't
she, Dillon? This is the first time I seen her up close. I
mean she's damn pretty. So how about you and me working something out?"

"Barry..." Dillon said, but Barry refused to be interrupted, draping his arm around Dillon's shoulders and
poking his chest with the hand that held the beer.

"No, now, I wouldn't ask this except she's so... *damn*
pretty. So how about it? The same deal you had with
Griffen. You know I'd take care of her..." He looked
wistfully at Thea, then at her breasts. "I'd take...real
...good care of her."

Dillon grabbed him by his shirt front. "Get away from
here, Barry," he said, his voice quiet and deadly. "Now."

Barry looked from one of them to the other, more
puzzled than warned. "What? See, see, Dillon, I'm going
to promise you just like you promised old Griffen. If
anything happens to you, Barry will step right in, see?
Whatever she needs doing, I'll do it. See, I wasn't *asleep*,
Dillon. I *heard* you."

"That's enough, Barry!" Dillon said, giving him a
shove backward. Barry sat down heavily on the table
behind him, causing the water glasses to slosh and a tray
of breadsticks to fall to the floor.

"What?" Barry suddenly demanded. "What! I ain't
good enough? You share her with your own kind and the
rest of us can go to hell in a pea-green boat. I'm as good
a man as you, Dillon! You promised, and I'll promise.
I mean, it ain't as if she was hard to look at."

"You're drunk, man!" Dillon said. "Leave it!"

"Listen, listen," Barry said earnestly, still not seeing
the peril he was in. "I'll promise the same way you did.
If anything happens to you, I'll take her, Dillon. Hell

I'll even say I'll marry her just like you—"

Thea abruptly stood up, her mind filled with another drunken man.

You're mine, Thea. Griffen gave you to me.

Oh, Griffen. I finally understand.

Strange, she thought, how detached she felt from it all. No, it wasn't strange. It was all too familiar. She was in that secret room again, and she had just bolted the door. Everyone was looking, but it didn't matter. Her eyes were locked with Dillon's. It wasn't his fault that she had wanted so desperately to believe him. She smiled, a smile she couldn't quite keep from trembling, a smile that made him reach out for her.

But there was nothing he could do this time. She was in her secret room, and she was going to stay there.

"Thea," Dillon said urgently as she picked up her purse. "You don't understand this, Thea!"

"Yes, I do. I understand better than anybody on this earth. You're a good friend, Dillon. To Griffen, if not to me."

She turned and walked away, hearing the commotion behind her but not stopping. She maneuvered steadily through the crowd to the outside door, stepping into the rain with Dillon right behind her.

"Thea, where are you going?" he yelled, catching her by the arm.

"Home," she answered, surprised he wouldn't know that.

"You have to let me tell you, Thea!"

"Dillon, please!" she cried, trying to get his fingers off her arm. "The only thing I was sure of in my life was that Griffen Kearney loved me. I don't want you to tell me! I don't want to lose that, too!"

"Thea," he said, pulling her around to face him. She

raised her arm as if she meant to hit him, then let it fall. "Thea, we have to talk. We didn't mean for Barry to hear. Listen!"

"No!" she said savagely. "I don't want to talk to you. I'm all right, see? No hysterics, no tears. I always knew there was a reason—something besides Caitlin. I just didn't know what. You made some kind of pact with my husband, Dillon. I should have guessed—Flora told me about them. She said your father gave you to Roddy if anything happened to him. I was too—what is it you say about Americans over here?—thick! I was too thick to see it."

"Thea, I can't stand seeing you like this!"

"I'm all right!"

"You're no' all right! Do you think I don't know? You look the way you did when Griffen—" He abruptly stopped. "We have to talk, Thea!"

"No! Dillon, I'm going home."

They were both getting wet.

"I'll take you then."

"No, you won't! Can't you understand? This is the end of it! My God, how have you stood it with Roddy and my dead husband both expecting you to tie yourself to me?"

"Thea, you're not going—"

"Dillon, *please!* I . . . I can't be with you now. It hurts too much." She tried again to pull his hand off her arm, and this time he let go. "You don't have to worry, Dillon. This isn't my first trip to Aberdeen. I know how to travel here. Please. Please, Dillon. Just let me go home."

She took a taxi to the train station, buying a ticket on the slow night train to Wick. From there, she could take the eight-seat islander plane into Kirkwall, and then, with any luck, the "post" bus that carried the mail and an odd passenger from Kirkwall into St. Margaret's Hope. At best she'd be traveling for the next twelve hours, and if she needed to cry, she'd have plenty of time to do it in. She made a telephone call to the phone booth in front of Roddy's, giving a message about her expected return to one of the Dunphy twins, and she boarded the train, sitting by the window in an empty compartment and waiting for the tears to come.

She sat dry-eyed for the entire journey, arriving in St. Margaret's Hope just ahead of another gale.

"Dillon's here," Flora said as Thea got off the post bus. "Had one of the oil company helicopters drop him off. Damn thing landed right on the beach."

But Thea fled the details, shutting herself away with Caitlin for the duration of the bad weather, blessing the fact that the storm would extend her solitude even if it hadn't kept Dillon from following.

She took care of Caitlin, and she worked on Flora's memoirs, listening to Tessa's sultry choice of music on her birthday tapes until the loneliness they evoked made her want to scream.

She tried to sort through the chaos in her mind, and there was only one thing of which she was certain. Whatever reason Dillon had had for forcing his way into her life, she loved him. He'd tried hard to keep his promise to Griffen; she'd give him that. He'd won her totally, and but for an American diver with a penchant for eavesdropping and one too many beers in him, she might never have known.

I love you, Dillon.

She could hear herself saying it, meaning it with all her heart the last time they'd made love. But because

she'd had his child, and because of his promise to Griffen, there had been no honorable way for him to get free
of her. Except for her to let him go. And she loved him
enough to do that.

She couldn't sleep at night. She kept drifting on the
edge of it, hearing the rain and the keening of the wind
and thinking that someone was calling her or that Caitlin
was crying.

She came awake with a start at a burst of rain against
the bedroom windows, and she strained to see the small
clock on the bedside table, trying to make out the po-
sitions of the blurred, luminous hands. Nearly dawn, she
thought, listening a moment for Caitlin.

"Thea?"

She jumped violently, turning over and sitting up in
nearly one motion.

"Dillon, what are you doing here?"

"Don't be afraid."

"I'm not afraid. What are you doing here!"

He was standing by the bed. She could just make out
his features in the early morning darkness. He heaved
his jacket off and let it drop to the floor, sitting down
on the bed in his wet clothes. "I can't stand it anymore,
love," he said, lying down beside her, crowding her,
taking her into his arms. "God . . . I'm so tired . . . don't
send me away, Thea."

"Dillon!" she said in exasperation. "Did it ever occur
to you that I might not *want* you turning up here dog
wet and trying to crawl into bed with me?"

"On, not in," he said wearily. "I've no strength for
in. I'm so cold, Thea. Let me get warm."

"Dillon," she protested one last time, returning his
embrace finally and bringing up a corner of her blanket
to cover his shoulders. He *was* cold. He was shivering.

"Look at you," she said, giving a sharp sigh. "What have you been doing?" His hair was wet and clinging to his face, and she brushed it back with her fingertips. He felt so good to her, and her arms tightened around him.

"The Dunphy twins ran aground in the storm. We've been trying to get them off their boat before it broke up—damn hardheaded old codgers."

"They didn't drown," Thea said in alarm.

"Ah, no," Dillon said. *"I'm* the one who's near drowned. They wouldn't get off the boat, the buggers. Too busy blaming each other for the mess they were in and trying to bash each other's noses. Archie fell overboard. Do you know how heavy a Dunphy twin is when he's wearing wool and he's just gone into the drink? God, I was ready to drown them both myself."

Thea laughed softly, and Dillon suddenly reached up to touch her cheek. He hesitated a moment, then tentatively pressed his lips gently against hers, the kiss deepening when she didn't resist. He sighed and pressed his face into her shoulder.

Oh, Dillon.

Thea held him quietly for a time, feeling him shivering from the cold and listening to the storm outside and to his breathing.

"You never would have told me about your promise to Griffen, would you?" she asked, not really knowing if he was asleep or awake.

"No," he answered.

"No?" she said incredulously, the temptation to forgive him going right out the window.

"It was between Griffen and me, Thea. It had nothing to do with you."

"Nothing to do—! Griffen was my husband!"

"Aye! He was. *Was,* Thea. And he was my friend for

the whole of his life. It isn't easy now, Thea. I'm . . . jealous of him, don't you see? I'm jealous of him in a way I never was when he was alive. I'm afraid I'm not the man he was, and I want to be. For you and Katy."

"You thought I'd never know, is that it?"

"Yes." His arms tightened around her. "I didn't think anyone knew. I didn't see how you could find out. It's all . . . daft, Thea. Griffen was—"

"What?" she asked when he didn't go on.

"Do you remember telling me that he was afraid?"

She remembered, and she remembered how angry she was at Dillon at the time, because he was alive and fearless—The Great Silkie.

"Sometimes a diver knows when he shouldn't dive, Thea. He can feel it. Griffen said to go out then was like climbing into your own coffin. I . . . didn't understand. I've never felt that. I knew the tiredness and the closed-in feeling, but I never knew that—that sense of doom or whatever it is. Griffen did. It got to the point that he couldn't dive. The crew chiefs won't hold it against a man a time or two, but if it keeps up, you're out of a job. They think you can't dive anymore, and most can't. Sinclair . . . can't.

"Griffen couldn't go out, but he said he'd be over it if I'd do something for him. I thought he wanted me to mother him along when he was out, until the feeling left. But that wasn't it, Thea. He was worried about you—and he asked me.

"'Take Thea for me,' he said. 'Give me your word, man.' I thought he was joking—he laughed a bit—in that way he had. But he wasn't joking, Thea. 'I have to know she'll be with a man who'll cherish her, a man who cares about her. You care about her, Cam,' he said. I didn't know what to say to him. I didn't know he *knew,* you see. That I . . . cared about you."

"Don't tell me any more," Thea said abruptly, trying to move out of his arms.

"You have to hear it, Thea," Dillon said, not letting her go. "You have to understand. I did care about you. You were always so . . . kind to me, letting me hang about you and Griffen when I had no place to go. If you hated it, it didn't show. I was Griffen's friend, and I was welcome in your house."

"Dillon," she said, feeling the tears beginning to slide down her face. Her throat ached with trying not to cry. "Why didn't he tell me?"

"Because you're an American and you'd never accept it and because he loved you. Griffen knew what was coming, Thea, and he prepared for it. His grandmother Kearney—you've met her—she's a *spaewife*, a seer. She told us about you when we were lads—'great love and a bride from over the sea.' I don't think she ever told him that the sea would take him—until he knew himself. Thea, I know how this must leave you feeling. Even I didn't know how resigned he was until I came back. His insurance—he didn't leave you the money because he'd trusted me to take care of you. And the night I went out drinking to Griffen's health—he'd left things for all of us in Roddy's keeping. What he left for me were his keys. He meant for me to have them. He meant for me to make my life with you."

"You . . . promised him?"

"Aye. I did. A few weeks before he died. He seemed the better for having my word on it. He was going out again. I was looking all the time for some sign that he wasn't all right, when it was Sinclair I should have been watching. I . . . don't forgive myself for that. After Griffen's funeral, I knew you wanted me away from the cottage. I knew you couldn't bear to look at me, but I needed you so. I loved you, and there was no one else on this earth who knew how I felt. I took advantage of your grief to try to hide from my own."

Thea raised her head to look at him. "You—you *loved* me?"

"Yes, *yes!*" he said, hugging her to him fiercely. "Didn't you know that? How could you not know? God, Thea, I was so ashamed of what I did to you."

"You didn't force me into anything."

"Didn't I? I didn't know how you would see it. I couldn't stay then to do what Griffen wanted. So I stayed away, until Roddy told me about Katy. Ah, love, I was so *happy*. We had a child, you and I, but you'd never told me."

He sat up on the side of the bed, and Thea moved with him, tentatively reaching to put her hand on his shoulder. His shirt was wet and cold to her fingers, and he gave a soft sigh at her touch.

"Now what are you doing?" she asked sadly. "You've made me listen—are you leaving?"

"No, no," he said, reaching up to put his hand over hers. "I'm ... afraid of you, Thea. Afraid of your kindness. Roddy always told us—Griffen and me, when we were boys—if we wanted a bachelor's life, beware the woman who is kind, the woman can hurt you and won't. I know what you're about to do. You love me, and you think I'm some wild creature that has to be set free. God, Roddy was right! A man has no defense at all against a woman who can hurt him and won't!" He turned and reached for her, burying his face into her neck. "Thea, Thea, when you said you were going home, you didn't mean America, did you?"

"I ... don't know," she said truthfully.

"Thea, don't leave me."

"I'm afraid, too, Dillon!"

"Why? Do you think a man doesn't know when he's ready to settle down? Griffen was a good husband to you, because he loved you and wanted to be married to you. But we were *alike*, Thea! Before he married you, he was one step behind me or right by my side or leading the way—through the Royal Highland Fiddlers or little French bird watchers or anyplace else we fancied. A man knows the difference in being with a woman he loves and being with a woman who's willing when he's got the need. He knows when he's ready to share his life, and he knows how to cherish that love if he's any man at all—the way Griffen did. The way I will."

"Dillon," Thea said, pressing her face against his. "I just don't know what you want!"

"I want *you!* I want the same thing the poet wanted—in the poem I sent you. I want to come home to you. I want to *always* come home to you."

"You can't stand being domesticated!"

"Thea, I love you! I love you, and you love me. Don't you?"

She pressed her face into his shoulder.

"Don't you!" he insisted.

"Yes!"

"Yes," he affirmed, kissing her hard. He tasted of saltwater.

He suddenly gave a tired sigh and flopped backward on the bed, dragging her along with him. "Oh, God, I am so tired," he said again. "You and the Dunphy twins have nearly done me in."

"Is that so?" she said, somewhat insulted.

"It is. I'll forgive you, though, if you'll get me out of these wet clothes," he said wearily.

"Seems to me I do that a lot for you."

"Oh, aye . . . and I like it, too."

Thea smiled, beginning to work on his shirt buttons, her heart bursting with love for him.

"Dillon," she said softly, making him roll over so she could cover him with the flannel sheet and a blanket. He stirred restlessly, throwing all her pillows off the bed and onto the floor.

"Thea . . ." he murmured. "You know I'm married."

"You're what!" she said in alarm, and he lifted his head to grin at her in the dim light.

"To you, Thea. *I'm* married to you. The irregular marriage isn't the shock to me it was to you; you're not used to being married without knowing how you got that way. I'll still take you to the *kirk*, lass—Roddy and his bagpipes and my mother and Flora and all of it—if you'll let me."

She hesitated only a moment. "I'll let you," she said, bending down to kiss him gently on the brow. Then she left the room to give their daughter a similar kiss.

Dillon was sleeping soundly when she returned, stirring briefly when she climbed in beside him. She fitted her body to his to keep him warm. The storm and the sea raged over the island, but she had him safe.

She suddenly remembered something she'd heard Roddy once say: Whatever the sea takes away, it gives better back again.

She pressed a soft kiss into Dillon's shoulder, loving him with all her heart whether their marriage was regular or not.

"I love you, Thea," Dillon said sleepily, and she smiled. Dillon Cameron had come home.